The Ashes and the Roses

Siara Brandt

Copyright © by Siara Brandt. First Edition. All Rights Reserved.

No part of this book may be used or reproduced in any manner whatsoever without written permission, except in the case of brief quotations embodied in critical articles and reviews.

ISBN: 978-1492765547

Printed in the USA.

*Whisper of a sweet surrender
To love so wild and so tender,
For we will e'er remember
The roses in September.*

Prologue

Near Cedar Mountain
August 9, 1862

The air hung hot and sultry in the open, very still, though from afar the deep thunder of cannonade continued. Daylight was fading fast with a full moon just beginning to rise over Cedar Mountain.

The scout's gaze searched the deepening shadows as he felt for the wooden canteen hanging from his saddle. He did not relax his vigilance as he raised the canteen to parched lips and drained the last trickle of warm water. He lowered the empty canteen, turned his face and gazed northward through the warm Virginia dusk.

Night had not put an end to the fighting. Fitful stabs of muzzle flashes dotted the darkness, like harmless fireflies from this distance. He could hear the far-off rattle of musketry along with the deeper roar of artillery. Stonewall's guns. And though the last of daylight was nearly gone, the General's fighting blood was roused. He would continue the chase and drive the Yankee Army north toward Culpeper.

The scout let his breath out slowly and removed the loosely-tied strip of cloth from his hand, exposing the saber slash across his palm. He pulled a clean piece of linen from his breast pocket. His heavy wool cavalry coat was unbuttoned against the heat, but he could feel, beneath his shirt, trickles of sweat coursing down from his chest to his belly.

He hoped it would rain. Enough to cool things off some. He frowned thinking of the heat that day. Like hell's fire. Men had died from the heat on the long, hard march here. But the General was a driven man and so for three days and three nights he had been almost continually in the saddle scouting the Union position.

Inured though he was to hard service, he could not remember ever having been so tired. In those three days he had rested only briefly. His muscles were stiff and aching with the strain. He had not eaten since the dark hours before dawn. He had been chased and shot at. And he had had a good horse killed under him in a fierce fight in a wheat field.

He turned his face to the side and spat, grimacing at the gritty taste of dust in his mouth. Thrown up by artillery wheels and by horses' hoofs and kicked up by the shoes of marching soldiers, the dust was everywhere, it seemed. He breathed it. It powdered his clothes and hair and clung to the sweat on his skin. His eyes burned from it.

He tied the ends of the new bandage and, with a frown still on his face, reined to the right. He knew his horse needed a longer rest, but he had his orders and the sooner he delivered those dispatches, the sooner the rest.

Darkness had fully descended by the time he reached the field hospital. The abandoned farmhouse was now crowded with wounded men. As he stepped inside, the familiar odors of straw, whiskey, sweat and blood mingled strongly. The sounds were familiar, as well. Moans and piteous cries filled the air. The shrieks were enough to unnerve any man.

Lantern light wavered fitfully over the pale faces of wounded men. Off to one corner the surgeon was busy at his work on the family's kitchen table, which was now slick and dripping with blood.

"Ah'm glad to see you alive and well," came a low greeting as the scout got down on his heels before an officer with bandages wrapped around one leg.

"It's not as bad as it looks," the other man replied to the question in the scout's eyes. "Hurts like the devil, though. Ah'll confess it," he went on as the scout handed over the dispatches.

For the next half hour the two men talked quietly together, discussing details of the scout's new orders. Finally the wounded man held out his hand. "Good luck, Jes," he said. "Take care of yourself. Ah'll see you No'th as soon as Ah'm fit to travel."

The scout stopped to fill his empty canteen at the well in the yard. He was leading his horse to the road when an ambulance filled with wounded men suddenly jolted out of the darkness behind him. As he drew aside to let it pass, his attention was drawn by a low voice from the shadows. "Wait a bit, Reb."

Moonlight was filtering through the trees. The leaves cast shadows across the faces of three men sitting along the roadside. They were prisoners, evidently, for they all wore blue.

"Could you spare some water?" one of the men asked. The scout saw that he wore the bars of a captain on his shoulders.

The scout lifted the dripping canteen from his saddle and silently handed it over to the man. The Yankee captain drew back slightly, revealing the other two men. One was young and beardless with fair hair showing beneath a dark blue kepi. He was cradling a wounded arm. A third soldier lay further back in the shadows. His face was colorless in the moonlight.

The men had not yet been attended to. The fate in store for them was undoubtedly a Confederate prison. Wounded as they were, it was a grim prospect at best.

"Will you do something more for us?" the Captain asked. "Will you try to get word to our families that we were taken prisoner?"

The Captain reached into his breast pocket and handed a daguerreotype to the scout. "My wife lives just outside of Washington. Her name and address are written there. She'll be waiting for word." The Yankee paused for a moment. "She is expecting a baby any time now and she has been ill. It will be hard on her, waiting and not knowing. If you can get word to her and let her know that I wasn't wounded, but that I was pinned under my horse and captured, she won't worry quite as much."

The Yankee might have easily escaped, the scout realized, but he had chosen to stay with his men. "I'll try to get a message through the lines," he said to the man.

The Captain handed him two more items. "Here is my watch and the names of these men with me. I- " His voice broke for a moment and he looked aside. "I would appreciate very much if you would try and let them know what happened to us."

The scout nodded. "My word. I'll do what I can." He frowned as the Captain held out a roll of greenbacks. "Save it, bluebelly, you're going to need that in prison."

The Captain nodded and handed back the canteen, but the scout left the canteen with the Yankee as well.

"Sir," said the Captain. "I am deeply indebted. I hope that one day I can return the favor."

The scout watched soberly as the Captain turned back to the other men. He saw him pass his arm beneath the head of the badly wounded soldier who lay in the shadows. He heard a low cough and a sound that he recognized as blood in the dying man's throat.

For a moment longer the scout lingered while the Captain wiped the blood away from the pale lips with a bit of cloth and gently smoothed the dark hair back from the waxen brow. All the while, the sounds of battle kept up a faint throbbing in the far distance.

The scout finally turned back to his horse. As he lifted his boot to the stirrup and swung his weight across the saddle, he could hear, very low and very gentle, the voice of the Yankee Captain who was speaking as he might to a child who is afraid of the dark while he leaned over the young soldier who was breathing his last upon this earth.

Captain Jesse Lucane, scout for the Confederate Army, stared ahead into the hot, windless darkness, wishing for rain to cool things off and put an end to the fighting. From out of the darkness there came to him, faintly, the scent of wild roses, a scent completely at odds with all the death and destruction that surrounded him.

With a weary sigh he turned his horse's head. After a touch of his boot heels, he headed North, towards Maryland, his old home, with a message for a Yankee woman who lived just outside of Washington.

Chapter 1

There is always hope where wild roses bloom. You can ignore them. You can trample them and cut them down. You can even burn them, but they will rise up out of the ashes and bloom again. Let your faith be like the roses, 'Scensia. Believe they will come back again.

Ascensia Marguerite McCay closed her eyes for a moment, wanting to believe her grandmother's often-repeated wisdom. But hope was not so simple a thing these days. And neither was faith.

As August yielded to September in a blaze of smoldering heat and blood-hot fury on the Virginia battlefront, the city sprawling northward from the banks of the Potomac lay tense and breathless. The wagons had begun to arrive during some of the hottest, most sultry days of a Washington summer. They were slow moving and cumbrous those wagons. Their white canvas covers seemed to pulse beneath a miasmic distortion of heat waves. Heavy, wooden wheels rumbled like sullen thunder across the planking of the long bridges that spanned the river, groaning beneath the weight of their burdens, the wounded and the dying gathered from the fields of the terrible battle raging southward.

Like two pale, disjointed serpents, the wagons stretched across the wide Potomac River to the Virginia shore and beyond, past the faint tracery of the Arlington Mansion that had once been the home of Robert E. Lee. They came from a maze of unknown places with now familiar names. Centreville and

Alexandria and Chantilly, the Rapidan River and the Rappahonnack. All made hallowed by the ghosts of thousands of souls who had perished there during two long years of war.

With agonizing slowness the wagons rolled into the city. With woeful prophecy they kept coming, in an endless procession, it seemed, as they disappeared southward into the misty reaches of the boundless distance.

Ascensia waited as she had waited all day. Not patiently, but with a restlessness that she could not completely control. Too far to hear the piteous moans and the curses, the pleadings and the prayers, the feeble whispers and the shrieks, she sighed and looked up from her task of rolling strips of linen for the wounded. She rose from her porch chair and with an accompanying whisper of silk skirts, walked to the edge of the veranda.

The air was still and sultry. Disagreeably so. As it had been for days. But there was a hint of rain in its breath today.

And it was hot. Hot just standing still. She had come outside hoping to feel a slight breeze, but none stirred. The curtains at the windows did not move. The leaves hung motionless on the trees. The only sound to disturb the dead calm of the afternoon was the shrilling of the locusts in the thickets along the river.

She lifted one hand and rested the back of it against her forehead, shading blue-violet eyes against the harsh glare of the sun. Eyes that some said were, at times, perhaps, too passionate for a lady to possess. Eyes that were troubled now as she gazed eastward.

She could see the houses and fences of Washington in the distance, and the darker patches of woods. There were far-away rows of tents gleaming white among the green summer hills. Over it all a constant rippling of heat waves gave to the whole landscape the illusion of movement.

Yet there was no change along the long, lonely length of road. Only a ragged veil of dust stirred up earlier by horses and wagons passing by, lingered to drift lazily into the tall trees that lined the road.

Ascensia straightened, waiting as the whirring song of the insects rose once again in the dead heat and gradually died away. In the silence, very faint and very far away, she heard the deep rumble of thunder from across the Potomac.

Also across that river the Union Army lay licking its wounds somewhere in Virginia. An Army that was still fighting for all anyone knew on the old Bull Run battleground of last summer. It was another loss for the North, another bitter defeat after a summer of disasters. More than ten thousand men in blue were said to have fallen.

If that was not distressing enough, rumor had also brought word that the Union Army was routed and was retreating towards the safety of the fortifications that surrounded Washington. And somehow, somewhere in northern Virginia, though it seemed no one knew just where they were or what they intended, it was feared that the Southern Army had gotten itself in a position to threaten the Northern capital itself.

The result was a terrible excitement in the city. Rumors of a raid on Washington had come down along the road all day. They were unreliable or unfounded rumors, perhaps, yet Southern cavalry had proven in the past that it was audacious enough to attempt anything.

With things so unsettled, it had been decided that Ascensia would go back to Oak Haven to stay with her cousin Hetty until the war was over. For the winter at least for Washington had become like a huge military camp and things would no doubt be even worse after this latest disaster.

She hated to leave Letty and the baby. After giving birth to her first child, Letty was still confined to her bed upstairs. Since her husband, Ascensia's cousin Eben, had been listed among the missing after the battle of Cedar Mountain, Letty had only grown worse. Thankfully, the baby, a girl, was thriving.

Ascensia turned to look at the man who had just come out of the stable. She watched him as he crossed the lawn to the house and waited for him to join her on the veranda.

"Hot today, 'Scensia," he said as he came up the steps.

Bromfield McCay was twenty-five, just two years older than Ascensia. Brom was still paler than he ought to be, she thought. Her cousin's expression was thoughtful as he turned to gaze down the road. He, too, was listening to another low rumble of thunder.

Only two months ago Brom had come up that road on a bed of bloody straw in the bottom of a springless wagon. He had been burning with fever and so weak that he could barely hold onto the dirty blanket covering him.

Shot from his horse by Rebel guerrillas in the mountains of western Virginia, he had been left for dead for two days before he had been found. Later he had told her that all he remembered of his journey back home was waking up to see her face above him while they carried him to the house.

"It *is* hot, Brom," Ascensia sighed.

Her head lifted as another low rumble of thunder sounded from across the river. But this time it was echoed by a sound so faint and far away that it seemed only a tremor on the summer air. It was the distant mutter of cannonade, she realized.

She listened with a sinking heart for it meant that the slaughter across the river was not yet ended. It also meant that the Rebel Army was near. Near enough for echoes of the battle to reach the city. She knew that Brom had also heard it. As she watched his face, she saw his frown deepen.

"It's hard," she said. "The waiting, I mean."

"Morgan's on your mind," Brom said.

She nodded. "I keep dreading the long night ahead. That we will hear no news. Like- before. Yet I fear the news that might come."

Her voice trailed off as she stared out at the road. "I have been thinking of Eben today," she went on. "Of how we all used to sit here on the veranda together on summer nights. Before the war. I was remembering one night in particular when he made lanterns out of fireflies for us. Do you remember that night?"

"Yes," Brom said quietly. "I remember. I think about him a lot, too." Eben and Brom had been close, even for brothers. And they had both been more like brothers than cousins to Ascensia.

She closed her hands around the railing before her as she listened to the muffled throbbing in the distance. At this very moment Morgan was out there in the midst of all the horrors of war. And while she tried not to think of it, her heart ached at the thought that he, and so many others she knew, might be wounded, or worse, and she was here not knowing it.

She looked at the ambulances in the distance, their white covers showing through the trusses of the Chain Bridge. There were times when it was frustrating to be a woman, because as a woman she could do no more than wait, even if the waiting seemed forever, even while the whole world was falling apart.

She remained on the veranda for a while, talking with Brom. She then went upstairs to check on Letty and the baby. When she came back downstairs, the sky had grown dark with storm clouds and the stillness had yielded to a breath of wind that was aloft in the trees around the house.

In the parlor the curtains were straining against their fastenings. Several pages of sheet music had blown off the piano. Ascensia picked up the pages scattered around the room. She was about to close one of the parlor windows when her hand froze upon the sash. Brom was outside talking to a horseman at the gate.

The storm wind moved through the leaves with a sudden prolonged gust. Lightning pulsed fitfully behind the black cloud masses that were now sweeping in from across the river. Ascenia waited for Brom in the front hall, dreading whatever news he might bring her. When he came back to the house, her hand trembled as she tore open the letter he handed to her.

My Dearest Ascensia,
Before receiving this letter, you will doubtless have heard of the recent battles that have been taking place around Manassas. But this will assure you that I am safe . . .

Ascensia closed her eyes for a moment. "It's from Morgan," she said. "He is all right."

Letty was calling for Brom who had placed a second letter in Ascensia's hand, one that was addressed to Aletta McCay.

"I'll be back down after I see what Letty needs," Brom said. He hesitated a moment and looked up at Letty's door. His glance lowered to the letter in Ascensia's hand. "I won't mention the letter to Letty yet. We'll open it first. And in the morning, if- "

A tremendous crash of thunder cut off his words. It shook the very foundation of the house. The first drops of rain came pattering down upon the hot, parched earth as Brom went up the staircase. Alone in the parlor, Ascensia opened the second letter.

She read the few lines that were written on the single sheet of paper, then glanced down at the name boldly scrawled across the bottom of the page. When she looked up, she was frowning as she stared past the window where the rain had begun to blur the outside world. The storm, with all its fury, had come shrieking down with a vengeance.

Chapter 2

Through the delicate lace flowers of her veil, Ascensia looked up at the high walls of Montfort Prison. It was a forbidding, dismal-looking place that reminded her of an ancient fortress. It had once been a warehouse. Now Rebel prisoners were confined within the towering brick walls.

Her gaze wandered over the boards that were nailed across the windows a moment longer before she sat rigidly back against the leather carriage seat. One gloved hand rested on a small wicker basket on the seat beside her. She bent her head slightly forward, staring hard at the letter in her other hand, frowning at the bold, masculine scrawl as if she were trying to visualize the man who had written it. For the letter, and the man, were the reasons for her being here in the dusk of this second day of September.

Her gaze lifted, swept the dreary environs of the town. Greville Crossing was nowhere at all. Just two roads that came together in a clearing, around which was gathered a collection of unpainted, rundown buildings, Montfort Prison at the center of it. Surrounding what somebody had decided to call a town was a seemingly endless and impenetrable expanse of forest and mountains.

A steady, unrelenting rain had fallen all last night. The downpour had been so heavy that by morning the roads had become nearly impassible. Cut up by horses' hoofs and wagon wheels until they were a treacherous crisscross of deep ruts and holes filled with water, the roads had caused many troublesome delays since leaving Washington.

To make matters worse, Brom had been thrown by a fractious horse, aggravating his wound so that he had to be left behind at a farmhouse on the way here. A friend of Brom's, a Lieutenant Armitage, who had been traveling with them, had escorted Ascensia the remaining distance to the prison.

Even with a reliable escort, it had taken a good deal of time and persuasion to convince Brom to allow her to continue on without him. This southern border section of Maryland was extremely wild and unbroken and guerilla warfare was carried on here with a vengeance, not to mention that it was in close proximity to some of the more active smuggling routes along the river. Brom knew very well what Rebel guerillas were capable of.

This Rebel, this Jesse Lucane who had written the letter, claimed to know something about Eben, however, and Ascensia felt that they had waited too long and had gone through too much already to find out what the man might know. They could not give up now.

Last night she had thought about Letty, sick at heart over what might have happened to Eben down in Virginia. If Eben was safe, then that news would do Letty more good than anything else they could do for her. If they heard the worst, well, then she and Brom had decided to bear the news in silence and wait until Letty was strong enough to bear the shock herself.

Brom had only reluctantly yielded to her decision, but he could not argue with the fact that Letty was in no condition to make any kind of a trip by herself. And now neither was Brom. The truth was that neither Ascensia nor Brom was willing to miss this opportunity to find out what had happened to Eben.

She turned towards Lieutenant Armitage who had just come out of the prison. "Miss McCay," he said, offering her his arm. "We can go in now."

Nearly half an hour later Ascensia was readjusting the black lace veil over her face while a guard escorted her up to the third floor of the prison. There had been a lengthy interrogation downstairs. Her wicker basket had even been searched before they would allow her to bring it up. They could take no chances with spies, she was told. They would give her no further details, but she learned that this Jesse Lucane was no ordinary Rebel soldier. He was a Confederate spy.

The guard stopped before a closed door at the end of a dimly-lit corridor. He fitted a key into the lock and the hinges creaked faintly as the door slowly swung inward.

The guard stepped aside. "He's in irons, ma'am," he told her. "So you don't have to be afraid. I'll be right here if you need me. You only have to call out."

Inside the small, candle-lit room, Jesse Lucane had been sprawled comfortably on a narrow cot against the far wall. He now rose and stood before her.

Immediately, she noticed several things. For one, he was tall. Her head would have just reached his chin. For another, his movements were unhurried and deliberate, and not self conscious in the least, giving her the impression that he was a man of uncommon self-possession. Even here.

His dark hair was worn long in the Southern fashion. The dark beard stubble shadowing his chin and jaw gave him a particularly villainous look. Dangerous was another word that came to her mind.

And yet, in spite of all that, she admitted to herself that most women would have considered Jesse Lucane to be a handsome man. A very handsome man. Despite a steady intensity in his gaze that she found to be most unsettling. And though her veil hid most of her face, Ascensia had the unnerving sensation that those unwavering eyes were capable of seeing right through the barrier of lace.

She drew a slow breath, forcing calmness, and cast a glance towards the shadowed corner nearest her. "I have brought you some brandy," she said. "And some decent food that may make your time here less- difficult and improve your- " She paused. "Your condition."

Still trapped by the man's silent scrutiny, she frowned at her unaccustomed, halting speech, bit her lower lip and set the basket on the floor. She was turning towards the last of daylight and the fresh air at the window when the sudden scraping of a boot heel against the floor and the soft clanking of chains startled her. Ascensia whirled back around at the same time that she felt the hard pressure of the man's fingers circling her upper arm.

"No need to shy so," she heard him say in a low voice.

The Rebel's hand had fallen away and he had stepped back, but Ascensia continued to stare at him as if he were a ravening beast about to spring upon her and devour her.

"It's not safe to get too close to the windows, ma'am," he explained. "The guards will shoot at times. Without warning."

There was a hint of the South in his voice, she noted. And there was another quality in it that she was trying to analyze when he said, "But I thank you, ma'am, for trying to improve my- condition."

She did not know if he was mocking her. Certainly there was something in his voice and in his eyes, a boldness that hinted at mockery. They were not dark eyes. They were blue, perhaps. Or gray. She was not certain in the dim candlelight.

"So you're Aletta McCay," he said.

She nodded, hesitating a moment before she spoke the lie. "Yes."

She hadn't been sure until this moment how she would approach the man or how she would get the information she wanted. He might refuse to tell her what he knew if he found out that she was not Letty and she was not willing to take that chance. Then this would all be for nothing and they would be back where they had started. Surely he had never seen Letty. Letty could not possibly know this Rebel personally.

He nodded. He did so slowly as if he were considering her but had not yet come to any conclusions. "Then you must have received my letter," he said. "I've waited a long time for you to come."

Ascensia frowned beneath her veil, not sure if she detected a slight narrowing of his eyes. She searched for something, some hint of emotion in the man's face that might give her an advantage. She could find none.

"I was beginning to think," he interrupted her thoughts. "That you wouldn't come at all."

"Your letter was delayed for some reason. In Washington. At the Provost Office. It reached me only yesterday."

"I can see how that might happen."

While he spoke, his eyes seemed to travel the length of her. It was done in a subtle manner. A manner in which he, himself, exhibited no self-consciousness at all.

Amazingly, Ascensia felt herself blush. She could feel the blood surge hotly into her face and she became intensely grateful, at the moment, for her veil.

"I'm surprised to see you looking so- *fit* after such a long and arduous ride, ma'am," she heard him say. The faintest trace of a smile touched one corner of his mouth, further confusing her.

"You had a pleasant ride from Washington?" he asked softly and Ascensia had the distinct impression that he was playing some sort of game with her. One which he was winning.

"Why, no," she replied stiffly. "It was not pleasant in the least."

"I'm sorry for that, but I have to admit, I'd find any kind of ride pleasant right now."

Ascensia stared at him for a moment. "Indeed," she remarked coldly. What was he implying? Was he hinting at something improper? She didn't know. She did know, however, that he certainly seemed arrogant for a prisoner. For a spy. God alone knew what terrible things he had done or what he was capable of.

"Sir," she began in a carefully-controlled voice. "I hope that you have not deceived me into believing that you have knowledge of my- my husband's fate."

"No, ma'am," he said soberly. "No more than you would try to deceive me."

Behind her veil, Ascensia's gaze dropped to the man's black boots. Cavalry boots, scuffed and worn by hard service. And circled by heavy chains.

"It's just that I'm having some trouble knowing how to deliver such an important message when I can't see your face."

Jesse saw her head come up the slightest bit. Under the dark veil he could discern nothing of the woman's upper face. However, below the fragile lace was a different story. He noted that her very sensuous lips exhibited a brief display of disbelief followed by a hint of temper. He didn't miss that. And following the temper, he was sure that her beautiful mouth curled with just the merest hint of scorn.

He admitted to himself that he was more than a little curious as to what the rest of her face looked like. In fact, he was downright obsessed with the thought of seeing if his imagination matched the reality. Her voice was soft and sultry. A man couldn't help but wonder.

"Am I to understand that you are asking me to remove my veil?"

Her tone was priceless. He suppressed a smile.

"I only want to make sure you understand everything I say to you."

The man's audacity roused a strange antagonism in Ascensia. It was a deliberate challenge.

She reminded herself that she had come here for information about Eben. That was all that mattered. She was so close and if she had to remove her veil, that was a small price to pay. She drew the lace back.

The Rebel fixed her with a look that made her lower her own eyes in confusion. Only for a moment, however. She forced herself to look directly into his eyes. "Will you tell me now?" she asked. "I'm- "

"A liar," he finished for her. "Because you're not Aletta McCay. Just who are you and what do you want?"

His sudden demand startled her. No man had ever spoken to Ascensia like that. And even though he had just called her a liar, she saw that it did not cause him even the slightest bit of embarrassment. His eyes were as steady as before. Moreso, perhaps.

He had known all along, she realized. *His* deception roused something new in her. Indignation. She had come into this dreadful prison with good intentions. She had traveled a great distance. She had undergone many hardships. She had been kind enough to bring him food. There was even a bottle of brandy in the basket. And he had deliberately deceived her when all the time he had known that she was not Letty.

She tried to speak, not only to justify herself but to put him in his place. All she managed, however, was, "You- you . . . "

He lifted one dark brow. It was not enough that he had just called her a liar. This mockery, this deliberate mockery, was the last straw.

"I *what?*"

"I suppose," she said, yielding rashly to her emotions, without thinking it through. "That a man who is not above spying could be expected to be so insolent. But I also suppose that you will lose some of that insolence when they finally do put a rope around your neck."

She was immediately horrified at her outburst. Never in her life had she ever spoken so callously to anyone like that. Never had she reacted so impulsively.

"Ma'am," he said soberly. "I'm not denying that my future existence might be somewhat shortened. But are you forgetting about Captain McCay? Don't you think that now would be a good time to tell me who you really are?"

Ascensia had turned her face aside as she tried to gather up her composure. When he mentioned Eben, she looked back at the Rebel. It took some doing, but she reminded herself that she had come here with a single purpose in mind. She explained in as few words as possible who she was and why she had come in Letty's place.

He ran his hand slowly along the dark whiskers on his chin. The chains there rattled softly. "Why did you lie?" he asked.

She stared at him across the shadowed room and answered simply, honestly, "It seemed less complicated that way."

"You've told me that you are related to the Captain," he said. "But I have no way of knowing if you're telling me the truth." He narrowed his eyes at the look she gave him. "You did lie already, ma'am."

"And I don't know that you really have anything at all to tell me," she flashed back. "You haven't offered a shred of information yet."

"That's true enough," he replied. "But I don't have any reason to lie."

"Of course you don't believe *me*," she said. "But you expect me to take your word. The word of a Rebel spy."

"Are you wondering whether I'm a spy or not?" he asked, a new interest in his eyes.

"I want you to know that who or what you are is of no interest to me. My only concern is Captain McCay."

She stared back at him, saw how the candlelight gleamed on hair black as a raven's wing.

"I might be a spy. Is that why you're afraid of me?"

"I am not afraid of you."

"Aren't you? You seem so." She wasn't sure, but suspected that he was making fun of her again.

"You are mistaken, sir," she informed him, mockery edging into her own voice. "If you think that I am afraid of a man in chains while there is an armed guard standing right outside the door."

He smiled faintly at that but held her gaze.

"And I think," she added. "That if you have any of the wrong kind of ideas, you will have more to think about than how to deliberately provoke me."

He breathed a low laugh, surprising her. And for a moment, Ascensia wondered at the change in his face. But while the smile softened the hard lines of his face, it never completely changed his eyes. She quickly made up her mind that as the smile lingered, it was more like a wolf baring its teeth in a snarl.

"Well, ma'am," he said. "Whoever you are, I have decided to trust you since my own future is somewhat uncertain. As you have already pointed out.

"I have given my word to get a message to Captain McCay's wife. So I have no choice but to trust you to deliver it and hope that my trust hasn't been misplaced."

Ascensia watched as he reached into his vest pocket.

"Here is the Captain's watch and a letter written to his wife."

Ascensia's heart clenched. He had Eben's personal effects. Did that mean that Eben had been killed? Or even worse, what if this man had killed him? Her voice was barely above a whisper. "He's- "

"Alive."

She closed her eyes for long moments, battling the impulse to display her joy, her utter relief at that one word. She could scarcely wait until she could tell Brom and Letty the good news.

He handed her Letty's daguerreotype and she knew it was the proof of her lie.

"Captain McCay was taken prisoner," he told her. "At the battle of Slaughter Mountain. Cedar Mountain you Yankees call it. He wasn't wounded, but he was taken to a field hospital with some of his men who were. Their names are also in that letter."

As he spoke, Jesse watched the play of emotions that crossed her face. They seemed sincere. He could almost believe her.

Ascensia folded the watch in her gloved hand. Looking up to see that the Rebel was still watching her, she quickly slipped all three items into her reticule. "I would like to thank you for your trouble," she said.

"There's no need," came the reply. "I gave my word to the Captain."

"In spite of that," she said with a slight frown. "I am grateful."

Uncomfortable with the silence that had suddenly settled between them, Ascensia was not sure how she ought to end things between them.

"And I am grateful," Jesse Lucane said and smiled at her bewildered look. "For the brandy and such that you brought me."

His smile faded but his eyes lingered on her face. In the wavering shadows of the small room, once again Ascensia felt strangely confused, oddly reluctant to let things stand as they were between them.

But there was no more left to say until he said softly, "Goodbye, ma'am."

The colonel in charge of Montfort Prison watched until the carriage had disappeared from sight. He pulled the dispatch from his pocket and reread his orders.

No mercy is to be shown to enemy spies. As an example, the Rebel, Jesse Lucane, captured on August 19, 1862, is to be duly hanged upon receipt of this order.

The Colonel folded the paper and put it back in his pocket. He had postponed the hanging for Miss Ascensia McCay. But now that she was gone, there was no reason to delay it further. He stood for a while gazing out at the darkness, frowning over the things that war demanded of a man. With a heavy sigh he turned and walked back into the prison.

Chapter 3

It was midnight. Ascensia heard the clock downstairs filling the house with its sonorous chimes. Twelve, she counted as she fastened the last button of her heavy cotton nightgown.

They sky was black and starless. It had rained again, but briefly. Now only the last mutterings of thunder could be heard in the distance. Closer, the leaves kept up a steady dripping outside the window. There was a pond nearby and the loud chirping of insects and the croaking of frogs filled the night.

Ascensia was surprised, but grateful, that Lieutenant Armitage had arranged such comfortable accommodations for her. She had not expected to see such a gracious home set in the midst of the wilderness less than half an hour's ride from Montfort Prison.

She parted the curtains at the window. The night air bore the fragrance of rain. It was also pleasantly scented with wood smoke because a small detachment of soldiers was camped in the yard below.

When she got into bed, she did not close her eyes but lay staring up into the darkness. There was a great deal to be thankful for. Eben was alive. He was lying in some dreadful Southern prison at this very moment, probably hungry and no doubt homesick. But he was safe and because he was an officer, there was a good chance that an exchange might be arranged.

She'd wasted no time in forwarding a message to Letty in Washington. And one had been sent to Brom. If Brom was able to travel, he would meet her here tomorrow and they would go on to Oak Haven together. If not, Lieutenant Armitage had offered to escort her there personally and Brom would join her later.

It had been a very long day and Ascensia was tired. Yet sleep eluded her. It was this unfamiliar place, she told herself, and the long day's events behind her which probably accounted for her sleeplessness. She went over the details of all that had happened once more, but in the end her thoughts kept returning to a single memory.

She saw the Rebel's face again in her mind. Jesse Lucane had aroused many conflicting emotions in her. He had made her angry. He had made her resentful. And indignant. And then he had made her joyful, relieved and thankful. Such a kaleidoscope of opposing emotions had left her feeling more than a little confused.

She didn't know why, in the small space of time that they had been together, he had been able to draw up such strong reactions from her. So easily. So quickly. She didn't know why she was still thinking about him at all.

There was something about Jesse Lucane that she could not completely define. He was not like other men. He was hard and unshakable. Cynical, perhaps. She wondered if he had always been so. Or if the war had changed him and made him the kind of man he was today.

Whatever manner of man Jesse Lucane was, he was now shackled like an animal and imprisoned for a treasonous act. The last of many probably. Condemned to death most likely, for that was the usual fate of spies. She found herself regretting the words she had spoken to him, but there was no way to call them back now. In any case, what could she possibly say to him that would change anything?

She understood that war was a grim game, one in which punishment, no matter how cruel it seemed, was considered to be justice. Still, she could not help but feel a deep sense of the tragedy of it all. She would never meet Jesse Lucane again. Not this side of heaven at least. In time she would forget a Rebel spy with eyes that reflected more than she was accustomed to seeing in a man's eyes.

As she lay there pondering his fate, however, she was troubled by something she could not completely understand. It was an elusive something that made her *keep* remembering. While she lay there in the darkness, she heard the first strains of a fiddle through the open window. Accompanying the music, a soldier began the words of the sad song, *Weeping Sad and Lonely*.

Weeping sad and lonely,
   Hopes and fears how vain.
When this cruel war is over,
   Hoping that we meet again.

The music was played beautifully. It was played slowly, with deep feeling. After the last verse, the soldier's voice died away though the fiddle continued to play. The last notes quivered lingeringly on the night air before they faded away like a dream.

Thunder rolled quietly in the distance. In the morning, Ascensia thought sleepily, she would tell them how much she had enjoyed the music. She would tell them how well they had played. In the morning . . .

And she finally slept as did the homesick soldiers who also felt the song weave about them like a spell. A slight breeze lifted and moved through the darkness. But save for the thunder which echoed in a very distant place, all was quiet along the Potomac on that most profound and most lonely of nights.

It is the unforeseen, however, which most often rules in the end. For Ascensia and the Rebel spy were destined to meet again after all. While they slept, there was more astir in the hushed whisper of the wind as it swept over the land than any of them imagined.

Some fifteen miles to the west, along the Union border where the Potomac lapped gently against the Maryland shore, a slight rippling sound disturbed the idle murmur of the river. Downstream, a night creature sat upright and peered through the darkness, instantly alert. Turning quickly, it scurried into the concealing shelter of the thick underbrush and disappeared.

The river itself could not be seen. Drifting layers of mist at first hid the phantom-like shadows. The shadows soon rose out of the water to become the dark shapes of men and horses.

The horses waded through the shallow water, then heaved themselves up onto the muddy bank where they stood dripping with river water. Except for the sound of the water and the slight clank of steel against steel now and then, both riders and horses remained as silent as the mist from which they had emerged.

The clouds broke and moonlight revealed an occasional gleam of accoutrements. It also lent a hungry glint to the eyes of those men who looked up towards the sudden moonlight as they sat their horses on the shore waiting for the others who were still coming across the river.

No word was spoken. Not even after they had all gathered. The men silently wheeled their mounts, climbed the steep slopes of the river bank, and soon vanished into the depths of the Maryland forest.

For a time the steel-shod hoofs of the horses made a heavy, muffled sound on the damp ground. Occasionally a hoof cracked over loose rocks. Eventually these sounds ceased altogether so that except for the hoot of an owl, the night was as deathly silent as before. And all that remained to give evidence that the riders had passed that way were the tracks they left behind. But these, too, would fade and soon be washed away by the rain that was yet to fall.

Chapter 4

Jesse sat motionless in his cell. His eyes were half closed as he idly contemplated the condition of his boot toes stretched out before him. He lifted a saber-scarred hand and raked it through his dark hair, ignoring the rattle of the chains. He had been confined in prisons before and this was not the worst of them. Still, these weeks of forced inactivity did not sit well with him.

He stretched his legs out slowly, lengthening the taut muscles, and glanced up toward the window as the branches of the trees outside shivered in a slight breeze that had just risen. Thunder rolled softly in the distance.

Tonight the past had been creeping up on him with images that moved before him like something half lost in a mist. He frowned, focusing in on a long-ago memory that he had tried hard to leave behind.

Going back to the old place would be like visiting a graveyard. The people he had known no longer existed. They were merely ghosts of a past that was now too painful to recall.

The restlessness that plagued him tonight had been even stronger in his early years. He had been rebellious and headstrong then. To a fault. It had led him into a hard and violent life. It occurred to him that he may have lived so hard for so long that he might never be able to settle into a quiet, domestic kind of existence. He did not know if he regretted it.

He settled back on his blanket. It was raining again. Softly. It had rained that night, too. The remembering was hard, but would not be denied as he closed his eyes.

He had come back more than once in those later years. But he still did not understand the strange coincidence that had called him back home that one night out of all the others. Life, however, often worked itself out in strange ways. Maybe a man could call it fate. He had lived long enough to know that there were things that could not be explained.

There had been no warm welcome waiting for him as there had been the other times. The only thing awaiting him had been death. The house was left. They hadn't been able to burn it because of the rain. But they had tried. The barn, however, had been filled with hay. He had ridden up to see a pile of smoking beams still glowing an angry red.

They stole what they could. And everything else they had touched had been destroyed. Or violated. And they had touched everything. He relived again that stunned disbelief, and felt now a helpless, hollow kind of pain at the memory of a gentle face framed by fair curls. And laughing green eyes. Eyes that haunted him still. Eyes that he had closed for the final time.

Military necessity, they had called it. Murder, he called it. And greed. It had all been for private plunder. He had stayed all night beside the grave he had dug, tortured by the thought of what she must have endured. He had shivered as much from the agony and the grief as he did from the rain that drove the cold deep into the marrow of his bones.

He frowned and shook his head, willing away further recollection. He could not dwell long upon it. She was dead and nothing could change that cold, final fact. He prayed that she was at peace.

His gaze wandered along the ceiling without really seeing it. A name breathed upon his lips as he closed his eyes. Pain etched itself across his features. "Be still in your grave," he whispered. "Be still."

Sometimes it seemed that the instinctive, driving need for revenge burned as strongly in him now as it did that night. They had worn blue, so the next day he had ridden south and enlisted in the Confederate Army.

Somehow he survived nearly a year and a half of bloody battles and deadly cavalry charges, of scouting and spying and smuggling, which summed up his service on behalf of the Southern Confederacy. He had been assigned to special detached service. A fancy phrase, he reckoned, that meant he was a spy. Eventually he was sent north to scout for Stonewall Jackson in the Shenandoah Valley.

He was back home now, accepting service along the Potomac because he knew the region so well. Unfortunately, he'd ridden right into a Yankee scouting party two weeks ago and he'd gotten shot in the bargain. The ball had glanced off his leather belt, tearing away a strip of flesh below his left shoulder. It was not a dangerous wound, but it was a painful one that was slow in healing.

He had been carrying a quantity of quinine as well and passes from several Confederate commanders. He realized well enough what his fate might be. And yet it seemed ironic to him that he had come home to meet it.

He lifted the bottle of brandy to his mouth and drank long and deep, feeling a stab of pain where his wound still healed. He settled back and let the warmth spread through him.

He had almost forgotten her basket left there in the shadows. Rubbing the back of his hand across his chin, he felt the harsh rasp of beard and grimaced. He reckoned he looked pretty rough. Rough enough to frighten young Yankee ladies. He needed a shave. And a bath. His hair needed trimming as well. He even had a bullet hole or two in his clothes.

He was aware, too, of other things that he had been without for a long time. He conjured her image. Veiled, perfumed, intense. He found himself wondering how she would look with her dark hair unbound and those fascinating eyes half closed with passion, her eager mouth awaiting his kiss.

She had wanted to improve his condition. He let his breath out shortly there in the shadowed room. It was followed by a smile of grim humor. Yeah, right before, as she had said, they put the rope around his neck.

If nothing else, she had amused him. He recalled the startled expression on her face when he had called her a liar. She had immediately exhibited disbelief. And then she had quickly grown indignant. He believed the indignation had amused him the most for it had given him a glimpse of a fiery spirit.

He took another drink and remembered the moment when she had drawn her veil back. She was more than pretty. She was damned beautiful actually and his masculine urges were not immune to her charms. But he knew many beautiful women. He also knew that she might well have been some campfollower they had gotten to find out what she could about him.

The shadow of a smile lingered. He would have liked to have taken a long, long time teaching her a few things about himself. Regrettably, that didn't have a chance of happening. Amidst the regret, he lifted the bottle in a silent, half-mocking salute. "To you, ma'am. Whoever you are."

As he lay there, an owl called out in the darkness. After a period of silence the sound came again, clear and distinct from the woods that surrounded the prison. This time Jesse straightened, listening more closely. His smile grew wolfish. Some of the night's loneliness fell away from him and it was like a release of old chains.

Deep in the wilderness of southern Maryland, several miles west of Montfort Prison, six Union cavalrymen and their prisoner made a silent procession through a dead-white world of drifting mist.

"Miserable night," one of the men grumbled. "Fog's so thick I can't see my horse's ears." The complainer cursed again, more profanely this time, and slapped wildly at a branch that loomed suddenly before him.

The voice ceased and only the soft clanking of accoutrements punctuated the dull, sloshing sound of horses' hoofs in mud.

The freshening breeze touched the prisoner's face and blew through the dark strands of his hair. His wrists were tightly bound and lashed to the pommel of his saddle. With ropes now, not chains. Two soldiers rode on either side of him, but the exercise and the rawness of the night air went a long way towards reviving Jesse's blood after the confinement of his cell.

The moon was visible at the moment though it continued to play hide and seek with the clouds. The moonlight, when it shone, afforded some light to guide the men. They were riding along the edge of a thick stand of pine trees. They were confronted by a sudden outcropping of rock. The ground on the opposite side of the trail fell away to emptiness where the mist rose thick and heavy. Jesse could hear water rushing over rocks far below. He knew the place.

"Evenin'."

The sudden voice from the misty darkness startled the men. They jerked their horses to a halt and strained their eyes towards the single horseman that had materialized in the path before them.

A black slouch hat was pulled low over the man's eyes. A full, dark beard covered the lower half of his face. He wore a blue Union overcoat. Union trousers were tucked into black cavalry boots, but more than one man's hand crept cautiously towards his weapon.

"You're wonderin', I reckon," the horseman drawled. "Well, forget about pulling your guns. Jest keep settin' there and y'all put your hands up."

The black muzzle of a carbine made its appearance from beneath the blue overcoat. At the same time several other riders appeared from the mist as the ominous click of weapons filled the silence.

The Union men raised their hands when they realized that they were surrounded by enemy soldiers. The sergeant at the lead, however, hesitated.

"Don't even think about it," the black-bearded Rebel warned him. "Don't touch that gun or Ah'll blow you clean off your horse."

The sergeant slowly raised his hands till they were level with his shoulders. Several Rebels rode forward to relieve the Union men of their weapons.

The black-bearded man grinned at the prisoner. "Howdy, Jes."

Jesse grinned back.

Sometime later, the group of Rebel horsemen were halted in a small clearing in the woods. The black-bearded giant, Lieutenant Wirt Blackford, handed a leather pouch to Jesse.

"Jes," he said with a shake of his head. "You've got the look of a wolf who's been starvin' for a long while. Ah reckon," the Lieutenant went on. "That prison didn't set well with you. Ah have had a taste of Federal jails myself. Ah suppose you were getting a little uncomfortable wondering if we would show up in time."

"Maybe a little uncomfortable," Jesse admitted.

The other men grinned. Jesse knew most of them. Officially they were all scouts. It was their business to ride just beyond the Union Army and keep track of its movements. But they all did some spying and smuggling as well.

Contraband goods, desperately needed in the blockaded South, were procured from various sources up North and were shipped down to the Maryland border to be ferried across the Potomac River. Guns, ammunition, uniforms, medicines, mail, information and even people, including escaped prisoners, might be sent at any time into Virginia.

It was a profitable business for some, a risky business for them all. The Potomac was situated between the two armies and the Yankees did all they could to make things lively for them. Consequently, they were all used to living on the edge of danger.

Perhaps the boldest of them all was Lieutenant Wirt Blackford. Jesse knew him to be fearless and dependable. They had scouted together in the Shenandoah for a time as well as in Maryland.

"Ah have received orders from Colonel Louvain," the Lieutenant said. "We're to provide Captain Bayne with horses and saddles. He's down at your- at the old house with some escaped prisoners. Most of them are pretty bad off. They'll be in desperate circumstances if a party of Yanks happens to find 'em. You are to meet with Captain Bayne as soon as possible. He's holding papers that have got to be on their way south tonight. You'll have to be especially careful. If a man was to show himself at the wrong time tonight, he wouldn't last any longer'n a rush light. Noble heah run into a group of riders on the way back."

"You get close enough to see who they might be, Noble?" Jesse asked the young scout.

"A might closer than Ah wanted to be, by God," Noble declared. "There were twenty-five, maybe thirty, of them prowlin' around below heah. Travelin' fast and quiet on the back trail by the old mill. That's not all," he went on. "There's a small Yankee wagon train at the Cade Mansion. It's guarded by about fifteen cav."

"They aware of anything?" Jesse asked.

"Don't believe so," the scout replied. "But Ah'm certain of one thing. They'll know about them before this night is ovah. Ah heard one of the riders say something about it while they were passing by. Don't know why they'd be interested at all. Unless they're carrying a payroll."

"We'll have to keep a close eye out," Lieutenant Blackford said as the men wheeled their horses.

"So-long, Captain," they called as they rode off. "See you in Leesburg."

Noble Young lingered after the other men had ridden off. Leather creaked as he shifted in the saddle, watching Jesse adjust the cinch on his saddle. "There's something else Ah thought you would want to know, suh."

Something in Noble's voice made Jesse look up.

"It's about John Lathrop."

Jesse's face hardened.

"It's no secret that Lathrop has been making himself a lot of money," Noble went on. "He has connections with some Yankee who's got influence."

Jesse's lips curved with contempt. "Smuggling can be a hell of a business," he said. "Sometimes it doesn't matter what a man's motives are as long as the money is good."

"You're right there, Captain," Noble said slowly. "But helping your country, well, that's one thing. Getting rich off of other people's needs, why that's something else. Ah reckon with you bein' in prison, you hadn't heard about Newell Law bein' killed."

"The hell you say. When?" Jesse asked.

"About the time you were captured. Newell and Rush were just coming up from the river to an arranged meeting place when Yankee soldiers fired on them. Newell was shot through the chest and Rush was hit in the arm. They managed to escape and tried to reach friends by traveling at night and hiding in the woods by day. But Newell got so bad that Rush took him to the house of a girl he knows. She took care of them. Newell died a few days later. Rush and the girl had to bury him in the woods in an unmarked grave. It about broke his mother's heart when she heard about it. Rush told me later that Lathrop was supposed to be at that meeting place but he never showed."

"You think it was an ambush?" Jesse asked.

"Rush sure thinks so. Those soldiers never gave them a chance to surrender."

"And you think Lathrop had something to do with it?"

"Ah don't know what to think," replied the scout. "Rush claims Lathrop was nursing a grudge against Newell. Ah'll confess that more'n once Ah have had suspicions about Lathrop."

Jesse's face wore a hard expression as he mounted his horse and gathered the reins.

"Sure it's a quiet night, suh," Noble remarked softly as he gazed up at the night sky. "But Ah'm thinking there's going to be a lot of howlin' before daylight comes."

As if to support his words, thunder rumbled ominously out of the darkness and rolled across the mist-shrouded forest.

"Seems like we're in for another rainy spell," the young scout remarked.

"Reckon you're right about that, Noble," Jesse said as he turned from his own contemplation of the heavens.

Noble touched his fingers to his hat and grinned. "Watch out for those two-legged wolves, Captain. See you in Leesburg, suh."

Chapter 5

To Ascensia, waking from a deep and dreamless sleep, the sound reverberating back from the hills had a quality of unreality about it. By the time she was fully awake, the faint echoes had ceased altogether.

It may have been thunder that had awakened her, she thought sleepily. It was not thunder, however, that she heard next. It was the sound of horses hoofs approaching at a gallop.

She rose quickly from the bed and groped about in the darkness for her shawl. Finding it, she pulled it around her nightgown. The next sound she heard made her freeze on her way to the window.

It was like no sound she had ever heard before. It was howling. It was like the sound of wild beasts on the scent of blood. This howling, however, came from human throats.

She sat down on the bed to pull her boots on and heard a burst of gunfire. Outside the open window, what had been a peaceful night had exploded in violence and confusion.

With her boots still half unlaced, Ascensia stood up and stared at the door. Heavy footsteps were coming along the hall. They stopped just outside her room.

The door was flung violently open, the lock proving no hindrance to the man standing on the threshold. A shadowed figure filled the doorway. The moment that the man stepped forward, the room was suddenly illuminated by a red glow from outside the window. Something had been set on fire.

The light grew. Ascensia could see the man's face clearly now. It was a coarse face, hideously scarred and unshaven. A kind of savage excitement etched the man's distorted features. She remembered all that she had ever heard about guerillas and knew that she was seeing one now.

The man did not speak. He grinned, however, as he focused on her. The grin widened as she looked at the gun in his hand. The black barrel suddenly swung towards the open doorway. Lieutenant Armitage had appeared on the landing.

The moment that the warning cry left her lips, Ascensia heard the huge crash of the gun. A crimson flame burst before the Lieutenant's face as he fell back against the wall.

For a moment Ascensia shut her eyes against the horror of the scene before her. It seemed unreal. Everything was happening so quickly, giving her no time to think. She was aware of the acrid smell of burnt powder in the room. And smoke. And the crackling sound of flames beyond the window.

When she opened her eyes again, the guerilla was jamming the smoking gun back into his holster. He turned back to Ascensia and stepped directly in front of her. Without a word he took hold of her arm and dragged her along with him, out of the room and into the hallway, past the Lieutenant who was lying motionless on the floor.

Ascensia fought the man all the way down the stairs. When she continued to resist, he slapped her hard across the face before he shoved her through the doorway to the veranda. He pulled her along with him to a horse that pranced and snorted at the rail. He jerked the reins free and mounted. Then, immediately reaching down, he lifted Ascensia and swung her up onto the saddle before him.

He gripped the reins with one hand. His other arm encircled her, crushing her ribs and pulling her hard against his chest. His boots thudded hard into the horse's ribs and the animal reared upright then came down again before it jumped forward into a bone-jarring gallop.

In spite of the moving horse, Ascensia tried desperately to free herself. She squirmed and twisted and managed to kick the man. Once. Twice. It must have hurt him because he grabbed a fistful of her hair and pulled her head back until she cried out.

"Try that again, Yankee witch," he hissed viciously beside her ear. "And I'll make you sorry you even thought of it." He gave her hair one last brutal wrench then urged the horse to an even faster pace through the moon-lit aisles of the forest.

Branches lashed painfully across her flesh. They tore at her clothing. The night was cold, but Ascensia's blood was pounding hotly through her body. She could still hear the sound of gunshots behind her.

The man pushed her over the horse's neck then leaned over her to avoid a low sweep of branches himself. As he straightened, he uttered a hoarse, strangled cry. Ascensia felt his hand tighten convulsively on the back of her nightgown before it loosened then released her altogether.

After riding furiously and recklessly for a few moments, the reins were jerked tight. The horse tossed its head wildly as it drew itself up into a rough, abrupt halt in a small clearing. The animal continued to paw the ground, prancing sideways while lit fought the bit.

Ascensia was able to slide out of the saddle. She landed hard on the ground but managed to scramble away from the deadly, iron-shod hoofs. She fully expected to be roughly treated. In fact, she expected to have to fight for her life.

But the man still had not dismounted. He was leaning far over the pommel, with both hands gripping it as he drew his breath in in deep, hoarse gasps. When he did dismount, he kept his hands pressed tightly over his chest. Those hands were covered with what looked like blood, Ascensia saw. A dark stain was also visible across the front of the man's shirt.

While she stared in indecision, the man fixed Ascensia with a savage look. He staggered forward and reached for her with a bloody hand. He managed to grasp her sleeve. She tried to pull away from him, sickened at the thought of his blood on her.

There was a brief struggle. He pulled her halfway down with him as he sank to his knees. To Ascensia's horror, he refused to let go. When he finally did release her, he pitched forward into the grass where he lay face down. And did not move.

Ascensia looked around for the horse, but it had bolted and was nowhere in sight. She glanced back at the guerilla. Her nightgown was damp from the ride through the woods. She still had her boots on, but they were loose because they were untied. She had lost her shawl, she realized, but could not remember where.

In fact, she could not seem to be able to think clearly at all. The memory of Lieutenant Armitage being shot flashed vividly into her mind and she covered her face with her hands.

For a moment the incoherence of her thoughts alarmed her. She lowered her hands to her mouth. She fought to remain calm. She had to stay calm. She didn't know if she could find her way back to the Cade Mansion. She didn't know what awaited her back there. But at the same time, she knew she couldn't remain here alone in the woods.

She heard another horse approaching. Quickly, she moved out of the clearing, backing up until she was concealed by the heavy brush. She inched her way even further back, keeping a tense watch on the clearing through the heavy screen of leaves before her. There was no moonlight just now so the woods were very dark. Maybe someone was coming to rescue her. Until she knew for sure, she would remain hidden.

She was so intent on what was happening in the clearing that she wasn't prepared for what happened next. Her startled cry was smothered by a hand that clamped firmly across the lower part of her face.

Panicking, she attempted to turn her face to the side to free it from the harsh pressure of the hand, but her head was pulled relentlessly back against a hard shoulder. At the same time, an arm encircled her like a steel band, pinning her arms at her sides.

Held ruthlessly in a man's grip, Ascensia was forced so hard against the length of his body that she could feel the buttons of his clothing digging into her back right through her nightgown. She still struggled, but the more she fought, the tighter his grip became.

"Keep quiet," came the low command as the man leaned close to her ear.

The hand over her mouth fell away without warning. In the next moment she heard the dull click of a pistol beside her ear as a horse suddenly burst into the clearing.

Certain she would be killed if she uttered a sound, she silently watched the horseman in the sudden flood of moonlight. He looked down at the body of the guerilla while his horse snorted and pranced restively, as if shying from the smell of blood.

Ascensia could not see the rider's face clearly. Only the lower half of it showed beneath the shadow of his hat brim. While she watched, a cold smile touched the man's mouth. He would be no rescuer, she realized in an instant. The smile expressed pure evilness.

The smile vanished as he looked up sharply. He turned to gaze intently at the woods in all directions around the clearing. Ascensia did not move. Neither did the man who held her. The only sound was the deep breathing of the horse as the rider pulled out his pistol. She heard the click as he pulled the hammer back. She watched as he took slow, deliberate aim and put four more balls into the body lying there.

Ascensia closed her eyes, fighting the sick feeling rising up inside her. She waited, like the man behind her, for the rider to depart. It was not long before he wheeled his horse and disappeared into the woods.

The man who held Ascensia did not immediately release her. Even after the rider could no longer be seen or heard, he continued to hold her. She could feel his gun where it rested against her upper arm. And the pressure of his arm across her breast had not lessened. The night was cold, but she was aware of the heat of his body where it molded itself against her, even through the layers of their clothing. She could feel, too, the man's thumb as it stroked her shoulder in a slow, almost caressing gesture.

That movement ceased abruptly, however, and she knew that the man was now focusing his attention on her. His chin brushed her cheek as he leaned forward.

"No screams," she heard him say before he let her go.

Ascensia whirled around to face the man. She stared through the moon-lit darkness, drew a deep and startled breath and released it in a single word. "*You!*"

Ascensia stared through the darkness as if it was impossible for the man to be there. Instinct made her take a step away from him.

Jesse Lucane grabbed her arm. "Stay put, honey," he warned. "I'm not in the mood to be chasing you through the woods."

Her eyes flashed. Her breast rose and fell. She wrenched her arm free, suddenly furious over the rough manner in which he had just handled her.

"Don't call me that," she whispered passionately. "And don't ever put your hands on me like that again or I promise I'll make you sorry."

He stared at her a moment. "Well, I believe you would try your best," he said. "But let's save it for later. It's going to rain again and I don't want to be out here in the woods when it does."

His eyes slowly raked her. "Judging by the way you're dressed, or *un*dressed, I'm guessing you won't want to be either."

Jesse saw the quick rise her breast under the damp nightgown as she drew an indignant breath. It was a questionable covering at best. It did more to emphasize her womanly curves than to conceal them. He recalled that his arm had rested there quite intimately and, if he cared to be perfectly honest with himself, maybe he had held her a little longer than had been necessary. He also admitted that he now found his thoughts wandering an unbidden, if compelling path that-

She drew one arm protectively in front of her, making him suspect that his wayward thoughts had, perhaps, found expression in his face.

There was something in the man's eyes that made Ascensia even more keenly aware of the fact that she was wearing only her nightgown. And that no corset and no petticoats, no other coverings whatsoever, had been between them when he had held her. She still had not shaken the feel of his hand over her mouth or the pressure of his arm around her.

"You are taking me back then?" she asked a little breathlessly, a little hopefully.

He shrugged out of the cavalry coat that he was wearing and handed it to her. She put it one because she felt stripped down to nakedness beneath the man's stare. It had been the same way with her veil. He seemed to have the ability to see right through any and all barriers.

"You'll go back," he told her. "But not just yet."

"What do you mean?"

"I mean that we're both going to have to adjust our plans."

Plans? She didn't know what he was talking about. "But you will take me back?" she persisted.

"After I take care of some business," he replied, watching her face a little more closely. It was hard to know what to expect from this woman.

Ascensia did not know exactly what he was suggesting any more than she knew how he had come to be there in the woods. But she certainly would not consider even the prospect of traveling to places unknown with an enemy spy.

"And where is it that you *think* you are taking me?" she asked as she stared back at him through the darkness.

"Ma'am, if I was inclined to discuss military matters with you, I would do so. But I am not."

That straightened her back, Jesse noted.

"I am not going anywhere with you unless you tell me where- "

"If I have to, I'll make you come with me," he interrupted in a voice that, perhaps, she should have interpreted as being a little too quiet.

"You will *make* me?" she echoed.

"Just that."

Apparently, he had no intention of discussing it further. He turned and held a low-lying branch aside for her. She reluctantly followed him for a short distance to a horse that was waiting in the shadows. She meant to pursue the matter. She meant to find out exactly what his intentions were. She was about to ask when he gathered the reins and mounted the horse.

He held his hand out. "Come on. I'll help you up."

She did not want to get up on the horse with him. That was altogether too much. The alternative, however, was to spend the night lost and alone in the Maryland wilderness with Rebel guerillas and murderers prowling around. Not to mention wild animals. And more rain.

Before she could voice a protest, he reached down and hauled her up to the saddle. He ignored her arguments about the impropriety of riding together *like heathens* and seated her sideways in front of him as if she were riding a sidesaddle. She immediately stiffened and grew quiet as she concentrated on keeping as much distance between them as possible. As the horse started forward, she had to grab the pommel with both hands to keep from falling off.

Even while they were riding, the Rebel would not tell her where they were going except to say that she would be safer and considerably more comfortable than she would have been had he left her wandering alone in the woods all night. He would not, he added, have been able to forgive himself if he had left her behind to fend for herself.

This last statement had a trace of mockery in it, the same mockery she had detected in the prison cell. He did give her his word that she would be returned, however, at his earliest convenience and she intended to hold him to that promise.

Somehow the man was able to find his way through the darkness. After perhaps half an hour had passed, they stopped before a house that had suddenly loomed up out of the forest before them.

The house had apparently been deserted for some time. Some of the windows were broken. Tattered remains of curtains streamed out of some of them. Far back in the shadows, a pile of blackened beams remained where a barn had once stood though ivy had already twined around the charred wood. And even further back, a lonely gravestone was half hidden by weeds. Ascensia, however, saw neither. The mist and the darkness concealed both.

There were several saddled horses tethered to the rail of the front porch. Standing on the porch were three men wearing gray uniforms. As the man behind her guided the horse up close to the porch steps, the men leaned forward to peer at Ascensia through the darkness.

"Why, it's a woman," she heard one of them exclaim.

There was a long, drawn-out silence followed by a quiet, "Evenin', Captain" as they dismounted.

Ascensia pulled the wool coat more tightly around her, summoning as much dignity as was possible in a nightgown and a Rebel's coat. She remained where she was, staring up at the house while the *Captain*, as she had just learned he was, started up the steps. He turned back to her when she did not follow.

"Come on," he said, impatience deepening his voice. He reached to take hold of her arm but she drew back before he could get a firm hold.

"Let go of me."

He obviously had not expected her to resist.

"We're going inside," he informed her, as if there was no debating the issue.

"Who's in there?" she asked.

What could only be described as a wolfish smile tightened one corner of his mouth. "Soldiers," he replied.

"Rebel soldiers?"

"Yes," he answered. "And you are going to keep quiet and do as I say."

He would have taken hold of her arm again, or at least attempted it, but she walked stiffly up the steps before he could do so.

At the head of the stairs she paused again. The soldiers on the porch suddenly swept their hats from their heads. They might be enemy soldiers, but Ascensia realized that she was in the company of men who were accustomed to treating women with some degree of respect. That, at least, made her a little hopeful.

The Captain gave her a long, narrowed look before he walked to the front door and held it open for her. He gestured her inside with a mocking sweep of his hand.

The interior of the house was dimly lit by candles. Some of the rooms were completely dark. Blankets had been hung over the windows to keep the light from being seen outside. From where Ascensia stood in the front hallway, she could see men lying on the floors everywhere. Wounded men. She could see bandages on some of them. Apparently they were sick as well for a dry, hacking cough came from one of the shadowed rooms.

A Rebel officer stepped into the hallway. He stopped abruptly when he saw Ascensia. His eyes registered even more surprise when he looked down at her nightgown below the cavalry coat. Plainly confused, and even a little embarrassed, his gaze sought the man standing next to her.

"I am glad to see you, Captain Lucane," he said, attempting to cover up his embarrassment. "I hope you didn't run into too much trouble on the way here."

"Some," was the Captain's reply before he silently led Ascensia to a small room at the back of the house.

Before he left the room, he told her to "stay put". She had no choice in the matter since there was no window and only the one door. A single tallow candle flickered on a small table. There was a chair against one wall.

Ascensia did not sit down. She paced the room. She lifted her hand to push the dark, tangled curls back from her face and noticed the dark stain on the lace of her sleeve. Blood.

She shuddered, remembering how that man had grabbed her, how he had done murder and then had been murdered himself. She wiped her hands against the wool coat, then crossed her arms at her waist and tried to will away her nervous trembling.

Jesse walked into the kitchen and leaned a gray-clad shoulder against the door jamb. His gaze wandered about the familiar room as he found himself suddenly confronted by the past. He brought those thoughts up short, however, and frowned as he considered the problem that had been thrust upon him. A Yankee woman. A willful, defiant one at that.

He had to make a decision about her. He couldn't let her wander about the countryside alone and he couldn't leave her here. She would be an added burden. These men would be moved as soon as possible, but most of them were too bad off to be able to defend themselves if they ran into trouble. And she, he decided, could definitely be trouble.

All she had to do was to light out of here and get word to the nearest Yankee. He had already formed several very definite opinions about her and he was convinced that she just might attempt it. He had observed, as well, that she watched and listened closely to everything that took place about her. She had seen and heard enough, he thought grimly, to make her a very dangerous female. He sighed, knowing there was only one decision that he could make.

He struggled with that decision even though he had already made up his mind. He glanced at Captain Bayne who had just come into the kitchen. "How many men do you have here now?" Jesse asked.

"Twenty-three."

Jesse nodded slowly. After a silence the other man asked quietly, "Have you decided what to do with her?"

Jesse let his breath out slowly. "I could just leave her here."

"But you are thinking that wouldn't be best?"

"I am thinking that it would not," Jesse replied.

"She has seen a good deal already," Captain Bayne pointed out.

"You're right," Jesse sighed again. With resignation this time. "I thought that it would be a good idea to keep her under my protection for a while."

"You're probably right about that. If she should happen to run across a picket in the dark, they would probably shoot before they asked questions. Especially tonight. I suppose you will force her, if necessary?"

"I imagine," Jesse replied slowly. "That it will be necessary."

"She'll be safer with you, Jes. It's unsafe for anyone traveling about tonight. And she's- " Captain Bayne left the thought unspoken and looked towards the room where she waited.

"I know," Jesse finished in a quiet voice while his mouth settled into straight lines.

Ascensia turned and looked up at Captain Lucane as he entered the room. She had a sudden sense of foreboding as he closed the door and leaned back against it.

"Ma'am," he began soberly. "You're not going to like what I have to say to you. But I want you to listen carefully. As things have worked out, I have no choice but to take you with me tonight."

For several long moments there was only the silence between them.

"Take me with you?" Ascensia repeated as if she wasn't sure she had heard him right. "What do you mean?"

"I mean it isn't safe for you to be roaming around by yourself right now. You have already seen what can happen to a woman alone in these mountains."

"Yes," she retorted a little breathlessly. "She could be kidnapped by Rebels."

He took a step away from the door. Except for a slight narrowing of his eyes, he ignored the remark. "In a few days," he went on. "You will be given an escort back to the Union lines and set free."

"A few *days*? I have allowed you to bring me here. But- " She held both palms out towards him as she spoke. "I am *not* going any further with you," she declared, meaning it.

"Ma'am, if I say you will go with me, then that is what you will do."

Jesse watched her face. She was definitely not accustomed to having men tell her what to do. As he stared down at her, he couldn't help noticing how beautiful her eyes really were, especially when they grew stormy, as they were now.

He had wondered how she would look with her hair down. And now he saw that the effect was damned distracting. His dark brows drew together in a frown.

"Buy why," she was demanding to know in a low, heated tone. "Must I go with *you*?"

"Someone has to make sure you don't get yourself into any more trouble. You did run into some already, you'll recall."

"You gave me your word that you would take me back," she reminded him.

"I have every intention of keeping my word," he told her. "It's just a matter of when- "

"I assumed that it would be tonight," she interrupted him. "And I- well, I shan't say what I think about your word."

He was losing patience with her. She knew it by the way he let his breath out suddenly. And by the way his body straightened. She knew it by the look on his face.

"I would very gladly take you back tonight if that was possible," he informed her. "But I have no idea what we would find back at that Yankee camp. And I am not about to send someone riding down there to find out. So you will do as I say."

She looked straight into his eyes. "What you mean," she said coldly. "Is that I am to be a prisoner because I have seen too much."

He looked back at her, just as if he was not affected in the least by the scorn in her eyes and in her voice. "If you prefer to put it that way," he drawled in a subtly mocking undertone.

"I was not aware, *Captain*," And he did not mistake the contemptuous tone in her voice. "That Rebels were in the habit of making prisoners out of defenseless women."

Defenseless? He thought of her as anything but.

"It isn't my habit," he replied tersely. "You might say you are a prisoner, for I'll make you do as I say. You may call it a misfortune of war, sweetheart, or whatever you like. You're right. Turning you loose would be dangerous. For us as well as for you. But don't get the mistaken idea that I like this situation any better than you do. I would most willingly leave you anywhere than have to drag you along with me."

"And just where is it that you intend taking me?" she asked, her voice low and trembling with emotion.

No sense trying to keep it from her.

"Across the river. To Virginia."

For a moment she appeared speechless as his words sank in. Then she muttered something under her breath that he couldn't quite catch. "You can't mean- "

"I mean, ma'am, every word I say."

His eyes did not waver as he looked down at her. Ascensia knew in that moment that whatever she might say to him was not going to make the slightest bit of difference. Nothing was going to alter the decision he had made.

Jesse had no more time for arguing with her. Before he left the room, he informed her that she would go with him, even if he had to drag her kicking and screaming all the way to Virginia.

Ascensia stood with one hand pressed tightly against her chest. There was a desperation in her eyes that a certain Rebel captain had not yet learned to read. She told herself that the only thing for her to do was to await an opportunity to escape and somehow reach the Union lines. He positively was not going to get her across that river. He just didn't know it yet.

Chapter 6

Ascensia had plenty of things she wanted to say to the Captain. But she maintained an icy silence as they rode through the darkness. She wondered that she had allowed him to drag her into the woods this far. Brom would be frantic at her disappearance. He would blame himself. He wouldn't know if she was dead or alive. And what would Morgan have to say about it? She thought about Lieutenant Armitage lying in the hallway outside her room and was haunted by the image.

They rode through the woods for what must have been an hour or more before the Captain halted the horse and dismounted. The animal needed a rest, he explained in few words, because it was carrying double.

Ascensia did not dismount. She remained on the horse, fully expecting to be forced to get off. But the Captain busied himself with adjusting the saddle straps. While she sat there, she realized that this might be her only opportunity to escape. They were getting deeper and deeper into the wilderness, farther and farther from the Union lines. Who knew what his plans for her really were.

She wavered in her decision, afraid of the consequences should she fail. But she also realized that the further they rode, the more hopeless her situation became. She was completely at the Rebel's mercy. He was an enemy soldier. A spy. There was no reason whatsoever for her to trust him. Hadn't he already broken his word to her? Hadn't he already threatened her? Forced her to do his bidding?

There had been a house not far back on the road. They had avoided the house. There had been lights in the windows and she was certain she could find her way back to that house and maybe find help there as well.

When the Captain turned his back to her, she knew that she could not waver nor could she hesitate any longer. She threw her leg across the saddle, gathered the reins and wheeled the horse.

The powerful horse reared up a little and turned its head. It was immediately jerked back down by a hand upon its bit that was stronger than her own. There was a desperate struggle as the horse fought the conflicting hands.

Recklessly, Ascensia lifted the trailing ends of the reins and brought them sharply down. Blindly. There was a vicious, whistling sound as the leather lashed the Captain alongside his face. Again she struck, this time catching him somewhere across his body. She could not tell where.

The blow had not been a light one. Jesse instinctively threw his arm up to ward off another one. His other hand meanwhile still maintained a tight grip on the bridle. He still controlled the steel inside the horse's mouth.

"Let go!" Ascensia heard him call out.

In that moment she also caught a glimpse of the Captain's face. Fear drove any mercy from her heart. She kicked out and caught him squarely across the chest with her boot. She immediately dug her heels into the horse's ribs and the animal leaped forward.

The Captain struggled mightily for a few seconds, but he was able to pull the horse down. With rough hands he dragged Ascensia from the saddle.

Jesse sucked his breath in sharply, then let it out slowly between his teeth. His face had paled and he was breathing shallowly. The she-wolf didn't know that when she had kicked him, she had torn his wound open again and that he was fighting pain that made hell's fire seem like a cooling summer breeze. He had let go of the horse but he continued to hold onto her.

No man had ever handled Ascensia the way the Rebel was handling her now and she was terrified. While he held her with one hand, she saw that his free hand was clenched into a fist. She thought that he was about to strike her.

"Let . . . go!" she whispered almost hysterically.

His response was to pull her closer to him. "Let you go? Hell, I'll hold you closer. Don't like it? I can do a lot more that you wouldn't like if you keep fighting me."

Jesse could feel the blood trickling down his chest. His wound continued to throb as if it had been seared with hot coals. He pressed his hand against it for a moment as he let go of her.

Ascensia drew back, watching him with wide eyes. The muscles worked in that hard jaw as he turned angry eyes on her.

"You've done your best to let me know that you don't like being told what to do," he said between gritted teeth. "But understand this. I have no intention of giving in to you." She refused to look at him. Or maybe she couldn't look at him. Which only made him angrier.

"You ought to realize that this inconvenience is preferable to what might have happened to you."

"Inconvenience?" she breathed as she looked up at him. "Is that what you call it?"

After a silence, he said with deliberate enunciation in every word, "Well, I'm telling you now that the man who rode off with you the first time would have *inconvenienced* you all the way to hell and back."

He expected outrage and was not disappointed.

"*You* were there, too," she flashed. "Those men were Rebels. And *you* are a Rebel. A Rebel *spy*." She said it as if it were the lowest thing on earth.

"I'm not denying that I fight for the South, honey, or that I have done things that you would consider to be spying. But I had nothing to do with that raid back there."

He didn't know if she believed him. Or perhaps it made no difference to her. He'd be damned, though, if he was going to sit here defending himself or trying to argue the point with her.

"Come on," he said abruptly, harshly. "We can't stay here all night waiting for it to rain."

They traveled on in stony silence. It seemed to Ascensia that half the night passed. An occasional ghost of light showed where the moon rose and then descended. The expected rain did not come but the air grew heavy with dampness. And it grew colder.

It was the roughest travel that Ascensia had ever endured. The Maryland wilderness seemed vast, impenetrable. But somehow her captor found his way through the mist-veiled night without getting lost.

She was almost numb with cold and fatigue when she was startled by a deep challenge from the darkness. She could barely make out the man in the shadows. He silently stepped aside and allowed them to pass.

They soon came to a camp where several low fires held the darkness back a bit, revealing crude little shelters and lean-tos beneath the trees. There were men sleeping in some of the shelters. Others were sitting around the fires.

None of the men were dressed alike. Some wore blue clothes. Some wore gray. Others wore a combination of both. But every eye that was not closed in sleep was now fastened upon her.

The Captain led her to an empty lean-to at the edge of the camp. "You can sleep here," he said as he tossed a wooden canteen onto the blankets. "There's water if you're thirsty. Better get some sleep. I'll be waking you soon enough."

Ascensia drank for the first time from a canteen. Exhausted and shivering, she laid down and pulled two heavy wool blankets over her. Though she expected to find the ground hard and uncomfortable, the blankets hade a surprisingly soft bed.

She had never been so tired in her life. Her head ached, but the rest was a blessed relief after the torturing hours of travel. As she lay there, her gaze wandered to Captain Jesse Lucane.

He was standing near one of the fires. He nodded as he listened to another man who was talking to him. Absently he rubbed the back of his hand along the side of his face and down along his jaw. She realized it was the side of his face that the reins had struck. The beard shadowing the hard, lean jaw seemed heavier than it had been-

Was it only yesterday? It seemed that more time than that had passed since she had stood before him in Montfort Prison. She frowned as she watched him. Evidently he felt no guilt over what he had just put her through. In fact, he seemed to have forgotten her entirely. He took off his hat and pushed his dark hair back from his face then grinned at something the other man said to him. He replaced the hat and lifted a tin cup to his lips.

She turned away from him. Took tired to keep her eyes open any longer, she pulled the blanket up closer to her chin.

In a little while the rain began to fall again. She heard it in the woods all around her. At first it was just a light ticking on the leaves, then it fell harder and began to pelt the canvas above her.

The sound of the rain seemed to fill her with a deep sadness. She wished that she was back home. She wished she had not witnessed the terrible things she had seen this night.

The memory of Lieutenant Armitage being shot came back to her. Other men had no doubt died as well tonight. Her mind, however, recoiled from further remembering. Her thoughts became hazy and disconnected as sleep claimed her at last.

Chapter 7

The singing of birds awakened Ascensia. When she opened her eyes, she saw the canvas roof above her. She frowned when she remembered where she was.

The first light of dawn bathed the forest in rosy hues. The air was very still with a trace of mist. The trees were dripping moisture. The scent of pine was strong around her. And grass. And the smell of wood smoke.

She rose stiffly from her crude bed and looked around. By daylight the woods seemed very different than they had last night. Men were eating breakfast around the fires. Others were busy rolling up bedding and blankets.

She straightened her clothing as best she could, conscious of the fact that it was her night clothing. She was trying to do something with her tangled curls when a soldier approached her.

He removed his hat and smiled politely down at her. "Ah'm Lieutenant Parrish, ma'am," he said.

He spoke with the soft accent of a Southerner. "Ah know you came in late. But Ah hope you were able to get some sleep."

"I did sleep a little," she replied, painfully embarrassed about how she must look.

"Ah reckon you are hungry," the soldier said. "Ah'll bring you something to eat."

He left her and returned with a tin cup in one hand and a plate of food in the other. The plate was piled high with ham and eggs and biscuits. Enough for a hungry soldier, perhaps, but far more than Ascensia had ever eaten for breakfast. She stared up at the plate of food.

"Ah'm sorry, ma'am. Ah'm certain these army rations are not the sort of refreshments you are used to. But we're not used to having ladies in our camp."

"I'm sure that the food is very good," she said as she adjusted the plate on her lap. She was grateful for his thoughtfulness and discovered that she was, indeed, ravenously hungry.

She ate sparingly, however, for Lieutenant Parrish had seated himself only a little distance from her. Though he seemed to be absorbed in repairing a bridle strap, she was certain that beneath his hat brim he was secretly watching her.

"Did you make this food for me?" she asked.

He flushed slightly and replied that he had done so.

"You are a very good cook," she said, then asked, "And are you a Rebel guerilla as well?"

He lifted his head and replied that he was a Confederate soldier. There was so much dignity in his voice and in his eyes that Ascensia lowered her own, feeling a little ashamed.

When she had finished eating, Lieutenant Parrish led her to a little pond in the woods where he told her she could wash up.

"Take all the time you need, ma'am," he said. "You won't be disturbed." He flushed deeply once again before he disappeared in the direction of the camp.

It was a quiet, secluded place, and though it was deeply shadowed by tall trees, the sun's early rays came sifting through the branches to fall all around her. Mist still clung to the surface of the water.

Ascensia took off the heavy cavalry coat and rolled back the sleeves of her nightgown. She caught up some water in her hands and washed her face and arms, lathering them with the soap the Lieutenant had left with her.

An attempt to flee into the woods would be foolish, although the idea had occurred to her. She had come too far to have any hope of finding her way back safely. Especially afoot. Besides, she was certain that the Captain would have her hunted down and brought back.

She gazed longingly at the pond, wishing she could wash all the dirt from her body. Instead she sat down and began to unlace her boots while she considered Lieutenant Parrish.

She believed that he was a gentleman. Certainly he had treated her with kindness and respect. Her instincts told her that in spite of being a Rebel soldier, he would be dependable. She decided that it would not hurt to act graciously towards the man so that his opinion of her would be a favorable one. Then, should she need a friend or defender in the future, she might be able to rely upon him. She frowned suddenly. She did not want him to share the Captain's unfavorable opinion of her.

At the edge of the camp, Jesse had just finished grooming his horse. He adjusted the saddle blanket and frowned. In a moment of weakness he found himself almost feeling sorry for his less-than-willing prisoner this morning. She hadn't asked for this situation any more than he had. Maybe he had been a little hard on her last night. He stopped and stared at the two men who had come to saddle their own horses.

"Mawnin', Captain," one of the men greeted amiably. "Anything wrong?"

"No," Jesse replied slowly as he picked up his saddle and placed it across his horse's back. "I just never saw you both clean-shaven at the same time before. Hardly recognized you."

Jesse himself had shaved earlier. But then he hadn't had the chance while he'd been in prison.

He also noted that both men had their hair neatly groomed. Their clothes had undergone some miraculous changes, too. He frowned for a moment at the feathers adorning the men's hats as he jerked a leather strap tight. He could not help overhearing the conversation between the two men.

"She certainly is pretty," one of them said.

The other agreed. "She sure took my breath."

Over the back of his horse, Jesse inquired tersely, "She up and about?"

"Sure," one of the men drawled. "Woke a while ago, just like sleeping beauty."

Jesse slipped the bridle on his horse and heard, "Ah don't believe Ah ever saw such eyes. Or hair. Long and falling all the way to her waist. We heah, Captain, that she is a Yankee girl that was caught in a raid and carried off by some rascals, damn 'em."

"But lucky for us," pointed out the other man.

"News sure travels fast in this camp," Jesse remarked tightly.

"Ah reckon she isn't too happy about the situation?" one of the men asked.

"She is not what you would call a willing guest," Jesse replied.

"You couldn't help it, Ah suppose, Captain. She is as handsome a girl as Ah ever saw."

Jesse stared at the man but did not reply. A scowl had settled upon his face by the time he had finished with his horse. He was beginning to think that he had made a mistake in bringing her here. A young female thrust into the midst of a group of restless, headstrong young men like these men were? It suddenly seemed like a dangerous combination.

She was good-looking enough to have already won their attention. And their admiration. It was just a matter of time, he figured, before they were clamoring for notice. The fact that she was a Yankee would make her even more interesting. If she seemed to be a helpless maiden in distress, she would appear irresistible to their chivalrous Southern hearts.

He walked into the clearing, looked towards the empty lean-to, and frowned as he muttered to himself, "Took his breath."

Ascensia waited for Lieutenant Parrish to return.

"Are you feeling better?" he asked when he saw her.

"Yes, but I'm afraid that my appearance hasn't improved any," she replied ruefully.

He denied her words gallantly. "Being dragged all night through the woods and sleeping out in the rain aren't easy things for any woman to have to endure."

He expressed further regret at what he called her unfortunate circumstances. "Ah'm sorry for the harsh treatment you suffered last night," he said. "Ah imagine it gave you a bad impression of Rebel soldiers."

"Some Rebel soldiers," she replied quietly.

He reddened beneath her steady gaze and fumbled with his hat brim. "Ma'am," he began as he looked up. "You do understand that those men last night were not Rebel soldiers? We don't condone what they did to you. This camp is hardly the place for you, either. But upon my word, while you are here, you will not be ill treated in any way. You are safe now."

"Yes," she said. "Safe in the hands of Captain Jesse Lucane."

The Lieutenant's eyes showed surprise. He had not failed to note the sarcastic undertone in her voice. "Ah'm sure Je- the Captain did what he had to do. What happened last night- "

"He is a savage," she burst out impulsively. "He treated me shamelessly."

"Ah will admit that the Captain might seem hard and unyieldin' at times. But Ah also know that whatever happened, he meant no disrespect to you. He did bring you heah safe and unharmed."

"He *forced* me to come here," she corrected him. "He threatened me. He admitted that I was a prisoner because I had seen too much."

Lieutenant Parrish looked even more surprised. "The Captain is some strong-minded," he said, obviously feeling a need to defend the man. "Ah won't deny that. But Ah have spent a long time scouting with him and- "

"You are scouts then?"

"Yes. Confederate scouts," he replied.

"And he is a spy as well."

"Some people would say, ma'am, that there is a fine line between scoutin' and spyin'. If the Captain seemed a little unreasonable last night, why- "

"Please," she whispered. "Do not remind me of last night. It was dreadful. I shall never forget- " Her voice broke as she recalled it. She was sincerely distraught at the memory. "I saw a man shot right before me." She covered her face with her hands.

"Try not to think of it," she heard the Lieutenant say. "You are safe now."

When she lowered her hands, he saw that there were tears filling her blue-violet eyes.

"Forgive me," she said. "I am not blaming you. I know that you had nothing to do with any of it. You have been nothing but kind to me, Lieutenant Parrish."

He let his breath out slowly. His gaze shifted to the forest behind her.

"What will happen to me, Lieutenant?" she asked.

"Why, Ah don't imagine you will suffer anything more than a long ride," he replied steadily, though the appealing, tearful look of her almost unnerved him.

A surge of tenderness and pity welled up inside of him. He thought about his own sisters. This girl had been outraged. And she needed protecting. Her lip quivered slightly as she looked up at him. Tears threatened to spill out of those beautiful, imploring eyes.

"And you will spare me any unnecessary distress if you are able?" she asked him.

"Ah would do the right thing, Miss, as Ah saw it."

"Miss McCay," she said. "My name is Ascensia McCay."

"Mornin'."

Ascensia gave a sudden start at the familiar voice behind her. Only when she had braced herself emotionally, did she turn to see the Captain standing a short distance away. His eyes were fixed on her face. He must have been listening, for it seemed to her that he had been anticipating her startled look. She resented the warmth suddenly flooding her face as much as she resented his unannounced appearance.

"And how is our Northern damsel this morning?" he asked.

"Better now," Lieutenant Parrish replied. "Ah was just assuring Miss McCay that she need fear no lack of courtesy nor any ungentlemanly conduct while she is in our hands. She has been through a great deal already." Although he had spoken amiably, Ascensia detected a hint of challenge in his words.

"She won't have to concern herself about that," said the Captain. "As long as you can get her to do what you say. She doesn't like to listen to me." He cast a meaningful glance in her direction. A meaningful glance underlayed with that familiar hint of mockery she had come to expect. And there was something in his eyes that seemed to be specifically meant for her alone.

"As long as she is treated with respect, Ah'm sure there won't be any problems," said the Lieutenant. "And, of course, we will treat her with respect."

"Nothing else but," replied the Captain.

Ascensia looked quickly from one man to the other. She expected to see anger smoldering in the Captain's eyes. But she saw instead that it was friendly bantering. These two were obviously close friends.

"I'd appreciate it, Lieutenant," said the Captain. "If you would see to Miss McCay's horse. I want to talk to her."

Ascensia watched the Lieutenant leave the clearing, then steeled herself for a confrontation when the Captain approached her. His hand reached towards her. His fingers curved beneath her chin. She felt the terrible, unyielding strength of that hand as he lifted her face to his.

"Tears?" he queried with an irritating drawl. "I wouldn't have thought you were the type."

She jerked her face away. Though he let her go, she continued to watch him warily.

"I assume that the Lieutenant is seeing to all your needs," he said. "He is mighty chivalrous when it comes to ladies in distress. But I reckon you are smart enough to have figured that out already. You won't be doing him any favors, though, if you get him feeling too sorry for you."

Her eyes changed. "Of course you would never feel the slightest bit of compassion for a woman who has been abducted, dragged through a wilderness and held prisoner against her will," she said in a low voice.

"You sure are feeling some braver now." His irritating drawl was in evidence again. "But you will be better off if you remember that you *are* my prisoner."

"How could I forget?" she breathed. "Everything that I have been through convinces me. You may have forced me to be your prisoner," she went on heatedly. "But that is as far as I surrender. I refuse to stand here and converse with you against my will."

She attempted to leave the clearing, but as she passed by him, he grabbed her arm and turned her around until she faced him.

"Not until we get something straight," he said with a voice that had lost all traces of mockery. "I reckon you already know that you are mighty fine-looking and I expect that you are used to having men pay attention to you. And I suppose you have practiced your feminine wiles enough times to know how to get your way."

"Feminine wiles?" she burst out indignantly.

He ignored her outburst and said, "But I am warning you now to restrain yourself while you are here as much as you are able. Don't imagine that my tolerance is without end. I won't stand for you disrupting this camp and making matters any worse than they have to be."

"Your- tolerance?" she sputtered.

He released her arm but she did not move. The insinuation of his words, the outright insult had sent her blood pulsing hotly through every nerve in her body.

Jesse was keenly aware of the change in her. With the Lieutenant, she had been shy and imploring. She was not so now. She was like a smoldering flame suddenly fanned to life. Her eyes were blazing. Her face had paled. As a contrast, her dark curls were hanging loose and wild, like a dark veil over her shoulders.

There was a bruise on her face and a scratch along one cheek. Her clothes were torn and muddy. Beneath the collar of his coat a bit of white lace from her nightgown was showing. All in all, she appeared a most bedraggled young lady.

Her eyes were stormy as she looked up at him through long black lashes. "I think, Captain, that you are a horrid man, or you would never say such things to me. I did not ask you to bring me here to this camp. It is because of you, *only* you, that I am here now. And you have the effrontery to insult me as well.

"Why, a gentleman would blush at the things you have said and done to me. You are the rudest, the most ill-mannered, the most insolent man I have ever met. And I- "

"And you, Miss Ascensia McCay, are the most provokingest damnyankee female that I have ever met," he interrupted her, angry at the sudden, almost overwhelming urge he had to cover her beautiful mouth with his to shut her up.

"You- you *Rebel*," she breathed, beside herself. "You have shown me that you are no better than a savage. But at least, at *least*, you could keep a civil tongue when you speak to me. You could at least pretend to act like a gentleman."

"Like Lieutenant Parrish?"

"He has shown me that he *is* a gentleman," she replied.

"Sure. When you flatter him with your soft voice and let him think you are all tears and weakness so that he thinks you need rescuing. From me. Hell," he breathed and turned his face from her for a moment.

"That is certainly not true, she said angrily. There may have been a spark of truth in what he said, but it was not the way he made it sound.

"Lieutenant Parrish has treated me kindly," she went on while her chin lifted a few notches. "Unlike you." Her eyes narrowed slightly. "I suppose you say such mean things because your conscience is troubling you. You are not half the gentleman the Lieutenant is and I suppose you are afraid that if I tell him how you treated me last night, he will realize what a brute you really are."

He gave a hard little laugh and said, "Tell away, ma'am. My conscience isn't grieving me about anything I did last night. But if you think you have something to tell him, then do it."

They faced each other for a few moments in dead silence.

He finally spoke. "Save your breath, honey. I haven't got the time to cross swords with you any longer. We're almost ready to ride. So I suggest that you finish whatever it is you need to do and get yourself back to the camp. Or I'll come and drag you back myself."

It didn't matter what he said, Ascensia told herself as he walked away. She didn't care how many mean and hateful things he said to her. Because somehow, sometime soon, she vowed, he would be sorry for each and every one of them.

Chapter 8

In an amazingly short time the camp had all but disappeared. The men had packed everything and were ready to ride. Ascensia was about to mount the horse that had been brought to her when the Captain walked up to her.

"I'll give you a hand up," he said.

"Don't touch me," she snapped.

"I was only meaning to help you. That's a big horse."

"I've ridden big horses before. And I don't want any help from you. Do you understand?"

"Sure," he replied. "You're still mad at me for what I said to you by the pond."

"You don't know anything," she retorted.

She snatched up the reins, then placed her hand on the pommel. As she lifted her foot to the stirrup, however, she found that she couldn't reach it. She jumped and might have made it all the way over the saddle, but the horse, most likely trained for cavalry charges, started forward at the same time that Ascensia's boot slipped from the stirrup. She landed hard on her backside on the ground and found herself staring at the Captain's black boots.

The other men were staring at her, but they were silent. It didn't take long for her to realize that most of them were trying in various ways to suppress their laughter. Above her, Captain Lucane made a half-smothered sound that made her suspect that he found the situation amusing as well. She looked down and saw that her black-stockinged legs were exposed to her knees.

She quickly jerked her nightgown back down and felt her cheeks flush hotly.

"You aren't hurt, are you?" she heard the Captain ask.

She glared up at him and saw a smile lurking about his lips, even though he was trying to keep a straight face. She quickly scrambled to her feet.

"Maybe she hurt somethin', Captain," one of the men said.

"Did you?" the Captain asked.

He was struggling even harder to keep the smile from showing. Ascensia, on the other hand, was struggling with a longing to slap the smile off his face.

"Ah'm glad you're not hurt," another man declared. "And really, Miss," he assured her in all seriousness. "That was the most graceful arm-flailin' Ah have ev' seen."

"It was for a fact," grinned the Captain as he boldly let his mirth show. "Reckon all that got hurt was your pride," he said as he passed one arm around her waist and lifted her easily to the saddle.

He mounted his own horse. When Ascensia glanced over at him, she saw that he had lost his self-restraint for he bowed his head and laughed outright as he spurred his horse to the head of the column.

She heard a smothered guffaw. Another man chuckled beneath his hat brim. And then, as if it were contagious, sounds of laughter could be heard up and down the entire column.

Lieutenant Parrish rode back to where she sat her horse. "Are you all right?" he asked.

"Yes, I'm fine," she replied stiffly as the line trotted briskly into motion.

They rode south, deeper into the Maryland wilderness. By midmorning the sun had retreated behind a cloud cover. The air grew heavy with dampness again and soon had a definite feel of imminent rain to it.

By the time they crossed the Potomac River, a perilous crossing that terrified Ascensia, it had begun to rain again. It came down lightly at first then turned into a steady, drenching downpour. For Ascensia, it was a most miserable, most exhausting ride into Rebeldom.

They covered mile after mile on Rebel soil. When night finally fell, Ascensia's eyelids had grown so heavy that she could barely keep her eyes open. She began to fall asleep sitting upright in the saddle. She would catch herself with a start and clutch at the pommel each time she felt herself begin to fall. When a halt was finally made, she peered sleepily up at a large building before her and focused on the sign beside the door. *Leesburg Hotel.*

She did not protest when the Captain helped her down from her horse. In fact, she was so stiff she could barely move and nearly collapsed into his arms.

Agony crept along her limbs. Her backside ached from the long hours in the saddle. She shivered, chilled to the bone from her wet clothing. She stood and watched in silence as the Captain tied the two horses to the rail. She followed him, without protest, into the lobby of the hotel.

The lobby was already crowded with men. Some of them were spreading blankets on the floor, preparing to sleep there. Ascensia found an unoccupied corner near a window where she leaned wearily against the wall.

She was desperate for a place to lie down and go to sleep. She could have dropped where she was and been perfectly content. Of course, she also wanted the warmth of blankets and clean, dry clothes. Most of all she wanted to be alone. Her blood was throbbing heavily through her veins, making her feel irritable and jittery.

" . . . and a room for the lady," she heard the Captain say.

"Just got the one room empty," said the clerk. "Every corner of the hotel is filled. And by morning there won't be a bed to be had in Leesburg."

"I haven't slept in a decent bed for a long while," the Captain sighed. "I guess the one room will have to do."

Ascensia brought her head up sharply. She pushed her dark hair slowly back from her face as she watched the clerk pass over the key. The *only* key. She immediately walked over to the Captain. "I- " she began, but he cut her off.

"Wait here," he said before he turned and left the lobby.

Ascensia stared after him for a moment then followed him outside. She limped stiffly across the porch and said in a low voice, "I want to talk to you."

He had been reaching under the horse to loosen the cinch. He glanced up at her.

"I won't stay in that room with you," she said. "It's not proper. And if you had any sense of decency, you would- "

"If you had any sense at all," he interrupted. "You would keep quiet. If you didn't hear me the first time, I'll say it again. Wait inside for me. We'll talk when I'm through here."

She drew a sharp breath but remained where she was, watching while he lifted the saddle off the horse and set it on the railing.

"You can't expect me to share a room with you."

He stared up at her through the darkness. His lips curled slightly. "It's you that's thinking all those thoughts, ma'am. Not me. I suggest you stop thinking about- " He hesitated slightly. "Such things and concentrate on the fact that you will be sleeping in a dry, comfortable bed tonight."

He turned and began to work with the saddle of the horse she had ridden, ignoring her and talking to the man beside him.

He had rudely dismissed her. She watched him turn his Rebel back on her as if she didn't even exist.

"Listen to me," she hissed.

"What do you want now?" he asked sharply as he turned back to her. She knew that he was angry. But she was angry as well.

"I didn't think that even you would insult a woman this way."

"Damnation. Is that all you think about? Get it off your mind. I said I'll talk to you when I'm through here. So go back inside."

Maybe she should have heeded the warnings. She heard the tone in his voice. She saw the muscle working in his jaw. But something drove her. "Is this how you are accustomed to treating Southern women?"

He looked at her and said in a level tone, "If they were to forget they were ladies, they might expect it. I'm saying for the last time, honey, that I'm too busy to be exchangin' shots with you at the moment."

The insult had its effect. And the mocking endearment fueled an already smoldering fire. Her nerves were raw, unstrung. She had been compelled time and time again to submit to every whim of this wild man. He had slept near her last night. And she had endured it. But that had been outside. This was something else entirely. She had no intention of yielding to him so easily now.

"Sir," she began in a voice that was low with suppressed emotion. "In the past two days I was abducted not once, but twice, by enemy soldiers. I was forced to ride through woods for hours in freezing rain. I was dragged across a raging river in which I nearly drowned. But the very *worst* of all," And she emphasized the word. "Is that I have been compelled time and time again to endure the company of a man who does not have the decency to pay a moment's attention to me when I say that I will not- "

"As far as your virtue is concerned," he interrupted abruptly as his eyes raked her. "You don't need to worry yourself about that. It isn't on my mind. Hell. I know you went through some hardships. But all that's over now. So why don't you save your breath?"

"If I were a man," she declared in a heated voice. "You would not treat me this way."

He leaned towards her with his hand on the rail. "If you were a man, I'd have knocked the squawk out of you by now."

She stood rigid as he turned away. A sudden gust of wind rattled the windows behind her and shook the rain from the trees above her. She shivered violently.

"Of course you can talk to me like that." Her voice was surprisingly steady for all the emotion surging through her. "A coward feels safe enough when he is threatening a woman. And you are a coward as well as a contemptible Rebel spy."

He swung back around. The men standing nearby were watching the exchange in silence.

One look at the Captain's face made even Ascensia fear that she had gone too far.

"You sharp-tongued little cat!" he exclaimed. "You had better watch how you talk about a man."

"Go ahead. Insult me. Threaten me. It's what I have come to expect from you."

"Keep quiet," he warned in a dangerously-suppressed voice.

"I will not."

He came up onto the porch. Ascensia could not withhold a gasp when his hand lashed out and imprisoned her wrist. He dragged her across the porch and did not release her until they were upstairs alone in the hotel room.

"Listen to me," he said after the door had slammed shut. "You want to sleep somewhere else? Maybe you would like to spend the night with Lieutenant Parrish. Or some of the other men. You won't be lonely, sweetheart. You'll get all the attention you've been begging for."

She drew her hand back to slap his face.

"Try it," he dared. "Try it and I promise you you'll be sorry you did. And say one more word about this room and you'll find yourself regretting that, too."

"I hate you," she whispered, trembling with the intensity of the emotion as she turned her back to him.

There was a long silence before she heard him say, "Had you waited and listened to what I had to say, you would have known that I never had any intention of sleeping here with you. So this was all for nothing."

She didn't say a word. Nor did she turn around. He might have explained. He might have told her so from the beginning.

After a little while the door slammed shut, making her jump and she knew she was alone. She bit her lip hard, trying not to cry. But she could not keep the tears from coming.

Angrily she wiped them away with the back of her hand. Anger was an easier emotion to deal with, she found. In any case, she was so tired that she seemed incapable of putting two thoughts together and having them make sense.

She dropped the sodden Rebel coat from her shoulders then lay down on the bed without undressing and pulled the blankets over her. Not a minute passed before she was sound asleep.

Chapter 9

"Ah would like to apologize, Miss McCay," Lieutenant said to her the next evening. "For everything. Ah want you to know how deeply Ah regret all that has happened."

"There's no need to apologize Lieutenant," Ascensia replied. "I don't know how I would have been able to bear any of it if you hadn't been there." She meant those words. Renn Parrish was one of the kindest, most thoughtful persons she had ever met.

She was feeling considerably better than she had last night. She had slept late and she had been able to take a bath and wash her hair. She had scrubbed off layers of Maryland and Virginia mud. Clean clothing had been brought to her room and the gown she was wearing was exquisite. It was a beautiful shade of deep blue, richly trimmed with black lace and sparkling jet. All the proper underpinnings had been brought, too, along with an embroidered, fringed shawl made of the finest black silk. There was even a pair of black lace gloves for her hands.

Still, Ascensia was plagued by uncertainty as she walked beside the Lieutenant. She had not seen Captain Lucane since that disagreeable scene last night. He had sent word, however, that Lieutenant Parrish would escort her to a Confederate wedding reception of she wished to attend.

She had definitely decided not to go. The invitation was a mockery. She also imagined it was a challenge on the Captain's part. He knew she wouldn't go. But after sitting restlessly in the hotel room all afternoon she had changed her mind.

It seemed that everything had been beyond her control during the past three days. She couldn't change all that had happened, but for some inexplicable reason, she wanted to present herself as she really was, now that she had some control over her appearance and her behavior.

Still, she hesitated when they reached the big white house where the reception was being held. "Maybe I should not have come," she said, looking up at the Lieutenant.

"You're promised me the first dance," he reminded her. "You're not going to disappoint me, Ah hope."

She relented, half reluctantly and when they entered the huge ballroom, Ascensia saw that it was already crowded with men in gray and women dressed in every shade of silk and satin. Chandeliers sparkled brightly overhead while the bride and groom got ready to dance the first dance of the evening.

"It's a lively crowd," the Lieutenant said with a laugh. "Ah expect everyone is in a mood to do some howling."

She smiled up at him. However, that smile faded when her glance happened to fall upon the Captain across the room. He did not see her come in so she was able to study the change in *his* appearance.

Cleanly-shaven, he wore the clothes of a Rebel captain. His black hair had been trimmed, but it was still worn long enough to give him that untamed look she had come to associate with him. Nothing, she decided, could ever change that latent air of danger about him. It was a part of who he was.

And he was handsome, she grudgingly admitted to herself. Very handsome. She bit her lower lip as she glanced at Lieutenant Wirt Blackford who was standing next to him because the Lieutenant was looking at her now. The big, black-bearded man leaned over and spoke some words to the Captain, who casually looked in her direction and smiled in his mocking, disagreeable way.

Across the room, Jesse raised his glass to his mouth and drank deeply. Miss Ascensia McCay had wrought some remarkable changes in her appearance, he noted as he watched her over the rim of his glass.

"She got mighty fine-looking after scraping all that mud off," Wirt commented beside him. "The little witch has a way about her. She's sure turnin' heads," he said, then snorted in disgust. "The boys are about fallin' over each other wanting to dance with her. Noble's been watching her since she came in. He'll be askin' her to dance before long. Just watch."

Jesse did watch her. He understood very well that this particular woman was capable of exerting a powerful effect over the men around her. He had seen enough evidence of it during the past two days.

She began a dance with Renn Parrish. She danced gracefully, with an abandon that held his eyes. It was not just that she was beautiful. She possessed a unique quality, an underlying sensuality that hinted at passion and innocence at the same time. An irresistible combination for most men.

His glass froze on its way to his mouth. He was suddenly remembering how he had held her in the woods and how she had felt in his arms. The scent of her and the softness of her womanly curves were not things that a man could easily forget.

And then an image of her on that bed in the hotel room flashed into his mind. He thought about her eager and willing beneath him while he kissed her panting mouth. Against his will, he thought about all that sensuality and passion unleashed for him. The image surprised him with its intensity. He cursed under his breath while Wirt turned to him with a questioning look.

"Well, would you look at the arrogant bastard," Wirt suddenly remarked. "Ah'll say he's got nerve comin' heah."

Jesse also watched the man who had just come through the doorway. His eyes narrowed slightly as he recalled the ambush in which Newell Law had been killed. Further knowledge hardened his eyes even more.

From across the crowded ballroom, Ascensia had observed the change in the Captain's face. His eyes had narrowed and grown hard with what she could have sworn was dislike. Contempt, as well, was evident in the lines about his mouth. That contempt was focused on a man who had just entered the ballroom.

Apparently the man was acquainted with Lieutenant Parrish for he joined their group though reactions to him were mixed. He was almost grudgingly introduced to Ascensia as John Lathrop.

It was the Captain's reaction to the introduction that interested Ascensia. It interested her enough that when John Lathrop invited her to dance, she accepted. Two dances later she turned to see Captain Lucane standing before her.

"You won't refuse me the next waltz, I hope?"

Before she could reply, he had passed his arm around her waist, giving her no chance to refuse. He whirled her out onto the dance floor and they danced in silence. He danced well. Not a false step, she noted. However, she sensed something simmering below the surface of his polite exterior.

"Having a good time?" he asked, looking down at her.

"I was," she replied.

His grin was wolfish. "I hope you didn't feel I was neglecting you," he said. "But then you haven't exactly lacked for partners."

She did not reply.

"I see the dress fits," he went on. "I thought the color might match those fascinating eyes."

Those eyes flashed as she looked up at him. She didn't know that he had personally picked the dress out. Had he picked out the underpinnings, too?

"Dare I hope that a change of clothing has improved your manners?" she asked, feigning unconcern. "Or would that be a vain hope? I almost imagine that you are finding it difficult to restrain yourself with all these people around."

He laughed and said, without looking at her, "I'll admit, sweetheart, that you have a way of making me forget myself."

"You have already proven, Captain, how useless it would be to even begin to defend myself. Tonight I refuse to be drawn into another battle with you. No matter how disagreeable you may try to be."

"Really? That's good because I thought we might discuss how busy you've been looking for a way to get back at me."

"I don't know what you are talking about."

"Sure you do," he said. "And I'm telling you now that if you keep flirting with John Lathrop, I'm going to drag you out of here, crowd or no crowd."

He suddenly released her. She had not been aware that the dance had ended. She was only aware of how contemptible the man really was.

"You get as mad as you want," he told her. "But you remember what I said. You hear me?"

"I hear you," she replied, angry enough to scream.

Lieutenant Parrish was suddenly by her side. He looked down at her with a questioning look for a moment before she heard called out: "Broom dance."

"I don't know about up No'th," the Lieutenant said with a smile as he led her out onto the dance floor. "But it's customary at weddings down here."

The Lieutenant whirled her expertly in his arms. Suddenly the music stopped and there was a mad shuffling of feet and the heavy stomping of cavalry boots as the men thundered around the room looking for a new partner before the music began again. In the center of the room a young soldier was left to dance with the broom. The music started up again. And abruptly ended, leaving another soldier to hold the broom.

As the men scrambled to find a different partner, there were good-natured struggles and outright thievery as the women were fought over. The hilarity was infectious and Ascensia was literally swept off her feet more than once. Her disagreeable scene with the Captain was almost forgotten and Ascensia had as good a time as anyone as the dance went on.

The sudden clatter of horse's hoofs drew everyone's attention. A wild yell rent the air as a horse and rider appeared in the doorway. Women screamed and, although some men protested, there were many others who seemed to appreciate the diversion.

The horseman doffed his hat and waved it with a flourish. "Ladies," he greeted drunkenly. "An' gent'men. Ah would like t'offah a- toast."

He raised a bottle to the crowd, then swayed a little in the saddle as he called out, "Heah's t' th' happy c'ple." He paused to take a long drink.

"An' heah's t' th' South'n Conf'dracy." He downed another gulp of whiskey, then whooped. "Ah'm Mar'land bound." He reeled in the saddle and his horse pulled back snorting.

The inebriated Rebel then began to amuse himself by singing a baritone rendition of *Dixie*. Halfway through the song, Captain Lucane stepped forward and grabbed hold of the horse's bridle.

The man squinted as he tried to focus. " 's th't you, Cap'n, suh? Don't worry 'bout me," he said. "Ah'll be a'right. Ef'n this hoss'd jes' stand still."

He leaned forward to listen to something the Captain was saying. "A'right," the man said, nodding his head. "Jes' le' me say a- a fond fa'well t' th' ladies." He bowed deeply and wavered for a moment. Sinking lower and lower, he slid off his horse and landed heavily on the floor.

Two men immediately rushed forward to seize the drunken man and lead him outside. The Captain leaped into the saddle to lead the horse back outside. The gaiety resumed, with even more abandon, it seemed, and before long the musicians had struck up another dance.

Chapter 10

Ascensia glanced quickly over her shoulder. She had managed to slip out to the back veranda without being seen. She felt a deep sense of relief as the darkness surrounded her. She wanted to be alone for a few moments. She wanted to collect her thoughts before going back inside. The ballroom had been growing almost uncomfortably hot. Out here there was almost a chill in the air. She hugged her bare shoulders with her hands as she looked up at the stars. The same stars she would have looked at if she was home.

"Cold?"

She whirled around and stared at John Lathrop.

"I didn't mean to scare you," he said.

He stopped closer and this time, when Ascensia shivered, it was not because of the cold. She didn't like the man. He was close enough for her to smell the whiskey on his breath, close enough to make her feel uneasy.

"When I saw you come out here, I knew it might be my only chance to talk to you alone."

She had no idea what he was talking about. She certainly had no wish to talk to him.

"I can get you back to the Union lines," he said in a low voice after glancing over his shoulder. "I'll take you off tonight."

She shook her head.

"You want to go back, don't you?" he asked.

"Captain Lucane told me that I would be taken back tomorrow."

"You trust him? You looked like you wanted to claw his eyes out when you were dancing with him."

"He gave me his word. But whether I trust him or not," she said evasively. "He would be furious if he knew that you had made such a suggestion to me."

"Hell. I'm willing to take a chance for you."

Either the man was drunk or he was terribly arrogant to believe that she would agree to go off alone with him. She wanted him to go away, but he moved even closer and laid his hand on her bare shoulder. She jerked her shoulder away.

"Why are you acting so cold all of a sudden?" he asked. There was a change in his voice that alarmed her. "Why, when you smiled at me earlier, it was all I could do to keep from kissing you right then."

He looked at her more closely, as if something had just occurred to him. "But maybe you and the Captain- " His words trailed off suggestively.

"Certainly not," she cut off his crude assumption. She started past him but he stepped in front of her.

He gripped her arm and jerked her towards him. "You can't just walk away like that. Maybe you need some convincing." Without warning, he pulled her into his arms and kissed her full on the mouth. She began to struggle, frantic to get away from him.

"Quiet," he whispered harshly as his mouth tried to clamp down on hers once again.

He released her suddenly, breathing a savage oath under his breath as a voice behind her said, "Let her go."

Ascensia turned to see the Captain standing behind her. He was not looking at her. His gaze was fixed on the man beside her.

"Thought I might find you here," the Captain drawled in a dangerously quiet voice. "Ignore a snake in the grass, and sooner or later he's going to strike."

Three Rebel soldiers stood behind the Captain. Ascensia knew by their backward glances that they intended to keep anyone else from coming out onto the veranda. She heard a reel begin inside.

"I don't remember asking you to interfere in my business," Lathrop said belligerently.

"But she *is* my business."

Lathrop sneered. "I'll bet she is. But the truth is, you've had it in for me for a long time."

"I've never had any use for traitors," the Captain returned evenly.

There was a long, tense silence. Lathrop's eyes blazed. "By God," he said hoarsely. "I won't be insulted. Not by you."

Ascensia glanced quickly at the Captain, who was still coldly contemplating the man.

"And I'll be damned if I take one more order from you," Lathrop further declared. "Unless, of course, you think you can make me."

"Oh, I can make you," the Captain replied. "And if you don't believe me, I can give you all the convincing you need."

"You can try," Lathrop smirked.

"My pleasure," Jesse drawled as he began to remove his coat.

"Maybe you don't like the idea of sharin' her," Lathrop taunted as he stripped off his own coat.

Ascensia paled at the words just as the Captain's fist struck the man's leering face. It was a hard blow and Lathrop's head jerked back.

"Shut your mouth," Jesse warned.

"Go to hell," Lathrop spat as his own fist lashed out.

Jesse countered the blow. At the same time his left fist came up to smash the man savagely in the face once again. Lathrop stumbled back but did not completely lose his balance.

"That was for Newell Law," Jesse told the man.

With an enraged roar, Lathrop lunged forward and the two men exchanged blows. It continued until Lathrop was driven to his knees. He was breathing hard and balancing himself with one hand on the ground. When he finally lifted his head, his eyes glared with a hatred that was unmistakable. He rubbed his sleeve across his mouth and looked at the blood from his bruised, raw lips.

Jesse waited for him to get to his feet. Although Lathrop must have realized that he would only suffer more if he met the challenge, he started to rise. Without warning, he suddenly cursed and pulled a knife from his boot as he leaped forward.

Momentarily caught off guard, Jesse threw up one arm to deflect the blade. While the men behind him protested such a "miserable trick," Jesse reacted.

He gripped Lathrop's arm and twisted it until the man howled in agony. His fingers opened and the knife dropped into the dirt. Jesse then drove his fist into Lathrop's jaw with tremendous force.

It spun Lathrop halfway around. He fell on his knees then threw one arm over the rail of the veranda for support, bracing himself as he attempted to rise. But he sagged back down again.

Jesse waited for him to recover. Lathrop did finally manage to get to his feet but he was a beaten man. He staggered uncertainly and leaned over. For a long time he remained in that position, laboring for breath. When he straightened, his face was a distorted mask of hate. His mouth worked as he muttered some of the worst language Ascensia had ever heard.

Finally he walked stiffly to his horse which had been brought out for him. He mounted with difficulty and threw one last malignant look at the Captain. His eyes then fixed on Ascensia's face. They slowly traveled the length of her as he drew his swollen, bloody lips back into a hideous grin. He savagely dug his spurs into his horse's ribs and the animal leaped forward into the shadows of the trees.

Ascensia drew a sharp breath as the Captain turned towards her. He closed the distance between them and, without a word, reached for her. With one hard jerk he pulled her close to his side. Silent still, he forced her off the veranda and into the darkness.

He let go of her only when they were back in the hotel room. He did not light a lamp. The room remained dark except for the moonlight that fell through the open curtains.

Ascensia remained standing where he had let go of her. She did not take her eyes off of him while he walked to the window and stood with his back to her. She rubbed her wrist, still feeling the hard pressure of his fingers. Keeping her eyes on him, she took a step away from him.

He must have caught a reflection of the movement in the window. Or perhaps he heard the rustle of her skirts. He turned and was standing before her in an instant. He forced her against the wall in the square of moonlight that was streaming through the window. He kept her there by placing his hands on the wall behind her.

He frightened her. She admitted it to herself. His nearness in the darkness, the violence of his movements, the anger that she sensed he barely held in check. All these things had their effect upon her.

"I reckon that was some romantic walk in the moonlight."

"That wasn't *my* fault," she said breathlessly.

He stared down at her. Suddenly he was gripping her upper arm in one hand. His other hand slid behind her neck.

She stiffened, alarmed. "Let go!"

"I can feel you tremble, Ascensia. Are you afraid of me?"

"No!"

He released his breath harshly. It was an expression of mockery that let her know that he did not believe her. "I think you are," he said. "I think you have always been afraid of me. I've been watching you all night. And you know what? I'm beginning to realize just how fascinating you really are. Contrasting, you know? You were so breathless laughing and dancing with Renn. And then I watched you flirting with Lathrop. And now you're different. All that warm friendliness has disappeared now that you're alone with me."

Ascensia struggled to free herself. But his grip did not loosen.

"What are you afraid of?" he asked.

"I'm not afraid. Let go," she panted. "I think you must be drunk."

"It doesn't take whiskey to get me all worked up when I'm with you. And this time you went too far. Suppose I hadn't found you when I did? Do you realize what might have happened?"

"Do you think that I don't know?" she blurted wildly. "I- He assumed all sorts of vile things. And it was not through any fault of mine."

"You're saying you didn't flirt with him to deliberately try and rile me?"

She could not completely deny the truth of what he was saying. But she did not deserve what had happened and she said angrily, "That horrid scene would not have occurred if you hadn't brought me here in the first place. And if he hadn't thought that you and I- that we- "

"That we what?"

"Oh," she stormed as she continued to fight him. "It doesn't matter. You don't believe me and I don't care what you think about anything."

His hand fell away from her arm but now the fingers of that hand curved around her waist. He leaned closer to her. She put her hands against his chest. "Don't," she whispered as her hand closed around his wrist, not knowing why she suddenly felt like she was fighting a different kind of battle entirely, that something had shifted.

She turned her face aside, desperate to escape him. His hand came up to hold her chin, imprisoning it so that she could not look away again. He tilted her head back.

"Look at me," he said in a hushed voice.

She was panting softly, staring not at his face, but at the darkness beyond him. It seemed she was fighting something inside herself now. Something she was terrified of.

His hand slid around to the small of her back. She could feel the hard muscles of his chest beneath her hands as he leaned even closer and breathed softly against her ear, "Reckon I'll make you forget his kisses."

She opened her mouth to protest, but he gave her no chance. He immediately covered her mouth with his own. No, she thought wildly as he kissed her. Yet where was her will to stop him? She ought to be outraged. Instead she felt a sharp, hot pang of need surge through her. Her resistance melted away in an instant.

He kissed her slowly. Deeply. Thoroughly. His mouth moved hungrily on hers until she was aware of nothing but the taste and the feel of him and the awareness of his hard body pressed close to her own. She wanted him there. She wanted him even closer.

When he finally pulled away, Ascensia realized that her hands were clutching his shirt front and that they were *both* breathing hard. She didn't open her eyes. She didn't dare open them. She was afraid she might reveal too much if she did look at him. He was her enemy. And yet, somehow, he was something much more than that.

Jesse watched the changes in her face. He saw the confusion and the uncertainty in her eyes when she finally did look up at him.

"You had no right to do that," she said, stricken as she began a slow descent back to reality.

"Nor did you," he whispered back, which confused her even more.

She struggled to remember who he was. Who she was. Deep inside her, she knew that he had taken something from her, something she could never get back again.

And now what would his reaction be? Would he gloat over his victory? Would she see the familiar mocking smile on his face? It was her first passionate kiss. It had been a devastating thing. And it had been with the wrong man. But she had allowed it. She hadn't stopped him. She hadn't even wanted to stop him. Guilt rose up to swamp her.

She reacted blindly, reacted without thought. She raised her hand and slapped him as hard as she could, as if that might wipe out the kiss that they had shared. As if it could undo her shameful response.

She would have hit him again but his own hand lashed out and imprisoned her wrist. He forced it behind her, holding it at the small of her back.

"Yankee witch," he hissed.

Maddened, she struggled wildly to escape him. "I'll- die," she panted. "Before I allow you to take such liberties again."

The writhing and twisting of her body roused Jesse as much as the kiss had. His blood ran high in response. With awareness. With need. With a whole host of other emotions he couldn't even begin to understand. With a violent jerk, he pulled her tighter against him, trapping her face roughly with his other hand.

He kissed her again. But this time it was with savage, ruthless demand. His mouth moved to kiss her face and her throat, then claimed her mouth again. When she moaned, he kissed her all the more hungrily. He might have sworn that, despite her struggle, she was responding, too.

When he finally released her, Jesse stepped back. He was breathing deeply. He had never known such an intense yearning as the one that consumed him now. He had never wanted a woman so badly that he forced her to yield to his desires against her will. But she had some kind of hold on him. He fought it. He fought it like he had never fought anything in his life.

Had she opened her eyes, she might have realized what she had done to him. But she did not. And when Jesse was finally able to leave her, he did so.

Long after he had gone, Ascensia was still standing against the wall in the square of moonlight. When she did open her eyes, she stared at the empty room as if she searched for some elusive answer to an equally elusive question. The darkness, however, yielded her no answers.

She lifted her hand to her mouth and touched her lips, then closed her eyes again. She was still tasting him and feeling the warmth of his mouth and the hard pressure of his body molded to hers. She was still fighting the shameful part of her that had wanted those kisses. And more. So much more.

Jesse lay staring up at the canopy of tree leaves above him.

"Ah'm all in," Wirt sighed as he sat down before the fire and pulled his boots off. "Don't believe it'll rain tonight."

"Doesn't have the look of it," Jesse replied absently. It was late and he was still awake, the cause of his sleeplessness still vivid in his mind. It had taken a lot of time, and a good amount of whiskey, to force his passions back under control. Her unexpected response had inflamed him. And had his pride and the circumstances allowed him to do so, he would have most willingly-

Hell, he thought to himself as he lifted his hand and raked back his hair. There had been nothing willing about it. Not on her part. He was fooling himself. His frown deepened as his thoughts ran on.

It was not, he suspected, simply lust for her that had driven him to be so brutal. Whiskey had been a factor. And jealousy, maybe, had been a part of it. Even though that confused him even more. He had no right to that emotion where she was concerned. In addition, there was his frustration at wanting her in the first place and *his* will having nothing at all to do with it.

Surprised and annoyed at such unfamiliar emotions, he nevertheless admitted them and hoped, sincerely, that by doing so, he could deal with them rationally. Tomorrow he would be rid of her. That ought to finally make her happy. And his life a whole lot easier.

"Lathrop's a man who won't let go of a grudge easy," Wirt remarked as he arranged his blankets. "You made him look bad. He'll be out for blood now and you can figure he'll jump at the chance for revenge when the time's right. He's that kind."

"I expect he will," Jesse replied, recalling that two nights ago he had seen Lathrop coldly and deliberately put four additional lead balls into the body of a dead man who had ridden off with a certain Yankee girl.

Noble Young was reclining on his side by the fire. He picked up a twig and stirred the embers, sending a shower of sparks aloft. "Captain?" he queried softly.

"Yeah?"

"You reckon she's got a Yankee up No'th who she is fond of?"

After a silence, Jesse breathed, "God help him if she does."

"She sure is uncommon pretty," Noble remarked quietly.

Jesse did not reply to that and the young scout went on. "Guess the Yankees are going to be stirred up soon's they see us crossing the river."

"They will," Jesse agreed.

The North would indeed be stirred up. In the morning the Southern Army would begin crossing the Potomac. The purpose of the invasion was to make the North experience war on its own soil in hopes that it would bring an end to the bloodshed.

Jesse knew that McClellan had just been given back command of the Northern Army and McClellan was always slow, always deliberate and cautious. He wouldn't be bold enough to strike a decisive blow against Robert E. Lee, who was boldness itself. It was clear to Jesse, therefore, what the campaign ahead meant and that knowledge was sobering to contemplate.

It did no good, however, to brood over such things, he reflected. It was all beyond his control and he had lived the kind of life where a man learned not to think too much about tomorrow or kick too hard against fate. No matter where it might lead him.

Chapter 11

Ascensia sat her horse alone, looking out over the Potomac River at a place called White's Ford. The aspens flashed above her. The sun was shining. The day was soft, the wind calm.

She was wearing a simple lavender calico dress. Her dark hair was primly braided down her back and tied with a piece of ribbon that matched the dress. From beneath her lashes she watched the long, gray columns moving northward.

It seemed like the entire Confederate Army was on the move. They were already wading the Potomac. They were the most ragged men she had ever seen. Many of them were barefoot. Still, they seemed to be in high spirits. She could hear the strains of *Maryland, My Maryland* from afar.

At dawn, Ascensia had observed crowds of people from the town turn out of their homes to greet the soldiers. Women and children had stood at the gates waving handkerchiefs and Secessionist flags. They had offered food and drink. Relatives, some of them were, and friends, and Ascensia could not help but feel a measure of sympathy for them, misguided though they were.

She frowned as she glanced down at the reins in her hands. Last night had been an endless torment of self-reproach, of regret and burning shame. While she sat there alone, the memory of what had happened returned to haunt her.

Lieutenant Parrish had come to the hotel room for her early in the morning. She hadn't seen Captain Lucane at all. Not since last night. She wondered how she was going to face him or if, in fact, she would have to face him at all. She had the answer to one of those questions when she lifted her face and saw the Captain riding towards her.

He reined in beside her. "Well, you're going home at last."

When she did not reply, he said, "Renn will be here soon."

He swung down from his horse and asked, "That saddle loose?" He placed his hand on the pommel and shook it. "I'd better tighten the cinch before you start out." Evidently he meant to act as if nothing had happened.

"Nice morning," he remarked as he reached under the horse. "Maybe we could manage to spend this last time together without tearing at each other," he said as he glanced up. "We seem to have the habit."

She gazed down at him. "I have no desire to tear at you, Captain."

After another silence, she asked, "Aren't you afraid I will tell what I have seen here?"

He smiled slightly, but did not look at her. "If I told you to keep it to yourself, would you listen to me? Besides, there are some Yankee scouts downriver that have been watching us all morning. The Union Army will know soon enough. And anyway," he said as he looked up at her. "You would disappoint me if you showed yourself to be anything but loyal to your country. Just as I am loyal to mine.

"If you'll move your leg," he went on. "I'll shorten this stirrup for you."

She lowered her eyes and noted the breadth of his muscular shoulders and the way his black hair fell over his collar and the sure strength in his lean hands as he worked with the leather strap.

All at once she was conscious of a strange little thrill and a breathless sensation when she recalled that hand upon her face, when she remembered the wild, hungry working of his mouth upon hers . . .

Confused, she turned her face towards the river, willing away the hot blood that began to rise up into her cheeks. "You are invading Northern soil, Captain. Our army will come to meet you."

"Yes, ma'am," he replied soberly. "They will." He had stopped and was also gazing across the river. He then moved to the other stirrup to adjust it. Finally, he shook the pommel and declared the saddle secure.

"You ought to be back within the Union lines tonight," he said. "I have no doubt Renn will get you safely through. There he is, coming now." He looked up at her. "I reckon we won't be seeing each other again. So let me wish you good luck."

After he had mounted his horse, she ventured a direct glance towards him. He swept off his hat and bowed to her. It was a surprisingly gallant and graceful gesture and his eyes, as he replaced his hat, continued to hold hers.

Lieutenant Parris rode up. "Ready, Miss McCay?"

She nodded. When she looked back to the Captain, his gaze continued to linger upon her face. And there was, perhaps, the slightest trace of the old mockery as his mouth curved into a faint smile.

"So long, ma'am," he said before he rode off, the sound of his voice staying with her long after he had wheeled his horse and disappeared into the endless stream of gray-clad men.

Chapter 12

The Southern invasion of the North brought about the battle of Antietam, or Sharpsburg as it came to be known in the South. The fighting along Antietam Creek would come to be known as the bloodiest day in all four years of the war. It was worse in suffering and loss of life than anything that had come before or anything that would follow.

Both sides had fought fiercely and savagely. But as night finally descended on that 17th day of September, the battered Rebel Army still held its original position. The exhausted Union Army also crouched nervously in the same position it had occupied in the early hours before dawn.

Over in the East Woods and around the Dunker Church, beside the Hagerstown Road and in the bloody, trampled rows of corn, down by the banks of Antietam Creek and the Stone Bridge was the appalling evidence that the ranks had diminished by countless thousands.

In the month following Antietam, a battle fought at Perryville, Kentucky cost the Union another 4,000 casualties. In December, more than 12,000 Northern soldiers lay killed or wounded on the frozen slope below Mayre's Heights beside the Rappahonnack River at Fredericksburg, Virginia. The slaughter at Fredericksburg was subsequently called a tragic, bloody mistake, little consolation for those waiting at home.

In Tennessee, as the year drew to a close, Federal losses were nearly 13,000 at Stones River. The armies spent the following months bracing themselves in winter quarters for the year to come.

1863 saw Vicksburg on the Mississippi River still in Confederate hands, still defiant and heavily fortified against the Union Army. In May of that year, at a crossroads called Chancellorsville which met at the fringes of the Virginia Wilderness, over 16,000 Union soldiers of the Army of the Potomac were added to the casualty lists as Joe Hooker, latest Union commandeer, lost his nerve in a confrontation with Robert E. Lee. The war had entered its third summer.

"I have missed you, Ascensia," Morgan was saying to her. It was the first time they had been alone in a long time.

"I have missed you, too, Morgan," Ascensia replied quietly.

Major Morgan Damon looked down at the profile of his fiancée. Ascensia was beautiful. He had always thought her so. It made other men envy him. She was innocent and even-tempered and patient. She came from a good family and she loved him. All qualities that would make her a good and devoted wife. A man in his position needed a proper wife.

A frown touched his face, however, as he noticed how distant her gaze was. Lately her moods puzzled him. She often seemed withdrawn and preoccupied. At times it seemed he could not reach her at all.

"Ascensia," he chided gently. "Here we are, together at last, and you are a thousand miles away."

"I'm sorry, Morgan," she said with a sigh. "I was just remembering a dream I had last night."

Ascensia felt a twinge of guilt. The single, lingering memory of that dream centered around a certain Rebel captain whose eyes were exactly the color the sky was at this moment. But she did not mention those details to Morgan. Morgan did not know anything about Jesse Lucane and she hoped that he would never find out. Morgan was leaving for Washington soon and he was telling her how disappointed he was that he would not be able to escort her to dinner that evening.

"There will be other dinners," she said.

"Yes," he said in a low voice. "In our own home." He looked down at her. "I am looking forward to that time, Ascensia. And I have to say that when I am with you like this, I don't feel at all like waiting until Christmas."

He looked around to make sure that no one was watching them from the house, then leaned over and kissed her. It was a hard kiss. A possessive kiss. But it did not have the affect on her that the other's had had and she was immediately afflicted with a renewed sense of guilt.

"I'm sorry," he said, mistaking her blush for something else. "We had better go in now. We don't want to make a bad impression by staying out here alone too long."

He took her arm and escorted her back to the house and asked, "You haven't forgotten that I want you to have a daguerreotype made, I hope?"

"No," she replied vaguely. "I haven't forgotten."

That night, in her bedroom at Oak Haven, Ascensia glanced at her cousin Hetty who was standing at the window. Hetty stood silent and pensive as if she was lost in deep thought. The lamplight glowed softly upon Hetty's rose silk dress and upon her ringlets of glossy chestnut hair.

"They are late," Hetty said, without turning. "But then Quillie rarely manages to get anywhere on time."

Hetty turned and smiled. The smile quickly faded, however, and she said, "Poor Quillie. She has been terribly worried about her brother."

Ascensia remained silent. She was certain that Hetty was thinking about her own brother, Holmes. At the beginning of the war, Holmes had been arrested and charged with relaying information to the Rebel Army. After being confined for a few months in the Old Capitol Prison, Holmes had been sent to Fort Monroe in Virginia where he was exchanged for a Union officer being held by the Rebels.

No one had heard from Holmes since. It was assumed that he had enlisted in the Confederate Army where his sympathies had always been. Some considered him to be a traitor. Hetty rarely spoke of her brother but she had always been devoted to him and Ascensia suspected she remained so.

They knew many other families who had been bitterly split by the war and among their Maryland acquaintances were other young men who had gone south to fight for the Rebel cause.

"Why, 'Scensia," Hetty said suddenly. "You have scarcely glanced in the mirror. Don't you want to see how your new dress looks?"

Ascensia turned to the mirror and absently smoothed the folds of deep green silk that fell from her waist. Beads of jet embroidered into the rich black lace that adorned the dress glistened with every movement. Her long dark curls fell in a satiny profusion over her bare shoulders.

"I knew that shade of dress would become you," Hetty said. "You will have every man falling at your feet tonight. Too bad Morgan won't be there to see."

Did Hetty mean too bad Morgan would miss seeing her in the dress? Or that he would miss seeing other men fall at her feet? She wondered because lately, sometimes when Hetty looked at Morgan, Ascensia would catch a glimpse of something that looked very close to dislike.

But it wasn't Morgan's reaction that Ascensia was imagining as she stood in front of the mirror. She gave a self-deprecating sigh. How long, she wondered, was she going to find her thoughts wandering back to the memory of a far-away Rebel? How many times was she going to re-live his kisses, brutal as they had been? And how many times was she going to wonder whether he had become another casualty of this cruel and endless war?

She couldn't help it. She didn't want to think about him, but it seemed she had no control over her thoughts. Or her memories. Months had passed and it seemed to her that she ought to have forgotten him by now. But that wasn't the case. In fact, it seemed that she was thinking about him even more.

"Here comes the carriage now," Hetty said with another glance out the window. "I do hope," she went on as she arranged her lace shawl over her bare shoulders. "That we can enjoy the evening. Even though I am sure we shall have to hear about generals, and battles and military strategies all night long."

On the staircase, Hetty glanced back over her shoulder at Ascensia and said, "I can't wait to see Quillie again. It will be such a comfort for all of us to be together again."

In the elegant entry hall of the Strode Mansion, Ascensia stood gazing into the adjoining room. Shimmering cut-glass chandeliers threw a flattering and lustrous glow over the guests. Soft laughter and the low murmur of pleasant conversation greeted the three young women as they were led forward.

Quillie fluttered her fan beside Ascensia and whispered, "Look at the way Leora Strode is watching you. She looks as if she would like to claw you to pieces. I suppose she is worrying that you look better than she does."

"Really, Quillie," Ascensia replied, frowning, but then glanced at Leora in spite of herself.

Leora Strode was a beautiful woman. She was the only child in a very wealthy family and so she had always been excessively indulged and spoiled. Leora was always dressed in the height of fashion. Tonight she was wearing an elegant gown that was covered in the most exquisite ivory lace Ascensia had ever seen. Fresh roses adorned her hair which was gathered up in elaborate coils and waves.

Ascensia smiled politely. She could not help noticing, however, that the smile that curved the corners of Leora's lips did not reach her dark eyes. Eyes that, for a moment, flashed with something very close to hostility.

Ascensia's attention was drawn by Quillie who was describing a new style of mantilla she had seen in Godey's Magazine. Ascensia, however, quickly lost interest in the subject of fashion and her gaze wandered around the room.

Her glance fell upon a small group of soldiers talking in the room across the hall. Brom was part of the group and he looked up and smiled at her. Lieutenant Armitage was there as well. Much to Ascensia's relief, he had survived the wound he had received that terrible night of the raid.

She did not recognize any of the other men. Not the ones that were facing her. She stared at one of the men whose back was towards her. He was tall and his dark blue frock coat fitted his wide shoulders well, she thought. The hair falling over the collar gleamed black in the light from the chandeliers.

Ascensia didn't know why the man held her interest. Except that there was something familiar about him . . . She chided herself severely for thinking about Captain Lucane. *Again.* Merely because this man had black hair, too, didn't mean it had to bring up another round of memories for her. Would she ever stop seeing his ghost?

But her breath caught in her chest as the man turned. She could feel the blood drain from her face. She remained frozen, rooted to the spot for the man in the room across the hallway really was Jesse Lucane.

There could be no mistake. Even though she did not understand how he could possibly be standing there dressed in the clothes of a Union officer. Before she could do anything, say anything, before she could even move, those pale gray eyes that she remembered so well had already locked with her own.

Quillie's voice seemed to come from a distance. "'Scensia?" she repeated. "You remember Colonel Jameson?"

Remember?

"I- yes," Ascensia stammered. "I remember you very well, Colonel."

She did not dare to look at the Captain again. Yet she was oblivious to anything else. What was she going to do? What was *he* going to do?

"Miss McCay?" Colonel Jameson was peering down into her face with a slight frown.

Quillie was also staring at her. "'Scensia, are you all right?"

Ascensia shook her head. First no, then yes. "Yes. I'm fine," she replied a little breathlessly. "I'm- fine. It's just that it has been a very busy day and it is terribly warm in here. Don't you think it's warm?"

"Yes, it *is* warm," the Colonel agreed.

"You look as pale as a ghost," Quillie said, looking worried.

Hetty asked if she wanted to lie down and rest upstairs for a while.

"No!" Ascensia cried, immediately regretting the sharp tone of her voice.

She forced herself to smile. She forced herself to appear calm. "Really," she said. "Everything is all right. I just don't want everyone looking at us."

Hetty looked around curiously. She looked back at Ascensia.

Though Ascensia tried not to look at the Captain again, it seemed that her eyes were drawn helplessly to that one place across the hall. Her breath lodged in her throat when she looked up to see Brom and Captain Lucane, or *whoever* or *whatever* he was, walking towards her.

"Hetty," Brom began the introduction. "You have already met Captain Wolfe. Captain, this is my cousin, Ascensia McCay. And Quillie Wells."

Captain *Wolfe* smiled at Hetty, then Quillie. "A pleasure," he said politely to Ascensia, the low, familiar voice sending tremors through her. She noted that not even the slightest trace of a Southern accent was evident. She barely managed to smile back at him and was saved from further distress when dinner was announced.

Ascensia took her place at one of the long, lavishly-spread tables. Brom sat to her right. Quillie was to her left. Captain Lucane, or Captain Wolfe as he was now calling himself, sat across from her and Leora sat beside him.

He held her gaze briefly after they were seated. After that she refused to look at him again, even though her thoughts were most definitely centered upon him. She was so absorbed in those thoughts that Brom suddenly leaned towards her and looked closely into her face.

"You're distracted tonight, 'Scensia," he said with a smile as he tugged at one of the long dark curls that fell over her shoulder. She returned his smile as best she could and was grateful when the champagne was served.

She immediately lifted the delicate crystal to her lips and sipped at the icy, bubbling liquid. Ignore him, she told herself. Don't look at him. Pretend he isn't even there.

While they waited for the food, the men immediately began a lively discussion of political and military affairs. Ascensia, meanwhile, congratulated herself over having managed to regain some of her usual poise. At least the champagne was helping her feel more relaxed.

She could scarcely believe the man's impudence in coming here, or in wearing that uniform. He was a spy, she reminded herself. Of course he would have the audacity to wear it. He could be arrested and hanged if he were caught. All she had to do was let them all know who he really was.

As for that, she should have exposed him by now. She wasn't sure why she hadn't done just that. The more time that passed, the more she would have to explain why she had waited so long.

She drank a second glass of champagne. She could feel the warmth of it flowing inside her. It brought with it a courage that she had not felt before. It brought a new defiance as well. There was a trace of color in her cheeks now and a sparkle in her eyes.

Those eyes narrowed over her glass. He might have amused himself at her expense before, but now- well, that was another story altogether. If he attempted to molest her in any way at all, he would quickly find that she held the upper hand. She tossed her curls over one shoulder, laughed at Brom's witty remarks and even had a conversation with Quillie about the latest fashions in Paris.

She glanced across the table to see the Captain lean close to hear something that Leora was saying to him. His low laugh reached her. A flood of memories came rushing back at the deep, familiar sound of it. He made a reply to Leora that Ascensia was not able to catch.

Leora certainly seemed interested in the Captain. She playfully tapped him on the arm with her fan, unabashedly and openly flirting with the man.

Ascensia's eyes narrowed. He was certainly treating Leora differently than he had treated *her* down in Virginia. Antagonism stirred within her.

"What was it that you do, Captain Wolfe?" she asked suddenly.

"Ma'am?"

"My cousin has mentioned that you are in the horse business."

That pale, unwavering gaze held hers for a moment before he replied, "I train horses for the cavalry."

"You must work very hard at it," Ascensia remarked. "Because, besides being a general nuisance, Rebel guerillas have proven to be reprehensible horse thieves."

"That is certainly true," Brom spoke up beside her. "Unfortunately, the Maryland wilderness hinders us down here and makes it easy for Rebel guerillas to draw their provisions from the United States government."

"You mean *steal* their provisions," Ascensia corrected him. "Captain *Wolfe*, certainly you find it frustrating to work so hard to train good horses merely to have Rebel traitors steal them. Who," she went on a trifle heatedly. "In spite of their talk of sacred honor, act more like ravening wolves who make off with everything they can get their hands on."

A look of bewilderment crossed Hetty's face as she looked down the table to where Ascensia sat. Brom, meanwhile, looked at her as if she had just announced her decision to fly to the moon after dinner.

"I understand how you must feel, Ascensia," Leora said as her fan fluttered gently before her generous bosom. "Especially after your terrible ordeal last fall. Why, it must have been awful being abducted by the brutes. Heaven knows what they put you through."

Leora accomplished what she had set out to do. She had meant to humiliate her. And her suggestive words had accomplished just that. Ascensia offered no further comments about Rebels. Or anything else for that matter. She spent the rest of the meal in virtual silence, enduring as best she could Leora's haughty manner and barely-concealed smirks.

After dinner, Jesse stood on the back veranda with several other soldiers who had gone outside for brandy and cigars. He glanced up, paying closer attention when one of the men asked, "Do you know who that dark-haired girl is? The one in the green dress."

"I don't need to ask who you mean," Another soldier replied with a grin. "She is fine-looking, isn't she? Her name is Ascensia McCay. She won't be Miss McCay for long though. She is supposed to be married before the year is over."

Jesse stared at the man's face for a moment before he asked, "And when is the happy event?"

"Christmas, I believe," was the reply. "Unless Major Damon can get her to move the date up. Of course, after you've seen her, you can't blame him for being impatient."

Jesse had managed to appear calm but beneath the surface some deeper emotion was responsible for the tightening of the muscles in his jaw and the slow clenching of his hand around the railing.

"That right?" he remarked casually, although his indifference was forced. "And just how long have they been engaged?"

"Since last year sometimes, I think. That's right. They announced the engagement last summer."

Someone mentioned some special apple brandy out back and the men eagerly went off across the yard to sample it. Jesse remained alone in the darkness. There was a cold light in the depths of his eyes. Eyes that narrowed with the flow of his thoughts. So when he had kissed her back in Leesburg that night, she had belonged to Morgan Damon.

"And I didn't even know it." The irony of it brought a smile to his lips, but it was a chilling smile. He didn't know what she was going to do about seeing him there. Really, that particular she-wolf had proven that she was capable of anything.

Still, as he thought the thing through, there came a feral gleam to his eyes as he straightened and said to himself, "Well, Miss Ascensia McCay, it's going to be a mighty interesting re-acquaintance."

Ascensia managed to slip away from the crowd after dinner. She passed the back parlor and saw that it was dark and empty so she went inside. She knew she had had a little too much champagne to drink and she had to have time to think and to clear her head. This sudden appearance of Jesse Lucane, or Jesse Wolfe, or whoever he was, had unnerved her.

She hadn't seen him for the past half hour or so. For all she knew, he had already left. That made sense. He had to be wondering if she was going to tell who he was. Maybe he was gone and she wouldn't have to deal with him. Maybe he . . . She suddenly whirled around and saw him standing in the doorway.

She drew a long, slow breath as he entered the room. She almost panicked.

"Let me out of here," she said. "I'll scream and every one of those soldiers out there will come running. And when I tell them who you are- "

"I reckon," he said quietly. "That if you thought it over, you would realize that it wouldn't be the best thing for you to do. I only want to talk to you."

"I don't see what we could possibly have to discuss." She was watching him closely, with wary eyes. She suddenly turned towards the window, shaking her head as she kept her back to him.

After a few moments of silence, she whirled back around to face him and demanded. "Who do you think you are?"

"A ravenin' wolf of a horse thief," he drawled.

"Oh! You haven't changed at all." Her hands closed into angry, frustrated fists at her crinolined sides.

"And you're still kicking against me."

"But there is a difference," she informed him, her chin lifting slightly. "We are *not* in Virginia now. And I am *not* your prisoner."

"No, you're not," he said, continuing to hold her gaze. "But all the same, I'm asking you to listen to what I have to say."

"Oh? This is the first time, isn't it, that you have *asked* me to do anything? You do have the habit of making demands. It is not *my* habit," she went on, touching one hand to her décolletage. "To oblige enemy spies."

"Yet you haven't told anyone who I am," he pointed out.

"I certainly didn't keep silent for your benefit," she informed him.

"Then I assume that the omission was for your own benefit?"

"*My* benefit?" she echoed. "I should think that you would realize that you have more to lose than I if your identity were revealed."

"Sure," he said slowly. But a certain familiar tone in his voice made her wary. "Then everyone would know about those days and nights we spent together."

"Spent together?" she breathed. "I would like to remind you, Captain, that you compelled me to stay with you against my will."

He nodded. "I did. Of course they'll understand how you didn't have any choice. And they will surely sympathize with you when they hear how I'd forced you to- well, to do all those things you didn't want to do."

She didn't like the way he was making it all sound. "I will not be threatened, if that is what you are trying to do."

"Threaten you? Why, I'm just reminiscing. You could explain it all, of course. I reckon all those nice guests out there would believe almost anything. And there's the way that I kissed you in that hotel room. Though I sure haven't forgiven myself for that."

She paled at his words. How could she explain it all in a way that wouldn't make it sound so sordid? Worse, how could she explain her silence when she had known all night who he was? The truth was she couldn't.

"Do you intend telling?" she asked in a voice barely above a whisper.

"Not if you don't mention it first," he replied.

"What is it that you want?"

"A truce," he said. "A cease-fire. If you think that over, I am sure you will agree that it would be mutually beneficial."

She was silent for a long time before she asked, "Why are you really here?"

She was surprised when he answered her immediately and apparently honestly.

"Smuggling," he said. "Medicines mostly."

She struggled with herself. She searched for options that weren't there. "Do you give me your word that no one will be hurt or killed by my silence or by your actions while you are here?"

"I give you my word," he replied soberly. "The only life at risk is mine."

And so, reluctantly, Ascensia entered into an agreement of sorts with a Rebel spy and prayed sincerely that no one would ever find out.

Chapter 13

The very next morning Ascensia was sitting on the veranda of Oak Haven after a leisurely breakfast with Hetty and Quillie. The weather was agreeable. The air was soft and Spring-like. She had been prey to many conflicting emotions last night. She was still sorting them out.

Jesse Lucane was alive and well, it seemed. It wasn't relief she felt, she assured herself. It was just that there had been so many thousands of men killed that it was only natural to wonder.

She was looking out at the pasture where the horses were grazing. Horses for the army were sometimes kept temporarily at Oak Haven, because of its location, before being sent west. Noticing the direction of Ascensia's gaze, Hetty explained that about twenty new horses had arrived last night while they had been gone.

Ascensia half listened while Quillie repeated all the gossip she had heard the night before. Brom had left before dawn to rejoin his regiment. It was always difficult for her to say goodbye to Brom.

Morgan had not returned from Washington. Alone in her room last night, Ascensia had realized how fortunate she was that Morgan had not been able to escort her to dinner after all. She would have had a very difficult time pretending that nothing was wrong when in fact-

She stared in disbelief at the man who was just now riding up the drive.

"Welcome to Oak Haven, Captain Wolfe," Hetty greeted.

"Morning ladies," the Captain returned politely as he removed his hat. He searched around in his saddlebags for a few moments then handed something down to Hetty. "Here's the sheet music that you wanted," he said to her. "And some books I thought you might all enjoy."

"How kind of you, Captain," Hetty said as she took the books from him. "Can we fix you some breakfast? We have already eaten but there is still plenty left."

He thanked her but said that he, too, had already eaten.

"Well, then," Hetty said. "Perhaps you would consider having lunch with us later."

"A man could hardly turn down the chance to enjoy the company of such charming hostesses," he replied with his own charming smile.

Ascensia felt the same antagonism stir in her that she always felt in his presence. She thought that he was about to accept Hetty's invitation. But after looking at Ascensia's face, he politely declined and told them that he would probably be too busy to join them that day. Tipping his hat, he bid them a good day and rode back down the drive toward the stables.

"What did he bring us?" Quillie asked with all the eagerness of a child at Christmas.

"Oh," she exclaimed excitedly as she picked up one of the books. "Godey's Ladies' Book. The latest issue. How very thoughtful of him. We'll have to do something for him in return."

After a silence, Ascensia looked up to hear Quillie remark, "Not only is he kind *and* thoughtful, but he is terribly handsome, too. Don't you think so, Hetty?"

"Yes," Hetty agreed with a laugh. "Terribly."

"Ascensia?"

Ascensia stared blankly at Quillie and then realized what she was asking. "He's- yes, Quillie. He's good-looking." She could barely grind the admission out. Jesse's looks were the last thing on her mind.

Well, he had certainly won them over, Ascensia thought to herself as she stood in the shadows of the wisteria vine. She was frowning as she bit her lower lip. She certainly had a few things to say to the Captain. But more than an hour passed before she was able to do so.

"What are you doing here?" she demanded later in the stable.

He turned and looked at her questioningly but she gave him no opportunity to reply.

"We had an agreement last night," she reminded him. "You said you were here to- " She glanced around to make sure there was no one else in the stable to overhear them. "To smuggle medicines. Now you show up here and prove that your word is unreliable."

"There's no need to get your feathers all ruffled up."

Her scornful look would have disconcerted most men. But Jesse Lucane was not most men. He leaned against the stall door behind him and regarded her lazily.

"You knew all along that you would be coming here to Oak Haven," she went on in an undertone. "But you didn't mention that last night. You didn't say one word about it."

"You didn't ask," he said. "And as for that, I have orders to train these horses for the cavalry and they're wanted by the end of the month. So that means I'll be too busy for fooling with you. Despite what you think, I have not come here to torment you. We agreed on a truce and I intend to keep my word." He glanced behind her. "But if you keep looking like you would like to run a saber through me, someone's eventually going to get to wondering why."

"You mean you have orders from the wrong government- " She paused. "*Captain Wolfe*. Or whoever you are. I don't even know your name anymore."

"You see? That's just what I mean," he said as he moved closer to her. "You're forgetting yourself. And talking loud enough for someone to overhear you. My real name *is* Jesse Wolfe Lucane." He touched his hat lightly with a trace of his old mockery in the gesture.

"Oh, you are so maddening!"

"But I haven't done anything," he protested.

She turned away from him, but as she whirled around, her skirt swirled against his boots and became caught on one of his brass spurs. She tried to pull it free but it was caught fast.

"I don't think this is funny," she snapped.

"Did I say it was?" He said it soberly enough but she was sure she saw his mouth twitch with inward humor.

She was still trying frantically to free her skirt when he got down on one knee before her. "Hold still," he said.

When he had freed her skirt, and after he had gotten to his feet again, he crossed his arms over his chest. She detected amusement in his pale gray eyes as he regarded her. She found it most irritating. She found *him* most irritating and took no pains to conceal it.

The sound of horses approaching made Ascensia step quickly away from him. She turned towards the open stable door, hastily gathered up her skirts and, with one last murderous glance over her shoulder, left the stable.

Jesse, meanwhile, did not move. There was a hard narrowing of his eyes, however, as he watched the officer who had just ridden up to greet Ascensia.

The weeks passed by. For Ascensia it was a period of getting used to seeing Jesse come each morning to work with the horses at Oak Haven. It was obvious that Hetty liked Jesse. And apparently the sentiment was mutual for they treated each other with an air of familiarity that was, at times, more than a little annoying to Ascensia.

Quillie was taken with him as well and he was often invited to join the ladies on the porch for a meal late at night before he returned to his camp. And why wouldn't they like him, Ascensia thought to herself. He was pleasasnt. He was agreeable. A perfect gentleman. Indeed, he seemed very different from the Rebel spy who had made off with her last fall.

And even though she fought it, at times even Ascensia found herself enjoying Jesse's company. Last night he had stayed to hear Hetty play the piano for an hour or so, waiting out the rain that had begun pouring down just before he was about to return to his camp. At one point, Ascensia had looked up to see him watching her with a quiet intensity that had had a strange effect upon her. But then, Jesse had always had an unsettling effect on her. Why wouldn't he still affect her?

Early mornings she got into the habit of spending time alone with Jesse walking the garden paths before anyone else was up. She even found herself looking forward to those mornings, enjoying them more than she had a right to. She consoled herself with the reminder that his presence was temporary, and that he would soon be gone and life would return to its normal routine.

Late one night he joined them on the veranda after Hetty insisted that he rest a while before returning to camp. He had put in a long, grueling day with the horses and he looked tired. Quillie had already gone to bed and Hetty had gone inside to fix him a packet of food to take back to camp with him as she sometimes did.

Jesse was sitting on the veranda steps in the dark. Ascensia was standing by the rail trying to keep her eyes from wandering in his direction. Neither had spoken for a few minutes. He got to his feet and was suddenly standing at her side.

"It's not exactly proper, my being alone here with you like this," he said, glancing at her face in the darkness.

"Most people would consider it improper," she replied quietly.

He laughed beneath his breath and said, "We have done a lot of things that most people wouldn't consider proper."

She didn't look at him. She looked instead at the moon just now rising above the trees beyond the stable.

He cast a glance over his shoulder, as if he was making sure that they were still alone. It was an intimate gesture somehow, one that made her feel like there was a bond between them that no one else shared.

"You're feeling restless tonight," he said and she was not surprised that he could read her mood so well. Jesse seemed tuned into her emotions more than anyone else had ever been in her entire life.

"I don't feel like going in yet," she admitted, closing her eyes and lifting her face to the star-strewn sky. A faint breeze blew against her, softly ruffling a few stray curls that refused to stay confined.

She opened her eyes. As she looked at Jesse from beneath her lashes, she silently agreed with Quillie. He was handsome. Terribly, dangerously handsome. She had always thought so.

He dropped his hand over the railing. Her dress brushed lightly against him. He did not touch her in any other way but somehow it made her more intensely aware of his nearness.

She watched him reach out and pick one of the white roses growing on the trellis near them. "Does it still bother you?" he asked as he lifted the rose to sample its scent. "My being here?"

"I am managing to tolerate it," she replied, *managing* to keep her voice light. But it was an effort. His low, husky voice seemed to move over her skin like a caress. Like he was touching her without actually touching her. She tilted her head back again, closed her eyes and concentrated on his voice, realizing how much she loved listening to it.

"In a few weeks I'll be gone and you'll be able to relax."

"Are you going back to Virginia?" she asked with her eyes still closed.

"Most likely." His voice had lowered even more. She imagined he was looking at her. And there was something else in his voice-

She shook herself mentally. It was good that he was leaving soon. She had already had one disagreeable scene with Morgan because he had seen her talking alone with Jesse one morning down by the pasture fence. Jesse was, and always had been, a disruption in her life.

But suddenly, unaccountably the prospect of Jesse leaving made her feel a sense of impending loss. When she should feel relief. It was something that confused her. She fought this gentler side of Jesse. She fought what it did to her.

She opened her eyes and searched his face in the darkness Her gaze lingered upon his mouth, and she was suddenly remembering the feel of it upon hers. And she found herself wondering if he ever thought about that night when he had kissed her. The night she had kissed him back. It was still difficult for her to admit that, but it was becoming less so.

She tightened her hand around the railing. "Don't," she told herself sternly. "Don't think about it. About him." Her wayward thoughts refused to obey, however. They drew her helplessly down a path of remembering that left her nearly breathless.

"Look!" he suddenly whispered and his hand fell upon her wrist. The fingers closed, with an iron strength, but gentle.

She, too, had seen the brief flash of light in the blackness of the heavens. His hand fell away but she remained standing very still.

"Did you make a wish?" he asked. "You're supposed to make a wish when you see a shooting star. The only thing is you have to think of it before it's gone."

He was watching her. He smiled faintly and his eyes lingered. But the smile faded and his face changed. He was looking at her so intently that she felt lost for a moment. She lowered her eyes guiltily, grateful for the darkness.

Hetty's footsteps in the front hallway announced her return. Jesse had moved away from Ascensia and she heard him tell Hetty that it was time for him to go.

Long after he thanked Hetty for the food and said his goodnight, Ascensia remained at the rail. Alone in the darkness, she reached out to pick up the rose he had left behind.

Chapter 14

Ascensia pulled the flowers from her hair, then the confining pins and combs. She sighed as the heavy weight of her curls fell past her bare shoulders to her waist.

There had been a military review that day and a ball in the evening. She should have been tired but that wasn't the case. She hadn't undressed yet. She felt restless. She felt confined. Unsettled.

She looked out of her window and her face suddenly grew sober as she contemplated the darkness. She sighed again. She could not deny it any longer.

Something had changed her. She was not the same person she had been. Her eyes searched the heavens as if she sought an answer there. The sky was filled with a million stars, but no answers.

She had not seen Jesse in three days. For all she knew he had already gone back to Virginia and wasn't coming back. She knew that would happen one day. He would ride away and never return to Oak Haven. She would never see him again.

She ran her hand along the window pane, not liking the empty feeling that the thought stirred in her. She wondered if he would have any regrets at not seeing her again. She wondered if he ever thought about her the same way she was thinking about him right now.

Her taffeta skirt rustled as she turned back to the room. With both her hands she brushed the loose curls back from her face then went still as she lifted her face to the image she had just seen in the mirror. Jesse was standing in the shadowed alcove of her room.

"What are you doing here?" she asked, startled but not as angry as she ought to be. "If you think I will allow you to come into my room like this, you are mistaken."

"Relax, Ascensia. I just want to talk to you."

"You couldn't have waited until morning?"

"Honey, fighting my way through a squadron of cavalry would be easier than getting to see you alone during the day."

She relented, but reluctantly. "All right," she said. "You're already here. You may as well say what you have to say. And then you have to leave," she added as sternly as she was able to.

I should not allow this, Ascensia told herself. I allow him too much. I would not allow any other man such liberties. Not even Morgan.

"You danced with a man named Quarles tonight," Jesse began. "You know who I'm talking about?"

She hadn't seen Jesse at the ball tonight and was surprised to hear that he had been there.

"Yes," she replied. She remembered the man.

"What did you talk about while you were dancing?"

By the way that Jesse was watching her face, she knew that her answer was important to him. She frowned as she tried to recall the conversation.

"The usual things," she answered with a slight shrug. "The war, the weather. He also talked about Hetty's brother, Holmes. He is fighting on your side."

"What did he have to say about that?" Jesse asked.

"He said it was a shame that his family had to suffer for his disloyalty and that we must all be wondering what has happened to him."

Jesse nodded and seemed preoccupied for a moment.

"What's wrong?" Ascensia asked, alarmed. "Does he know who you are?"

"No," Jesse replied. "He would have had me arrested by now. But Quarles' presence here may mean that he suspects something." His voice trailed off as if he was speaking to himself. He looked at her and said, "You ought to know that Quarles has had people arrested and thrown into prison merely because of his suspicions. And more than once the man has been motivated by personal interests.

"Should I be caught," he went on. "Don't admit ever, to anyone, that you knew anything about me. No matter what happens, you deny any knowledge of my real identity."

He had her worried and it showed in her face.

"I just want you to have the right answers," he said, then smiled. "We don't want you to end up confined in the Old Capital Prison alongside of me."

"I wish this war was over," she said earnestly. "Everyone is paying the price. I know that there really are women confined in the Old Capital Prison. Women who have smuggled mail and many other things through the lines. Women who have even spied for the South. I don't understand why they would take such risks."

"Some do it out of loyalty," he said.

"And others?" she questioned.

"There are some who just seem to like the thrill of it."

"And do you find it thrilling?" she asked.

"It has its moments," he replied as he sat down at the foot of her bed.

He grew serious and said, "To be honest, I have seen women who were cooler in dangerous situations than the bravest soldier. Sometimes the right woman can carry a thing though when it seems hopeless to a man."

"And do men find that kind of woman- interesting?"

"There are women that could seriously distract a man if they set their mind to it," he replied.

"And have any of them seriously distracted you?" she asked, standing before him.

He looked up at her. She turned away and shrugged her bare shoulders. She did not know why she had asked that question. She regretted it immediately.

"What would you like to know?" he asked.

She was not sure what it was that she wanted an answer to. Finally she said, "I suppose I am wondering if you treat other women in your life the same as you treat me."

He smiled. "I don't reckon, 'Scensia, that there is another woman quite like you. We have always had our little games."

"They are dangerous games," she whispered, sitting on the bed but leaving a distance between them.

"And just how did you get into the spy business?" she asked.

"Circumstance, honey. Just circumstance," he replied.

"And does circumstance often put you in the company of women spies?"

"At times," he answered honestly.

They stared at each other for a moment. And then she said, "It's something that I certainly don't understand."

She bit her lower lip for a moment and asked, "If I were a spy and you were in possession of certain military information, if I wanted that information, and if I tried- seducing you into giving it away, would you be tempted into doing so?"

"Depends."

"On what?"

"Depends on what kind of a man I was."

"Suppose," she said. "You were a man who had already half decided to hand over that information."

There was a long silence. Ascensia began to feel somewhat foolish until she heard him say in his softest tones, "I would be tempted."

She smoothed the folds of her skirt. She did not dare to look at him.

"Ma'am," he said in a low voice. "I have been waiting outside for your signal. I have just gotten into town after a long, lonesome ride. And I have that information you wanted."

She looked at him. The suggestive drawl in his voice frightened her, but it was a game, she told herself. It was just a game. She could stop playing at any time.

"I would be most grateful," she whispered back. "Is this where I use my *feminine wiles* to get what I want?"

He smiled, remembering that day in the forest when he had accused her of using them. "Yes, this is where you use them."

He reached to touch her unbound curls and said, "I've never seen a woman with such beautiful hair."

"And of course you have seen a good many of them with their hair down?" she asked, waiting for his answer.

"None like you, honey," he replied. His fingers touched the side of her face almost reverently. His thumb trailed lightly across her parted lips.

Caught in the spell of the game, she whispered in her most sultry voice, "I find you most- intriguing, Captain." She boldly laid her hand on his shirt. She felt the warmth and the hard-muscled male flesh beneath it. Felt his heartbeat.

"I find you most beautiful," he whispered back. "And most desirable."

Her hand slid up over his shoulder. She felt the strength in the muscles beneath the fabric, wanting to explore further. She felt the quick rise of his chest and was aware of a change in his eyes. A sharp thrill coursed through her as she realized that what she was doing was having an effect upon him. He reached up and restrained her wrist. She made a half-hearted attempt to pull free of his grip.

"If you are going to pay for that information," he said as he pulled her fingers to his lips and kissed them gently. "Then I reckon we can agree on a price that will be mutually satisfying."

He turned her hand over and kissed the open palm. His eyes never left her face.

Ascensia watched, mesmerized. It was as if Jesse had cast some kind of spell over her. A spell that made her feel strangely weak and helpless.

He leaned towards her and whispered, "I'm wondering . . . "

She stared into mist colored eyes that held her captive.

"What it would be like to kiss you," he finished.

"But you have kissed me."

Were they still playing the game? Or weren't they?

He leaned closer and his lips lightly traced the delicate line of her jaw with slow, feather-light kisses. Her eyes slid shut. It didn't count. Not really. He wasn't kissing her mouth.

"When I kissed you before," he said, soft-voiced. "It was because I was angry." He kissed the sensitive place beneath her ear and she slipped a little further from reality. "And I wanted to hurt you. But I'm not mad now."

"You were a savage," she replied in a ghost of a voice, remembering not only his violence, but what the kiss had awakened in her as well.

"I know," he said. "But I want to make you forget all that."

He leaned closer to her. His breath fell warmly upon her lips, mingling with her own. She knew what he was going to do and she waited an eternity for his mouth to touch hers.

He kissed her slowly. Sensuously. This kiss was not at all like the ones that he had forced upon her that night in Leesburg. He was gentle now. He was so, so very gentle. As his mouth continued to move over hers, an almost painful longing rose in her breast, a longing she could drown in if she wasn't careful.

When he drew away, her eyes were still closed. "I shouldn't have let you do that." She opened her eyes but kept them lowered to his chest. "You promised that you would leave when you were done talking."

"You want me to leave?" he asked.

"Yes."

He reached up and rested his hand caressingly on the back of her neck. "Who said I was through talking?"

She still did not look at him, so the fingers of his other hand lifted her face to his. She looked into his eyes, felt herself lost in the misty depths of them.

"Ma'am," he whispered huskily, re-stoking the illusion of the game. "I find you most distracting."

While his mouth closed over hers again, she felt his arm slide around her waist. The hand behind her neck slid down to her bare shoulder. It rested there while his thumb slowly caressed the bare flesh above her dress.

"We- " she breathed between his now-hungry kisses. "Jesse, don't . . . "

She tried to protest but her voice faded to a sigh, whispering his name again, whispering it like a plea as his mouth caressed her throat then traveled along her shoulder.

She had forgotten what it was she wanted to say. She did not resist when he pulled her against him. In fact, the feel of his body roused a new hunger within her, a hunger that drew her mindlessly along to the edge of a very steep precipice. She wanted to fall. With him.

I will allow this only a little longer, she thought with the last remaining shred of her resistance. Just a little longer.

His hand came up to hold the side of her face. And when he began to kiss her again, there was a new passion in him. A new hunger. She lifted her face to his, matching the hunger now, not fighting it. Not having the will to fight it. The world had faded away and nothing mattered any more except Jesse and the feelings he was awakening in her.

Her senses were so filled with the things that his mouth was doing to her that she was only dimly aware of it when he lowered her to the bed.

"Remember that first night," he breathed softly, stroking her lightly for he could feel her momentarily grow tense. "When I held you in the woods?"

His mouth closed over hers again, briefly. When he pulled away, she was panting softly. And his breathing matched hers.

"Well, I wanted to do all these things to you," he confessed as he slid his hand up between her breasts.

She closed her hand around his wrist. "J- Jes," she breathed so quietly that he barely heard her.

She would stop him, she promised herself. Soon. But she was too overcome at the moment by the mounting intensity of the exquisite need that Jesse was rousing in her.

He was breathing harder when he drew back. His hand slid down to her hip. He pulled her against him. Instinctively she pressed her softness against the hard male heat of him. She sighed and pressed harder, wanting a closer contact.

Even with the layers of petticoats and taffeta between them, the intimate contact brought a deep groan from his throat. The knowledge that she could make him feel the same things she was feeling drove her to a new boldness.

Each new awareness, each new sensation seemed to meld into one consuming, irresistible need. Almost desperate for a release that she did not yet understand, Ascensia moved more fully against him. She returned his embrace. She held him. She kissed him back, responding to the same passion that drove him. A passion that merged and became one.

She would never know what might have happened next. A knock on her bedroom door startled them both.

She moved quickly away from Jesse. Dazed, still breathing hard, she sat up on the edge of the bed. When she had recovered a little, she went to the door and leaned against it. She opened it a mere inch and looked out to see Hetty standing in the hallway.

"I was passing your room," Hetty said. "And I thought I heard you cry out."

Ascensia closed her eyes. "It was only a dream," she said, hoping Hetty would not notice the trembling that had suddenly seized her, or that she had not yet undressed.

"Were you already asleep? I'm sorry if I woke you."

"It's all right, Hetty."

"Goodnight, 'Scensia," she said quietly. "I'll see you in the morning."

Ascensia closed the door and locked it. She did not turn. She was too ashamed to face Jesse. She stiffened when she felt his hand upon her shoulder.

"I should be going," he said as his hand fell away.

"Yes," she whispered. She did not turn around.

It wasn't until she heard his bootsteps on the bare floor of the alcove that she turned towards the empty room. Her eyes were drawn to the bed.

Shame rose up to torment her. She had wanted him to do all those things. She had wanted more. She still wanted more. And she belonged to another man.

Chapter 15

The darkness around her was deep. Fireflies danced around her like stars. Her partner held her in strong arms, leading her in a slow waltz. She lifted both of her arms and slipped them around his neck, leaning even closer to him.

He was holding her in the most intimate way and when she lifted her face and opened her eyes, she saw the image of a face with eyes the color of the morning mist. Eyes that could see right through her. Eyes that were capable of seeing down into the depths of her soul.

"But you are a Rebel," she said, noticing with some astonishment that they were dancing in a prison cell.

"Yes, ma'am," came the low, drawling voice. "And you came to bring the key."

"You will only use it to steal horses," she protested.

He laughed deep in his throat and agreed that he would steal them, but only from across the river. Then he admitted that he wanted to steal something from her as well. She had brought a basket of white roses for him and the petals were drifting down around them. She could see them in the moonlight. His half-naked body pressed harder against her, making her realize that she was clad only in her nightgown.

"But if you come across the river," she said in a voice that was almost a sigh. "They will arrest you."

His strong arms only held her tighter as he lifted her against him. "Then we'll both be prisoners," he said. "But I can't free you yet. You know too many secrets," he whispered low and soft and hungrily against her ear as she surrendered to the warm hunger inside her, and to him.

Ascensia awoke suddenly but it was a long time before the feeling of the dream dissipated. The intensity lingered. It kept pulling her back.

She got out of bed in a distracted state of mind and stared miserably into the mirror as a flood of guilt and remorse washed over her. She touched her mouth. It felt sensitive, almost swollen from Jesse's kisses. Should Morgan ever find out-

The thing to do, she told herself, was to forget last night ever happened. But could she? Would she just be able to forget? And how was she going to face Jesse again? Jesse would be gone soon, she reminded herself. And then she would have no choice but to forget.

On the following day, Morgan came. Ascensia was sitting on the veranda swing in the early dusk. Morgan was standing with his back to the rail, discussing plans to have her visit his headquarters in the fall.

Her gaze drifted away and she stared out across the yard. She suppressed a sigh and suddenly realized that she had been tapping her foot in an impatient way. She stopped the motion.

She glanced up at Morgan. She studied his profile. Morgan was ambitious. He had a promising future ahead of him. Morgan was, as she had been told countless times, all that a woman could desire in a husband.

But the word desire conjured up the image of Jesse. She didn't feel those intense stabs of longing when Morgan looked at her, while a mere glance from Jesse was enough to-

Stop this, she told herself. Stop and listen to what Morgan is saying.

"You'll come then?" he asked.

"Yes," she replied. "If Hetty will go with me." As he sat down beside her, she asked impulsively. Do you really think I will be a good wife, Morgan?"

He smiled indulgently. "Of course you will be a good wife," he promised and his hand closed reassuringly over hers as if to make it certain. Then, with a quick look around to make sure that they were alone, he leaned forward and gave her a kiss.

"And why wouldn't you be a good wife?" Morgan laughed as if she were being very foolish. "You will learn to cook and keep house. *Our* house. And I am sure you will be very adept at those things. I have no doubt you will be a very good wife."

Cooking and cleaning. But what about passion? Ascensia wondered. She could not seem to be able to imagine Morgan kissing her until she was weak with desire the way Jesse could. She bit her lip, trying to will away the unwanted thoughts.

Morgan finally rose to leave. Ascensia stood silent while he took her hands and said his goodbye. She tried to smile but the smile was something she had to force.

When she was alone and the dusk was deepening around her, she shivered suddenly though the wind was quite warm against her. She struggled to regain the self-control that had been taught to her throughout her entire life. She was not successful, however. She felt hopelessly, helplessly torn between being sensible and her wayward desires.

Night had fallen. Out of the profound darkness, a soft mist surrounded him. It was only after Jesse had made the sudden, almost impulsive decision to ride back to Oak Haven that he realized how bad things had gotten with him.

With the memory of that night in her room still running like a fever in his blood, he knew that it was Ascensia drawing him back to Oak Haven. He could no longer deny that he was eager to be near her or that when she was absent from Oak Haven, he was plagued by a sense of regret at not seeing her there.

He had admitted to himself that the idea of seducing her because of Morgan Damon had occurred to him. But he knew he couldn't hurt her. Not for revenge or for any other motive. So he had decided that the only reasonable thing to do was to stay away from Oak Haven as much as he was able so that he might distance himself from her. Ascensia was proving to be a dangerous distraction when all his senses had to be alert to the business at hand. Too much rested on his clear thinking. Lives were at stake.

Still, he wanted her and he found himself helplessly drawn in spite of it all. And the compelling notion that she wanted him as well drew him inexorably on like a moth to a flame. So with that one irresistible thought working its way deeper into his soul, he urged his horse towards Oak Haven.

The night lay deep and silent around her. She had managed to keep herself busy for the past few days. With everything that had presented itself. Reading, needlepoint, music, anything that was a potential distraction. Still, Ascensia had not been able to find relief from the whirlwind of emotions churning helplessly inside her. She stood on the veranda and lifted her face to the intense darkness of the sky. Boundless, it seemed. Depthless. As depthless as the sea of emotion inside her, it seemed.

She had tried to be logical. She had tried reasoning it all through, but she was finding that sometimes there were things that defied logic and reason. She closed her eyes and sighed before the terrible truth that refused to be banished from her thoughts.

She had never understood women who had been reckless in following their hearts. She had always scorned women who had fallen foolishly in love with the wrong man. She had always considered it to be a weakness. But was it really weakness? Or did it take a special kind of courage to surrender to the true wishes of the heart? Could she admit the desires of her own heart even in secret to herself? Only if she had the courage. And the honesty.

Truth, she was finding, was an agony. Yet truth was bliss. And as necessary to her at the moment as breathing. She could no longer deny her heart. She wanted to see Jesse again. She needed to see him.

How long had she tried to deny the truth? Since the very beginning perhaps. All the yearning, all the longing that her heart felt for Jesse made no sense at all. She only knew that if she was near Jesse, if she looked into his eyes that were like no others she had ever looked into, reason fled. To be replaced by something else entirely.

And the thought that he would leave someday soon and that she would never see him again, seemed unbearable to her. Yearning swept through her with a renewed intensity. She ached to be with him. Right now. At this very moment.

As if in reply to her wish, the quick gallop of a horse broke the stillness. She could see very well who the rider was. Her heart had memorized every detail about Jesse. Even in the darkness.

For a long time she stood on the veranda, waiting while he dismounted at the stable. And then, though terrified at the thing she was doing, she stepped down into the yard.

Jesse was standing by the pasture fence. He watched her silently as she approached. For a long while neither of them spoke.

"You're up late," he said finally.

Her arms were crossed at her waist. Her head was bowed. "I couldn't sleep," she said, keeping her gaze averted from his. Sleeplessness seemed like a common problem for her these days.

"I couldn't sleep either." He paused. "I have been thinking about you. About what you have been thinking since we last-talked," he said, his voice fading as his gaze focused on her eyes that were now watching him.

"So have I," she replied, shifting her gaze up to the dark sky.

She was intensely aware of every detail of the night around her. It was as if everything was being indelibly imprinted upon her memory. She heard the low chirping of crickets in the grass. The mist was soft and translucent around them. It was very beautiful, like a shimmering veil that transformed everything. It blurred the white fences and the edges of the house. Even the moon, glowing like a great pearl above them, seemed to be melting into the velvety depths of the sky.

Ascensia heard Jesse release his breath in a sigh as he took a step closer to her. His very nearness had always been a potent thing. It had power over her now.

She closed her eyes while the last shred of sanity started to slip from her like a discarded gown. This was not the man she was *supposed* to love. It wasn't the man she *wanted* to love. But she could not deny her feelings for Jesse any more than she could have changed the course of the moon across the sky. Something filled her so deeply that denying it was more of an agony than facing it.

He reached out and his hand closed around hers. It was a very deliberate action. An intimate one. The familiar male scent of him surrounded her immediately. It drew her further into the sphere of his being.

Tomorrow there might be regrets. Tomorrow there would assuredly be a price to pay. She knew that. She could not help but know it. But right now she needed something that went far beyond what a hundred or a thousand tomorrows could bring. Fate had brought them together, she believed. Fate had been leading her to Jesse since that very first day in Washington when his letter had been placed in her hand. Was it foolish for her to believe that? If so, then she was more than willing to be a fool.

Jesse could feel her fingers tremble beneath his hand. His other hand came up to gently cradle the side of her face. It was a reassuring gesture. And somehow for both of them it was a gesture of surrender. Of finality.

With her eyes still closed, Ascensia leaned into the touch. Jesse knew what this cost her. But there was no way to deny that what drove her also drove him. It was there in the kiss he leaned over to give her. It was in the way she returned the kiss.

As he pulled her into his embrace, Ascensia felt Jesse rest his chin against her temple. She glanced at the house over his shoulder. It was late. No lights burned there.

Without a word, Jesse let her go. Silent still, he untied the blanket from his saddle then took her hand. He led her down the path behind the stable. Stopping at a distance from the house, he spread the blanket on the ground.

Turning back to her, he ran his hand down the silken tresses of her hair. He didn't know how he had gotten so lost in this woman. "You don't know what you do to me," he said softly, almost as softly as the wind breathing over them.

But she did know. He was doing the same thing to her. When he guided her down to the blanket, she did not resist. In the moonlight, she saw that he was frowning. He shook his head slightly. It was as if he, too, was struggling with this thing that had caught them both off guard.

"When you want to go back to the house," he said. "Tell me and I'll take you back."

As she nodded slowly, her eyes never left his face. He leaned forward and kissed her again. When he drew back, he said to her, "We have right now, 'Scensia. I can't promise you anything more than that."

"I know," she answered back. "But I- " She searched for words to describe all that was in her heart. Would he understand that this moment was enough for her if that was all she could have. That having nothing was unbearable to her, because she had already come so far.

That was not to say that she wasn't afraid. She was terrified. But right now, the yearning in was stronger than the fear. Nothing in her life so far could compare with what she was feeling at this moment. She had never felt more alive, more herself.

When he kissed her again, she responded with a desperate hunger, one that seemed to be quickly finding its own expression. One that seemed to be intent on satisfying its own need, without reason or logic being any part of it.

As for Jesse, he had imagined her like this. He had been right about her. Ascensia had hidden depths. There was an underlying passion, a sensuality in her that could reach deep inside a man and possess his soul. He knew very well what was happening to him. But there was no turning back for him either. He, too, had come too far.

He strived for patience. But patience got lost somewhere between the demand of her kisses and the feel of her body pressed against his. His hand slid down her throat to the top button of her dress. He began to undo the buttons. When the dress was finally out of the way, he lowered her to the blanket then lay down beside her.

By now she was as impatient as he was. She worked at the buttons of his shirt and when he had removed it, she moved eagerly against him, running greedy kisses along his jaw, his shoulders, his chest.

There was a ragged edge to his breathing as he said, "I couldn't stop thinking about you when I was gone."

"And I kept waiting for you to come back," she whispered back.

Her mouth pressed kisses against the hard contours of his chest, then moved lower to his belly that was lean and taut with muscle. He was hard and powerful all over and it seemed she could not get enough of the feel or the taste of him. She would never be able to get enough.

He opened her camisole and she found the damp night air against her sensitive, suddenly-freed breasts to be a highly erotic sensation. But it was nothing compared to the hard pressure of Jesse's unclad chest against hers or the exquisite sensations that he evoked when his thumbs flicked lightly across her nipples. He followed that with the sensuous touch of his tongue exploring her body as she had explored his. By the time he had worked the last of their clothing loose, they were both panting with need.

"Is this what you were waiting for?" he whispered above her.

She arched her throat back. "Yes," she sighed. "Is this what you came back for?"

"It might have been on my mind," he confessed, his voice trailing off as she pushed up against him. At his response, she drew in her own shivery breath and became his willing prisoner as his mouth captured hers once again.

She realized she had power over him, too. She could make him as needy as she was. She could hear it in the change in his breathing. She could feel it in the force of his arousal as he sought her most secret, most sensitive place.

She wanted to know his body fully, wanted to give him the same pleasure he was giving her. She wanted to yield everything. There was no hiding, no pretense, no falseness between them. Only love and need, so deeply felt that she thought she might drown in it.

"Jesse, I- " she panted between kisses, unable to express all she was feeling. "Make me forget there is anything or anyone else in the world."

"There isn't, honey. There's just you. And me."

He masterfully stoked her fire till it burned hotter. Till it threatened to consume her.

"There's only this," he whispered against her lips, drawing her with him.

"And this."

He kissed her so deeply that it felt like he was ravaging her very soul. And when she was ready, when she was aching with need, when she was greedy with need, he filled her with his passion.

The world shifted. It changed. There would be no going back. Ever.

Matching the slow, deep thrusting of Jesse's body, Ascensia rose to meet him with instincts that were timeless. She moved against him with an abandon she had never known. And when at last the final release came, it shook them both with its intensity. It blighted them with a consuming fire that worked its way deeply into both of their souls.

And for a time everything else in the world did seem to fade away. It was as if they had waited for this moment forever. Ascensia found herself in the sharing. She lost herself there as well.

As she drifted slowly back from the stars, Jesse continued to hold her and to kiss her. But his kisses were gentle now, lingering, loving. He smoothed the dark, damp curls back from her face and kept her close to him. This was her first lovemaking and every moment, every detail would be held in her memory, he knew. And he wanted her to remember it. Always.

She sighed beside him and stretched like a contented cat. He eased over onto his back and breathed his own deep sigh as he contemplated the heavens. "I don't want to take you back," she heard him say.

With her eyes closed, she smiled wistfully and ran her hand lightly down his sweat-dampened chest. "You haven't heard then. The war is over. No one wants to fight any more."

He smiled lazily beside her. "You must be wishing on falling stars."

"I did actually," she confessed. "I wished on one over your shoulder when we were- "

He lifted one dark brow as he turned to look at her. "And here I thought I had your undivided attention."

She smiled against his strong shoulder. "It must have been the moment I found myself out among those stars."

He turned onto his side and gathered her close. Sleep would have suited Ascensia. A very long sleep in Jesse's arms for a sated sensation, as if sweet honey flowed through her veins, had overtaken her.

She did not sleep, however, for after a while Jesse began to kiss her again. And the hunger that she had thought had been appeased began to rise in her again, as it was obviously rising in him.

They made love again that night. But the night had to end. As Jesse helped her dress, she could not help but notice that he was quieter than she had ever seen him. In fact, he had never seemed more sober. And she, too, was fighting something that felt very much like sadness welling up inside her.

She watched Jesse fasten the last buttons of his shirt, trying not to yield to a deep sense of loss, for she could not shake the feeling that she was losing him. When he was fully dressed, he put his hands around her waist and pulled her close to him, letting his arms enclose her in a last lingering embrace.

She stood on her toes and kissed him long and softly, reluctant to let him go. He sighed and said, with gentle chiding. "'Scensia, daylight's coming on."

It was her turn to sigh. She didn't want to let him go.

Jesse didn't want to go, either. Yet someone had to keep thinking clearly. The night was nearly gone. But Lord, she could make him want, he thought as he heard the first bird sing out in the woods.

He gathered up the blanket. By the time they reached the pasture fence, more birds were voicing their presence in the trees around them. They would have to hurry. Morning wouldn't wait. And the war sure as hell hadn't been called off because everyone had decided to stop fighting. No matter how much they both wanted that to be true.

There was, in the misty gloom around them, a faint scent of wild roses, and just before she made her way to the house alone, Jesse heard Ascensia quietly say something about hope where wild roses bloomed. Her voice stayed with him, but he was aware that it had held more sadness than it had held hope.

Chapter 16

Ascensia wandered the garden paths of Oak Haven alone. The house was full of guests and lights were streaming out into the night everywhere but she felt more comfortable with the darkness surrounding her. The tedious conversation and the endless gossip wearied her tonight. Smiling politely through it all and pretending interest had become a strain for her.

Nearly a week had passed since that night with Jesse. And she had not seen him in all that time. There were things she wanted to say to him. There were things she needed to hear from him. She pulled her skirts away from the shrubs that grew thickly along the path. She walked further from the house, deeper into the shadows of the trees and on towards the stable.

She stopped abruptly when she heard a low voice from the darkness ahead. It was Hetty. She was speaking to someone else and because she did not want to eavesdrop, Ascensia turned and intended going back to the house. But she stopped. The voice that replied to Hetty was Jesse's.

"I don't want you involved in this any deeper than you already are," she heard him say. "Now that Quarles is here asking questions, we will have to be very careful."

"You know how important this latest shipment is," Hetty said. "You know what it means."

"Yes," Jesse replied. "But I don't want to risk your neck to get it. That last venture of yours was entirely too dangerous."

"I intend to be careful," Hetty replied with confidence. "I haven't been caught yet."

"You were almost caught the last time," he said. "Sometimes, Hetty, you are too reckless."

"Reckless?" Hetty laughed. "*You* warn *me* about being reckless when you are the boldest man I have ever met. Yes, bold. And even reckless at times.

"And lately," she went on. "There is something about you that worries me. You have changed, Jesse. And I am afraid . . . "

Ascensia heard him let out an impatient sigh.

After a long silence, Hetty asked quietly, "Is it because of *her*?"

The emphasis on the word made Ascensia listen more intently. She waited for his reply.

But none came and Hetty said, "I see you have no answer for me. You know that this will only make more trouble. I sense something between you and her, Jesse. I have sensed it all along. And you know how I feel- "

"Let it go, Hetty," Jesse interrupted, low voiced.

"No, Jesse. I will not. I will speak plainly. I can't help but wonder why you are interested in Ascensia. You at least owe *me* the truth. Is it because of Morgan Damon? Is it vengeance, Jesse? You want revenge and so you will use her to get it?"

Breathlessly, Ascensia awaited his reply.

"Yes," he admitted harshly. "I'd like to reckon with Morgan Damon." Ascensia was shocked at the bitterness in his voice.

Hetty said, "You chill my blood when you look like that. Your hatred is still as strong, isn't it? You still can't forget."

"Would you expect me to forget?"

Ascensia closed her eyes. The chill in her heart grew till it was colder than the night air around her. Blindly she turned and made her way back to the house. She could not bear to hear more.

She closed her bedroom door and stood with her back to it. "What have I done?" she whispered to the darkness. Agony washed over her. "What have I done?"

Jesse had never cared for her. He had been motivated by revenge. And she had made it so easy for him. She had given herself willingly, eagerly. To a spy. To a traitor. A man who knew very well how to deceive and to lie to get what he wanted. And the thing that he had wanted? Revenge. Nothing more than that.

She wondered, too, how Hetty had come to be involved with him. The worst possible thought came to her. Were they lovers? She stood in the darkness, white-faced and trembling. She felt stricken inside. He had used her. When she thought of how she had gone to him, she felt sickened. And when she recalled her boldness, her breathless passion, she moaned aloud. All along he had been cold and calculating and false.

Damn him, she cried silently. Damn him. She buried her face in her hands as the tears fell hotly.

"Hetty," Jesse replied quietly. "She's come to mean more to me than that."

Surprise showed on Hetty's shadowed face. "How does *she* feel, Jesse?" she asked. "Do you know?"

"I- " he began then frowned. He would not speak a word of what they had shared that night. Not even to Hetty. "There *is* something between us," he confessed, then sighed. "Hell, Hetty. I didn't want it. Lord knows, she didn't want it. But it's there and I can't deny it."

"And was this *something* there even when you dragged her shamelessly down to Virginia?" Hetty asked, a softness in her voice belying the accusation.

"Yes, Hetty. Even then."

Something changed in Hetty's eyes as she watched Jesse's face. Then her brows lifted as if at some secret realization as an ironic smile touched one corner of her mouth.

It was a dismal day. A drizzling rain had fallen since before dawn with a sullen, hopeless sound upon the sodden ground. A mournful wind kept it company.

Ascensia awaited Jesse's return. She did not wait with eager anticipation, however. She did not wait with loving expectation. She looked at the sky through the parlor window. Wispy gray clouds moved swiftly beneath the darker cloud mass. Thunder rumbled softly.

She had managed to have a note delivered to Jesse asking him to meet her in the spring house. She pulled her shawl over her head and went out into the rain. As she entered the little stone building, her hands felt as cold as the chill wrapped around her heart.

She thought over what she would say to him. Again. When she remembered the conversation she had overheard, when she remembered how he had betrayed her, she felt the knot of pain coil a little tighter inside her breast.

The words that he had spoken had destroyed everything. Nothing could make it any different. But if her fragile courage did not desert her, she would at least have her pride. Maybe he won't come, she thought. Maybe ...

She heard someone coming up the path and her heart immediately began to pound harder. She heard him speak her name. She turned around and saw his tall, dark form filling the doorway. As his eyes held hers, for a moment weakness threatened her.

"You sent for me?"

"Yes," she replied and was surprised to find that her voice was steady. She took a deep breath. "I have made a decision," she began. There was nothing left but to get it over with. "I don't want to see you again. And I don't intend to have- what happened ever happen again."

"What's wrong, 'Scensia?"

Wrong? Everything was wrong, her heart whispered.

Trembling, on the verge of breaking down, she nevertheless lifted her eyes and saw that he was frowning. As those mist-colored eyes continued to watch her, she lowered her own eyes to his chest. He seemed to have some terrible power over her. In spite of her resolve. In spite of all she knew. Her gaze dropped to his boots.

"Ascensia- " he began.

"What we did was wrong," she said abruptly. "It was all wrong."

"That's not how you felt before. You wanted- "

She looked up at him, a flash of wounded pride blazing in her eyes. And perhaps defiance was evident in her voice as well when she interrupted him. "I know what I *thought* I wanted. Before."

He remained silent and she became aware suddenly of the sound of rain beating down harder on the roof. A low, lingering peal of thunder accompanied it.

"Don't you understand? I don't want to see you again."

"So you can live happily ever after with your Major?" he asked after a silence.

She vaguely registered the emotion behind the huskiness in his voice. But she was struggling with her own raw emotion.

"Yes," she whispered quickly as she gazed past the window. She looked back at him and, remembering the pain he had caused her, said coldly, before she looked away, "But that isn't any of your concern."

She might have had her own revenge had she looked at him then. She might have seen how deeply her words had carved into him.

But she was staring beyond the window as she asked, "And when do you intend leaving here? I don't feel comfortable with you coming around and reminding me of- of all the things that I intend to forget- "

She didn't finish. He cut off her words to say that he had finished here and was leaving anyway. She felt the knot of pain twist a little tighter in her breast.

"So we're both free," he said. "And you can do all the forgetting you want, sweetheart."

Her gaze remained at the window. "Don't call me that again," she whispered. "Ever."

His face registered nothing as he stood looking down at her. For long moments he remained silent. Then he turned and walked away. It was an abrupt departure. The only goodbye was the sound of his boots crossing the stone floor.

The door banged shut. Soon after, Ascensia heard the sound of horse's hoofs. When that sound had finally faded into the sound of the rain, she was still staring past the window.

He was gone then. He was gone and out of her life forever. It was what she wanted. But as she listened to the lonely sound of the rain, she looked suddenly forlorn. Desolation seemed to grip her.

Forever. Oh, Jesse. She knew that he had taken something with him when he had gone. She looked around at the empty room, then bowed her head in silent misery, feeling as if she might fall apart if she dared to move.

Thunder cracked loudly overhead. The sound seemed to free all the emotion trapped inside of her. Her lower lip began to quiver as tears started to slip silently down her cheeks. She was filled with a sadness so profound it seemed like the depths of the sky could never hold it.

PART II

Chapter 17

The bloodshed at Gettysburg was enough to stagger the senses. The entire nation, though divided, shared something in common. It shared the same suffering and death, the same grieving, the same loss and mourning.

When the gunfire died away and the smoke settled over the rolling hills and valleys surrounding the little Pennsylvania town, the evidence of the fury and the violence of the three-day battle was appalling. More than 50,000 men were dead, wounded or missing.

Even after such losses, the Southern Army still had not been destroyed, not even after the Union forces had scattered them like chaff before the wind in a last, desperate charge on the third and final day of the battle.

After all the bleeding and the suffering, the weary Southern survivors gathered their wounded and their dying as best they could and began a slow, agonizing retreat towards the swollen Potomac River and Virginia.

Had the Union's latest commander pursued the exhausted, battered Rebel Army, he could have destroyed it. But he did not and the war would last for two more years. Two more years of growing malice and bitterness on both sides.

Two weeks after Gettysburg, Jesse was sitting silently in the parlor of a deserted farmhouse. There was a hard look about the group of Rebel scouts that were with him. The uniforms they wore were faded and tattered. The men were spattered with mud. And they were exhausted.

They had scarcely slept during the past two days and nights. Most of that time they had spent out in the rain in the woods. In addition, they had had some unpleasant little skirmishes with Yankee cavalry, losing one killed and two wounded. There were a dozen of them left. They had lost some good men at Gettysburg.

Gettysburg. The word left Jesse with a cold feeling inside. It seemed to have left them all feeling a little stunned.

Things were getting desperate for the South. Vicksburg had just fallen. Starved out. Most of the Mississippi River was now in Union hands, effectively dividing the Confederacy in half.

Throughout the South it was becoming more and more difficult to procure even the barest essentials of life for both civilians and soldiers alike. The Northern blockade was slowly and surely strangling the life out of the Confederacy.

They were running out of food and ammunition. There would not be enough shoes and clothing to keep the men warm during the long winter months to come. With poor food and poor clothing, almost as many men seemed to die of sickness as they did from Yankee lead.

Horses were becoming scarce as well. He had seen their carcasses piled high and burned in huge bonfires after battles he didn't care to count. It was such a damned waste.

The South had always believed that it was fighting for its rights. And though outnumbered, Southerners generally felt that they would prevail. It was possible, Jesse thought grimly, if determination and bravery were enough. But the reality was that they were not enough. The North was just as determined.

The firelight flickered over his sober face. Determination and Southern pride had sustained them so far. But they weren't going to stop hunger and sickness and Union lead. Those things were killing good men. And what good were rights to dead men or to their mourning widows and starving children?

He drank the last of the coffee in his tin cup and then lay back on his blanket. He stared up at the ceiling above him, his dark brows drawn into a frown. He felt worn out, almost sick with weariness. His gaze ran along the deeply-shadowed rafters.

Struggling against the exhaustion had become a habit. It had become a way of life. He wondered if he would ever be able to relax again, or let go of the eternal need for vigilance.

The rain began to beat down a little harder on the roof. And hearing it, a deep sense of loneliness took hold of him. Damn, he thought, forcing it back down inside. I won't let this get a hold of me. I can't. He was just overtired. That was all. He wouldn't let himself fall prey to thoughts of regret. And her.

For a long time he lay there, fighting the thing that he was determined to keep buried. He lifted his hand and pushed back his dark hair. It was his last gesture before sleep finally claimed him.

He awoke the next morning and looked out on a world shrouded with mist. Daylight had seeped over the land with a somber tint. The air was still. Still as death, Jesse thought as he leaned against the open doorway. The sudden thought made him frown as his gaze wandered idly across the wooded stretch of countryside. He rubbed the back of his hand slowly across his unshaven chin.

Wirt grunted behind him as he tugged at his boots. "Ah haven't seen a bit of sunshine for a week now."

"No," Jesse commented, his eyes narrowing slightly as he thought, *and not a bird song to be heard either.*

He straightened slowly from his relaxed stance while his gaze swept the deep shadows of the heavily wooded section to the right. Suddenly his muscles tensed. All his senses had become alert. He saw it again.

Wirt went still behind him and, before he asked the question, Jesse answered, "Somebody's signaling out there."

Wirt quickly awakened the other men. A few moments later, they saw a rider emerge from a dense thicket and ride straight towards the farmhouse.

"That's Noble Young," Wirt said beside the door. "An' it looks like he's been shot."

The young scout pulled his horse to a sliding halt in front of the house and slid to the ground.

"Yankees," he called breathlessly. "They are setting an ambush. Ah was at Ransford's house and Ah saw them pass on the road. Soon's they passed, Ah took a short cut heah. But you are already surrounded."

He spat and then said with venom, "An' Ah saw John Lathrop riding with them. Only he saw me first an' put a bullet in mah a'm."

Wirt swore viciously as he began to bind up Noble's wound. There was an angry murmur from the other men. They had been listening and they now began to peer carefully through the curtains on the windows.

The men already knew what they had to do. Jesse gave the order. They leaped into their saddles and formed a battle line, grimly awaiting further orders.

"Ah suppose they think we will surrender," one of the men muttered.

"Ah suppose they are wrong," Wirt said.

To a man they silently agreed to fight.

"Might as well die quick here than die slow in a Yankee prison," one of the men remarked. "They won't give us any quarter."

"Wouldn't want to miss the opportunity of sayin' a hello to Lathrop," another said darkly.

There was a harder look to them all as they shared a glance at that sentiment. They tightened their grips on their reins. The horses pranced a bit and pricked their ears up, familiar with what was coming.

"When I give the order to charge," Jesse told them. "I want you to ride right through them and break for the woods."

There was a silence. Then Wirt's booming voice called out, "Draw sabers."

The thin whistle of steel cut through the morning stillness.

"Boys," the Lieutenant ordered in a voice like growling thunder as he rose up in his stirrups and pointed with his saber. "Forward." With a Rebel yell, the line charged forward.

When they were halfway across the open field, a sheet of crimson fire blazed out of the trees. There was an immediate, deadly reply.

As his horse leaped for the woods ahead of him, Jesse became aware of the sun breaking into a patch of blue sky. Shafts of sunlight were suddenly falling through the trees and glistening on the wet grass and foliage. It warmed him.

He reached the woods and immediately found himself surrounded by enemy soldiers. The clash of sabers rang out.

Two of his men, he saw, reached the safety of the woods. One scout fell from his horse. He got to his feet and Jesse saw that a ball had passed through both cheeks. The blood was streaming from his mouth. Jesse lifted his pistol and shot the Yankee who was about to put a saber through the man.

Another scout rode back out of the woods and, reaching out his arm, managed to help the wounded man up into the saddle behind him. Both of them safely reached the cover of the woods.

Jesse looked around and saw a young scout named Waite fall back off his horse. The riderless horse pranced sideways, snorting with a wild-eyed look before it bolted into the trees.

The scout staggered to his feet. One arm was hanging limply by his side. He looked up at Jesse and tried to make his way over to him. The boy stopped, however. Blood suddenly spurted from his chest and appeared on his lips. He pitched headlong into the weeds and lay motionless. There was a dark stain between his shoulder blades.

Jesse turned in his saddle and with a cold, bitter rage, aimed his pistol at the man who had just shot the boy in the back. John Lathrop. The hammer came down with a dull click.

Immediately, Jesse cocked his pistol again. But by now he had been surrounded by half a dozen men in blue who had their weapons trained upon him. For a moment, a reckless look flashed into his eyes. Then, with the muscles jumping in his jaw, he lowered his arm.

They forced him to get off his horse. His arms were roughly seized and jerked behind him then tightly bound.

"Don't kill him," he heard Lathrop say. "The Major will want that sonofabitch alive."

Jesse looked at the dead scout who was lying on the ground not far away. He lifted his gaze to Lathrop who still sat his horse. The color slowly receded from Lathrop's face when he saw the look in Jesse's eyes. It seemed to hold a promise for him. A deadly promise.

Chapter 18

The door closed behind Jesse with a hollow echo, shutting him off suddenly from the outside world. The gloomy, foul-smelling place that was to be his prison resembled some ancient dungeon.

It was deep and narrow with high stone walls. His gaze ran along the ceiling, which was so high that it was lost in shadows. Along the upper reaches of the far wall were several small, barred windows through which daylight streamed. The light, however, seemed to lose its cleanness as it filtered down through the murky gloom.

In the center of the room, the light from a single, smoky lantern only accentuated the deep shadows. The floor of the prison was rough and uneven. Pools of water had gathered in the low places.

The air was damp and cold. The walls gleamed with moisture that seeped through cracks that were like great scars in the stones. The place was crowded with Confederate prisoners.

Jesse's mind recoiled at the thought of being shut in here. He could sense a hesitancy in the men behind him as well as they stepped forward.

The fetid, musty smell of the prison was pervasive. It seemed tainted with the odors of dampness and rot, of sickness and unwashed men. Jesse could feel the stench surrounding him, filling his throat and his lungs.

The other prisoners sat huddled at the edges of the dull glare of the lantern and beyond. They gazed up with wary, apathetic expressions as he walked by. Their filthy, unshaven faces seemed to reflect only hopelessness.

The small group of captured scouts found an unoccupied corner and sat talking quietly among themselves.

"Shooting would be too easy on the bastard," one of them muttered, voicing the sentiment that was uppermost in their hearts.

"Ah sure would like to see him strung up for the dirty, sneaking traitor that he is," another remarked passionately.

"He's probably counting his blood money right now," another spoke up. "Well, Ah want to watch his face when he sees the reward *we* give him."

"We owe it to the ones who aren't here with us now," said one of the men whose brother had been killed in the ambush. "The sonofabitch won't have even a squeak left in him after Ah get through with him," he vowed as he leaned back against the wall.

The next morning, Jesse woke stiff and sore upon his uncomfortable prison bed. He rose and walked over to the water bucket, dipped his tin cup down inside and raised the murky liquid to his mouth.

The water had a disagreeable taste that reminded him of the stench that filled the air. He managed to swallow a mouthful and found that it didn't settle easily in his stomach.

There was not much to occupy the long hours that followed so he sat talking with the other men. Towards the middle of the day, they received their first meal.

It consisted of hard bread, accompanied by a weak, nasty-looking substance that the guards called soup. Jesse ate it though it didn't come anywhere near satisfying his hunger. With such sparse, unhealthy food, he realized that in very little time he would be as worn and starved-looking as the other men.

That night, as he lay on his bed, he stared up at the darkness for hours, intent on devising some plan of escape. There seemed to be no easy means to accomplish it, however, and gradually he drifted off to sleep only to have someone's hand rudely shake him out of the fitful slumber he had fallen into.

"Someone wants to see you, Reb," the guard said.

He was taken to a small office. Sprawled in a chair with his coat unbuttoned and his muddy boots thrust out comfortably before him was John Lathrop.

He was regarding Jesse with a gloating expression. "Don't think that I haven't been looking forward to seeing you again," he said with a sneer. A small scar beside his mouth grew more noticeable.

Jesse's eyes narrowed as he contemplated the scar. He remembered the beating he had given the man one September night long ago. Lathrop caught the look and his hand involuntarily lifted to his mouth.

A cold smile touched Jesse's lips and he drawled softly, "Still as arrogant and self-serving as I remember you."

The coolness of the man, the quiet confidence he maintained even now enraged Lathrop for it was evidence of depths of character that were lacking in his own makeup. Beneath the hatred was envy.

"But you don't look so good, *sir.*" Lathrop emphasized the word. "And I believe you brought some of that prison stink in with you."

"Maybe," Jesse said slowly. "But I don't reckon I'm as rank, say, as a traitor."

"Go to hell," Lathrop spat out and Jesse knew he had hit a nerve. Lathrop then attempted to affect a careless unconcern as he laughed quietly and said, "You sure weren't smart getting yourself caught that way."

"I'm smart enough," Jesse drawled meaningly. "To know that a traitor's life isn't worth more than a rush light."

Bootsteps sounded sharply outside in the hallway. Both men looked at the officer who stood in the doorway.

Major Morgan Damon entered the room. He was followed by two rough-looking Union soldiers. Jesse watched him with eyes that were as hard as saber steel. Deep inside him burned a bitter hatred. A hatred that had been intensified by the man's relationship to Ascensia and now by Damon's role as captor.

He is enjoying this, Jesse thought. He has been looking forward to it.

The Major entered the room and stood silent behind the desk. He read through some papers in his hand then threw them down on the desk before him. "You have had a taste of our prison, Captain," he began in a smooth voice. "Not a pleasant experience, I'll wager." His eyes froze for a moment as they met Jesse's.

"You don't have to go back, however," he went on. "You can tell me who was involved with you in the smuggling operation near Oak Haven."

"You can go to hell," Jesse replied quietly.

For a fleeting moment, rage flashed across the Major's face. He controlled it, however, and said, "I thought you Rebels knew enough to be able to discern what was advantageous- "

"Not all of us," Jesse interrupted. "Are completely without honor or decency." His eyes flickered briefly to Lathrop then settled back on the Major. "Thought you would have learned about honor and decency while fighting us a couple of years back."

The Major's head lifted sharply. His eyes had a narrowed look as he said, "I can tell you this, Captain. That if you do not tell me what I want to know, *you* will learn very shortly what a disagreeable future awaits you."

Jesse smiled but there was no mirth in it. Cold hatred flamed into his eyes as he said cuttingly, "Won't be so easy as before. You're not making war on a woman now."

The Major went rigid. He had been about to light a cigar but the hand holding the Lucifer before his face suddenly stilled. There was a silence in which neither man's glance wavered.

"That's enough," said the Major. "Say one more word and I will have them buck and gag you."

He lit the cigar then looked at the bayonet that one of the guards had thrust against Jesse's throat. Into his eyes came a merciless, sardonic gleam. "Perhaps," he began thoughtfully. "The persuasion of steel would convince you that insolence will get you nowhere."

He puffed on his cigar several times. Smoke unfurled before his face as he narrowed his gaze, he said, "Or maybe my men could give you a more lasting lesson. I will give you one more chance to tell me what I want to know."

Jesse held the man's gaze and remained silent. The Major nodded to one of the guards and immediately Jesse felt himself seized roughly from behind. The other guard stepped in front of him. Without a word, the man hit Jesse hard in the belly. He continued to hit him for several minutes, delivering vicious, brutal blows to his face and body.

The guard paused for a moment to rub his fist, then demanded, "You ready to talk yet?"

Jesse shook his head slowly. "Be damned," he whispered and, seeing the hand draw back again, he turned his head aside to lessen the blow. As the powerful fist connected with his jaw, Jesse's breath left him in a groaning sigh. His mouth felt numb now, but he tasted a warm rush of blood. The bastard sure could hit, he thought.

As the beating continued, the Major watched for signs of fear. He had seen it in other men's faces and he had enjoyed it. He was frowning, however, for the Rebel had not yet cried out to make them stop.

"I can put an end to this," he said as Jesse took another blow to the belly. "Beg me. Beg me to make them stop and they will."

Jesse shook his head and the man in front of him stepped back quickly from the spray of blood.

"Beg me," the Major repeated, watching intently. "Beg me, you bastard, or I will have them kill you."

Jesse glared with savage hatred. "Like she did?" he whispered and there was a terrible passion behind the words. He didn't even see the fist coming but it exploded in his face and the room whirled around him. He sagged . . . coughed blood . . .

"You will beg," the Major's voice came from a distance.

Jesse grinned and then felt a vicious back-handed blow to the side of his face. There was a low, rushing sound like wind inside his head. He had dropped down to his knees and he knelt there, swaying.

"Get him up."

Someone grabbed a hold of his hair and yanked his head up roughly. He was hauled to his feet and shoved back against the edge of the desk.

He braced himself for the next blow and then some part of his mind remembered that no one was holding him. He raised his right arm and caught the blow with his forearm. And then with a fierce feeling of satisfaction he drew his left arm back and drove his fist forward. He heard it connect solidly with the guard's jaw.

Jesse's bloody mouth drew back into a grin as the man's head jerked sharply and he staggered back. The guard stood rubbing his bleeding mouth with his hand.

Yeah, Jesse thought. Worth it. Worth every damned bit of it. He tried to clear his head in the silence that followed. But with a snarl of rage, the man was upon him again.

"You're going to pay for that," the guard gritted between his teeth. "You hear me?"

The beating went on, savagely, relentlessly, and with a renewed fury. Jesse suddenly felt a fierce agony deep inside. The breath was forced from his lungs. He could not catch his breath. He was badly hurt, he knew. He was fading into darkness and could not will himself to rise up out of it.

But as he lay there on the floor, helpless and at their mercy, a tiny flicker of consciousness still remained. He could feel, again and again, someone's boot kicking him brutally in the ribs.

The Major's voice seemed far away when he said, "That's enough for now. We don't want him dead. Not yet."

Only then did the merciful blackness finally wash over him.

Chapter 19

The summer waned. It was well into September and many times in the early dawn Ascensia would waken to the songs of the birds in the branches outside her window. She would lay very still, caught in the spell of some dream and the helpless longing that lingered from it. She would stare past the lace curtains in the alcove and know a yearning in her heart for a time when she would listen to the birds and not remember...

"This will pass," she would whisper to herself. "This will pass."

Things had changed between her and Hetty. They had changed because of Jesse. Hetty, of course, did not understand Ascensia's cold, distant manner. But she was aware of it.

"Ascensia," Hetty began while they sat together in the back parlor one afternoon. "I hope I didn't wake you by practicing the piano so early this morning."

"No," Ascensia replied quietly. But Hetty had awakened her and Ascensia had listened to the same song that Hetty had played for Jesse one night long ago.

"I have not heard you play lately, 'Scensia," Hetty said as she looked up.

Ascensia gave a little shrug. "I haven't been in the mood."

Hetty had been sewing and the clicking of her scissors suddenly stopped. "'Scensia?" she began. "I have been worried about you. You look so pale and worn out. Even Leora Strode mentioned it after church last Sunday."

Ascensia frowned. What business was it of Leora's anyway, she thought with vexation.

"And yesterday," Hetty went on. "I saw you leaning against the fence by the pasture. And you looked so sad that I- " Hetty paused and looked intently at her cousin. "'Scensia, I know you and I know that you are ill or you are worrying yourself sick over something. I can't bear to see you like this. But I cannot help you if you will not confide in me. If you would just tell me what it is that is troubling you- "

"Hetty, I am fine. Really. Don't trouble yourself over it, Hetty, because, really, there is nothing wrong."

The days passed and a whisper of winter breathed over the land. The nights grew cold enough to keep a fire in the hearth. One night was particularly wintry but a cheerful fire was burning and casting its flickering light upon Ascensia's face as she sat before it. Her eyes were fixed upon the flames as Quillie sat talking beside her.

Leora Strode had come for a visit as well. Entertaining Leora all day had been rather a strain. Ascensia had no inclination towards idle chatter lately. However, she forced herself to pay attention to what Leora was saying.

"Some of the Rebels escaped unfortunately. But two were killed on the spot. Six were wounded or taken prisoner. And," she paused for effect. "Among them was a certain Rebel captain named Jesse Lucane."

Hetty had gone still.

"Who," Leora went on. "Was really our very own Captain Wolfe. Who was actually a notorious scout and spy. A very dangerous man. Imagine."

"Was the Captain wounded?" Hetty asked quietly.

Leora shrugged her silk-clad shoulders. "I don't know. I only heard this from Levi Hedlin who saw the men as they were being sent in by rail some weeks ago."

"Do you know where they were sending them?" Hetty asked.

"To be hanged, I suppose," Leora replied.

"Oh," Quillie exclaimed. "That is a terrible thought, even if he is a Rebel."

"Well if he does hang?" Leora said petulantly. "To think how he fooled all of us. If these traitors are going to carry on like that, they will find out that they must expect punishment accordingly."

Hetty asked no more questions and let the subject drop. Ascensia did the same. But it was all she could think about for the rest of the evening.

Later, Hetty joined Ascensia on the veranda in the cold, windy darkness. In spite of her resolve to remain silent, Ascensia asked, "Hetty, do you know where they will take him?"

Hetty shook her head. Without looking at Ascensia, she replied, "Maybe to the Old Capital Prison. But they will probably not keep him there long."

After another silence, Ascensia asked, "Are the prison camps as bad as they say?"

Hetty looked at her through the darkness. "They are worse than you could imagine."

Hetty went back inside to her guests. Ascensia, warming her hands in her skirt pockets, felt something inside one of them. She slowly drew it out.

It was a white rose. The rose that Jesse had left behind that night. It was faded and withered now. But a hint of sweet fragrance lingered in the fragile petals as she lifted it to her face.

Chapter 20

The weeks wore on and lengthened into months. Each day was exactly the same as the one before it. Time became a vague, elusive thing. Day and night ceased to have any meaning save for the feeble light that filtered weakly through the barred windows of the prison.

It used to trouble him. He used to be bothered by the uncertainty of whether it was the gray of dusk or dawn that lighted the small patch of outside world. Only the sound of the rain, as it fell now, was a certainty from beyond the distant windows.

Jesse's beard had grown quite full. The bruises on his face were almost healed, except for a small cut on his chin that was slow in healing because it had been so deep.

He lifted his hands and rubbed one of them across his jaw. His hands trembled. Both of them were shackled together. At first he had spent countless hours trying to free them. But he had been forced to give that up because his wrists had become raw and bloody. Such things did not heal well in this place.

He now sat as listlessly as the other men. Each day of imprisonment claimed a little more of his strength. He could see its effect upon the others. Their wasted forms and haggard countenances, he knew, only reflected his own appearance.

They were waiting for their meal. Like caged animals, they spent their time waiting for food even though it was food that Wirt declared he wouldn't feed to a dog at home. The bread was so full of worms, Wirt maintained, that if the guards would just leave the door open, it could crawl in by itself.

Jesse gazed about him. He could calculate which ones would survive. Which ones might endure the starvation and the cold and the sickness. That Alabama boy now, the homesickness alone would claim him. Jesse could see it in his eyes.

Jesse laid back and closed his own eyes. He closed his mind against those thoughts, seeking sleep which was the only escape from this reeking hole. As long as the rats did not awaken him by scurrying across his hands and face as they often did. It was so easy to drift off . . .

He suddenly found himself in the swamp near his home. It smelled of decaying things and he could hear the whining of flies and mosquitoes in the darkness all around him. He found that he was confined in some way. A fence kept him from getting out of the swamp. He looked to see a gravestone with his name upon it. He had to get away, he knew, though he was not sure what it was that was after him in the darkness.

He took a step forward and the thick mud was suddenly sucking at his boots. He realized his hands were bound. He could not help himself. Water surged up to his knees. He struggled but could not pull himself free. He tried with all his strength to take another step. He was terrified to realize he was going to drown.

He heard his own voice calling out and he came awake with a jerk. A nightmare, he told himself. Just a nightmare.

He tried to relax. He tried to slow the pounding of his heart. But he could still feel the terrifying sense of the dream like the terrible reality of captivity that surrounded him.

The next day as they were finishing their meal, one of the prisoners came around and whispered that there was to be an escape attempt that night. They were to wait for darkness beyond the windows. They had all heard this same thing before and nothing had ever come of it. They were inclined to disbelieve it now. As was expected, nothing happened that night.

The next night, Jesse was sitting with his back against the wall. His head nodded as he dozed. The same soldier got down on his heels beside him and repeated the message.

"What'd he say?" Wirt asked.

"Another prison break," Jesse replied.

Wirt muttered something beneath his breath and then went back to sleep.

Someone said quietly, "Might just as well be shot by the guards. Couldn't be much worse'n slowly starvin' to death day after day."

Hours passed. Nothing happened. Then, as the guards opened the door, some of the prisoners acted impulsively and rushed forward. Though feeble and emaciated, the men were desperate. They managed to wrench the guns from a few of the guards.

One of the guards resisted and was bayoneted just outside the door. Another guard raised his gun. Before he could shoot, a prisoner clubbed him in the head with a carbine and the man slumped to the ground.

Jesse sprang forward and grabbed hold of the back of the shirt of one of the guards who was trying to escape up the stairs. He swung the man around and held him by the throat to prevent him from giving an alarm.

"You goddamn Rebel son- " the man began but Jesse's fist exploded in his face and the guard slid to the floor.

Jesse moved quickly to help another prisoner who was fighting desperately with a guard upon the stairs. A gun roared and the prisoner was shot through the arm. However, they quickly subdued the guard and made their way up the stairs. Dripping blood from his wound, the man in front of Jesse made his way to the landing.

Shots suddenly exploded nearby and the man clutched at his chest and fell back with a cry. Jesse came to a sudden halt as the black muzzle of a carbine pressed into his chest.

"Like to try it, eh?" the guard snarled. "Come on. Try it, you Rebel bastard."

Jesse knew it meant certain death. In the dim stairway, powder smoke hung on the air, but except for the groans of the wounded, everything was perfectly still.

The prisoners were forced back into the cell. As the door slammed shut, a kind of madness came upon Jesse in the familiar, fetid darkness. He had tasted a moment of freedom and now he longed to cry out his rage and frustration. He wanted to tear at the confining walls with his bare hands. He wanted to lash out at the men who had trapped them here like animals. Instead he sank down upon his bed and shuddered impotently with the intensity of his emotions.

The prisoners, meanwhile, cared for their own wounded as best they could.

"Someone got a Bible?" came an anxious whisper from one corner. "Mah friend is shot bad and he wants to hear the Scriptures."

"Ah know the Word," another voice quietly replied in the darkness.

And as the men gathered, someone else declared, "That's something we all need to hear."

Jesse clutched his meager, threadbare blanket closer about him. He was shivering. It was a very cold day. The Southern men were not used to northern winters and they were suffering very much. They could do nothing about it except to remain wrapped up in their blankets and move about as little as possible. It was so cold that they had to break through the ice in the water bucket to get a drink.

Each day of bitter cold and hunger was taking its toll. And how could they be expected to resist sickness under such conditions? All around him, Jesse could hear the continuous hacking of men who were coughing their strength away.

He lay on his bed, aware only of the cold. He had been so uncomfortably cold for so long that he felt as if it would never be possible for him to be warm again. Stay here much longer, he thought grimly to himself, and I'll be cold all right. For good.

He was, he admitted to himself, not only filthy and starving and cold. He was afraid. He didn't want to die here. That was all he could think of. He didn't want to die in this place.

He frowned at his manacled hands. Morgan Damon had not killed him outright. But he had succeeded in bringing him down gradually.

He suddenly thought about her. Again. The bitter lines deepened around his mouth. Maybe they were married by now.

But I had her first, he thought savagely. I had her first and you can't change that, you bastard.

Maybe he had gotten her pregnant. One corner of his mouth drew back into a truculent snarl. He would like to see her try and explain that.

The man on the bed next to him was delirious. He was raging about his crops again. They were doing all they could for the man but he kept getting worse.

"God," Jesse prayed. "Help us through this."

The man who had worried so much about his crops was dead before the next morning. He had died while still out of his head with fever. And Jesse was sick now. He was so weak and so trembly that he could barely lift his tin cup.

By the next day he was even weaker. His imagination began to play tricks on him. He began to hear voices though he knew that they were inside his head. His mind wandered. Strange how the pain and confusion that whirled through his brain made him speak his thoughts out loud, things that he wanted to keep to himself.

He was weaker than he could ever remember being in his entire life. What chance did a man stand? The cold was wearing him down, too. He could not seem to be able to fight off the cold and this sickness at the same time. His throat was so swollen that it was an agony to swallow. He ceased to eat. He could not get the ice-cold, strong-tasting water down. Mind getting as weak as my body, he thought.

In short time, he sank even deeper. His dignity became a pitiful thing as he clung to his last ounce of self-respect. As he lay there helpless, he had moments when he couldn't control the fear. He hated this miserable, hopeless existence. Living had become a physical and mental agony. Yet he clung to life. His heart continued to beat. His breath continued to rasp out of his lungs.

Night now, he thought in a moment of clear thinking. No light coming through those far-away windows. But he thought he could see very faintly the twinkling of a star. Make a wish, he thought. Make a wish. But you have to do it before it's gone. And while he thought about the wish, Wirt, sitting beside him, worried about the smile that touched Jesse's mouth.

Death would come to him presently, Jesse knew. No decent burial. His lifeless body would be carried off to the dead-house and he would be buried alongside all the others. And would she ever know that he had died? he wondered fiercely.

Someone was there. Wirt was beside him. A hell of a way to die. A hell of a place. "Tell her I died," he whispered intently. "Tell her that I ... "

He turned slightly, groaning as the movement brought a renewal of the pain in his head. The pain was searing his brain, making connections of thought that he had no control over. He wondered vaguely how much time he had left. His fevered brain conjured wild images that left him raving. He relived old, bittersweet memories.

"'Scensia," he muttered in the darkness while his tortured thoughts seemed to thunder inside his head.

Jesse survived. Somehow he managed to recover. One day the guards came into the prison and began to bind the prisoners with ropes. The guards did not explain anything and some of the prisoners feared that they were being taken out for execution.

A little while later, for the first time in many months, the men were standing outside of the prison. They waited in the yard, looking up at the same building that they remembered looking up at so many long months ago.

Jesse felt the freshness of the cold air against his face. Clean, pure, sun-bright air. He experienced an odd sensation of faintness. The cold air hurt his lungs. His legs felt unsteady. He drew a shaky breath as he got in line with the other prisoners. For long moments he closed his eyes. He was not used to daylight.

The guards informed them that they were about to change prisons.

"You mean we're leavin' this yere fine hotel?" queried one of the prisoners.

They were marched to the outskirts of the town to the railroad station where they huddled against the station wall on the wide platform. However, it offered only meager protection from the cold.

There were a lot of blue uniforms guarding them and Jesse noticed someone peering out of a window of the house across the street.

Noble Young was standing beside him and he declared, "Ah'll die if'n any girl sees me lookin' the way Ah do."

They were, in fact, being watched by a crowd of civilians. They were a tattered, filthy, starved-looking group that looked more like wild beasts than men, Jesse thought as they were herded like cattle onto the platform.

He leaned back against the station wall in his ragged gray clothes, his long, unkempt hair blowing across his cheek. His eyes, however, were clear and full of light as he looked out at the mountains in the distance.

They would have to spend the night sleeping on the platform, the guards informed them, for they were to take the morning train. The night grew bitterly cold. Jesse wrapped his threadbare blanket around him and sat down on the ground, sharing his blanket with another prisoner who did not have one. The temperature dropped steadily and the wind was piercing through the tattered blanket. The two men shivered through the night.

In the morning, the sound of the train woke Jesse. It shook the platform as the wheels rumbled over the tracks. The heavy doors were slid open and the prisoners were herded into several box cars. Their destination, the guards finally told them, was Fort Delaware, the most dreaded of all Northern prisons.

The train clattered loudly over the rails, rocking back and forth with a rhythmic motion. The men were crowded together in the darkened interior of the car. The cold wind blew through the cracks along with the black smoke and cinders from the engine.

The car swayed as it lurched along the tracks. Wirt swore suddenly as he cracked his head against the hard wood wall beside him. Jesse set his teeth against the jarring motion.

The train ran through a tunnel, roaring in the cavernous darkness. Jesse was sitting near the half open door. Wirt was beside him. On the other side sat one of the guards. Noble sat behind the guard.

Night fell. The train continued to move along, slowing down as it climbed a hill. They had passed no towns for a long time. Jesse was fully awake and he watched the ground rushing by beneath the train. He narrowed his eyes as he studied the landscape in the distance.

His manacles had been removed. He had been working at the ropes that bound him till his hands were free. He knew some of the other men were doing the same, and that someone, somehow had managed to secretly pass a small knife among the prisoners to assist in the task of removing the ropes. Wirt was free and Noble soon would be.

The descent from the tracks was almost a sheer drop. The height was dizzying. But there were concealing trees and brush growing thickly along the steep embankment. The risk lay in gaining a secure foothold before dropping all the way to the bottom. It was a risk all right. But the horrors of Delaware Prison were a certainty.

Jesse had decided that he would escape or die attempting it. A glance passed between him and Wirt. Wirt looked back at

Noble and the other men. Jesse's face was suddenly wearing the old, reckless look and the men looked to him.

The guard also looked at Jesse. He had always been more wary of this prisoner than any of the others. He was now aware of a change in the Rebel's eyes.

All right, Jesse said silently to himself. He stretched his legs out a little further.

The guard called out. "Get back there."

Jesse ignored him and cast a last glance to the treacherous drop beneath him. He pushed himself halfway out of the car, straining to hold onto the opening with one hand. In his weakened condition, it was no easy task.

"Halt!" he heard the guard shout.

Not a chance, you damned fool, Jesse thought as he swung free and let go.

A ball zipped past him and he knew he had distracted the guard. That would give the other men an edge.

At once he was sliding. For a long time he could not get a foothold in the soft dirt. Then he staggered, falling and finally dropping to one knee in a sprawl where he sat down, breathing hard.

Looking up, he could see the dark figures of other men leaping from the train. Guards in the other cars were shooting. Streaks of red flame spurted from their weapons.

For a while Jesse remained where he was. He was trembling from the exertion and he was hoping that Wirt had made it. And Noble. He wished they all could have made it.

He watched the light of the train probing the darkness in the distance. He could hear a rustling sound in the brush nearby and the low murmur of voices. He could hear Wirt calling. "Jesse. Where are you?"

And Noble's voice, "That you, Wirt? Captain? Ah'm ov' heah. And some others."

Jesse stood up. The cold night wind blew clean against his face. He had hurt his hand but he didn't think it was broken, and his side and leg were pretty scraped up. But he had made it relatively unscathed.

The men gathered into a little group. A group of tattered, feeble men. One of them had been grazed by a ball while jumping from the train. But it was not a dangerous wound and no one had sustained any serious injuries. And Jesse was pleased to see that more men had escaped than he had thought possible.

It was the dead of winter and they were a long way from Rebel lines. But slow grins touched every mouth. They might be weak and hungry and lost, but they were free.

Chapter 21

The sky was hanging low to the earth. A cold drizzle had been falling since late morning. Towards evening, the wind veered and the mist changed on a sudden to a freezing rain.

As the Union cavalry patrol rode up the muddy street of the little mountain town, the young captain riding at the head of the column was troubled by indecision. Two of his scouts had ridden in earlier with reports that Rebel cavalry had been seen gathering in the woods a few miles southwest of his location. As a precaution, he had sent a message alerting his commander of the situation.

He had grown even more alarmed when a third scout rode in less than half an hour ago informing him that Rebels had appeared in force across the river only eight miles to the south.

As the column halted before the little telegraph office, the wind whistling along the wires caused him to draw his greatcoat closer about him. He frowned, biting his lips beneath his mustache. He knew that something was up but he had no way of knowing exactly what it was. And so he had another message sent in advising his superiors of the possibility of an attack. The problem was, he didn't know where exactly that might be.

The rain turned to snow before nightfall and the countryside was soon blanketed beneath a covering of white. Ascensia sat wrapped in a cloak of deep blue velvet. Her hair contrasted darkly with her pale cheeks as she gazed out of the train window.

"What a gloomy sky," Hetty remarked beside her. "It certainly has a look of winter to it."

The train was crammed with people. Women's hoops were crushed. Soldiers were sitting in the aisle. Ascensia settled back in her seat and thought about Morgan waiting for her. He had been so anxious for her to come visit his headquarters. In fact, he had practically arranged everything so that she had had barely any say in the matter.

Later, as she and Hetty stood in the crowd at the station, they found that Morgan was not waiting for them. Instead, he had sent a detail of soldiers to escort them to his headquarters. Ascensia and Hetty stood on the cold, wind-swept platform while their trunks and bandboxes were loaded onto a government wagon.

The wind was like ice as it swept across the flat meadow that stretched out from the station. It rattled the station windows and swept the snow up against the unpainted walls. The snow, blowing out of the darkening sky, stung Ascensia's face so she turned away from it.

She wrapped her cloak tightly about her and gazed out at the red signal light shining out beyond the falling snow. Her eyes swept the mountains in the distance. Suddenly she caught her breath sharply, which caused Hetty to turn and look towards the mountains, too.

On a far ridge off to their right was the dark silhouette of a horse and rider.

"There is someone up there," she said to Hetty.

"Yes, there is. What a magnificent tableau," Hetty exclaimed.

It was magnificent, Ascensia agreed. Horse and rider remained poised up on the ridge as if the man was watching the scene below him. They were very far away, but she could see the animal's arched neck. She could see its mane and tail as they were blown by the wind.

The man leaned slightly forward and the horse started forward, breaking suddenly into a graceful lope along the crest of the ridge.

"You'll see them now and then," said one of the soldiers. "But you don't have to worry. The only Rebels on this side of the river are scouts and small groups of cavalry."

He had meant to reassure them but Ascensia was aware of a new uneasiness in the men. As they blew on their hands for warmth, she was quick to discern that beneath the shadows of their hat brims, their eyes continually searched the dark stretches of woods all around.

It was late when they finally got started. The snow was falling harder. It seemed to hush all sound. Ascensia heard only the soft hiss of the snowflakes as they struck her hood while her gaze lifted from the meadow to the mountains beyond, somber and brooding and wreathed with shadows.

Jesse remained silent as he warmed his hands over the low fire and listened to the report of the scout who had just ridden in. His hat brim lowered as he asked in a low voice, "And the people on the train?"

"On their way," was the reply.

"You see to the telegraph wires?"

"Wires are down, Suh. Won't be any messages getting through."

Jesse nodded slightly. He stared at the dark circle where the snow had melted away from the fire and listened to the hiss and the pop of burning wood. He could feel the old, familiar stirring of his blood as he watched the driving snow continue to fall out of the darkness.

If all went well, they would quickly surround the town and capture Major Morgan Damon and hold him prisoner in exchange for two Confederate scouts who were still in his hands and who were now sentenced to be executed.

At Jesse's order, the men mounted their horses and struck out northward. The sound of the wind whispering through the pines surrounded them and drowned out the thudding of horses' hoofs on the snow-covered ground.

Ascensia peered absently over the flickering candle flames. Her brows were drawn into a distracted frown as she watched the tiny yellow lights reflected in the window. It seemed as if they were floating in the black sky outside.

Morgan had arranged a lavish dinner. Everything was prepared to perfection. From the tender, delicately-roasted chicken to the light, flaky biscuits that were dripping with freshly-churned butter. She raised the exquisitely-cut crystal glass to her lips and drank another sip of wine.

As she lifted her heavy silver fork, however, she was suddenly assailed by a sense of guilt. Remembering the snow and the bitter cold outside, she shuddered and wondered if Brom was warm tonight or if he or any of the other men had enough to eat.

She had been surprised to see how comfortable Morgan's headquarters were. She gazed around at the elegantly-furnished room. The house had belonged to Confederate sympathizers, she had learned. But she did not know what had happened to the owners of the house.

Morgan had not yet returned though several officers and their wives were present. After dinner, Ascensia asked if she might go down to the library and pick out a book to read. While she was looking over the vast selection of books available, a soldier came to tell her that Morgan would not return until very late.

The horsemen had filed off the road where they gathered in the shelter of a stand of trees. Snow dusted their hats and greatcoats. It clung to their hair and mustaches and the manes of their horses.

Through the trees below, Jesse could see the bridge and the river running like a dark scar through the white snow. Beyond the bridge, the lights of the town were lit against the darkness. His gaze fixed on the big white house at the far end of the street.

He couldn't keep himself from thinking about her down there. He had to force himself to control the restlessness that made him eager to confront her.

"The pickets have been captured," Wirt informed him.

Jesse threw a glance towards the man beside him. "Then let's go get us a hostage."

In the front parlor, the ladies chatted in unconcern as their full skirts swept the fine Brussels carpet. The officers had already gone to the back parlor to drink brandy and smoke cigars.

One of the women went to draw the heavy brocade draperies more closely over the window. "Goodness," she exclaimed as she looked out. "How heavy the snow- "

She uttered a little cry as her hand went to her mouth. She continued to stare out the window as if she could not believe what she was seeing down below. "There are Rebels riding along the road," she said breathlessly.

"It must be our men," one of the other women replied, unconcerned.

It was dark outside and snow was falling. A mistake could be easily made.

"They are Rebels, I tell you," the woman insisted. "And they are looking this way." She jerked the curtains closed and stepped away from the window.

Hetty went to look for herself. Her eyes widened in surprise. "Why, they- " she began and then looked harder at the men. "They certainly look like Rebels."

The woman beside her labored a moment for breath, then burst out, "What should we do? Should we stay here?"

Things began to happen quickly after that. Men in gray suddenly burst into the room, pistols drawn. Other men were already searching the house. The heavy thump of bootsteps could be heard on the wooden floors and on the stairs.

A Union officer stepped into the parlor, cigar in hand, and demanded, "Who is in here?"

He stopped short and stared at the gray-clad man holding a pistol before him.

"Ah am," was the quiet reply.

The officer's mouth dropped open in disbelief. "By God. You are a Rebel."

"Yes," replied the other man. "And you are a prisoner."

The officer was forced to join the other men while the Rebels continued their search of the house. A Confederate officer, meanwhile, stepped before the women and removed his hat. He was young and handsome and so he quickly gained their full attention.

"Ladies," he began, and then proceded to calm them with a speech about Southern chivalry, assuring them that they were in no danger.

"We never make war against women," he said. "Especially not such pretty women."

Downstairs in the library, Ascensia had heard the sound of horses outside. She looked out the window, expecting to see that Morgan had returned. What she saw instead were Rebel horsemen.

She turned quickly to a young Union Lieutenant who had come into the room. "What should we do?" she asked.

"Don't worry, Miss McCay," he said. "I won't let any harm come to you."

"Sure. If you do just what I say."

Even before she turned, Ascensia experienced a jolt of emotion that took her breath away. She whirled around to see Jesse standing in the doorway.

They continued to stare into each other's eyes until Jesse's gaze shifted to the man standing beside her. With a slight thrust of his chin and a jerk of his gun, Jesse motioned for the Lieutenant to move to one side. When the man did not obey, Jesse's eyes narrowed dangerously.

"Step away from her, Lieutenant. And keep your hands where they are."

The Lieutenant looked uncertainly at Ascensia, then reluctantly stepped away.

"Now hand over your pistol," Jesse ordered.

The Lieutenant refused. "I will not do it."

Ascensia's eyes had been fixed on Jesse's face. She now glanced quickly at the Lieutenant. At that moment, Jesse reached out and jerked her to his side.

She could feel the tension in him. She could feel the unyielding strength in the hand that gripped her arm.

"It would be a shame if the lady had to watch you get shot," he said.

"No!" Ascensia cried. "Don't. Please."

Jesse was looking down at her face when another Rebel appeared in the hallway behind them. "He's not here, Captain."

"Where is Major Damon?" Jesse demanded of the Lieutenant.

The Lieutenant did not answer. As Ascensia stared up at Jesse, she began to understand. He had come for Morgan. He had come for revenge. The same revenge that had always motivated him.

A sudden, fierce antagonism ran through her as she remembered how he had betrayed her. "Morgan is gone," she told him. "He is safely away from here. And from you. I only wish that I was, too."

Some emotion flickered across Jesse's face but it was quickly replaced by something else. "Well, then," he said as he looked down at her. "I'll just have to change my plans."

"Watch the Lieutenant," he told the other Rebel. He tightened his grip on Ascensia's arm and led her up the stairs.

"Where is your room?" he demanded as he hurried her down the hallway beside him.

Inside her room he let go of her. She turned and instinctively backed up, her eyes riveted on Jesse as he went to the huge, mirrored armoire.

He flung open the door and began searching through her clothes. He jerked out her blue velvet cloak and tossed it onto the chair beside her.

"Put that on."

"Why?"

"I need a hostage to hold in exchange for some of my men. The Major isn't here. So I'm taking you."

She stared at him, speechless for a moment before she burst out, "You are mad if you think you can just walk out of here with me. This town is full of Union soldiers."

"Who are already surrounded and captured by *my* soldiers."

"Morgan will- " she began angrily.

"He isn't here," Jesse interrupted harshly.

He stepped towards her and grabbed her face. She tried to pull away but he held her chin in a viselike grip. She winced but his steely eyes held no mercy as they blazed into hers. "You're my prisoner. The sooner you realize that, the better off you'll be."

He let her go and she backed away.

"Where is it you think you are taking me?" she asked. "What are you going to do?"

An involuntary little glint had come into Jesse's eyes. "Guess you'll have to wait and see."

She stiffened.

"You heard what I said. Get that cloak on."

She pulled the heavy cloak over her shoulders, not knowing what else to do, thinking that somehow this wouldn't really happen. They would be stopped before they even got outside the door. Downstairs Jesse steered her towards a side door and said to her, "We'll go out this way. We don't want the Lieutenant getting himself killed over you if he decides to be brave."

A little while later Ascensia was sitting on a horse and looking down from a ridge to the town below. The air was sharp and cold as she breathed it in. The snow was still falling.

The men had set the bridge on fire to prevent pursuit. It was already burning briskly and she watched the flames flare up against the night sky. She turned to see Lieutenant Renn Parrish ride up to Jesse a little distance away. She couldn't hear what they were saying, but the Lieutenant looked angry.

Renn reined his horse in with a jerking motion. "Look here," he said. "What kind of a damned fool thing is this, bringing her along? Ah don't understand- "

"Then I won't waste my breath explaining it to you," Jesse interrupted.

The Lieutenant stiffened in his saddle. Jesse turned his face to the side and swore beneath his breath. He looked back at the Lieutenant and said, "The Major wasn't there. So I'm taking her in his place."

"Well, it's hardly her fault if he is gone, is it? Why don't you do the decent thing and send her back now while you can?"

Jesse did not answer. Both men looked down as the bridge collapsed into the river with a loud hiss of steam. A silence followed. Jesse gave the Lieutenant a narrowed look before he twisted his reins and rode his horse over to Ascensia.

Chapter 22

The men rode hunched forward as they pushed towards the mountains. They had turned up their collars and pulled their hats down low against the icy blasts of winter wind that moaned through the branches of the trees around them.

Riding at the head of the column, Jesse was barely aware of the cold or the driving wind and snow. She hadn't spoken one more word to him. She wouldn't even look at him. She sat huddled down in her saddle, a most miserable-looking prisoner.

This was hardly the way he had planned things. The truth was that taking her was not resting easy on his mind. He was having a hard time justifying it even to himself. He had lost his head somehow when he had seen her standing in the library with that pale-faced, bespectacled lieutenant who was so intent on protecting her. From him.

And when she had taunted him about Morgan Damon, she had only added fuel to the fire and made matters worse. He had given in to a malicious desire to make her regret the things she had said to him.

Hell, he growled to himself and glanced back, wondering what she was thinking about. Probably about getting back to her precious major.

Rage surged through him anew, causing him to sneer savagely beneath his hat brim. Be damned if I'll oblige her and hurry their little reunion, he thought darkly.

Ascensia shivered as the raw wind blew snow beneath her hood. Her face felt frozen. Her feet and hands had grown numb long ago even though one of the men had given her his gloves to wear.

They had burned the bridge and the snow was already covering their tracks. Pursuit would be delayed. But someone would come to rescue her.

Hours passed before a halt was called to rest both horses and men. They dismounted in the shelter of some trees. Although Ascensia could not feel the wind, she could hear it above her in the tree tops.

The men soon had several low fires burning. They gathered around the snapping branches as they heated water for coffee. She looked up to see Renn Parrish walking over to her.

Across his horse's back, Jesse watched her. She was standing near one of the fires with Renn. She was holding her hands out over the flames to warm them. Her hood had slipped back and he could see white flakes of snow against her dark hair.

Renn handed her a tin cup of steaming coffee. Another man came forward to offer her an extra blanket to wrap herself in. Jesse jerked the leather saddle strap tight. A short time later he took a deep swallow of his own whiskey-laced coffee and then suddenly threw the remaining contents of his cup on the snow with a quick flick of his wrist.

Ascensia had turned from the fire but she stopped dead when she saw Jesse standing in front of her. The other men seemed to drift away from them. It was what they always did, she suddenly realized, when Jesse came near her.

"I suppose," she said in a voice as cold as the snowflakes falling around her. "That you think you have done a very bold and daring thing."

"I'm beginning to regret it more and more," was his reply.

Suddenly, resentfully, she blurted, "Morgan will come after you. When he finds out what you have done, he will come after you."

She had made a mistake. She realized it as she looked up at him. She noticed a faint scar on his chin that had not been there before just before he grabbed her arm and dragged her away from the others. In a small clearing they were hidden from the other men by the trees.

"I don't give a damn about what Morgan Damon is going to do," Jesse began in an savage voice. "But you mention his name once more and I'll slap it back down your throat. Do you understand?

"Do you?" he demanded, the muscles jumping in his jaw.

"Yes," she replied just as passionately.

In spite of his harsh words, Jesse could not help noticing, as he looked down at her, how pale she looked, how drawn. He had noticed it back at the house, too. He knew, too, that the dresses that women wore nowadays could hide a great deal and he asked abruptly, "Are you pregnant?"

Stunned by his question, she turned her face aside. She swallowed, recovered and her lips curled with a bitter scorn. "Don't you think you should have made that inquiry a little sooner?"

He grabbed her shoulders. "Answer me. Are you carrying my child?"

"No," she hissed. "No, thank God, I am not. And if I was with child," she said as she looked straight at him. "Why would you assume that it was *yours*? Unless of course you think that I couldn't- "

She had been about to say, *couldn't even think about being with any other man.*

But he must have thought she meant to say something else entirely.

"Don't," he warned between clenched teeth.

She should have heeded his warning. But something drove her. She was battling not only with him, but with herself because deep inside her, when she had first seen Jesse standing in that doorway, some traitorous part of her heart had reacted in a way that had been completely at odds with what she *wanted* to feel. What she *ought* to feel.

"I wish I never had to see you again." She sounded almost desperate, and half breathless. He was bringing up too many conflicting emotions. Things that she thought she had buried long ago. "I wish you were still in that prison."

He grabbed her again. And though she was fully aware of his anger, she faced him boldly. He didn't act on his anger. Just as suddenly as he had grabbed her, he let her go, half thrusting her away from him. She stumbled and fell in the snow.

His immediate impulse was to pick her up and brush the snow off her. And to his disgust, he found himself wanting to hold the faithless little witch and kiss away all the bad feelings between them. But when she got to her feet, she glared so hatefully at him that all he did was to turn his face away from her and tell her curtly to get back to the camp.

By the time Jesse had walked back to the horses, he saw that she was helping herself to his canteen of whiskey. She defiantly met his eyes as she lifted the canteen to her lips.

Ascensia tilted the canteen higher. She almost choked, however, when the strong liquid seared a path straight down to her stomach.

"You didn't offer," she said when she had finished coughing. "And I need something to keep me from freezing to death." She walked back to her own horse and mounted without help.

Jesse slung the canteen of whiskey over the pommel of her saddle. "Maybe it'll help keep you quiet," he muttered.

It was like a nightmare, Ascensia thought as the horses started out again. It was like some horrible nightmare. It was as if time had gone backwards to their first days together. It was as if they had never been lovers.

But if she could not forget that, she also could not forget the way he had deceived her. He had been false when he had held her and kissed her so tenderly. The real man was savage, brutal. Hadn't he just proven that to her?

Gradually she began to feel a little warmer inside the heavy cloak. She was feeling a little better, a little less uncomfortable. I might be able to survive this, she muttered to herself as she took another drink from the canteen. It didn't seem to burn as much as it did before. She could feel her muscles relaxing. She could feel her blood warming.

Hours passed and still they traveled. Every now and then Ascensia would drink more of the warming whiskey until she did not seem to feel the cold at all. But she was growing so weary that she had to carefully wrap her hands around the pommel because she could not seem to keep from nodding her head and dozing a little. She also could not keep from swaying a bit in the saddle.

Sometime later, she opened her eyes, realizing that the horse had come to a halt. She saw a house before her. She slid down from the saddle and found that it was a long way to the ground. As she stood swaying, someone caught her and she looked up, trying to focus on Jesse's sardonic face.

He scooped her up and took her into the house. With her still in his arms, he climbed a staircase, pushed a door open with his boot and dropped her down onto a soft, warm bed.

"Where are we?"

"Quiet," was his only reply. Soon afterward the door slammed shut.

Downstairs, Jesse drank what little whiskey she had left in his canteen. Renn, who had been moodily absorbed in the flames leaping in the fireplace, got up and stood before Jesse who was jamming the cork back into the canteen.

"What you are doing is wrong," the Lieutenant began. "You can't go dragging her along, forcing her to ride with a bunch of men like some- some- "

"Campfollower?" Jesse supplied.

Renn stared at him. His jaw tightened. "She's not like that."

Jesse's eyes narrowed slightly as he regarded the Lieutenant. "Don't trouble yourself about it."

"Ah just will trouble mahself about it," Renn flashed.

"Well, I'm ordering you not to," Jesse flashed back. "I don't reckon that I'm accountable to you for the decisions that I make."

Soon the front door slammed shut and Jesse stood alone outside, silently damning her. Damning himself.

An hour later he returned to her room. She was fast asleep. He walked to the bed and stood staring down at her. She lay there, sleeping peacefully. Of course she'd had enough whiskey to keep her sleeping peacefully for a long time.

Part of her hair had come loose. The soft, dark curls were trailing across the white embroidered pillowcase. He reached out and lifted a curl that lay close to her face. His hand lightly brushed her cheek.

She stirred slightly but didn't open her eyes. The lamplight softly bathed her face. She was as beautiful as he remembered. The hunger that he had barely managed to control suddenly leaped like a flame inside him. He was immediately hot and hard with need.

He was surprised at how much he still wanted her. His mouth yearned to taste the wild sweetness of her kisses. Kisses that he remembered very well. He clenched his hands to keep from touching her as his gaze wandered over her body.

He recalled how it had been between them, how intense. It had been a long time since he had had a woman. There had been none since Ascensia. And after the long months in prison, his desire was easily aroused. Too easily aroused.

He frowned suddenly as he thought about the things she had said to him. "Damn you, 'Scensia," he whispered and his face grew hard as he looked down at her. He reached out and pulled the quilt over her before he left the room.

Ascensia's gaze ran along the shadows of the trees flickering across the sloping canvas above her. She could hear the ringing of an ax. She could smell wood smoke. Men's voices came from a distance and, occasionally, male laughter punctuated the talk.

Three days had passed since she had been kidnapped. Today, she had spent the entire morning sitting alone in a tent. She had slept here alone last night. When someone knocked on the tent pole, she pushed the flap back and stared at the soldier who stood there.

"You must be hungry, ma'am," he said. "Ah have brought you everything you might need to fix a meal. You can cook, can't you?"

She stared at the man for a few moments. "Yes. I can cook."

After the man had walked away, however, Ascensia stood outside the tent with a rather bewildered look on her face as she stared at the camp kettles and pans. She had never cooked over a campfire before. She was hungry, however, and since cooking for herself seemed to be her only means of nourishment, she would have to at least try to prepare a meal.

She took some flour, made a batter and added more water until the batter seemed right. She set that aside and put some grease in one of the pans and placed it over the fire to heat up.

Meanwhile, she sliced the meat and when the grease seemed hot enough, she added the meat to the pan. While she sat waiting for it to cook, she looked at her surroundings.

She was in a Confederate camp. There were about a dozen tents. The land sloped down to a small stream. On the opposite bank the land sloped up again into an area of dense pine trees. The smoke from the fire began to burn her eyes, so she moved her camp stool to the left.

There was a house across the dirt road at the edge of the camp. It was a large, white, two-story house with a wide porch that wrapped around two sides. There had been no activity around the house all morning. But just now a scantily-clad young woman stepped outside.

Ascensia's eyes widened in shock as a soldier walked up to the woman, put his arm around her waist and went inside with her. She looked down at the sizzling meat. She turned it over and saw that it was charred black. Soon the other side was burned as well. The biscuits turned out as hard as rocks.

She looked down at the unappetizing meal she had just prepared. Cooking over a campfire was not as easy as she had thought it would be. To make matters worse, no matter where she sat, the wind would veer around and blow the smoke into her face, stinging her eyes so badly that she couldn't keep the tears from rolling down her cheeks.

In a little while the soldier returned. He didn't say a word as he stared down at the food. He ran his hand across his jaw and reckoned in his Southern drawl that cooking over a campfire did take some getting used to.

He looked at her tear-streaked face and said, "Well, it's nothing to cry about. It took me a long time to learn how. And Ah- "

She gritted her teeth in exasperation as she stormed past him and disappeared inside the tent. Later in the day, after she had finished the meal the soldier had brought her, she began to feel more and more uncomfortable with the cold. In fact, she was feeling quite miserable. The sun had disappeared behind the clouds. A chill wind now shook the tent walls.

She had been told by the soldier that the Captain had left the camp early that morning. But he had also left word that there was a room up in the house for her. Nothing would make her stay there, however. She knew very well what that place was and what went on inside.

So she sat miserably on the camp bed with a wool blanket wrapped around her, listening to the wind rising higher as the day wore on. She pulled her numb feet up off the damp ground and tucked them up under her. The tent flap was suddenly pulled aside and Jesse stepped inside, bringing a little more of the cold air in with him.

He looked at her shivering, blanket-wrapped form and frowned. "You're cold," he said, stating the obvious.

And why wouldn't she be? She glared silently up at him. The temperature had dropped dramatically in the last hour.

"I left word that there is as room up at the house for you."

"I am not going up there," she snapped.

Colder in here than it is outside, Jesse thought. "If you– " he began.

"I am not," she interrupted tersely. "Going to argue with you."

"Suit yourself," he said.

Her mouth set a little tighter as she kept her face averted from his. Yet no matter how hard she tried, she could not seem to be able to keep her anger inside. Hours of having nothing whatsoever to do to occupy her time had not improved her mood.

She watched as he tossed his hat onto the little table at the back of the tent. "You sleep in the barn with the rest of the animals last night?" she asked tartly.

He glanced over at her but let it pass.

"I suppose I should consider myself fortunate," she said in a voice that dripped with sarcasm. "That I didn't have to share a tent last night with a man who is without virtue or honor, a stealer of horses and women."

There was a little mirror hanging on the back pole of the tent. Jesse stood before it, frowning at his reflection in the glass. He needed a shave. He ran his hand through his long dark hair. He did look pretty rough. Exactly like a stealer of horses and women might look. He looked at her and said, "I thought you didn't want to cross swords with me."

She glared silently back at him. He sat down and laid his pistols on the table, preparing to clean them.

"Prison doesn't seem to agree with you," was her next remark as Jesse sat down.

"And how's that?" he asked without looking up, but wondering, as he had wondered before, how she knew that he had been in prison.

"The first time I met you, it was while you were confined in a prison. You forced me to go with you then after you escaped. It seems that there is something about captivity that makes you want to abuse women."

A heavy gust of wind struck the tent and sent a shiver through the canvas walls.

"I know why my presence here makes you act so disagreeably," she went on.

He leaned back in his chair and regarded her steadily while he ran a rag over one of his pistols.

"It is because your conscience is troubling you," she said.

"Really."

"Even a man like you has to feel some remorse over subjecting a woman to all this hardship. And to *you*."

"I told you there is a room at the house- "

"And I told you I won't stay there," she flashed.

"Fine," he said. "Then we don't have to discuss it any further."

The wind rose and the tent poles groaned.

"I am sure, however, that *you* have been up there."

He looked up. He raised one dark brow while his eyes held hers. He had not failed to note the malice in her voice. "Does that bother you?"

"Bother me? I don't care in the least what you do or who you do it with. In fact, if it keeps you busy and away from me, that suits me even more."

"I suppose," he said coldly. "That you are mad because I haven't been around to run and fetch for you since Renn isn't here to do it."

"Run and fetch?" she fumed as she got to her feet. "Why, you are the last person I want to run and fetch for me. I suppose Morgan will do that for me."

Jesse had gotten to his feet as well. In the silence, Ascensia could hear quite clearly the wind as it rushed through the branches above the tent.

"Really?" he breathed in a dangerously low voice. "And just how much running and fetching would he do for you if he knew that I'd already bedded you? How would he feel if he knew how breathless you got when I touched you, how eager you were when I- "

Her hand lashed out. Though Jesse saw the movement, he did nothing to stop or avoid her hand. After she had struck him, he caught her wrist and held it in a ruthless grip while his other arm pulled her body hard against him.

A shiver ran through her. It was something that had nothing to do with the cold. She heard the renewed fury of the wind in the moments before he kissed her. She squirmed to free herself but his arm tightened around her, trapping her against his chest.

"No," she panted after the kiss. Against her will, however, her body had already begun to respond to him.

The knowledge that Ascensia wanted him even though she was struggling against it, made Jesse even more savage in his demand. Yet even while he kissed her again, he knew he had to stop before things went too far.

As abruptly as he had pulled her into his embrace, he let her go. It was so unexpected and so sudden that Ascensia was still standing with her eyes closed and her lips parted. She opened her eyes and stared up at him, dazed, bewildered.

Out of his own frustration, Jesse said cruelly, "Doesn't take much to get you wanting it again, does it?"

She heard his words only, not the breathless, ragged edge to his voice. And soon she found herself standing alone in the tent, staring at the tent flap through which he had disappeared.

"You're wrong," she sobbed out loud. "You're so wrong about me."

And yet she had responded to his kisses. Brutal as they were. Even while she hated him, she still wanted him.

Jesse had walked to the edge of the camp. He stood leaning against one of the trees where there was no one to see how badly he had been affected.

His hands were trembling. He drew his sleeve across his brow. Sweating. Hell. He alone knew what it had taken for him to walk out of that tent.

Don't think about her any more, he told himself. Think about anything else. He hated this weakness. He cursed her for the faithless, provoking little cat that she was.

What was wrong with him? There were plenty of other women he could have right here. Right now. Any one of them could please him without all the turmoil that that one female always seemed to be able to rouse in him.

He looked back at the tent and frowned as he realized that he had forgotten to take his pistols with him.

The moment he stepped back inside the tent, he heard her voice. "Is this what you came back for?"

She was holding one of his guns in her hands. The black barrel was pointed squarely at his chest.

"Put your hands up," she whispered low and tense in the dim light.

She looked quite- distraught. And a distraught female with a loaded gun in her hands was a dangerous combination.

Definitely a dangerous combination. He slowly raised his hands until they were level with his shoulders.

"I want you to back out of here."

He did as she said.

"What's going on?" one of the men sitting at a nearby fire asked in alarm as he half rose.

Ascensia glared at him with such stormy eyes that he fell silent.

At that moment Wirt Blackford walked around one of the tents. Seeing her, he stopped short. "Lord!" he exclaimed. "She's armed."

"Ma'am, that pistol may be loaded," another man warned her.

She pulled the hammer back and fired deliberately. Again and again the balls tore splinters off one of the trees behind Jesse. There was a great scuffling among the other men as they scattered.

Jesse, however, didn't move. His eyes never left Ascensia's face. She threw the pistol at his feet and coolly informed them all that the gun was now empty.

She then walked past Jesse and ran up the steps to the house, brushing past a man who had just stepped outside inquiring, "Who's shooting?"

A moment later the slamming of the front door seemed nearly as loud as the pistol shots had been. Two of the door's window panes shattered.

There was a long silence back at the camp till Wirt suddenly exclaimed, "Why, did you ever see such a damnfool female? What got her back up this time? By God, if she isn't the worst damned shot Ah ever saw. She emptied that pistol at you, Jes, and missed every single time."

Chapter 23

"Why, yes. The last room on the right is empty," the woman in the crimson satin dress informed her. "I'll have hot water sent up for your bath. Captain Lucane said that whatever- "

Ascensia groaned as she went quickly up the wide, curving staircase. She slammed the door behind her and stood with her back against it, staring at the richly-carved furniture, the heavy brocade draperies, the ornate fireplace and the huge bed.

At least she was alone, she thought. And warm. She crossed the room and stared into the long mirror. She jerked the pins from her hair and felt the heavy mass of it tumble loosely down her back.

She took up a brush and began pulling it through the tangled curls. She cried out as it caught at a snarl and then slammed the brush down hard on the dresser.

"The wretch!" she stormed out loud. "I should have killed him."

She closed her eyes and took a deep breath. I won't let him get me this angry, she told herself. She picked up the brush again but the anger flared in spite of herself. Well, she thought with some satisfaction, all the hours Brom had spent teaching her how to shoot had been useful after all.

She walked across the room and pulled the armoire door open. She stood frowning as she examined the dresses within. Disapproval straightened her lips. Something else, however, was responsible for the narrowing of her eyes as she pulled out a black silk dress.

She held the dress against her and looked in the mirror. Her gaze shifted across the room to the ornate bathtub and then she laid the dress on the bed. She looked at the bottles of perfume on the dresser. And for the first time in days she allowed herself a smile.

Night had fallen and Jesse was sitting downstairs at a table with several other men. It was a lively group. Several bottles of whiskey on the table were already half empty and the men's unrestrained laughter filled the room.

"The way she looked when she emptied that pistol at you, Captain," one of the men laughed. "Ah reckoned you were a goner."

Jesse smiled then downed the remaining whiskey in his glass with a single swallow. He felt its warmth flaming through his belly.

"Yeah," agreed another man. "She came a'rarin', Captain, with blood in her eye."

"She's damned dangerous," Wirt declared. "Touchy as gunpowder. You never know when a spark is going to set her off."

"Well," laughed one of the men. "The Captain sure sparked her today."

"You see the boys scatter?" Wirt hooted as he slapped the table with his broad hand. "They were hopping around like chickens on a hot griddle."

Jesse joined in the laughter, declaring that he would rather make a stand alone against a ten-gun Yankee battery than to have to brave the wrath of that one female.

"She can't cook wu'th a damn," Wirt said with a wave of his hand. "She made some biscuits this mornin'. Hard as iron. Looked like something shot out of a cannon."

"But she's pretty enough not to have to know how to cook," one of the men pointed out with a grin. "A man could overlook it and be satisfied just lookin' in them eyes of hers."

As he stretched out his leg muscles, Jesse's glance roamed to the staircase that led to the upstairs rooms. He grabbed the bottle before him, poured more whiskey into his glass and drank it down. He could feel it glowing inside now and knew that he was getting a little tight. He heard Wirt call for more whiskey.

"So she finally came in to roost," Wirt remarked. "You know, it's funny, Jes. When she was shootin', she missed you. But she hit that tree behind you. Every single time. Dead center." Wirt's dark eyes rested on Jesse as he lifted his glass to his lips.

"Yeah?" Jesse breathed. "Glad I wasn't standing in front of that tree." He laughed but his thoughts were wandering back to Ascensia.

He couldn't seem to be able to get her out of his mind. He had tried, God knew. He took another drink, needing to ease the tension in him. The whiskey didn't seem to be doing anything, however, about the arousal that kept mounting steadily inside of him.

His eyes began a leisurely search of the room. If he had a woman tonight, it would be the sensible thing to do, to take care of this damned hunger inside him. Since there were so many available, and willing, women, he didn't know why he hadn't done so already. Maybe if he did, he'd be able to get that she-wolf out of his mind.

"Who's in on this hand?" one of the men asked.

"Not me," said the man next to Jesse. "Ah'm goin' upstairs." He was grinning as he stood up. He turned and went up the staircase with one of the girls.

Wirt looked at Jesse. "Got a restless look in *your* eyes, Jes."

Jesse lifted a dark brow and smiled.

A red-haired girl brought more whiskey to the table. She brushed against Jesse as she leaned over. She was very pretty. Her green eyes were bold, seductive and her lips were curved into an inviting smile as she looked down at him.

"What's your name?" he asked without really caring.

His arm went around her waist and he gave a little jerk. She laughed as she fell into his lap, pleased by the attention the handsome Captain was suddenly paying her.

Ascensia hesitated before the bedroom door. She glanced back at the mirror. The black silk dress was more provocative and more revealing than anything she had ever worn. Her breasts rose like a deliberate invitation above the daring décolletage. The dress pulled in her waist and flared over her hips, boldly emphasizing her curves in a way no other dress had ever done.

Her dark curls fell in a wanton tumble over her bare shoulders and down her back. She had decided not to pin it up. The other women here, apparently, did not bother with pins.

She imagined Jesse's reaction. That reaction was the reason she had put the dress on in the first place. If he was going to treat her like a campfollower, then she would dress the part. Oh, he would be angry all right. As she contemplated his anger, she found the courage to open the bedroom door.

The sounds from downstairs immediately grew louder. Three men were coming up the stairs. They stopped on the landing when they saw her. When they grinned, her courage failed her and she retreated back to the room.

One of the men, a young Confederate officer, had followed her inside before she knew what he was doing. He closed the door behind him. As he walked a circle around her, his eyes took in every inch of her.

"Ma'am," he drawled with a deep Southern accent. "That dress sure is beautiful. *You* sure are beautiful. But Ah expect you already know that."

He stepped closer to her. "Ah'm in a hurry," he said. "But Ah can pay you well. And, ma'am, Ah- Ah really want you."

He meant her no disrespect, she knew. He didn't know any better. Actually, despite the circumstances, he seemed quite refined and gentlemanly.

He placed his hands on her waist and she knew he meant to kiss her. She was spared having to make an explanation when the door was suddenly flung open.

Jesse stood on the threshold with a half-empty bottle in one hand. "What the hell- " he froze at the sight of Ascensia with the soldier.

His gaze ran the length of the dress and his mouth straightened in an unpleasant line. "And here I thought," he said with a deceptively soft voice. "That you'd be lonely without me."

He looked coldly at the young officer. Ascensia slowly and deliberately slipped her hands up along the soldier's arms to his shoulders. The action made the man's hands tighten involuntarily on her waist even though he kept watching Jesse.

"Ah'm- " the man began.

"Leaving," Jesse finished for him.

The man looked uncertainly down at Ascensia.

"I've already paid for her," Jesse said.

The young officer stepped away and quickly offered an apology. After he had left the room, Jesse slammed the door and slid the bolt into place.

His eyes raked her. "You sure are full of surprises, aren't you? I'll confess it," he said as his gaze continued to roam slowly over her. "You'd make one hell of a whore, honey."

His words shocked her, but she was determined that he would not ruffle her composure. Not this time. No matter what he said or did. Her eyes narrowed very slightly as she said, "He was very handsome, don't you think?"

She may have seen the change in Jesse's face, but she didn't understand exactly what it was that caused the muscles to tighten in his jaw.

He stepped closer to her. "You do these things to deliberately provoke me, don't you?" His breath was strong with whiskey.

She shook her dark curls back with a toss of her head. "You're drunk," she said.

"Drunk? Hell. Sure I am."

"You burst into this room, shamelessly drunk and reeking of whiskey and you- "

"*Me* shameless?" he broke in. "I find you dressed like a whore, standing in the arms of a soldier. A *stranger* to you." Damn, it was bothering him. "And you call *me* shameless."

"I don't have to stand here and listen to this. Why don't you go abuse one of the other women? There is a whole house full of them."

"Thought one would help," he muttered as he turned his face aside, trying to clear his thoughts. "But I changed my mind. Hell," he said as he looked back at her. "What did you think I would do, seeing you like that?"

He lifted the bottle to his mouth, waiting for an answer.

"Don't you think," she said, watching him. "That you have had enough?"

"No," he replied and took another slow, deliberate drink. "I haven't had nearly enough."

His gaze focused somewhere below her face. "Sure is a revealin' dress. Course, sweetheart, I have seen you in less." He grinned drunkenly. "Sweetest Northern territory I have ever had the pleasure of ridin'."

She stiffened and drew her breath in sharply. "Oh, you are no better than a savage."

"Hell, honey," he interrupted. "Why do you have that dress on if you don't want to get a man all- worked up?"

He reached out and pulled her with him to the bed. He sat down and kept her there standing in front of him. She began to struggle but he said warningly, "Be still, 'Scensia, or I'll lay you down on the bed and keep you there until the fight is out of you."

She stopped struggling, though reluctantly. Very slowly he ran his hands along the tantalizing curves concealed by the black silk. She trembled as she felt the hard strength and the heat of his hands through the thin fabric. When he pulled her closer, she fought him again.

His hand reached up and closed around the curls at the back of her neck. "I meant what I said. If you don't stop fighting me, I'll- do what I said."

Her body went still. Her hands were closed in fists that remained against his wool-clad chest.

"That's better," he whispered in a husky voice. "Really," he went on while the back of his strong, saber-scarred hand slid slowly down her bare shoulder. "You can be damned distractin'. You make a man forget himself."

His lips pressed kisses where his hand had been wandering. He freed the first hook that held the front of the dress together. Her fingers closed around his wrist.

"Jesse, don't," she warned.

"Don't what?" he asked in his softest voice.

She remained silent. Her softly rounded flesh rose and fell before him.

"Don't do what?" he persisted. "This?" he whispered.

She barely managed to nod as he undid several more hooks and the dress loosened. He kissed the sensitive flesh of her breasts where they rose above the black lace. Her eyes slid shut.

"You still want this, 'Scensia. When I'm gentle with you. And even when- when I'm not. I felt it in the tent. I feel it now."

The catch in his voice made her slip a few notches further from reality. The harsh reality that stood like a barrier between them. And yet she was still afraid. Afraid not only that he would continue his seduction, but that he would stop his seduction. And leave her as he had left her before in the tent. So she summoned up her will against him, fragile as it was. She remembered the words he had said to her in the tent and she repeated them to him now. "Doesn't take much to get you wanting it, does it?"

He shook his head. "No," he agreed. "Not much. Not with you."

He stood up and held her against him. She didn't want to but she leaned into the hard masculine strength, felt the evidence of his arousal, hot and hard against her. No, she thought, I don't want this. She shook her head where it lay against his shoulder, seeking the denial inside herself. A denial she knew wasn't there.

"You get me this way. I can't help it," he murmured in a slurred voice against her hair.

"Did you forget how it was between us?" he went on, tantalizing her with his words until her whole body was almost aching with need.

She hadn't forgotten. No matter how hard she had tried, she couldn't. Still it was not an easy surrender for her.

"I never forgot, Jesse," she whispered the admission softly against his shoulder.

"Neither did I," he breathed.

"This is where we always end up," she whispered.

"No, 'Scensia. This is where we begin," he said very soberly in spite of his drunkenness.

She drew back slightly and dared a look up into his eyes. Eyes that had always had the ability to see deeply into her soul. How many times had she feared that he had died? She knew with a certainty that of all the things she was feeling at this moment, most of all she was grateful that he was still alive. She was grateful with every fiber of her being.

Thousands upon thousands of men had lost their lives in this war. And she had never been able to bear the thought that Jesse might be one of them. She couldn't bear the thought of never having the chance to see him again. And she admitted to herself that gratitude for his life being spared had been her uppermost thought when she had first seen him standing in the doorway of the library of Morgan's headquarters.

They were together again. Fate, it seemed, had not given up on them. She reached up and lightly traced the scar on his chin. As she continued to look at the face that had haunted her dreams, she knew what was deepest in her heart. She loved Jesse. She loved him with all her heart and her soul. She would always love him.

And she did not want to live the rest of her life without him. Nor with regret. Her hands slid up along his arms and circled his neck. She lifted her face and kissed him and knew that she had surprised him.

He deepened the kiss while his hand came up to hold the side of her face. He rested his chin against her hair for a moment. "You want sweet words, 'Scensia?" she heard him whisper. "Well, you've made me feel like no other woman ever has. And I- love you."

When he laid her down on the bed, Ascensia felt herself going back in time. To a summer night that had changed her forever. Everything in between faded away. Helplessly they gave in to the passion that was stronger and more enduring than the hate and the hurt and the mistrust. They forgot the war and everything else that had ever come between them.

When Jesse woke much later, he frowned as he tried to focus on the ceiling. He was struggling against the effects of the whiskey and having a hard time overcoming the mist that was enveloping his senses.

His hand was closed over the one that lay upon his chest and he turned to look into blue-violet eyes. She was not a dream this time and she was watching him. And in those eyes was reflected all the love and the longing and the tenderness that her heart was capable of.

Wirt turned as the door suddenly swung open. Jesse walked slowly and uncertainly into the stable. He had his pants on and his coat. But the coat was unbuttoned and his chest was bare beneath it.

Jesse weaved a little, evidently having trouble walking steadily. Wirt knew that he had had a lot to drink tonight. All day Jesse had seemed moody and preoccupied, but smoldering, too. Like a powder keg about to go off.

When Jesse had gotten up from the table, he had left a very angry red-haired woman sitting alone while he disappeared upstairs. Now, however, Jesse was grinning with a kind of cocky, pleased-with-himself look.

"Jes," Wirt said. "Ah never have seen you so tight."

Jesse's grin grew wider. "That's so," he agreed then laughed to himself as if amused at the thought. "Sure never felt like th's before."

"That girl's got you goin' round and round, Jes."

"Isn't me, Wirt," Jesse peered intently at him. " 'S th's room that's goin' round 'nd round."

Jesse leaned his back against a post, almost missing it. "You know," he went on. "She- she's the most appealin' lil' thing when she's- mad. Like lightnin', you know?"

"Dangerous like lightning, too," Wirt remarked dryly.

Jesse nodded his head. "Dangerous Y'nkee, for a fact," he agreed soberly. " 'nd she's fully armed, too," Jesse confided to his friend. "W'th deadly weapons. She fair terr'fies me with those eyes an' th't mouth. And if it's true what they say about the first stroke bein' half th' battle, then I reckon- then I lost the battle. And if you d'dn't know that, then you sure didn't know th'- the depths of my heart," he quoted seriously, placing his hand over his heart.

He laughed again. "She can provoke a man to a lot of things. Maddenin' she says I am. Sa- s'vage."

He sighed. "The lady, she admires chiv'lry. Can't intimidate her. Can't win 'er by force. An' if anyone should know th't, it'd be me." His thumb pointed to his chest.

Jesse shook his head. "But damn, Wirt, when she forgets she's mad- I'll tell you," he said confidentially. "For all her rantin' and ravin', she likes me, too. Like to run a saber through me s'metimes. And she'll shoot at me. But . . . sometimes, Wirt. Sometimes."

Jesse leaned back, trying for the post again, but missed it, lost his balance and sat down heavily in the hay. He tried to get up again but he didn't succeed. He laughed at himself. "Shoot, Wirt. Le's get s'me more whiskey. Soon's I get up." But he only leaned back and said, "Reckon though I'll stay here for a minute an' sober up some first."

"Sure, Jes." Wirt looked down at him. "You lay there for a while."

Jesse let his breath out in a long sigh as he lay back and closed his eyes. He lay there muttering to himself beneath his breath. Wirth could barely catch the slurred words, but he made out, "My sweet 'Scensia. Lord, honey, I don't know what you've done t' me."

Wirt stared thoughtfully down at his friend. He had heard Jesse's delirious mutterings about the girl while he had been sick in prison. What was memory and what was imagined fantasy conjured by his fevered brain, Wirt hadn't known. But he had heard enough tonight to realize that she had come to mean more to Jesse than Jesse, sober, would admit to himself.

Chapter 24

When Jesse had managed to get his emotions somewhat under control, he turned from the window. He was still frowning darkly, dangerously. His jaw was tight with anger as he watched the man who was speaking.

"There will be no exchange, Captain Lucane," the man repeated. "She is being escorted back to the Union lines as we speak."

"Where?" Jesse asked, low-voiced.

"At the usual exchange point," Colonel Dunmore's eyes narrowed a bit. He had never liked the headstrong young captain.

"I don't know what you were thinking, Captain," he went on. "Have you thought how this looks? Abducting a young woman and holding her hostage."

"I don't give a damn about how it looks," Jesse interrupted. "What I thought about was getting my men out of a Yankee prison before they had ropes around their necks.

"Well, you picked the wrong girl," said the Colonel. "She has friends and family in high places. Lord knows her reputation is going to suffer because of what you have done. If she wasn't already engaged to a Yankee officer, I might have to think about making *you* marry her."

Jesse looked up.

"The Major will be waiting for her at the exchange point," the Colonel said as he pulled out his watch. "I dare say, she may already be on Northern soil."

He looked at the Captain. "Naturally we intend to keep this entire affair as quiet as possible. Major Damon is agreeable, of course."

"Of course," Jesse muttered beneath his breath.

"What, Captain?"

"What did she say," Jesse asked quietly. "When you told her she was going back North?"

"Why, she was happy to hear it, of course," the Colonel replied. "Why wouldn't she be?"

The Colonel frowned a moment, recalling that actually the girl had not seemed quite as enthusiastic as she ought to have been. But he wasn't about to tell the arrogant Captain that. There was jealousy behind the antagonism that stirred him. Everywhere he went the Captain turned women's heads without even trying. "Unless, Captain, you think there isn't a woman around who can resist you."

When Jesse's head lifted, the Colonel saw the muscles in his jaw grow even tighter.

"Not that she isn't a fine-looking girl," the Colonel went on. "In fact, I will confess that I was imagining more than a pleasant ride through the countryside when I was sitting next to her in the carriage."

Jesse's face hardened as the man described his lewd imaginings. Then, with all his anger and frustration behind it, Jesse reached across the desk and smashed his fist into the Colonel's leering face.

Ascensia sat with her head bowed over her hymnal. The early sunlight falling through the open church doors behind her touched her dark hair like a halo.

"Lo then would I wander off and remain in the Wilderness. I would hasten my escape from the windy storm and tempest . . . "

These were dark days. In May of 1864 there was yet another attempt to take Richmond and bring the South to its knees. The armies clashed in the Virginia Wilderness. More than 4,000 Northern and Southern soldiers were killed. Another 21,000 were wounded or missing.

In spite of the horrifying casualties, the new Union commander, Ulysses S. Grant, refused to retreat. He committed himself to a grim and deadly game of war with Robert E. Lee in an attempt to force his way into Richmond. As a result, thousands more were added to the casualty lists.

"It's a beautiful gown," Quillie said to Ascensia. "You will be the most beautiful bride, 'Scensia."

Quillie held the long lace veil up against Ascensia's dark curls and declared that it was the most exquisite lace she had ever seen.

"Morgan was so thoughtful to send it," Quillie sighed. "You will both be so happy."

Ascensia, however, was far from being as assured about her future happiness as Quillie was. Her room at Oak Haven was strewn with new garments which were a constant reminder to her of the wedding, which seemed to her like some dark, forbidding date that loomed on the calendar.

She had only put the dress on because Quillie had insisted. Because poor Quillie was still worried sick about her missing brother and Ascensia didn't have the heart to refuse her. The wedding was a diversion for Quillie right now.

Ascensia was standing in the middle of the room, gazing at her reflection in the mirror. She looked at the gown with its richly-embroidered, tight-fitting bodice and folds of beautiful lace.

How can I wear this? She thought. How can I let this go on, or pretend that nothing has happened? That Jesse never happened? Yet she could not bring herself to say the words that would bring shame and disgrace upon herself.

Of course she couldn't go through with it. She couldn't marry Morgan. He would know that she had been with another man. Of course, he would realize who the other man had been. And she would not be able to lie about it.

"A few weeks more and you will be Mrs. Morgan Damon," Quillie said and Ascensia looked away from her reflection. That name spoken out loud made her close her eyes and bite her lips.

"You had better get out of that dress, Ascensia," Hetty said quietly. "Morgan will be here soon."

"Yes," said Quillie. "Take care that Morgan does not see you in your wedding dress. You don't want to start your marriage out with bad luck. You have already had to postpone it once."

Quillie left the room. Ascensia stood as if in a daze as she pulled the veil from her hair. She waited for Hetty to help her undress. But Hetty stood staring out the window.

Ascensia started almost guiltily as Hetty turned. "I suppose we had both better stop daydreaming," Hetty said. "You have to get dressed for dinner tonight."

Ascensia returned home late that night. It was well after midnight and the house was quiet. Everyone had gone to bed except for Ascensia and Hetty who sat talking in Ascensia's bedroom.

"I never wanted to go in the first place," Ascensia to Hetty who was watching her face closely. "I know the gossip that has already been whispered about me. And now this- " She paused. "This has just made matters worse," she whispered, looking up. "I didn't mean for any of this to happen."

Morgan had taken her to dinner and then to a play afterwards. In the vestibule of the theater she had listened to Leora Strode's subtly-veiled insults as long as she was able. And then, when she could not bear to hear more, she had reacted impulsively. She had slapped Leora.

"You can't imagine the look that Leora gave me. Even before I slapped her," Ascensia said in a hushed voice. "There was hatred, Hetty. For a moment it was so strong that it startled me. And Morgan was fairly fuming."

"I dare say," Hetty remarked quietly.

"We had the most disagreeable ride home. Morgan didn't say one word the entire time. Not one single word. He was so angry. When he left, he told me he didn't understand my behavior at all. And yet I feel that he should have- " she paused, searching for the right words. "I don't know. He should have been more understanding and supportive of me. Leora treated me viciously, Hetty. And Morgan just allowed it."

Ascensia didn't understand Morgan's behavior, either. He was bolder now than he had ever been. He was more possessive of her, more critical than in the past. He made more demands of her and seemed to expect her to never question him.

"Are you all right?" Hetty asked.

"I'm fine. I'm just tired. But it is a relief, too, Hetty, when you can say what you really feel."

"You have been through a great deal lately," Hetty said. "Maybe everything is just catching up with you."

"Yes," Ascensia said as she closed her eyes and leaned her head back against the chair. "So much has changed," she said in a voice scarcely above a whisper. "So very much. People change, too."

"Why, yes," Hetty said. "People must change." She stopped and gave Ascensia a searching look.

"It seems, Hetty, that a lifetime has passed since I- " Ascensia's voice faltered. "Since I first left Washington. We can't go back. I thought I could. But I can't. Sometimes a person changes here," she said and laid her hand upon her heart. "Things inside of me have changed."

She closed her eyes again. She had to forget Jesse. She couldn't live the rest of her life like this. But his memory kept haunting her.

So far she had managed to keep it all hidden deep inside. But how long could she do that? How long before she fell apart? She looked at Hetty as a sudden flash of lightning outside the window illuminated her face.

A shiver ran through her. Something inside of her felt very fragile. She tried to will away the pain but she felt almost paralyzed by the thing pressing down on her heart.

He hadn't even said goodbye to her. He had had her sent away without giving her a second thought. All she was to Jesse was a means for him to satisfy his lust. Why had he said he loved her? Why speak those words if he hadn't meant them?

"Ascensia I have to talk to you," Hetty began. Something in her voice made Ascensia look up.

"You should know, 'Scensia. You should know everything."

Thunder rumbled in the distance. They both grew silent, listening to it.

"You already know that there are still strong ties between families and friends in spite of this war," Hetty said. "A long time ago I began running mail through the blockade. I would place the letters in a hollow tree near the river and they would be picked up. A lot of other people did the same thing at the beginning of the war. No one thought much about it.

"People would buy up medicines and other things badly needed in the South," Hetty went on. "And send them down to the Potomac. The Rebels would come across the river and buy them. I did the same thing."

"But that is considered smuggling, Hetty," Ascensia said. "Suppose you had been caught?"

"I was safe enough," Hetty replied. "I even had quinine and morphine hidden in my hoops a few times and got it safely through the Union pickets."

"But, Hetty, our country- "

"Our country?" Hetty interrupted bitterly. "*Our country* is invading the South. And the South feels that they are defending their homes. Their rights. What kind of a government would declare medicines as contraband of war? What about the women and children who suffer, even die, without them? Did they start this war?"

" 'Scensia, do you know how many men have had to have an arm or a leg amputated without chloroform?" Hetty asked feelingly. "Can you imagine the agony? Am I so wrong to do what I can to alleviate the suffering?"

"No, Hetty," Ascensia replied with as much feeling. "No, you aren't wrong."

Hetty frowned as she glanced out the window. "Last summer I began helping escaped prisoners. They needed shelter and food until they could make their way south." She bowed her head for a moment. When she looked up, there was a haunted expression in her eyes. "I have seen men sick and faint from starvation, their wounds untended. Many of them had neither a coat nor a blanket to keep them warm in the winter. How can anyone justify such inhumanity? I have vowed to myself," she went on in a low voice. "To do all that I can to ease the misery. I shall continue to do so until the stubborn men who started this war finally find a way to end all of this madness."

"What about Holmes?" Ascensia asked. "Have you heard from him?"

A shadow came into Hetty's dark eyes. "Holmes is- " She closed her eyes for long moments. "My brother is dead," she whispered.

"How?" Ascensia asked, her own voice unsteady.

Hetty continued to stare straight ahead. "He was wounded in the first year of the war. He might have lived had there been medicine available."

"And you never confided in me, Hetty?" You bore your grief alone? How terrible it must have been for you."

Hetty's face looked suddenly forlorn. Her lips quivered slightly and Ascensia saw that she was crying.

"It was," she admitted. She wiped the tears away with the back of her hand. "Then I met someone. He came here one day after he had been wounded. He came with another man. I dressed their wounds as best I could but one of them died. He is buried out in the woods. We buried him together. But we couldn't even put a marker on the grave."

Hetty bit her lips as she remembered. "The other man lived," she went on. "And I have come to love him, 'Scensia. He didn't want me to keep on smuggling. He knew that he couldn't stop me though and so he helped me and did all that he could to make sure that I was safe. 'Scensia, I love him," Hetty repeated, closing her eyes.

Ascensia remained very still for a long time. Hetty did not know how her confession had affected her. "And how does he feel?" she asked without looking at Hetty.

"He has told me that he loves me."

"Oh," Ascensia said faintly, struggling with the pain. She was sorry for Hetty but she could not keep the bitterness from her voice when she asked, "And you think it will be easy loving a Rebel?"

Hetty's dark eyes flashed. "No. I never thought that. But love hardly comes along only when we command it to, does it?"

Ascensia had no answer. Not for Hetty or for herself. She knew very well what it was like to love the wrong man.

"I'm sorry, 'Scensia," Hetty said quietly. "I didn't mean to talk to you that way. But I love him more than I ever imagined I would love anyone."

Hetty picked up her reticule from the table beside her. She took a daguerreotype from it and held it out to Ascensia.

Ascensia looked at the picture. It showed a handsome, dark-haired man with steady eyes. But the man in the picture was not Jesse.

"His name is Rush," Hetty said softly.

"I had thought that- " Ascensia began half to herself.

"Thought what?" Hetty asked.

"Nothing," Ascensia replied. "What about Jesse?"

Hetty looked at her blankly.

"Jesse helped you, too, didn't he?" Ascensia asked without looking at Hetty. "I know that he hates Morgan. Is that why he came to Oak Haven?"

"No," Hetty replied. "Jesse was here because of the smuggling. He didn't know that Morgan- He didn't even know that you- " Hetty paused, then began again. "Yes. Jesse does hate Morgan. Oh, 'Scensia, I never meant to hurt you. But if you knew what Morgan is really like, if you knew the truth about him and what he is capable of and the wickedness that is inside of him, you would reconsider this marriage."

Ascensia stared at Hetty, waiting to hear more.

"Morgan is not the man you think he is, 'Scensia. Ambition is one thing. But Morgan is obsessed with money and power. He desires them above all else. He has been trading with the Rebels. And making a fortune at it. That is not all. He has been unfaithful to you. There have been other women. Leora is one of them. That is why she hates you so much."

Hetty watched the changing emotions on Ascensia's face. "There is more." Hetty's voice lowered. "There is something else. At the beginning of the war, when Morgan was stationed west of here, he did all that he could to punish anyone who sympathized with the South. And some that did not. I have heard that he enjoyed making people feel helpless and at his mercy.

"There was a girl," Hetty went on. "Who was alone one night. Soldiers went to her house. They- they abused her terribly. She died after. Morgan was there. Morgan was one of the men. He gave the orders."

"Hetty, how do you know all this?" Ascensia asked in a ghost of a voice.

"Because that girl was Jesse's sister."

In his cell, Jesse stopped his restless pacing. He listened to the voice out in the hallway.

A Confederate officer walked in and said, "Jes, if Ah had known earlier, Ah would have gotten you out a long time ago. If Colonel Dunmore had his way, though, you'd be in here for good. He's still mad as hell about you hitting him."

The guard came with the key. As Jesse stepped outside the cell, he vowed to himself that this was the last time he would spend behind bars.

Chapter 25

Ascensia stopped as she approached the open stable door. She was surprised to hear Morgan's voice though she did not recognize the voice that answered him. What Hetty had told her made her step back into the shadows. She did not want to see Morgan.

"Stokes is impatient for the rest of the shipment," she heard the other man say.

"Tell him he'll have it the day after tomorrow," Morgan replied.

Ascensia shrank deeper into the shadows as the other man walked to the stable door and stood gazing out. He spat a stream of tobacco juice and walked back inside.

"Where is Lathrop?" Morgan asked. "I expected him back by now."

"Foolin' with some woman. He can't leave them alone," was the reply. "He says he's found out where some of that group that rides with Jesse Lucane is hiding out. About twenty miles west of here is a farm owned by a man named Holt. They've got a temporary camp in the woods nearby. "

"Get a group of men together," Morgan said. "You know who to pick. When Lathrop gets back, have him lead you to the camp. Burn the house and everything else that belongs to that farmer. Make sure he realizes just how dangerous it is to help Rebels. Make an example of him."

"You're sure Lathrop is trustworthy?"

"I have used him before," Morgan replied. "He has proven valuable to me in the past. He is trustworthy as long as he is paid well. And I am paying him very well. If you even suspect he is going to lead you into an ambush, however, shoot him on the spot."

After a silence, Morgan inquired. "What about Lucane? Is he at the camp with the others?"

"I don't know," replied the other man. "I know Lathrop would like to see him dead though. He hates Lucane like poison and the feeling is mutual. Lucane has it in for you, too, ever since- I mean, since you had him beaten in prison, his hard feelings can't have improved any. There's a Rebel named Rush Duganne who has been prowling around lately, too. Lathrop says he's trouble and expects him to be at the camp with the others."

"You make sure and pursue them vigorously," Morgan said. "You tell your men that they are to shoot to kill. If Lucane is there, you personally take care of him. I want them killed. Every one of them, even if they try to surrender. Report that they refused to give up."

Ascensia did not stay to hear more. Hetty had been right about Morgan. She was shocked to hear that John Lathrop was near. Suppose he had seen her and recognized her?

She was conscious, however, of one fact above all others. Those men would be ambushed and murdered if she did not do something to prevent it. Rush Duganne, the man that Hetty loved, was there. And maybe Jesse was there as well.

"We must warn them," she told Hetty later. Ascensia had already made a decision. "They are at a place in the woods near the house of a farmer named Holt. Do you know it?"

"Yes, I can find it," Hetty replied.

"We will have to hurry," she said.

Hetty stared at her. "You would help them? You would help Rebels?"

"What Morgan intends is murder."

"It means a long ride, 'Scensia. A dangerous ride. We will have to get past the Union pickets," Hetty told her.

"Of course we may not succeed," Ascensia said half to herself. "But if we do not try- "

" 'Scensia, I can go alone. There is no need for you to come, too."

Ascensia's blue-violet eyes grew stormy and her voice was low as she said, "I can't marry Morgan. Not now. And I couldn't sit here knowing that you were out there alone."

"But you- "

"Hetty, there is nothing that will stop me from going."

"Have you considered, 'Scensia, how it would be? If you go with me, you can't come back for a long time."

"Yes," Ascensia replied. "I have thought of everything."

After Ascensia quietly closed Hetty's bedroom door, she went out into the hallway to her own room. She whirled around before she closed the door and breathed, "Morgan, you startled me."

"I thought you would be in bed by now," he said. "But since you're still up, you could have come down and visited with me."

Lightning flashed outside, briefly lighting Morgan's face. He had been drinking, she realized. There was something in his slow smile that chilled her, but she was determined that he would not suspect anything.

She forced herself to smile. "Of course I would have come down to see you if I had known you were coming here tonight."

"I'm glad I can use the office in the stable," he said as he moved closer to her. "It makes things convenient for us."

"I'm glad, too."

"Soon, Ascensia, you and I will be going to bed together." He ran his hand up her arm and she forced herself to endure the touch without flinching.

When he put his arm around her, she did not push him away as she wanted to. She even managed a little laugh as she whispered, "Morgan, someone will see us."

"All right," he said, kissing her once. "I guess I can wait. You'll be mine soon enough."

"Are you ready?" Hetty asked later as they sat their horses. Hetty searched Ascensia's face in the shadows of the trees. "You know you can still change your mind."

"I won't," Ascensia replied as she gathered the reins and cast an anxious glance towards the road. Morgan had ridden off but he might return at any moment.

Ascensia and Hetty shared one last look, then, without another word, they led their horses out onto the road.

For hours they traveled through the dark woods. Storm clouds gathered overhead. Thunder growled threateningly. Lightning began to flash in vivid streaks against the darkness. Ascensia could see no lights and no dwellings.

"We shall have to be very careful now so we don't get lost," Hetty said. "This stretch of road is as confusing as a maze but the house is not far ahead."

They drew their horses up in the road a little distance from a white farmhouse.

"There are no Yankees there now," Hetty told her. "Or we would have been warned away by a white cloth hung in the attic window."

Hetty dismounted and went up onto the porch. She knocked quietly at the door. The man who opened the door looked them over suspiciously. When Hetty explained why they had come, he suddenly exclaimed, "Well, I'll be damned."

He led them into his house where several Rebel soldiers who had been eating a meal peered curiously at them from the kitchen.

"You ladies sit down and rest a while," they were told. "The boys will take you along with them to the camp."

A little while later, Hetty was lifting a tin cup of hot coffee to her lips when one of the men in the camp informed her, "There's Rush now, comin' with some other men."

Ascensia felt an unexpected jolt of emotion. She searched the faces of the men who had just ridden into the camp. But Jesse was not among them.

Hetty ran over to one of the men who had dismounted. She was immediately wrapped tightly in the man's arms. Ascensia saw the surprise in his eyes as Hetty spoke to him. Several times he glanced in Ascensia's direction.

After Hetty introduced him, he said, "Ah want to thank you for coming with Hetty. Ah'm grateful for what you have done for her and for all of us."

Ascensia felt her hand clasped firmly in his. He would take them both down to the Valley, he told them, where his family lived, where they would be safe.

Chapter 26

Dusk was deepening into night as Jesse rode along the tree-lined road. A light rain was falling upon him. The camp was bedded down for the night in a little stretch of woods. After Jesse had watered and fed his horse, he walked up to a little sheltered fire and leaned back against a tree. He could smell bacon frying. The hollow feeling inside him reminded him of how long it had been since he had eaten.

Wirt walked over to him and handed him a plate of food. "Heah, Jes. Reckon you could use something to eat."

They sat down together and ate in silence. Jesse has changed, Wirt thought to himself. Lately it seemed that Jesse was driving himself far too hard. He looked worn out and preoccupied.

"Yanks still on the move?" Wirt queried.

"They are," Jesse replied absently, frowning as he ran his hand slowly across his unshaven chin. Every day he had seen the black columns of smoke from burning homes and barns, a grim reminder of the advance of the Northern Army.

"Reckon we're in for some hard work tomorrow," Wirt remarked.

"Sure," Jesse replied. "We'll fight again."

He looked up across the low glow of the sputtering campfire. The rain was falling steadily through the trees. Out there in the darkness were all the men that could be scraped up to defend the Shenandoah Valley.

They had fought the Yankees again and again, killed them by the thousands. Yet in spite of all the killing and dying they were no closer to winning this war than they had been three years ago. They fought well and it seemed that a Northern victory now and then only strengthened Southern resolve and determination.

Except they never stop coming, Jesse thought. He had seen their bodies piled in heaps. He shook his head at the appalling waste. He was tired of fighting. He was tired of having to command men, tired of having men die because of his orders.

He took a long drink of whiskey from his canteen then jammed the cork back in place and laid down under the relatively dry canvas shelter.

He was back in the Shenandoah Valley again. Farther away from Maryland but the memories were still alive. He hated it, but he still remembered.

He looked at the deep, rain-slashed gloom beyond the fire. Damn it to hell. I can't keep thinking about her like this, he told himself.

There would be another fight tomorrow. Maybe this time he wouldn't be walking away from it. He was only beginning to realize that what bothered him the most was the thought that he might not live to have even the possibility of seeing her again. He would never have the opportunity to tell her- Hell, he didn't know what he wanted to tell her. Things just seemed unfinished between them.

While the rain steadily pelted the canvas above him, the fire popped and snapped and a feeling of desolation took a deeper hold of him. It wasn't fear. He did not fear the battle, nor did he fear death exactly. He had gotten so used to those things. But a premonition of death – his death – had gripped him and he couldn't shake it off.

Maybe it was because of the dream. Twice it had awakened him. In his dream he could see the blue hills in the distance. They seemed very far away. Turning, he would see a red flag fluttering through the tree branches. A light would suddenly burst overhead and he would feel himself falling. He could feel himself dying while he turned to see Ascensia far, far from him. Beyond his reach.

He closed his eyes and his mind against further reflection. All around him, in the wet darkness, the camps grew hushed as the men laid down to sleep. Some of them for the last time. Right now, a gloom that was as tangible as the rain seemed to descend upon the earth.

The next morning Jesse was sitting his horse and looking over the Rebel lines which were posted in entrenchments behind rail breastworks. It was not yet noon. The rain had ended and a pale mist was rising from the ground. Down below him was a field of clover. Beyond it were dense trees and underbrush.

Jesse slowly buttoned his coat. He turned his face to the north to see a column of smoke rising above the trees in the distance. As he did so, every feature of his face stood out unusually clear and distinct in the early light. Wirt looked over and was struck by something in Jesse's eyes, something that made a chill pass over him.

"The Yankees do hev a fondness fer burnin' things," someone said.

Down the line, to his left, Jesse could hear a band playing the strains of the *Marsellaise*. The music stopped and suddenly all was silent in the wet woods along the crest of the hill.

Jesse could hear birds singing in the woods behind him. Here and there amid the leaves he could see the gleam of bayonets as the men awaited orders.

A line of skirmishers was sent out. Jesse's hand tightened on the reins. He pulled the brim of his hat lower over his eyes. If they lost today, then most of the Shenandoah Valley was lost as well. And that rift between the right and left wings of the army bothered him. If the Yankees managed to break through . . .

He saw movement in the woods beyond the clover field. He heard the sharp crack of musketry.

"Heah they come," someone muttered low and tense.

A long line of blue infantry came pouring out of the woods. They were moving through the knee-high clover and advancing up the hill. Jesse could hear the thud of ramrods being dropped down rifle barrels all along the Confederate line. He laid a hand reassuringly on his horse's neck. The word was shouted up and down the breastworks and the entire Rebel line exploded into one continuous sheet of flame and thunder.

The volley took its toll. Scores of men fell. But the Yankees came on. They began to fire up the hill. Balls tore into the rails and the trees around Jesse. The enemy artillery added its deep roar to the battle and the exploding shells sent fragments tearing into the ranks of human flesh and bone. The air was soon filled with smoke and thunder and fire.

Jesse watched the Yankees rise and surge up the remaining distance to the crest of the hill. "Fire!" he could hear the Rebel officers shouting.

The fighting grew desperate. The men fought savagely as the two forces clashed in hand to hand combat. Bayonets were used. Rifles were used as clubs. Some men fought with their bare hands.

A cavalryman beside Jesse suddenly flung up his arm and fell back from his saddle. Half his face had been blown away.

Another man fell back against a tree, a ghastly hole in the middle of his forehead.

A ball struck Renn's shoulder, wrenching him out of his saddle. He scrambled to his feet in the smoke and, with Jesse's help, managed to seize the reins of his horse and get back in the saddle.

Jesse felt a sudden, sharp pain in his upper leg. He looked down to see blood spreading across his pant leg. He didn't feel much pain yet.

Wirt's horse was hit next. The powerful black lunged backwards with a piercing scream.

Another ball slashed Jesse across the cheek. He could feel the side of his face grow hot from the wound. He drew his arm across his face and his sleeve came away bloody.

Without warning, a heavy ball of lead lodged into Jesse's chest, taking his breath as he reeled in the saddle. He could feel the viciousness of it inside him as he pressed the flat of his hand against the hole.

For a moment, Jesse's thoughts wandered. He lifted his gaze and saw the blue hills. He saw, too, as he turned, the red folds of the Confederate flag through the trees and the smoke.

Artillery burst right above him. Fire exploded. And thunder. Something inside Jesse seemed to burst as well and he tried to grasp his pommel because he thought that he was falling. Or somehow the ground was rising up to meet him.

Death awaited him, he knew. "If you would escape this," he told himself. "Then ride . . . out of here."

He was still mounted. But there were bleeding men on the ground all around him. His horse was prancing and snorting. Wounded, perhaps. It reared upright.

And then he was hit again – he wasn't even sure where this time – and his breath left him with a groan as he sank.

His body hit the hard ground. He could feel the pain jar all through him. He was lying on his belly. He opened his eyes and lifted his head slightly. A man looked down at him with a pitying glance as he ran past.

A breathless, deep agony pulsed inside his chest. He tried to rise but could not. "Jesus," he gritted.

The light seemed to suddenly fade. All around him the thunder grew quieter. He felt himself drifting and for a moment he was looking into a face with blue-violet eyes . . .

He tried to hold onto the vision but could not. His strength and his consciousness were fading away with the blood that was flowing from his wounds and he slipped into darkness.

Chapter 27

Ascensia looked out of the window. The sound of distant artillery had awakened her. They had expected fighting somewhere. The Shenandoah Valley was important to both armies. She frowned as she laced up her corset, having to hold her breath to pull it tight.

She fastened the buttons up the front of her dress and found that the fabric was straining a little tighter against her breasts. She was also feeling ill again this morning. It was just a vague queasiness that came and went upon waking. This morning, however, she was feeling, perhaps, a little worse.

Mrs. Duganne called from downstairs to say that breakfast would soon be ready. Kate Duganne was Hetty's mother-in-law now for Hetty and Rush had been married. Ascensia was grateful that the woman had been kind enough to welcome her into the household as well.

In fact, Ascensia was more than welcome for Mrs. Duganne had three young children still at home and she needed help in caring for them and running the farm. Her husband had died during the first year of the war. Two grown sons, besides Rush, were in the Rebel Army.

After Ascensia helped seat the children at the table, she sat down and unfolded her napkin. The smell of bacon frying filled the kitchen.

"I'm sorry I overslept again," Ascensia said, yawning. "I am usually up early. But lately I- " She broke off as Mrs. Duganne set the breakfast on the table.

Ascensia sat staring at the plate of food before her. Suddenly growing pale, she covered her mouth with her hand and ran out of the kitchen.

She stood on the back porch with her eyes closed as she fought the terrible nausea that swept over her. She felt, suddenly, too warm though a cold sweat had broken out upon her brow. For the first time in her life, she felt as if she was about to faint.

One of the children had followed her out and was looking up at her and holding onto her skirt. "Mama," the child called. " 'Scensia is looking pale and sickly."

Hetty and Mrs. Duganne came out to the porch. They insisted that she go back upstairs and lay down.

"You will feel better after you have rested," Hetty said. "She was up sewing very late last night," she told the older woman.

"Yes, you will probably feel better after you have rested," agreed Mrs. Duganne, but there was a strange look in her eyes as she watched Ascensia go upstairs.

In her room, Ascensia loosened her clothing and lay down on her bed. She lay very still and miserable for a long while but eventually she did fall asleep. It was late morning when she awoke again feeling much better.

Two soldiers were eating in the kitchen downstairs. One of them was Mrs. Duganne's son. They had been sent home to drive off all the stock they could so that the Yankees could not steal it.

The battlefield was not far away, they told the women. General Jones had set up a battle line near Piedmont and the Union forces were advancing against them. That advance was being contested along the road leading south and that was what all the cannon fire had been about.

Later in the day, a messenger rode up to the house with news of disaster. General Jones, he said, had been killed. The

Southern Army was routed and the remnants of it were falling back to Fishersville. Staunton would surely fall.

Within the hour, Mrs. Duganne received a letter from a neighbor in town frantically asking for help in caring for the wounded men that had been brought to her house.

The three women quickly packed up everything they thought would be of use, then started out for town. They found that every house along the road was taking in the wounded. Men were lying everywhere. On the porches, in the yards and along the roadside.

They stopped the wagon in front of a large white house with a picket fence running along the road. Ascensia and Hetty got out of the wagon and stood waiting at the gate. They both looked at the woman who had come out of the house. There were blood stains on her dress.

"Thank God you are here at last," she said. "We are just about desperate."

She handed two buckets to Ascensia and Hetty and said that they could begin helping by giving water to the wounded men.

It was bad enough outside but they could hear terrible shrieks of agony coming from the house. Ascensia and Hetty glanced at each other as they filled their buckets at the well. Neither spoke.

Kate Duganne soon came outside and asked Ascensia if she would help inside. As they stepped up onto the porch together, a piercing scream from the house made them both pause.

"It is hard, I know," Kate said. "But you must try and be brave. For them."

Wounded soldiers lined the front hallway. The parlor to her right was filled with them. Even the staircase was crowded with men. There was blood on everything. It stained the wood floors and the carpeting. It was smeared on walls and furniture. There were trails of blood leading from room to room.

Ascensia made her way carefully, drawing her skirts aside, afraid that she might brush against someone's wound. In the kitchen, Kate silently handed her another bucket filled with water.

Left alone in the kitchen, Ascensia was overwhelmed for a moment by the suffering that surrounded her. There were pleading eyes and there were hopeless ones. Some of the men were asking for water. The cries of others almost unnerved her. "Someone. Please . . . help me," begged one voice.

"Oh . . . God . . . God . . . " was the pitiful cry of another.

A young soldier lying in a corner of the kitchen whispered feebly, "Mother." The man beside him begged in a quivering voice for someone to shoot him.

Imploring eyes sought her on all sides. "Ma'am, can you give me some water, please?" and "Ma'am, my friend here . . . "

She knelt down by one then, rising, went to another. She was soon working with a fierce energy. She was shocked at the heartrending scenes around her. These were human beings. Yet they were suffering the worst kinds of agonies with no one to care for them and no one to comfort them.

They were dying alone, too. She went out onto the back porch and stared in horror at a young lieutenant who lay gasping out his last breaths before death. A private lay dead in a corner, dead before his wound had even been looked at.

Stripped of all the glory and the grandeur, this was the sickening reality of war. This was what remained. Horror and suffering and violent death.

She worked hard all through that day. Night fell and darkness filled the house with shadows. Lantern light wavered fitfully over the faces of the men. The moaning sounds did not cease. The hushed voices of the women mingled with the sounds of suffering. Every now and then a whispered prayer or a sob would rise.

It was the shrieks from the dining room, however, that were the hardest to bear. The doctor was working in there. Ascensia would always lower her eyes when she had to pass that open doorway. In a huge barrel outside the window were piled arms and legs that had been amputated. She had heard someone say that they had run out of chloroform.

In one of the upstairs bedrooms she came across a Confederate captain who was cradling a younger soldier in his arms. The wounded man had been shot in the head. They had bandaged the wound but nothing more could be done for the man. Though he was still alive, he was unconscious and his life was slowly fading away.

Ascensia knelt before the Captain and asked if there was anything she could do for him. He shook his head slowly. But the stricken look in his eyes affected her deeply.

As she left the room, she heard the Captain's words as he gathered the young soldier closer and she realized that they were brothers. "Goodnight," the Captain whispered. "Don't be afraid. I'll stay with you. I'll stay till you go to sleep."

Thunder cracked out in the darkness. Ascensia stood in the front hall, looking out the open door. Lightning lit the sky in the distance. She suddenly lifted her face and prayed fervently. "Help us. Help them."

It began to rain, a soft ticking sound at first. Then it began to beat down harder till it was drumming steadily on the roof above her.

It was falling, too, upon the men lying outside in the yard. Some of the wounded had little makeshift shelters of canvas or blankets which had been put up earlier to keep them out of the sun. Many of them, however, still lay exposed to the rain and she could hear their piteous groans out in the darkness.

Kate Duganne came to the door with some old quilts and several pieces of carpeting. Together the women did what they could to fix crude shelters over the men.

Ascensia bent over a pale-faced soldier and tried to secure a piece of heavy quilt over him. She straightened with difficulty. Her back was aching. Her hair and dress were soaking wet.

The yard was soon drenched. She stepped through the water-filled wagon ruts and felt the water soaking through her boots. The hem of her dress dragged through the mud. She looked out through the darkness and saw that there were lights lit in every house down the road as far as she was able to see.

"Give me strength," she prayed. "Don't let me think about how tired I am." And she went on working with a grim determination while the rain continued to beat down upon her.

She looked up to see more wagons coming slowly down the road. More wounded men arriving. And she thought, "Jesse. Oh, Jesse. Where are you in all this?"

They took the men out of the wagons and laid them in rows. She looked to the side of the house. Some of the men who had died lay in a row there, beneath a soaked wool blanket. She looked away.

Cavalry came riding along the road. Someone near the gate called to her. "Ma'am, can you help a wounded man here?"

The wounded man was leaning over his pommel. His coat was bloody and his face was pale beneath the dark brim of his hat. She gave a little cry as she recognized him.

"Why," Renn Parrish exclaimed as he looked down at her. "Ah nev' thought to see you down heah."

She hastened her steps to keep up with the two men who were helping him to the house. There were men behind her and she turned. One of them was Wirt Blackford. She quickly searched the faces of the other men but did not see the one she was seeking.

"Where is Jesse?" she asked.

Wirt looked at her but said nothing. She looked at the other men's faces but they glanced away. She looked back at Wirt and felt a chill colder than the rain seep through her veins.

"There's no other way to tell you," Wirt began in a rough voice. "He was killed."

For a moment the faces of the men blurred before her. She leaned against the porch rail and might have collapsed if one of the men had not rushed towards her and put his arm around her to hold her up.

Yet Ascensia was scarcely aware of the action. She kept telling herself that they had made a mistake or that she had heard wrong. Jesse couldn't be dead. And yet the reality of death was all around her.

"Are you all right?" the soldier who was holding her up asked her anxiously.

"How?" she asked in a dread whisper. "When?"

"Ma'am," implored the man beside her. His own voice was rough with grief. "Ah think you ought to sit down for a while first."

Ascensia shook her head a little wildly. "I need to know."

"Ah saw him fall," another man said quietly. "I saw him hit. More'n once. After he fell from his horse, Ah saw him try to get up. But he never did."

"Where is he?" they heard her ask.

After a pause, Wirt said in a stricken voice, "Still there on the field. But Ah'll be goin' to look for him and bring him back."

As the men were riding away, Wirt turned back to the house for a moment. She was still standing at the rail while the rain fell upon her bare head. Even in the darkness he could see how pale she was. She had shed no tears for Jesse, but it seemed to him that the life had gone out of her as well.

Long after the men had disappeared down the road, Ascensia stood with her hands tightly gripping the rail. She still felt faint. She lowered her head, feeling the rain beating down upon her, trying to think only of the rain . . .

She experienced a fluttering sensation inside her breast. And for a moment it seemed as if she were suffocating while the sharp pain settled like a knife that was slowly, agonizingly piercing a wound deep inside her heart.

Jesse can't be dead, she told herself. He can't be like those men lying under that blanket. He can't be cold and still and— She closed her eyes tightly.

She could hear the wounded men all around her. In a daze, she turned, locking it all inside her because she knew she couldn't bear it if it got hold of her.

She saw a little group of men lying huddled under a bit of canvas. She walked over to them.

They were dying men. Nothing could be done for them. No time could be spent on them while others might be saved.

She knelt down beside the man nearest her. Both of his hands were pressed against the wound in his stomach. She knew that he would be dead before the night was over.

She sat down in the mud beside him. He looked mutely up at her. His mouth was drawn in a tight grimace of pain and she pushed her own pain deeper inside.

He won't die alone, she vowed silently. She cradled his head in her lap. She leaned closer to hear his simple request. She could just catch the faint, whispered words. And while the rain beat down hollowly on the canvas above them, she brushed his hair gently and began to sing softly for him.

While I draw this fleeting breath,
When my eyelids close in death,
When I soar to worlds unknown,
See Thee on Thy judgment throne,
Rock of Ages, cleft for me,
Let me hide myself in Thee . . .

There was a haunted look to Ascensia as she stood in the hallway. Her eyes were drawn to the dining room where the lantern light revealed a man lying on the table. The surgeon was bending over him.

The table was slick with blood. It glistened in the eerie light. It dripped down to the floor below and ran along the cracks in the wood.

There was no medicine. They gave the man a drink of the family's brandy. There was nothing else to give him.

Ascensia backed up to the staircase. Her hand gripped the railing. She watched the doctor remove the crude, bloody bandage around the man's leg. With a sponge – the same one that had been used on a hundred other men's wounds – he wiped away the blood. He began to probe the ragged hole with his fingers while the soldier gritted his teeth to keep from screaming.

The man's flesh glistened with sweat. She saw the rapid rise and fall of his chest as the surgeon wiped the blade of his knife against his coat to clean away the blood from the last surgery.

She jerked away and shut her eyes as a wave of horror surged through her. She tried to take a deep breath of air, but could smell only the sickening odor of blood. She was going to be sick. With a fierce effort, she held back the bile rising in her throat.

Suddenly it was too much for her. Suddenly she knew she couldn't bear to hear the shrieking, or see the spurting of blood, or hear the grating of the bone saw or the thump of the leg as it fell into that huge wooden bucket.

"Hold him down," she heard, then the maddened curses of the man, "God . . . Oh, Jesus."

Blindly she turned and stumbled up the stairs. As she reached the second floor landing, she heard the scream. It became a wail, a horrible, horrible sound that echoed and re-echoed through the house.

She stood on the landing, faint and swaying while that scream echoed in her ears. Then everything seemed to fade into nothingness and she drifted into a black void where she could not hear or see or feel anything.

Chapter 28

Out of the mist in which he was drifting came a murmur of low cries. The air around him was sulpher-tainted. He was lying on his belly, he realized, with his right arm outstretched. With each breath he took he could feel pain deep inside his chest.

Jesse lifted his eyelids slightly and focused on the grass in front of his face. He could feel soft blades of it against his lips. The damp earth beneath him felt cool against the side of his face where the ball had cut across it.

His mouth felt dry. When he ran his tongue across his lips, he could taste the mud that he was lying in. He was thirsty. Terribly thirsty.

With an effort, he lifted his head and saw several bodies lying around him. Some blue. Some gray. He tried to push himself up with one arm. But the movement made him suck in a raspy breath and go still.

He knew, though, that he would have to see to his wounds soon, no matter how much pain it caused. He brought his hand back slowly and carefully and found where the ball had entered his chest.

He barely ran his fingers over it, but the pain was intense, made him breath hard for a moment. The blood was still trickling out of the hole, running warmly against his fingers.

He heard a groan not far away. He looked up to see a Yankee soldier sitting against a tree. The front of the man's shirt was covered with blood. His hands were red where he held them pressed against his chest.

"You're alive," the man whispered faintly. "I'm shot through the chest. You?"

"Chest, too," Jesse managed. "An' leg."

He could hear faint cries from other wounded men. All of them were probably so badly wounded that they had been left for dead. And he had been left with them. He had to get up, he knew, or he would bleed to death.

He managed to turn onto his back. But a warm rush of blood flowed out of his wound and with it more of his strength. The pain and the effort had been so great that he slipped into unconsciousness once more.

Jesse sensed light flickering before him. Fitful flashes that came and went. At first, when he opened his eyes, he had to close them again. The pain throbbed fiercely through his head.

When he lifted his eyelids again, he saw only blackness before him. Gradually he could distinguish the darker shadows of the trees above him. The branches seemed to sway as if by the wind. He could hear a whispering sound through the dense foliage around him.

He attempted to turn his head and a kind of crimson agony burst inside his brain. For a long time he drifted in the haze of consuming pain.

"I'm sure not dead," he told himself with grim humor.

He had lain on the battlefield for a long time though. It was night now. There was only darkness with that strange, elusive light. Thunder muttered lingeringly and he realized that it was lightning he had seen.

The first numbness of his wounds had worn off. He hurt all over. The wound in his leg felt hot and raw. He could feel a slow, throbbing agony inside his chest.

He tried to move and discovered that he was weaker than before. A kind of pervasive trembling consumed him throughout his body. His voice was maddeningly faint, scarcely more than a whisper as he tried to call to the Yankee.

He turned his face, gritting his teeth against the shards of pain that pulsed through his head. He heard himself groan. With an effort, he focused his gaze where he thought the man had been.

For a moment he could see only the intense darkness beneath the trees. A brief flash of lightning suddenly revealed the Yankee. He was still slumped against the tree. His face was ghastly pale. His mouth sagged open. His eyes stared ahead without seeing.

Jesse closed his own eyes and laid back. He heard the thunder again, more ominous in this place of death. He realized then that there were no more cries out in the darkness.

Fever seemed to be coming upon him. He ran his tongue across his lips and they felt dry and raspy. He had to get out of here. He had to move or he would die. He would be like- He forced himself not to think about it.

He gritted his teeth and turned onto his side. The pain was like a raging fire. He lay still for a long time, weak and trembling and panting against the agony. Then, carefully, slowly, he began to drag himself over to the dead Yankee.

It took him a long time to crawl the short distance. It took most of his strength. He reached for the canteen. He had to pry the strap from the man's stiffened fingers but he got the canteen to his lips and sipped weakly at the liquid inside.

He coughed a little and closed his eyes, almost smiling with gratitude. The water was laced with whiskey. Maybe it will take away some of this God-awful pain, he thought.

He became aware of voices. They were faint sounds against the greater noise of the wind in the trees. Light flitted beyond the brush. Lantern light, Jesse realized. Off in the darkness, not far away, were search parties. Likely they were Yankee search parties.

He had to get away before they found him and took him to another prison. Safety lay south. But he was not sure which way was south. There was a heavily wooded area not far in front of him, beyond the dead Yankee.

He tried to rise. He fell back again, not able to stifle a moan. He knew he would have to drag himself the distance.

Out of the darkness came the soft snort of a horse. Jesse opened his eyes and heard the quiet rattling sound of a bridle chain as if a horse was shaking its head. He turned in the direction of the sound and saw the horse standing not far away.

The reins were trailing on the ground. There was a canteen on the saddle and the horse was healthy enough to be eating grass.

Slowly, Jesse got himself up on one arm. He brought his good leg forward though it seemed to take forever. When he tried to move his other leg, the pain that leaped both in his leg and in his chest sickened him. He wouldn't allow himself to stop, however. Even though he had to clench his teeth tightly together to keep from crying out.

He finally stood, wavered. The blood was welling from his chest, it seemed, with every breath he took. He drew his breath in as deeply as he could and held it. Everything around him began to spin and he half fainted. His knees almost buckled under him. He stood with his head hanging down, his face dead white.

The horse nickered. He was afraid the horse would move off or shy beyond his reach. He wouldn't be able to chase it down.

He started forward and at last was able to clutch at the bridle strap, but it had taken almost everything out of him. He leaned against the saddle, willing himself not to black out.

His hand slid along the reins and he reached up for the pommel. He gripped it. But the horse did not like the smell of blood on him. It shied and walked around in a half circle.

Jesse would not let go of the reins, however. He pulled on them and stopped the horse from going any further. Still holding the reins, he reached up with his other hand so that he was gripping the pommel with two hands. Then he slowly raised his left foot and felt his boot slip through the stirrup.

"Just one pull and I'll be up," he told himself. "Just forget the pain."

With all his remaining strength, Jesse pulled himself up into the saddle. He continued to hold the pommel with both hands, swaying as the pain tore through him. He was just barely conscious. He had a strange, breathless feeling. He knew the ball had jarred inside his chest. He could feel the blood flow out in a hot gush.

How much more blood could he lose, he wondered? How much longer did he have before he bled to death? He was so maddeningly weak. His head ached and there was a sick feeling in his belly. He was nauseated, too.

He nudged the horse with his boot. But the animal did not move. He dug his heels in harder. "Come on," he muttered savagely. "Move."

The horse started forward, breaking into a torturous trot. As Jesse sagged low over the pommel, he thought, "Have to bind up those wounds . . . "

He hoped that the horse would head south. They would retreat south. Had to ride around the cliffs near the river . . . and find the road . . .

Instinct was all that kept him mounted. He kept drifting in and out of consciousness. He was riding through the woods.

Because he was incapable of avoiding the trees or guiding the horse, he had to endure the lash of branches all around him.

The blackness kept creeping upon him though he tried to fight it. He would wake to find himself leaning far down over the pommel. He would feel it digging into his breast bone. He knew he was not going to be able to last much longer. He was burning with fever and he had been alarmed to discover that his thoughts were beginning to wander.

He sank lower and lower. Finally, clutching blindly at the pommel, he slid from the saddle and fell heavily to the ground.

He lay still in the high weeds that surrounded him. When he tried to move, he found that he could not. He became confused. He thought that he had been on a scout and had fallen asleep and had to get up and make his report. Suddenly he could feel the cool rain falling down upon his face. Weakly he moved his arm to shield it.

He lapsed into a half-conscious state that maddened him with its wild visions. He jerked awake with a start, thought that he had laid down to sleep on top of a huge black snake and that the serpent was digging its fangs and its poison deep into his chest.

During a moment of awareness, he heard his own voice calling for water. He thought that he was back at his old house in Maryland and that someone was waiting there for him.

Out of the black void that surrounded him, he lost all sense of time. Time was endless, he saw clearly now. There was no beginning and no end. But now was his time to die. And who would blame him? He had tried . . .

Someone was moving about in the wet weeds near him. Over the rain, Jesse could hear a woman's voice calling. "Here. I've found him."

He wasn't quite sure if it was real or if it was a dream. But he heard the voice again and turned towards it.

He noticed the woman's dark hair first. It was unbound. Wet from the rain, it hung over her shoulders in thick coils. He could not focus in on her face. He only saw her dark eyes staring at him.

" 'Scensia," he whispered faintly. "Get me away from here."

Of course, there is no way to be certain of the exact date that your baby will be born," the doctor told Ascensia. "But you must rest and take care of yourself. You can't work as hard as you have been. Do you understand?"

"Yes," Ascensia replied vaguely as she stared out of the window. Her mind wandered off to the night that they had spent together. And now because of that night, she was carrying his child.

Jesse's child. She imagined a little boy with dark hair and mist-colored eyes. But Jesse would never know.

And she remembered, too, that she had once told him that she didn't want to see him again. Ever. And now it was forever.

Chapter 29

The Confederate cavalrymen sat their horses a little distance down the road and watched the man in gray come riding back under a white flag of truce.

"Not there," the man said as he reined in his horse. He glanced briefly at the barn behind him which had been turned into a Yankee hospital. He had searched among the wounded. He had looked at the faces of the unburied dead who were lying in rows behind the barn.

They had searched throughout the countryside for Jesse. They had stopped at countless houses filled with wounded men. They had ridden back and had looked for him over the trampled, bloodied battleground and among the shattered railpens. They had searched the brush and the thickets.

They had done all they could to find Jesse's body and take him back so that they could give him a decent burial. But they had not found him.

"There's one more house up this road where there's supposed to be a few wounded men," a scout said. "We might try there."

Wirt nodded as he stared through the trees ahead. He looked down at his hands as they clasped the reins. Bowing his head, he wept openly for his friend.

The wagon slowly made its way up the road. Ascensia braced herself as they jolted over some deep ruts. "Sorry," said the boy beside her as he gritted his teeth against the lurching.

Kate Duganne's twelve year old son, Will, had offered to drive Ascensia back to town to see how the wounded were doing while he picked up some supplies for his mother.

Most of the wounded men had made their way out of town already. They had escaped as best they could, preferring to endure anything rather than remain to be captured and sent to a Northern prison.

There were about fifteen badly wounded men left behind, however. All of them were completely helpless and would probably eventually be taken prisoner. Renn's wound had not been serious enough to keep him behind. He had gone with the other men.

Ascensia was still staying with Kate Duganne. But Hetty had gone away with Rush. He had been badly wounded and needed close care. They had loaded him onto a wagon and both he and Hetty had headed south where they would be safer with relatives.

Hetty had cried half the night at the thought of leaving Ascensia behind. They all agreed, however, that a long, hard trip would not be the best thing for her right now. Will left her at the house and drove off to pick up the supplies.

"I told you they are corrupt, wicked villains," Ascensia heard from the kitchen. "They are searching all the houses. They will come here, too. Of course, they act brave enough when they ride up to a house where there are only women and children," the woman went on. "They even searched my bedroom. Looking for contraband, they said. And you should see the mess they made of the carpets with their spurs and their muddy boots.

"And then," she continued indignantly. "They had the effrontery to demand that I serve them breakfast this morning. Of course I refused."

"What did they do then?" another woman asked.

"Why the oaths I heard would make a sailor bush," was the reply. "They are just as insolent as can be. And they will come here, too. You may count on that."

They did come. After helping to serve the wounded men breakfast, Ascensia looked out the window to see a crowd of blue-clad soldiers marching by the house. Later, Rebel prisoners were halted by the fence. Several Union soldiers were standing guard over them.

Ascensia went downstairs and met a Union soldier coming out of the kitchen. He was carrying a sack over his shoulder that was overflowing with potatoes and other food supplies.

"What are you doing with that food?" she asked and followed him to the front porch.

"Confiscating it," was his abrupt reply.

"Confiscating?" she echoed. "Don't you mean stealing?"

He dropped the sack on the porch floor and turned back to her.

"You would take food from wounded men?" she asked in disbelief. "How are we supposed to feed them?"

"Those wounded men are Rebels," he replied. "They are prisoners of war now." He walked past her and went back into the house.

Ascensia was right behind him as he flung open one of the bedroom doors. Several wounded men were in the room. The man looked boldly around. Finding nothing in there to suit him, he went back into the kitchen.

She followed him and asked in an angry voice, "Are you more proud of stealing from defenseless men? Or from women and children? Because you are doing both."

He ignored her but muttered something about damnable female Rebels. "Give me the key to that cupboard," he ordered her.

She quickly snatched the key from the wall where it was hanging.

"Give me that key," the man repeated.

She faced him defiantly. "You may try and take it from me. But I won't give it to you."

He pulled out his pistol. Without hesitation he took deliberate aim at her.

Ascensia steadily returned his gaze. "Of course you would murder a woman over a sack of potatoes." With the key still in her possession, she walked out of the kitchen.

"Give me that key," he shouted. "Or you are going to die over a sack of potatoes."

He followed her out onto the veranda and banged the door loudly. It drew the attention of the men in the road.

"Damn you, I'll shoot!" he warned, brandishing his pistol before her.

She called him a coward but would not give in. Even the guards in blue were abashed at the man's behavior. The man glanced over at them. Controlling himself somewhat, he lowered his pistol.

He couldn't bear her getting the best of him, however. As he looked into her defiant face, he snarled and stepped closer to her. He put his hand out and grabbed her bodice while attempting to pry the key from her hand.

Out by the fence, the Confederate prisoners were hurling threats at the man. Several of them pressed boldly through the gate and started towards the veranda. They were prevented from going further by the guards. The man had let go of

Ascensia but an angry warning still rose from the group of prisoners.

"Hey, bluebelly," one of them called. "If you were brave enough to pursue us as hard as you pursue defenseless women, you might have a chance of winning the war."

The man on the veranda replied that the Southern women were as bad as the men. He had faced many a Rebel, he said with a sneer, and had found that they sure could run.

"Yeah," retorted one of the prisoners. "And you found that out while you were looking over your shoulder."

The man eventually left with his sack of potatoes. He never did get the key from Ascensia. Throughout the afternoon the women in the house waited for something more to happen. But though Union soldiers continued to pass along the road, they were not disturbed further.

The afternoon was drawing to a close and Ascensia went outside to draw some water from the well. She was tired. Mindful of the doctor's orders, she set her bucket down for a few minutes and rested in the shade.

She looked at the sunlight slanting down through the trees and pushed a stray curl back from her face. She looked up to see a horseman on the road. He was a dark shadow in the bright light that was falling around him. As she continued to watch the man, she froze as the blood drained out of her face.

She knew that he had seen her. She knew because he suddenly wheeled his horse and sat in the middle of the road watching her.

She went back into the house. She walked into the kitchen where she stood breathlessly staring at the doorway. She heard the front door open and the sound of bootsteps slowly approaching the kitchen.

"Surprised to see me?" Morgan asked softly.

He was watching her face closely. His eyes were hard and coldly speculative. "You can imagine," he said. "How surprised

I am to see *you*. Everyone has been wondering what happened to make you and Hetty disappear the way you did.

"What have you been doing?"

"I- " she faltered. "I have been taking care of the wounded men here."

"Rebels," he said and one corner of his mouth drew back in an ugly sneer as he considered her. "You're fond of Rebels, are you?"

As he stepped into the kitchen, she involuntarily took a step backward.

"What's wrong?" he asked between his teeth, barely holding his anger in check. "Aren't you happy to see me?"

"I- " she began then fell silent.

"Didn't you think I would be worrying about you? Wondering all this time about you. About my bride to be." The words were forced from him with bitterness. "And I find you here-

"Look at me!" he demanded savagely.

After a silence, he gritted, "You can't do it, can you? You can't look me in the face."

He suddenly reached out and grabbed her arm. "It's true," he breathed with disgust. He let go of her arm, almost shoving her from him. He half turned from her, then suddenly swung around to face her again.

"I know that it was Jesse Lucane who rode off with you that first time. A man named Lathrop told me. And all the time that he was at Oak Haven," Morgan went on. "You knew who he was. Yet you didn't say a word. Why didn't you, Ascensia? Why didn't you say anything if you knew he was a Rebel?"

"I couldn't," she whispered. "He was- He- "

"He was having you then, wasn't he? You let him bed you while you were engaged to me. You whore. You damned lying whore." His face was contorted with so much hate that it frightened her.

"And then because he hadn't had enough, he came back for more. And you spent all that time riding with him and his men. How many of them- "

"It wasn't like that," she broke in.

"How do you even dare stand there before me?" he breathed. "You ought to get down on your knees and beg me for forgiveness."

Her head lifted. She met his eyes and said, "You like to see women humbled, don't you?"

He stiffened. His eyes narrowed.

"I know about what happened to that girl," Ascensia whispered. "I know what you did. How can you explain that away?"

He looked down at her and said coldly. "Maybe some of the men got a little rough. But it was her fault. She fought too hard."

Ascensia stared at him with revulsion.

He gave an ugly little laugh. "*You* are judging *me*? *You*? A whore like you? Why, the Rebel bastard probably did the same things to you."

"Jesse never forced me to do anything," she blurted and immediately realized that she had made a mistake. She had never seen such rage in any man's face.

Morgan stood speechless. But his hands were clenched as if he wanted to put them around her throat. Frightened, she backed away. He lunged towards her. Grabbing her hair, he jerked her head up towards him.

"You deceitful bitch!" he hissed through his teeth. "I will make you beg. Do you know that? I will make you get down on your knees and beg."

Ascensia choked back the impulse to cry out, terrified by the look in his eyes. He suddenly released her and stepped back. Union soldiers had entered the house.

They took most of the food and they took off some of the wounded men as prisoners. Ascensia had no way of knowing what would become of them. She went back to Kate's house that day.

She was sitting in one of the upstairs bedrooms watching the sunlight fall across the four-post bed. Noble Young was sleeping peacefully on the bed. The sheets were stained with his blood. But she was relieved to see that his bandages were not soaked with blood this morning. The bleeding had finally stopped. He looked terrible, but Ascensia felt certain that he would live.

Wirt Blackford and some other soldiers had brought Noble here two nights ago. He had been shot and couldn't ride any further. They didn't know where else to take him. She had done all she could to help him. Maybe she had saved his life. But she worried that Union soldiers might come at any time and take him away.

Each new day brought word of house searches and arrests and other outrages. Three nights ago someone had broken into the barn and stolen the horses. No one had been aware of the theft until the next morning. It was frightening to realize how vulnerable they were. Ascensia and Kate were alone with the children. The only man in the house was twelve year old Will. And Noble.

A slight breeze stirred Noble's hair as she sat watching him. She walked to the window. The morning sun was warm upon her. The wind beckoned like a compelling whisper, stirring old memories. She raised her hand and clasped it against her breast. Suddenly she was filled with remembering. She drew a ragged breath and let it out slowly along with the tears. She bowed her head as a name quavered upon her lips. "Jesse."

On that same sun-lit morning, a dark-haired woman was looking down upon the haggard face of a wounded soldier. He was still unconscious.

She walked over to the curtains and parted them for a moment as she looked out. The light bothered the man. It made him frown and murmur a protest as he turned his head.

She placed her hand on his forehead and his own hand moved to push hers away. Suddenly he was breathing deeply. His delirious voice filled the room. "Forward," he said in a loud voice.

In his fevered brain, he was in the midst of the fighting again. For days he had rambled on this way, muttering orders or talking wildly of the battle. Since they had found him, she had feared that every moment might be his last. But a faint spark of life still flickered within him. It would not go out.

"Send so- " he would often whisper, slurring the words together so that she could barely make them out. And she wondered who he wanted them to send.

She sat down beside the bed. She picked up her Bible and began to read to him. Her soft voice must have reached through the fever somehow for it seemed to comfort him. His lips still moved, but his deranged mumblings had grown quiet.

As she read on, she glanced over at the rise and fall of his chest beneath the white bandages. Yesterday she had washed his shirt and mended the holes in it. That had been her comfort.

His voice rose again. He raved incoherently and she cooled his brow with a cloth that she dipped in the pitcher on the table.

"Sounds like he is still fighting the Yankees," came a man's voice from the doorway.

The man came into the room and shook his head. "By God, Ah wouldn't have believed he would live this long."

The woman pressed the cloth to the man's face and said quietly, "I was thinking about Cole. Hoping he didn't die hard. Lingering on for a long time like this one."

The man and woman were silent for a time, thinking about the son that they had lost. "I hope Cole had someone with him," she murmured.

The man laid his hand comfortingly on his wife's shoulder. It was the woman of her. It was as if somehow this spared life could make up for the loss of their only child.

"Soon as we can, we'll go on up to that Wilderness," he said to her. "And we'll bring Cole back home if we can."

He squeezed her shoulder, but there was a catch in his voice when he said, "Ah got to get that work done." As he limped out the door, he could still hear the whispered words that fell from the man's lips as he wiped a tear from his eye.

Chapter 30

The hand stirred where it lay against the white sheet. He was aware of the quiet first. The deep, soft, comfortable quiet. He was lying on a bed, he realized. He opened his eyes slowly and gazed about. He frowned slightly, recalling someone near him. Even in his dreams he had been aware of the presence of someone close by.

Maybe he was in a hospital. He could be a prisoner in a Union hospital. That thought made Jesse tense up. But the tightening of his muscles caused the pain to stab through him and he lay still. Wherever he was, he wasn't in any condition to do anything about it.

His gaze wandered along the ceiling. He watched the leaf shadows where they danced against the sun-lit wall. His gaze roamed slowly around the unfamiliar room. He was in a bedroom. Early day, he thought. Near noon by the light.

He was not in a military hospital then. But he wondered just where he was, and who had brought him here. He frowned, lifted his arm carefully and ran his hand along his bearded face. He could feel intense pain along the muscles of his chest. He could feel the tightness of bandages wrapped around him and knew that his wounds had been dressed. They had probably bandaged his leg as well. He wondered, with a sudden panic, if he had lost it.

With an effort, he lifted his head and saw that his leg was still intact. He had to lie back down again because he was so weak. "Where in God's name am I?" he wondered as the door suddenly opened.

"You awake now?" a man's voice asked after a silence.

"Reckon I am," Jesse replied. "Where am I?"

The man did not have a chance to answer for a woman had come into the room. She immediately walked over to the bed and laid her hand upon Jesse's forehead. "Why, you are looking so much better this morning, Captain. Are you in much pain?"

"Some," Jesse whispered weakly. "Feel it inside when I breathe."

"I shouldn't be surprised," she said. "The ball tore very deeply into your chest. We got it out but you had three other wounds as well."

"You were at death's door for certain," the man said. "But something reached out and plucked you back to life. Ah can't explain it. Maybe someone praying for you had their prayers answered. My wife sure did her share of praying."

"How'd you find me, bring me here?" Jesse asked.

"Your horse wandered into our yard. When we saw the blood stains on the saddle, we went out to look for you. My wife found you lying out in our pasture. She's been caring for you night and day."

"I'm grateful," Jesse breathed. "Have I come a long way then?"

"Pretty far from the fighting," the man replied.

"What about the battle?" Jesse asked.

"We hear that General Jones was killed and that the Yanks are in Staunton. We have been worried that they would come here and find you. But they haven't come yet," the man went on. "Ah have been taking care of your horse. Got him hid deep in the woods."

"You have lost a lot of blood," the woman said. "The best thing for you to do, Captain, is to rest and get stronger. You have had a long, hard fight back. We surely intend to do our best to keep you safe. Right now let's see if you can keep some food down. And then I would like to change your bandages and apply some fresh herbs to your wounds."

"Yes, ma'am," Jesse smiled faintly, too weak to do anything but lay there and obey the woman.

The woods lay still and sultry in the heat. There was a faint haze hanging over everything. And silence. Only the shrill screech of the locusts rising now and then broke the stillness. And the quiet sounds of the children playing.

Ascensia had rolled the sleeves of her calico dress back. Her skirt was tied up to keep it from dragging in the dirt. She took one of the children's shirts from the laundry basket at her feet and hung it on the hemp line to dry. She had washed her hair that morning and it was loose and curling down her back as it dried in the warm sun.

She suddenly straightened and looked towards the North. A black spire of smoke was rising up into the cloudless sky.

She looked towards the road and saw that Will had also stopped and was looking in the same direction. He turned and she knew that he was looking past the first bend in the road, a section that could not be seen from the house or the yard.

He came running back to the house. "Soldiers, 'Scensia," he panted. "Yankee soldiers comin' up the road."

They hurried the other children into the house. Kate told them to go upstairs. Ascensia went up with the children and called, "I will see to Noble."

She made the children go into one room. She then went to Noble's room and told him to stay quiet, that there were soldiers coming down the road.

Ten year old Augusta Duganne had followed Ascensia into the bedroom. She was frightened and she whispered, " 'Scensia, what will we do?"

"Everything that we can," Ascensia replied as she looked out the window.

The road in front of the house was filled with mounted soldiers in blue. They rode up to the gate and then came right into the yard. Some of them dismounted and walked up to the house.

Noble was looking over Ascensia's shoulder. He asked for his pistols.

"No," she whispered. "No. You couldn't possibly defend yourself against all of them. You would just get yourself killed and maybe one of the children as well. We will have to think of something else."

Noble was still very weak. They helped him across the room and concealed him behind the heavy draperies. Ascensia threw a heavy quilt over the blood-stained sheets.

They waited tensely and heard a loud knock on the front door. Ascensia opened the bedroom door slightly and saw Kate talking to an officer in the front hall. Several soldiers were standing on the veranda behind him.

"Ma'am, are you Kate Duganne?" the officer inquired.

"Yes."

"Is it true that your husband and two of your sons are in the Rebel Army?"

"Yes," Kate replied. "I have never denied it. Only my husband died defending his country and I have *three* sons in the Confederate Army," she informed him.

"I have orders to search your house and the outbuildings, ma'am."

"Whatever for, Captain?" Kate asked.

"For contraband."

Kate hesitated as long as she dared then opened the door wider. There was little she could do, she remarked to the officer, to stop armed men from forcing their way into her home.

Ascensia closed the bedroom door and looked at Augusta who was terribly frightened. They could hear the opening and closing of doors downstairs. The stairs creaked beneath the men's boots.

Ascensia did the only thing she could think of. She quickly unbuttoned the bodice of her dress. As she unfastened the last button, the door was flung open. She gasped in outrage as a rough-looking soldier stared at her.

She clutched her gaping dress together and pushed the man back out into the hallway, then shut the door behind her.

"Get out of my way," he said. "I have orders to search that room."

When she did not move, he grabbed her arm and tried to pull her aside.

"Oh," she cried indignantly, but she still stubbornly refused to move. "You insult me. If you do not take your hand off of me, I will- "

The man laughed down at her. "You will what? You're a stubborn Rebel. But you sure are a pretty one."

She struggled to free her arm but went still as a deep voice demanded, "What's the trouble up here?"

A Union officer had come halfway up the staircase. He looked at her unbuttoned dress then flushed and looked away as he removed his hat.

Ascensia thought to herself, *He has looked at me and he is gentleman enough to look away.*

"Why, this man," she said to the officer. "Has insulted me. He- "

"She won't let me in that room, Sir," the soldier interrupted as the officer came up to the landing.

"You can see that I am not dressed," Ascensia went on. "And there is a young girl in that room who is positively frightened to death."

"I am sorry, Miss," the officer apologized. "But he was acting under orders."

"Do you order your men to go into a lady's room while she is dressing?" she asked with a tremor in her voice that was not at all feigned.

"Certainly not," the officer replied with a slight frown. He turned to the soldier. "Did you see anyone else in there?"

"Well, I saw another girl standing in there, Sir. But- "

Just then one of the other children came out into the hall, held onto Ascensia's skirt and tearfully whispered something to her.

Ascensia looked at the officer and said, "Sir, your men have already frightened the children. They are afraid that you will take them away as prisoners."

As she looked down at the child again, she noticed it. There was a dark patch on the carpet. Noble's blood. She moved to hide the stain with her skirt and stood with one hand still holding her bodice together and the other hand resting upon the child's head.

She scarcely dared breathe as she looked at the officer again. He was frowning down at the hem of her skirt. He then looked up at the closed bedroom door. He had seen the blood. She was certain of it.

But while his eyes moved back to her face, he ordered the soldier to go back downstairs. "We aren't here to frighten children," he said.

"Sir, you are a gentleman," Ascensia said softly, gratefully. "Thank you."

"Ma'am," he said as he looked at her. "I hope you understand that anyone found hiding any- contraband will be severely punished if they are caught. I should tell you that there will be more soldiers coming after we are gone. You understand, ma'am?"

She nodded, both of them understanding each other perfectly well. The officer put his hat back on, then turned and went back downstairs.

Chapter 31

Ascensia lay in her bed staring up at the darkness. She hadn't slept well in a long time. Night brought too many memories. But no one else slept well at night either. The darkness had become something to be feared. At any hour soldiers might come and burn the house over their heads.

They burned in retaliation. And they burned in wantonness. Many women and children were left homeless and facing starvation.

The Northern Army was sweeping through the Shenandoah Valley and stripping it clean. What the men did not take for their own use, they destroyed so that it could not be used by the Southern Army.

There had been more arrests. A neighbor's son had been taken into the woods and shot without a trial. He was a guerilla, they charged, though the boy was only seventeen.

Ascensia and Kate had decided that Noble would be safer out of the house. Ascensia and Will fixed up a little shelter for him in the woods where he now stayed day and night and she breathed a great deal easier because of it.

Tonight, however, Ascensia felt more uneasy than usual. Kate had gone to help a neighbor who was about to have a baby and Ascensia was alone in the house with the children. She finally did fall asleep only to be awakened by Augusta leaning over her.

"Wake up, 'Scensia. Look out the window."

She could smell the smoke even before she looked outside. She saw the red glow off in the distance. While she watched, another light sprang up to the left.

"That must be Mrs. Hunter's house," Augusta said to her.

"Wake the other children," Ascensia told her.

They all quickly dressed. Ascensia told the younger child that they had decided to camp out in the woods for the night with Noble.

"Just like soldiers?" the little boy asked.

"Yes," Ascensia replied. "And you must make sure to keep very quiet so that the enemy soldiers do not learn our position. No matter what happens, a soldier must be very, very quiet."

When they were ready, Ascensia gave them each a hug and sent them off with their blankets. She watched until they had disappeared in the woods with Will. She had stayed behind to gather more things that they would need for the night. She had decided that she would stay with the house so that, if it was possible, she would save it from being burned. While she was packing food from the cupboard, she turned with a little start as she heard the front door open. Will walked into the kitchen.

"I told you to stay with the children," she said.

"I want to help," he said with a shrug.

She sent him upstairs for more blankets then finished packing all the food that Will would be able to carry. They had already hidden some food in the woods during the past few days.

She locked everything up that she could. She was walking past the parlor when she heard the floor boards creak behind her. She turned, expecting to see Will, but someone's hand clamped roughly over her mouth. She was pushed up against the wall. When she lifted her eyes, she was staring up into Morgan's face.

"Afraid?" he whispered as his eyes probed hers. "Maybe you were expecting to see someone else. Were you?" he demanded harshly. "Were you waiting for your Rebel lover?"

"When I take my hand away," he went on. "I want you to keep quiet. Understand?"

"Understand?" he repeated and his fingers tightened cruelly over her face.

She nodded.

"That's better," he whispered as he brought his hand up against the side of her face and breathed softly, "Whore."

He was anticipating her fear, she knew. He was enjoying subduing her. She heard someone on the landing upstairs and tried to cry out a warning. But Will came hurrying down the stairs.

Morgan lifted his pistol and fired. As the weapon roared, the force of the ball threw Will against the staircase wall. He slid down to the bottom step where he collapsed and lay still.

While Morgan kept his hand upon Ascensia's arm, he kept his gun pointed at the boy. But Will did not move. He remained still while Ascensia stared in horror at the dark stain spreading across his shirt.

Outside, she could hear the sound of horses approaching the house. Without another glance at the boy he had just shot, Morgan tightened his grip on her arm and forced her outside to the veranda. He jerked her up to the railing and stood watching the soldiers who were riding into the yard.

They were rough-looking men. They were unkempt and unshaven, and bold-eyed, too, as they turned to look at Ascensia standing on the veranda with Morgan.

Every saddlebag was bulging and overflowing with items of every description. Hams hung suspended from pommels. There were even articles of women's clothing. The delicate, white lace of a petticoat trailed out of one saddlebag, making a startling contrast against the black boots of one rider.

Ascensia turned to look at Morgan. He rubbed one corner of his mouth with the back of his hand and grinned down at her in a mocking manner. She noted that, while Morgan had always strived for perfection in his appearance, he was now carelessly dressed. His coat was unfastened. His face was unshaven. She could smell the whiskey on his breath. He was not the Morgan she used to know.

He slipped one arm around her waist and drew her close to his side. He laughed softly as she stiffened. She admitted to herself that she was frightened. Frightened at what she had seen in his eyes, and what she saw in the eyes of the men sitting their horses in the yard below her. And she was frantic to see to Will.

She looked past the men, startled to see two of them dragging Noble across the yard. He had heard the shooting, she realized, and he had come to the house to see what was wrong.

"He's already been shot," one of the soldiers called out to Morgan. "Should we finish the job? Or should we leave him hanging from one of these trees to show the rest of the Rebels what we do to 'em when we catch 'em?"

Noble met her gaze, but only briefly. In that one moment she had seen the anguish in his eyes. While her own fears were for Noble, she knew his were for her.

Morgan let his breath out in a short, ugly laugh. "Leave him as an example," he replied.

Ascensia shot a glance up at Morgan. His expression was hard, unfeeling. One of the men brought a horse forward. Another tossed a rope across a limb of one of the big oak trees in the yard. Soon, a noose dropped below the dense foliage.

"No," Ascensia whispered as Noble's hands were jerked together behind him and bound tightly at the wrists. They forced him up onto the horse and then positioned the animal beneath the noose. One of the men spurred his horse forward and slipped the stiff rope over Noble's head. He tightened it with a rough jerk.

"You can't do this, Morgan," Ascensia began wildly.

Morgan watched her face but said nothing. After lifting his eyes from her, he nodded to his men.

With a sharp lash, one of them drove the horse out from beneath Noble. Ascensia watched with helpless horror as he slid off the horse's back and dropped towards the ground.

Noble was still alive and he was struggling. She struggled with Morgan and tried to get to Noble. But Morgan held her back. The men watched Noble as if they were enjoying some hideous game. They let him hang until he was almost unconscious then lowered him to the ground. As soon as he had revived, they repeated their cruel torture.

Frantic, Ascensia realized that Morgan's gun was pressing against her side. She moved her hand toward it. Her fingers touched it, were about to close around it, when Morgan became aware of her intent. His hand closed around her wrist, tightening brutally until she winced with the pain.

"Please, Morgan," she begged. "Please. You must have some mercy in you."

"Mercy?" he echoed in a strange voice. "I can put him out of his misery right now if you want me to." He drew his pistol and leveled it at Noble.

"You . . . " she blurted wildly. "You are- " She suddenly stopped herself.

Something in Morgan's face warned her. He was drunk and he was dangerous. Very dangerous. Morgan was like a wild beast and his blood-thirsty impulses sought only the merest of excuses to be satisfied. He would kill Noble, she knew. He would kill him without hesitation, without regret, if she said the wrong thing.

He watched her. He waited. His lips curved slightly as his eyes gleamed with malicious triumph. "Now beg me, Ascensia," he ordered softly. "Beg me and I will let him live."

"Please," she said simply. "Please."

Morgan put his gun away. "Now you are being more sensible, Ascensia," he said. "I would hate to have to teach you such a, shall we say, irreversible lesson. You had better watch what you say to me and how you say it if you don't want to see him dead. I want you to realize that I am in control here. It is up to me whether he lives or dies. And you, of course," he added with a chuckle.

He turned from her, snapped out an order and his men left Noble lying on the ground. This time Noble did not regain consciousness. He lay motionless while Ascensia started fearfully, waiting for him to move.

"He dead?" Morgan inquired in a bland voice.

"Naw," was the reply. "Just ain't too lively right now."

"Morgan," Ascensia began. She forced control into her voice but she was trembling. "Let me look at him. And the boy in the house. They need- "

"No," Morgan interrupted with angry impatience. "And if you ask me again, I'll put another bullet hole through both of them."

It was no idle threat. She knew he meant what he said. As she looked helplessly out into the darkness, another fear stabbed like a knife blade through her heart. Please, she prayed, make them stay hidden.

The men set fire to the barn. Some of them entered the house. Noble was still lying where they had left him. The yellow firelight from the burning barn lit his still,, dark form.

She tried to see Will but Morgan blocked her view. She would not look at Morgan. When he stepped in front of her, she turned her face away. That angered him and he seized her arms and jerked her up against him. Then one of his hands came up to grip her face tightly.

"That hurt?" he jeered when he saw the pain in her eyes. He did not lessen his grip, however. "You've got only yourself to blame, you know. This is all your fault. Whatever happens." His eyes narrowed slightly. "What are you thinking, Ascensia?"

"That I never knew you at all," she whispered as she looked back at him.

"I can say the same."

"What are you going to do?" she asked.

His lips curved into a smile, a smile that seemed to convey a promise of evil. "Make you even sorrier," he said.

He released her, suddenly, almost violently, and turned his back to her as he stepped to the front door. She could hear the other men inside the house in their search for whiskey and valuables. When they were satisfied that they had found all that was worth taking, Ascensia was forced to mount one of the horses. The light of the flames from the burning barn glowed upon her face as she rode across the yard. She could feel the heat.

As they passed Noble, she looked piteously down at him, not knowing whether he was alive or dead. She worried about Will who might be dead as well, and the children who were alone out in the darkness.

After they had ridden away and the night grew silent again, except for the popping and hissing of the fire, a terrified girl sat crouched in the woods with her hand held tightly over her little brother's mouth to keep him quiet. She stared towards the house with wide eyes. In their depths was reflected the flames and the haunting terror of helplessness.

Chapter 32

The first frail light of dawn diffused the darkness. The leaves trembled with the merest whisper of a breeze. As Jesse finished saddling his horse, his hat brim lifted slightly. He frowned as the words sank in. "You mean Ascensia is here?"

"She's here," Wirt replied. "After the fight at Piedmont, we took some of the wounded men to one of the houses they had set up as a hospital. We rode up and saw her there in the yard. We were just as surprised to see her as- "

"Why is she down here?" Jesse asked, still frowning.

"Ah'm not sure," Wirt replied. "Things were pretty confusing at the time."

"Ah saw her, too, Captain," one of the other men spoke up. "Ah was a prisoner at the time and the Yankees had halted us along the roadside. Ah was leaning against a fence when Ah saw her. Ah was looking mighty hard to make sure it was her. You remember a girl like her.

"A Yankee had just come out of the house carryin' some food they had set aside for the wounded men inside. She followed him and told him that he was stealing. When she refused to give the bastard a key he wanted, he threatened to shoot her right there. You ought to have seen her. Why, she stood there, just as cool as you please and told him just what she thought of him. And she made that Yankee back down.

"Anyway, he thought better of doin' any harm to her under the circumstances. There were a lot of prisoners and we were about to jump that fence and tear him to pieces, guards or no guards."

"She asked about you, Jes," Wirt said, and the other men looked uneasy.

Jesse noted their expressions then looked at his lieutenant.

"Course we thought you were dead then," Wirt went on. "And not knowin' any better, we told her that."

Anticipating Jesse's unasked question, Wirt said, "She went white. Just about as white as the rail she was holding onto. Kinda slumped like and we had to hold her up."

"Where is she now?" Jesse asked in a low voice.

"Stayin' at Pinewood with Rush's family. Noble's there, too. He got shot and we had to leave him there. She's been taking care of him. Ah have been worried, though, about the both of them. There have been a lot of Yankees swarmin' around over there burnin' and raising hell in general."

"How long will it take us to get there?" Jesse asked as he mounted.

Some hours later, the group of Rebel scouts had pulled their horses up on the wooded hill overlooking Pinewood. They were a silent group. Only the breathing of their horses could be heard in the stillness. They had run hard for even from afar the men had smelled smoke on the air. And they had seen the destruction and the burnt remains of other homes on the way.

Through the fragile mist, they looked down upon the white house that stood in a clearing below them. They did not look at each other. Nor did they offer any comments as they passed what was left of the barn. The blackened heap was still smoldering.

Without an order being given, each man drew his pistol. Keeping a careful watch on the woods surrounding them, they started down the hill.

Jesse noted the condition of the house as he guided his horse through the thick weeds. His gaze lingered on the gaping doorway and the shattered windows and the family's possessions strewn across the front yard.

He dismounted at the gate and walked into the yard. It was only after he had stepped up onto the veranda that he saw the two children. They were huddled against the wall in the far corner. Their terrified eyes were fixed on the gun in his hand as they held tightly to each other.

He holstered his pistol and walked over to the children. He got down on his heels and quietly assured them that no one would hurt them. Then he stepped over to the open doorway.

The older child, a girl, rushed past him and dropped to her knees in the hallway at the bottom of the staircase. She looked back over her shoulder at Jesse. Above her head, the wall was smeared with blood.

Jesse got down beside her and looked at the boy lying at the foot of the staircase. The boy's shirt was open to expose a dark, ragged hole below his shoulder. Jesse guessed she must have been trying to do what she could to dress the wound when they had ridden up and frightened her.

It was a bad wound but it was high up and so he believed the boy had a chance. Jesse reassured the girl as he reached down to help her.

"I wish I'd had a gun," she said in a fervent voice. "I would have killed every one of them. But I had to keep my brother quiet."

She stopped, and with quivering lips stared ahead as if she were seeing it all again. "We were so close we could see them.

And hear them. We could see what they did. Everything." Her voice was breathless and Jesse frowned as he watched her.

Some of the men had come to the doorway behind them. They carefully carried the boy into a downstairs bedroom and gently laid him upon the bed there. The boy moaned and showed signs of returning to consciousness.

One of the men motioned silently for Jesse to come out onto the veranda. "We found Noble, Suh." The soldier's voice was hoarse, and vibrant with emotion. "He's alive, but he's bad off. They- "

"They tried to hang him." It was the girl. She stood in the open doorway and Jesse saw how small she was, how she came up only to his chest. And how young she looked with the daylight full upon her face.

"More than once they tried," she went on and Jesse knew she needed to speak. "After they left, we dragged him to the side of the house because we were afraid they would come back. But we couldn't drag him far." Her voice caught for a moment. "It was only because she was there that they didn't do it all over again. She begged him and he told the others to stop."

Jesse's body grew rigid as he stood watching her.

The girl's hand suddenly covered her mouth as she uttered a little cry. "They took her. That man- that Yankee. He forced her to go with them."

"Took who?" Jesse asked in a hollow voice, dreading but already knowing the answer.

" 'Scensia," she replied and as she stared up at the soldier's face, she was both awed and frightened by the look that came into his eyes.

"How long ago?" she heard him ask in a hoarse whisper.

"I don't know. It was dark. We had been asleep. I- I- " she broke off, moaned. "Oh, what will happen to her? And the baby?"

"Whose baby?"

Augusta barely heard the man's question this time. "Hers," she whispered, ashamed to speak of such things to a man. "She's with child."

Jesse's eyes lifted as if he was seeing something in a far distance. Behind him, Wirt stayed silent. He kept his distance but watched Jesse's face closely as he went into the house.

Jesse's boots sounded with a hollow echo on the wood floor as he stepped into the kitchen at the back of the house. He was surrounded by a deep silence.

All around him was wanton destruction. Dishes were strewn across the floor, smashed into a thousand pieces. Curtains had been torn down. They lay twisted and muddied where they had been trampled by Yankee boots. The windows had been shattered. Chairs were overturned. And out there, somewhere, Ascensia was with the men who had done this. Ascensia with child. He bowed his head for a moment, his eyes closed as he struggled for control.

There were no signs of life about the house. A few chickens had scattered, squawking madly as the horses pounded into the yard. The house looked deserted. Some of the men dismounted and went up to the front porch. Some waited on the steps that led up to it. A loud crack shattered the stillness as the door was broken open.

The men swarmed inside. From the yard, Ascensia could hear the shuffle and stomp of their boots throughout the house. She could hear their voices, too. Voices that were rough and brutal and coarse. One voice declared with a laugh that it was a shame that there were no Southern girls at home to welcome them. Another called out that they had found more whiskey.

Glass shattered. Heavy objects crashed to the floors. The windows were broken from inside and the men began throwing the contents of the house into the yard.

It was wanton destruction. It was bold thievery. He men were like wolves on the scent of blood. Wolves with no restraint upon their greed or their hungers.

Morgan led her to the stable. He left her there under the guard of two of his men while he went back to the house. The men looked at each other. They grinned slyly and made no attempt to conceal their lewd stares.

"She sure is fine-lookin'," one said.

"Is," agreed the other.

The man nearest her suddenly reached out with a snake-like movement and seized her wrist. She jerked to free her arm, but the man quickly stepped so close to her that she was trapped between the wall behind her and his body. For a moment, as he pushed his body up against her, terror froze her.

"You're not going to be unfriendly, are you?" he said while the other man looked on.

As the man continued to press against her, her hand was reaching along the wall behind her. Her fingers sought the heavy leather bridle she had seen hanging near her. Her hand tightened around one thick leather strap. Driven by desperation and panic, she suddenly raised it up and swung it across the man's face.

He howled in pain. Both hands went to his face. The blow had had all her terror and her strength behind it. Suddenly free, she turned and ran towards the open door. She stopped when she saw Morgan standing in the doorway.

"We were just- " one of the men behind her immediately began to explain. But Morgan cut him short with a curt order and the two men left the barn.

For a time Morgan stood silent. He suddenly grabbed a fistful of her bodice and yanked her close to him.

Ascensia reacted impulsively to Morgan's rough handling. "I'm glad that I found out in time what you are really like," she breathed passionately.

He turned his face to the side for a moment. Then suddenly, viciously, he hit her face with a hard, back-handed blow that jerked her head back.

Stunned, Ascensia stared up at him. Pain stung her cheek, pounded in her head. Tears blurred her eyes. She lifted her hand to the side of her face, wondering that this was the same man that she had almost married.

Morgan was not finished, however. He spun her around and led her over to a pile of straw where he forced her to lay face down. He pulled her wrists up roughly behind her back and with quick, jerking movements, tied her hands behind her with a length of rope. She cried out as it cut painfully into her flesh.

"And I am glad," he hissed between his teeth as he turned her over. "That I know what you are really like."

He sneered as he looked down into her face. "You had me believing that you were so innocent, so *virtuous*." He emphasized the word with a savage, derisive drawl. "Not too virtuous, though, to play the whore for that Rebel sonofabitch, were you? And where did it get you?"

She knew that his rage was building. She tried to twist away but he threw one leg over her, straddling her.

"Where did it get you?" he repeated. His eyes never left her face as he ran the back of his hand slowly along her cheek. She stiffened.

"Still so very proud, aren't you?" he said slowly, his breath hot and rank with whiskey. "Well," he whispered with his face close to hers. "I'll take that out of you soon enough." His eyes grew hard and speculative.

"You're wondering, aren't you?" He chuckled to himself as if the situation was to his liking. "Since there aren't any Rebels around, I'm going to give you a chance to see how Northern men compare to your Southern boys. A lot of them. All of them, in fact."

He laughed again as Ascensia stared up at him. He seemed immensely pleased as he read the comprehension in her eyes. "And after they have all had you, after I have watched you be humbled, then it will be my turn. And I promise that you will remember everything that I do to you, and that you will regret your very unfortunate decision to invite another man into your bed."

Morgan's passions leaped inside him like an uncontrollable fire. He found those passions immensely satisfying. He found them wildly exciting. He was aware of a new strength. He wanted to take her against her will. He wanted to possess her more thoroughly, more completely than that Rebel bastard ever had. He would make her sorry for every thought of the Rebel that had ever entered her head.

Ascensia closed her eyes tightly as Morgan looked down at her. She thought that he would rape her then and she didn't know how she was going to bear it.

He suddenly released her, however, and stood up. He yanked her to her feet and led her back outside, then jerked her around so that she was facing the men.

One of Morgan's arms slid around her waist. He pulled her tightly against his body. Even though Ascensia kept her own eyes lowered, she knew that the men were watching her. They were silent. Too silent, it seemed.

Morgan ran his other hand slowly down the length of her unbound hair and she stood rigid, feeling the rope cut cruelly into her wrists, concentrating on that rather than on how her soul was filled with revolting horror for what Morgan intended for her.

She willed herself not to think about it. "I will get away," she told herself. "Somehow I will get away."

"We'll just let them whet their appetites a little longer," Morgan breathed close to her ear. "That way they'll be good and ready for you."

Chapter 33

Wirt looked across his horse's back and frowned. "We can't keep this pace up much longer, Jes," he said. "We'll all need fresh horses soon. Hell, you've got to at least stop that bleeding. Ah can see it starting to show through your vest now."

They had halted at a farmhouse to rest both men and horses. Wirt continued to watch Jesse, who ignored his suggestion and ordered his lieutenant to see if the people who lived in the house had anything that could be used for bandages.

"And get me some whiskey if they have any," he added. "I'm out."

Wirt looked at him for a moment longer then shook his head and stepped up onto the porch. Jesse's face was drawn with more than weariness and worry. He hadn't fully recovered from his wounds and this hard, relentless search was beginning to tell on him. He was hurting in a bad way, Wirt knew. He was using the whiskey to keep the edge off the pain. Jesse would bear it in silence, though, Wirt was certain, and nothing but death was going to stop him.

Jesse took a long, deep drink of the whiskey that had been offered by the owner of the farmhouse. He was silent as he sat on the porch and allowed Wirt to help him re-bandage the wound in his chest.

"Ah don't like the way you look, Jes," Wirt began again. "You need some rest. You're fightin' some pretty mean pain. Ah can see that plain enough. And you won't be any good to anyone if you- "

"You're ridin' me just like an old woman," Jesse growled. Then he sighed and shook his head. "No, Wirt. There's no way. We can't slow down. You know that. She's already been with them so long- " His voice broke off, the disturbing thoughts left unfinished as he looked off into the woods.

"Then let us go after her," Wirt urged.

Jesse shook his head. His jaw muscles were tightly set as he got to his feet and walked over to his horse. He was battling an overpowering sense of futility, of helplessness. He had been battling it all along. He had seen enough brutality in this war to know what some men were capable of. He knew what Morgan Damon was capable of.

The girl at Pinewood had heard Ascensia say that name and she had repeated it to Jesse. Ascensia was with Damon now and maybe the man knew things that wouldn't be good for him to know. At least not good for Ascensia.

His frowned deepened as he thought over the other things the girl had told him. Her baby. His baby. Maybe. Or was 'Scensia already married to that Yankee bastard and carrying his child? No. The scene that the girl had described had been too brutal. And why was Ascensia down here anyway?

He didn't have any answers. All he did know was that she was in trouble and he was going to do all he could to find her. If he was not already too late. If that was true- His teeth set hard together. He wasn't going to let himself think that way.

At that moment he looked up and saw a horse loping towards him. It was Renn Parrish. Jesse had sent scouts out and so far their reports had kept them on the trail of the men.

"Found tracks that head west," Renn told Jesse who mounted immediately. "Then they strike off sharply to the south. Ah figure Ah know a way to save a whole lot of time."

"Let's ride," Jesse called out. But the men had already mounted without his order.

Because of the darkness the men were forced to a maddeningly slow pace. The horses had run far. They were lathered and breathing heavily so the men halted in a small clearing to rest the exhausted animals. Two scouts rode ahead in the hopes of procuring fresh horses from a farmer who lived nearby.

Jesse had ridden ahead of the others, seeking solitude. He dismounted and stood motionless beside his horse. He stood with clenched hands, blaming himself, yielding to the full, crushing weight of his helplessness.

The images that his mind conjured were torture to him. He sickened at the thought of what she might be enduring right now. It might be too late. He knew he might have to face that. His strength was failing. He was near used up by the search. And it was slow going in the darkness.

He raised his face to the sky. "God," he prayed. "Help her."

His voice died in the soft whisper of the wind that swept over him and was swallowed by the silence which was deep and undisturbed save for the low chirping of the crickets. Then he heard, faint but quick, the distant gallop of a horse. He unslung his carbine.

He stood there waiting, straining his eyes through the thick night shadows. He suddenly relaxed his grip on his carbine when he saw who the rider was.

"Seen 'em, Jes," Renn called quickly. "They're not far. She's with them. Ah think she's all right. But they're- Well, she won't be for long."

Jesse did not wait to hear more. He leaped into his saddle and the two men galloped forward into the darkness.

The night air felt damp and heavy in her lungs. Ascensia could feel the rough fence post against her back where Morgan had left her tied. The flickering light from the burning outbuildings created fitful lights and shadows which defined the curves of her face. Even in that uncertain light, she looked drawn and pale. There was an ugly bruise already showing along the side of her face where Morgan had hit her.

She was watching the man who had just come out of the house. She was watching warily from beneath her lashes. He held a woman's white nightgown against him while he pranced about the veranda in drunken revelry. In his other hand he dangled as lacy camisole.

The other men laughed at his stream of obscene jests. Her glance darted to one of the other men. John Lathrop. He had joined them earlier. Since then he had ridden at Morgan's side.

They had all been drinking heavily. The shadows leaped, writhing and distorted. The firelight glowed red upon their faces. Morgan was as coarse and as brutal as any of them. She refused to meet, yet was aware of, the occasional glances that he cast in her direction.

The roof of the barn suddenly collapsed. Flames shot upward. The black smoke was tinted red. It billowed high against the sky and was shot with sparks that floated on the heavy night air.

Suddenly the laughter and the loud jests died away. The men on the porch talked among themselves in lower tones. More significant to her, they turned in her direction.

A huge, bearded man in a long blue Union coat stepped down from the veranda and walked towards her. In the midst of his unshaven face, she saw the gleam of uneven teeth as he smiled down at her.

He squatted down and began to untie her from the post. He forced her to her feet and pulled on the end of the length of rope that still bound her hands. He began to lead her along with him to the house, taunting her with little jerks of the rope.

When they reached the veranda, she looked at Morgan leaning against one of the veranda posts. He lifted a bottle to his mouth and watched without interfering as she disappeared inside.

The two men had left their horses behind. They were now moving towards the crest of a steep, wooded hill. They carried their carbines as they climbed. Lured on by the red glow beyond the trees above them, they skirted the heavy brush yet were careful to keep to the shadows.

Suddenly they could see the tongues of fire that reached up to the dark sky. After a few more moments of climbing, the burning outbuildings were in full view below them. They could hear the crackle and hiss of the fires. They could see the dark shapes of men and horses around the house.

Jesse saw her, too. His entire manner, as he crouched upon the wooded slope was like that of a wolf. A vengeful wolf who was intently watching the scene below.

While he took in every detail of what was happening down below, he reached down and quickly removed the spurs from his boots. Beside him, Renn silently copied his movements. Then they began their stealthy descent down the hill.

Drawn into the front hallway, Ascensia heard bits of broken glass crackle beneath her boots. At the bottom of the staircase, she stopped, refusing to go further and began fighting the rope.

The house was deeply shrouded in shadows. But the red light from the fires outside filled the rooms with a weird, pulsing light. She had never been so terrified. Exhaustion added to her terror. She had been up nearly all night. She felt breathless. Her heart was pounding wildly within her chest.

As she hung back, resisting the rope, the man turned back to her. The light penetrating the window beside her lit his bearded face as he began to force her up the steps, one at a time.

After he had closed her in an upstairs bedroom, he said, "Relax, girl. You can't change this."

She backed up until she stood in a corner of the room. All the while she struggled frantically to loosen her hands from the rope. To one side a massive armoire blocked her escape. The man came forward and reached out to touch her breast. His calloused fingers rasped harshly against her dress as she flinched from the touch.

"I'll untie your hands," he said. "Then you- "

As soon as he had done so, Ascensia twisted free and darted away from him. He moved quickly, however, and grabbed her from behind. He threw her across the bed, easily turning her onto her back and straddling her.

"I've been ready for you all night, girl. You damn well better know I'm not going to just let you walk out of here."

His face lowered to hers. He reeked of sour whiskey and tobacco. He tried to kiss her but only rasped her cheek with harsh whiskers. She strained beneath him. She fought with the desperation of a trapped animal fighting for its life. She clawed at his face but he caught hold of her wrists and drew them above her head.

"You want it rough, that suits me, too," he panted.

John Lathrop had come into the room. He sat on the bed and closed his hands tightly around her wrists. Dazed, she looked up, breathing hard, panicking when she found that she couldn't move at all.

"She sure is a wild thing," laughed the man above her.

Lathrop agreed, and said, "And I'm anxious to break her in." He leaned close to her face. "It's been a long time."

"Keep her still," the man above her told Lathrop. "While I get her dress up." As he jerked at her petticoats, he asked, "Where's the Major? Thought he wanted to watch this."

"The boys found some gold buried in the flower beds and you know how the Major is when it comes to gold." Lathrop grinned and leaned close to her face once again. "Now we're going to show you a few things," he said.

Ascensia lay helpless. When her clothes had been half stripped away, she yielded to the terror that she had been fighting all along. She screamed. It was a scream that echoed hopelessness in the face of unspeakable brutality. When the sound had died away, only the sound of harsh breathing filled the room as the man above her reached down to unbuckle his belt.

Jesse took advantage of every shadow as he made his way down the hill though everything in him urged him towards recklessness. They hadn't run into any pickets. Careless, he thought. Or maybe too damned drunk.

He stepped up onto the back porch of the house and flattened himself against the wall. He leaned against it, breathing hard. A cold sweat had broken out beneath his shirt. His wound throbbed like hell's fire. He watched Renn cover the distance to the porch. When he reached Jesse's side, both men glanced at each other for a moment before Jesse opened the back door and entered the house.

There was no challenge and they stepped cautiously into the kitchen, then moved quickly down the hallway. The side rooms were black voids that gave forth no sound. Nothing moved. Only the light from outside writhed like a living entity in the darkness.

When he reached the bottom of the staircase, Jesse looked up towards the upper landing. The light lit up his face. As his hand came down upon the railing, he heard her scream.

Something made Lathrop look up. Something that made him catch his breath in startled amazement.

Ascensia, too, turned to look towards the doorway and saw the man she had never expected to see again. Jesse was standing there. Jesse, alive and well and looking back at her.

Jesse's gun was in his hand. Lathrop had let go of her. He moved his hands towards his own pistol.

"Don't," Jesse warned. He motioned with his gun. "Move away from her. Both of you."

Lathrop eased back. He held both hands away from his body.

"Now, set your guns down easy. On the bed," Jesse ordered. "And stand over there against the wall."

Both men obeyed, but not fast enough to suit Jesse. "Quick!" he said savagely. "Now turn. Face the wall and get your hands up against it. Higher, damn you!"

"You don't think you are just going to walk out of here?" the bearded man asked over his shoulder.

"Keep quiet," Renn snapped as he stepped across the room to pick up their weapons. "Or you won't be walking out of here. Ever."

Renn was backing away from the bed when the bearded man suddenly turned and struck out at him. The Lieutenant countered the blow with his forearm but the man continued to grapple with him until Renn raised his pistol and struck him on the side of his head.

The man's head jerked sideways against the wall. His legs doubled under him and he collapsed to the floor without another sound.

Jesse, meanwhile, had come up behind Lathrop and had slammed him up against the wall. "Go ahead," Jesse told him. "Try something. I'd just as soon kill you now."

Lathrop offered no resistance, however, and Renn set about tying him to the bed and gagging him. Jesse looked down at Lathrop who uttered a muffled curse behind the gag.

"Like it, you damned traitor?" Jesse asked. He leaned close to the man and said in a low voice, "You've got her to thank for being alive. If she wasn't watching, I'd- " His last whispered words made the man on the bed grow pale and still.

Ascensia's eyes were riveted on Jesse. He took his jacket off and wrapped it around her. He frowned as he gently touched the side of her face.

"We'd better get out of here," Renn said in a low voice.

In the deep shadows of the back porch, Jesse stood beside Ascensia. He brushed the clinging strands of hair from her pale face. He could feel her tremble slightly. "You all right?" he asked in a low whisper.

She nodded, her eyes lingering on his face.

"We'll get you out of here," he said and with an effort forced his gaze away from her.

Renn, who stood in the deep shadow of a stack of firewood, motioned silently. Looking in the direction that he indicated, they saw the shadow of a man standing off to one side near the horses.

They reached the shadows cast by the firewood. "Keep quiet," she heard Renn's low warning. "Ah'm not alone. If you make one sound, Ah'll kill you real quick. You understand?"

The blade of Renn's knife was pressed against the man's throat.

"Yes," she heard the man choke out.

"Listen carefully," Renn went on. "We're going to ride out of here. But Ah'll have my gun on you every second. If you yell out, even once, you're a dead man. You hear me?"

The man nodded.

Jesse lifted Ascensia to one of the horses. He gathered the reins and mounted behind her. Renn snatched the reins of another horse and leaped into the saddle.

Ascensia shot a glance at the man Renn had warned. He stood motionless, watching them. He had not called out, nor did he try to stop them now.

But as the horses leaped forward, they were seen by other men. She heard shouting as they wheeled the horses about. Gunshots burst out of the darkness. A man suddenly appeared out of the shadows to their left.

"Get off that horse," he snarled and reached towards them.

"Not a chance," Jesse muttered behind her while his arm lifted and his pistol boomed.

She caught a glimpse of Renn as he fired his pistol behind them. He shouted something and they were soon racing through the forest at a thundering gallop.

Riders suddenly burst from the woods beside them. This confused her and she knew that they would not escape. But then she heard a loud cry and realized that it was the Rebel yell and that they were safe.

Jesse kept the horse at a steady pace as they made their way through the dark woods alone. The sounds of battle faded behind them. Ascensia was aware only of the clean, clear darkness surrounding them and Jesse's arms around her. Taking a long, deep breath, she tilted her head back and noticed for the first time that the sky was filled with stars.

Chapter 34

The weeks lengthened into months. Long months of winter and war and waiting. Ascensia walked to the kitchen window and looked out at the snowflakes that were falling silently against the glass.

It was still hard for her to imagine that she was married to Jesse. It had been a brief, hurried ceremony. He had ridden off almost immediately afterwards and she hadn't seen him since. The Southern Army was so harried by the Union forces and so hard-pressed for men that none could be spared.

Two months ago she had received word that Jesse had spent some time in a hospital with a wound that they assured her was not dangerous. He had already recovered and had rejoined his men.

The pine forest in the distance was sifted with white. Snow lay in deep drifts around the house. She sighed. So much had happened. So much had changed.

Miraculously, Will had survived his wound. Noble had recovered as well. John Lathrop had been sent to a Southern prison camp. Morgan had been killed. He had refused to surrender and so he had died as violently as he had chosen to live.

Ascensia's eyes suddenly changed and the trees blurred before her. She lifted one corner of her apron, yielding for a moment to the tears. The same snow was falling on Renn's grave. He had been killed only four weeks ago in a skirmish when a ball had pierced his heart.

With her own child inside her, Ascensia thought of another mother's pain. She prayed for the woman whose son would not be coming home. And for the sisters mourning their brother.

She dried her eyes after a time and set about making lunch. Wirt had been staying here at Hetty's home for almost a month. He was recovering from a wound in his leg and Ascensia had spent her time taking care of him.

Kate Duganne and the children were here as well. Rush had brought them down because he felt they would be safer here together. This morning, however, only Wirt was around to keep Ascensia company. Everyone else had gone to church and then they planned to go visiting after that.

Heavy and awkward now with the child that grew within her, Ascensia had stayed behind. But she was feeling a restlessness inside her today. She had felt it earlier, since the dark hours before dawn when she lay awake in her room contemplating all that needed to be done before her baby was born.

Now as she stood alone in the kitchen, she placed both of her hands against the small of her back and kneaded the uncomfortable tautness that had been bothering her vaguely but persistently for a while now.

She could hear the wind picking up outside though everything inside the house was very quiet. Wirt was out in the barn feeding the animals and gathering more wood for the fire.

She sighed heavily and finished sweeping the kitchen. When she glanced out the window again, she saw that the wind was driving the snow a little harder. It rushed against the glass window panes with a soft hissing sound.

She built up the fire in the stove and set the cloth on the table. She was reaching for the plates in the cupboard when the ache in her back suddenly intensified. It grew and tightened around her swollen stomach. Then, as quickly as it had come, it faded.

She wrapped a shawl about her head and put on her heavy mantle so that she could call Wirt in to eat. She pulled the door open and stepped out onto the snow-dusted veranda. The icy wind blew against her cheeks and tossed the ends of her mantle.

She was about to call for Wirt when the pain started to rise again. It was worse than before. She drew a breath of cold air slowly between her parted lips and grabbed the porch rail as she waited for the pain to pass.

She heard the banging of the stable door. Heavy bootsteps came up the walk towards her. She looked up and saw Wirt with his dark hair, beard and coat dusted with white snowflakes. He stopped when he saw her, then hurried towards her.

"When did it start?" he asked when they were back in the kitchen.

"I'm not sure. I've felt strange all morning."

"Looks like we'd better get things ready," he said as he pulled off his coat. "Ah don't reckon Hetty and the others will be coming back for a while. Maybe not till tomorrow. Snow's coming down harder and the wind's picking up."

"But it isn't time, Wirt."

"Well, that baby of yours thinks it is," he said, watching her closely as she gasped and tightened her fingers around the arms of the chair she was sitting in. When the pain had subsided, he said, "We better get you upstairs."

"But, Wirt," she protested. "You- you can't deliver my baby."

He knew by her crimson face how difficult this was for her, how embarrassed she was. "Sure Ah can," he assured her gently while he laid his hand on her shoulder. "Ah delivered a baby once. So, girl, Ah reckon Ah can deliver your baby."

Hours passed. The only sounds in the silent house were the ticking of the clock and Ascensia's hard breathing and now and then the reassuring sound of the man's low voice. The snow was still falling steadily outside.

The pains had progressed steadily. They lasted longer and grew more intense. Now and then Wirt would press a cool cloth against her face.

"Wirt," she asked anxiously. "Do you think everything will be all right?"

"Sure," he assured her. "We've both been through some rough times. We'll get through this, too." He grinned. "Won't Hetty be surprised when she get home."

Ascensia smiled faintly. "What time is it?"

"Heard the clock strike two some time ago," he replied.

Ascensia drew in a deep breath as her stomach began to grow rigid again. "Oh, Wirt," she breathed. "It hurts- so much." She closed her eyes and lay for a long time fighting the pain.

"I'm so tired," she whispered when she was able to. "If I could just sleep for a while. Just a little while. How much worse will it get, Wirt? How much longer?"

"Wish Ah could tell you that, 'Scensia."

"Wirt?" she questioned. "Tell me about the other baby you delivered. Whose was it?"

"Mine," he replied quietly. "It was a little girl."

She turned her face to look at him, surprised.

"She died when she was three," he replied to her silent question. "Died of fever along with my wife. It was a long time ago."

Ascensia bit her lip and he knew that the pain was coming again. "I'm sorry- " she gasped. It ended in a moan and she writhed on the bed a little.

"No time between the pains," she panted, aware of nothing at all except that the agony was going to consume her body again. "Scarcely any time at all . . . between . . . Oh, dear God . . . "

She arched her neck and gripped the sheets in her fists, letting out a cry that she could hold back no longer.

"Don't worry," some part of her brain heard Wirt say. "Ah'm right here. You won't believe me now. But after that baby comes, you're going to forget all this that's happening now."

She could feel his large, rough hand gently stroking the damp hair back from her face, soothingly. She gazed up into the dark-eyed, bearded face and heard him telling her to try and relax, that it would soon be over.

"But I- " she gritted. "I- can't- bear any more." She tightened her hand around Wirt's and felt it clench reassuringly around her own.

The sky was growing dusky outside the window. She could see the driven snow as it rushed against the glass. Like flecks of silver. Like his eyes, she thought, and she cried out again in pain, "Jesse . . . " as she had once cried out in love.

"Jesse's really all right, isn't he, Wirt?" she asked anxiously. "You haven't tried to spare me because of the baby?"

"Ah promise you, 'Scensia. Jesse's all right," he replied.

Pain lingered in her now, lingered as if it would never go away. She felt an overwhelming need to push the child from her body. Each time her stomach tightened, she pushed. The urge was instinctive, a thing she could not resist. She strained again and again until she lay back exhausted.

"You're doin' fine. Just fine," she heard Wirt say. His voice sounded husky, excited.

She kept pushing, harder and harder until suddenly there was a release. Suddenly there was no pain left in her body. She lay for a long time, wondering and anxious, but hearing only silence.

And then she heard a baby's cry. *Her* baby. When Wirt walked around to the side of the bed, he was holding a small bundle against his great chest. A softly mewling bundle that was tightly wrapped in a white blanket. That bundle suddenly became very vocal.

"Well, jest listen to him squallin'," Wirt whispered proudly. He looked at Ascensia and grinned broadly. "You've a boy, gal. A dark-haired boy."

She smiled. Her eyes filled with tears as he handed the baby to her. She cradled him on the bed beside her, against her heart, and hushed his crying. She gazed down with wonder at the sweet little face. She smiled at the two quivering little fists. She ran her fingers lightly over the silky black hair and cradled him more tightly to her. Protectively. Lovingly. Her child. Her son. And Jesse's.

"He looks . . . " she began but was too overcome with emotion and her voice caught in her throat.

"Got the look of his Pa," Wirt finished with a strange catch in his own deep voice.

While the storm continued to rage outside, Wirt built up the fire. The flames leaped and cast a warm glow over the three of them till Ascensia, weary and happy and contented, drifted into a deep and peaceful slumber.

Sometime later, she awakened to hear Wirt's voice downstairs. "Come on upstairs, Hetty. Ah want to show you something." She heard his heavy footsteps creaking on the stairs. A moment later, Wirt stood grinning in the doorway.

"Well, what- " Hetty exclaimed as she stared in astonishment at Ascensia and the tiny baby nestled in the blankets beside her. She threw off her wrappings and went over to the bed with a wondrous look on her face.

"A boy," Wirt declared behind her.

"Oh," Hetty exclaimed. "Why, he is just the prettiest little thing I have ever seen. What did you name him?"

"Renn," Wirt told her softly. "We reckoned we'd call him Renn."

Chapter 35

That winter passed. The first winter for some. The last winter for countless others. It had been a long winter but April came and, in spite of the war that had laid waste to the country for four long years, Spring burst out across the land.

The Confederate Army abandoned the trenches of Petersburg and, yielding up Richmond, began its last march. Exhausted, half-starved, Lee's warriors nevertheless continued to defy a foe that outnumbered them five to one.

They fought at Namonzine Church and Amelia Springs and again along the banks of Sayler's Creek. They were pushed steadily westward by the Union forces. Relentlessly pursued, they turned and fought again at High Bridge and Farmville. Finally surrounded, with no hope of reinforcements or supplies, the Southern Army made its last stand at Appomattox Courthouse.

On a warm and balmy April day, Palm Sunday, 1865, the guns at last grew silent. In the morning stillness, a white flag fluttered up from the Confederate lines. Robert E. Lee surrendered his Army of Northern Virginia.

Hetty uttered a little gasp as she stood up from her chair on the veranda. "It's Rush," she breathed excitedly. "I know it's Rush."

Hetty stared intently at the men who were just coming over the hill in the distance. "It is. And Jesse and Wirt, too." She turned to Quillie, who had also stepped to the rail. "You're going to meet them at last."

Ascensia had also gotten up from her chair. She was holding Renn against her heart, a heart which wa suddenly beating much faster at the sight of the men.

Hetty had already gone down to the road to meet Rush. As soon as he dismounted, she threw her arms around his neck. He lifted her a little as she buried her face against his shoulder. Hetty and Rush were very much in love. Hetty had just found out that she was expecting their first child. Rush did not know yet.

The men took their horses to the pasture before coming to the house. Ascensia waited in the shadows of the budding rose vines, the blood beginning to warm her face when Jesse came up the steps. She wasn't sure how things would be between them.

Their eyes met the moment Jesse stepped up onto the veranda. But only briefly. It seemed he looked right through her. There had been neither warmth nor welcome in his eyes.

Rush was greeted by his mother and the children and Hetty was still holding onto his arm with both hands as if she could not bear to let him go. He smiled a greeting in Ascensia's direction while the children tugged on his coat. Even Wirt acted more warmly towards her as he took Renn from her arms and fussed over him with a deep affection.

Jesse hung back, however. When Hetty introduced Quillie to everyone, Ascensia watched Jesse's face. She was confused by his manner. He did not look at her again, nor did he speak one word to her.

She believed that Wirt, too, noticed that something was wrong. She saw him give Jesse a strange look. She frowned and looked down at Renn, who was staring with wide, clear gray eyes at the man who was leaning against the veranda rail.

"Well, ladies," Wirt called out. "Do you reckon you could feed some hungry men? We've come mighty far."

The women spent the next two hours in the kitchen preparing the most appetizing meal that they could devise. The men, meanwhile, used the time to bathe, shave and put on clean clothing.

The meal, from beginning to end, was a strained affair for Ascensia. Everyone else talked and laughed as they had not done for a long time. Even the children were allowed to be louder and more boisterous than usual. Ascensia, however, sat quiet.

Jesse was sitting across the table from her. He was polite to everyone else, especially Hetty. But for all the attention he paid to Ascensia, she might not have existed at all.

"Why, yes, I do remember."

Ascensia looked up as Quillie replied to Hetty's question. "I do remember the Captain being at Oak Haven."

Hetty laughed mischievously. But though Quillie smiled, Ascensia knew that Jesse hadn't made a very favorable impression upon her today.

Though Brom and Eben had brought Quillie down, they were not here now. Ascensia was almost glad that they weren't. They would be back later in the evening, however, and she found herself wondering if this mood of Jesse's was going to last until they returned.

She glanced up as Jesse laughed in reply to something Hetty had said. Seeing a hint of Jesse's old wayward smile, a terrible longing took hold of Ascensia. There was an impatience in her to be alone with him, to make him change the way he had been looking at her.

Maybe he was simply tired. Maybe the surrender had been difficult for him. After four years of fighting, some men found peace a hard thing to adjust to.

Jesse happened to look at her then and a change came over his face. But not the change she had been looking for. A hard speculation narrowed his eyes. It set her back, the intensity of that look.

Hetty was eager to be alone with Rush. She was scarcely able to conceal it and she began clearing the table as soon as everyone was finished eating. While Ascensia helped wash the dishes, Jesse and Wirt spent time outside with Renn.

Worn out from the excitement, Renn fell asleep early so Ascensia put him upstairs to bed. The house was quiet when she came back downstairs.

She paused in the doorway of the back parlor. Jesse was in the room alone. His back was to her as he stood looking out the window. He did not turn when she entered the room though she was certain that he had heard the rustle of her skirts. He was holding a bottle of brandy in one hand.

She walked to his side and detected the same coldness in his manner that she had been aware of earlier.

"It's getting a little cool," she said. "We'll probably need a fire tonight."

Jesse did not reply and she said, "I'm glad you were able to spend some time with Renn."

"Jesse," she admonished softly, frustrated because she could get no response from him.

He turned towards her and leaned one shoulder against the window frame. He gazed down into her face and she almost thought that there was, for a moment, something hungry in the look. He turned back to the window, however, and asked, "Where is everyone?"

"Gone for a walk," she said. "Hetty and Rush went riding. They wanted time to be alone."

"I'll bet," Jesse said in a way that made her frown.

"Jesse," she said, staring up at his profile. "They are married and they love each other. Rush has been gone a long time. So have you," she finished in a quiet voice.

"Sure," Jesse drawled and his gray eyes narrowed a bit as he stared out the window. "And now I'm back."

There was a half sarcastic, half bitter note in his voice that confused her. He lifted the bottle to his mouth and took a long, slow drink while he kept his gaze on some distant point beyond the window.

"You have had a lot to drink."

"Maybe. But that's what I brought it for," he said as he turned his gaze on her and deliberately took another drink.

She noticed the scar on his wrist. His shirt sleeve had pulled back a little, revealing it. She placed her hand lightly on his arm. Is this where you were- "

His other hand closed around her wrist. He held it tightly for a moment. "It's nothing for you to worry about," he said coldly as he took her hand from his arm.

"What's wrong?" she asked, hurt by the action.

"Nothing," he replied, but the muscles in is jaw were tight with some unexpressed emotion.

"Something is bothering you."

"And what do you think that could be?" he asked.

"I don't know," she replied. "You haven't bothered to tell me."

The twilight had deepened around them, darkening the room. Jesse turned and for one brief moment gazed into her face. In that one moment he had noted how the setting sun touched her face and hair and he resented the temptation to take her in his arms. That resentment came close to manifesting itself in anger. He fought it down. He was tired and the last thing he wanted to do was to fight with her.

Damned if she wasn't going to persist though. She wasn't going to let it lie and he suddenly knew that he wasn't going to be able to stand here and calmly discuss what was wrong with him without making a fool of himself. Just like he knew the brandy was hitting him pretty hard now. He was suddenly feeling a hell of a lot drunker than before.

"We haven't had a chance to talk," he heard her say and knew the signs and knew, too, that she was getting a little angry with him.

"I think you are working very hard at getting drunk," she went on. "And maybe if you would put that bottle down and-"

"Put it down? Hell, I'll put it down." He set the bottle down hard on the window sill. "That make you happy? *Wife?*"

He'd done it now. He shouldn't have said it like that, but it came out all the same. And it sounded as bad to him as it must have sounded to her.

She stared up at him and he could see that she was getting pretty wrought up. And that was dangerous, he knew. Always was dangerous between them. Could lead to anything.

"I would be happy," she said. "If you would stop acting like- like you have been and talk to me."

"Talk?" he breathed huskily, growing more and more aware of how close her body was to his. "I can think of something I'd rather do than talk."

Then, because he was pretty drunk, and before he was aware of what he was doing, his fingers caught her chin and lifted it. Immediately his mouth was moving against her lips. Fiercely. Possessively. At that moment Jesse didn't care any longer about the thing that had been gnawing at him.

At first Ascensia responded with a wild hunger of her own. She felt herself swept away on a tide of aching need. It was what she had yearned for all along.

When Jesse drew back, however, there was still no warmth in his eyes. There was lust, however. He laid her back on the desk behind her, then leaned over her. He whispered in a ragged voice that he still wanted her. But there was no gentleness in him.

Afraid that someone would come into the parlor, Ascensia whispered, "No, Jesse."

"Why not?" she heard him mutter as he ran kisses along her throat.

Her hands slid up along his shoulders, feeling the hard strength and almost yielding to her own need. But she said, "Jesse, *don't*."

"Why not?" he asked again.

"For one thing you're drunk," she began.

"Maybe," he admitted. "But this is the way we've always gotten along best. Around all the rest. And you're my wife now. You're supposed to take care of my needs. Unless- "

She pushed him off of her. She stood rigid. "Your *needs?*"

He was looking down at her. It was hard to shake off wanting her so badly. But he was also aware that he had, in spite of his intentions to the contrary, made a fool of himself.

Ascensia had wanted him as well. But wife or not, she wasn't here as a convenient means to satisfy Jesse's crude lust. She wanted more. If he thought that he could treat her as coldly as he had, and then expect her to be willing and available whenever and wherever, then he was very much mistaken.

"You're a contradiction, 'Scensia." He frowned. "Thought the way you were panting a little while ago, that you wanted it, too."

He saw the change in her face.

"I wouldn't be contradictory at all if you didn't give me reason to be."

She turned angrily away from him. Immediately, he stepped close behind her. His hands were on her shoulders and she heard, "What do you want, Ascensia? You want me to tell you that I am aching with love for you, that all the time I was away I couldn't think of anything but getting back to you and making love to you?"

"Only if you mean it," she almost cried out. But she said nothing. It was what she had wanted to hear. To herself she admitted it. But his last words were spoken with such a bitter, mocking tone that she knew he didn't mean them. He was mocking her. Deliberately mocking her. And she hadn't done anything to deserve that.

She shook her shoulders free of his hands. He did not touch her again. She immediately realized that she was disappointed because he did not. She had waited so long for him to come back. She had worried about him and she had anticipated so much. And now she felt cheated.

"I'm wondering why you came back in the first place," she said half to herself.

"Maybe I shouldn't have."

It wasn't the answer she wanted to hear.

"Maybe it would be best if I just rode out of here tonight."

After a long paused, she said, "I suppose if that is what you want, then maybe it would be best." When she turned to look at him, his face was a mask of indifference.

"It seems to be about all there is left for me to do."

She did not understand him. She did not understand him at all. She said, "I have no intention of forcing you to stay."

"I reckon, then, that that's all we have to say to each other."

She stood alone in the parlor for a long time after he had gone. Hetty came into the room.

" 'Scensia," she began. "I have been looking all over for you. I thought that tomorrow we could- " She stopped and looked at Ascensia's face. "What's wrong? Where's Jesse?"

"Gone."

"Gone where?" Hetty asked. "Why, he's coming back, isn't he?"

"No," Ascensia replied.

"But I don't understand," Hetty went on. "Of course he is coming back."

Still battling with a sea of conflicting emotions, Ascensia did not reply. Finally she said, "I don't think that he is. And, really, I don't care if he ever does. I- " She choked off whatever she had been about to say, then turned abruptly and left the room.

Chapter 36

A slight breeze kept the leaves on the trees in constant motion. A tin cup of coffee was setting on the edge of the step beside Jesse. He stretched out his leg and his boot heel dragged a little in the dirt as he looked out across the open space before him.

"What do you meant it's going to be lonely without her?" he asked Wirt, then reached down to pick up the cup.

" 'Scensia's goin' back to Maryland," Wirt replied. "Her and the boy."

The tin cup halted halfway to Jesse's mouth. He turned to look at Wirt for a moment. He frowned slightly as he looked back at the meadow and contemplated the news in silence. The coffee was forgotten.

He made no further comment, and Wirt asked, "Well, what are you going to do about it?"

"There isn't much I can do about it," Jesse replied.

For all Jesse's seeming indifference, Wirt knew better. Jesse's frown and the tightening of the muscles in his jaw betrayed strong emotion. Jesse suddenly snatched up a stone lying in the dust between his boots and tossed it with a quick flick of his wrist. "Maryland," he breathed. "Why's she going back there?"

"Probably because it's the closest thing to a home she's ever known. The way she talks, it seems like she spent some happy years there when she was a child. I suppose she thinks Renn will be happy there, too. And maybe she feels like she can't stay here with Hetty and Rush forever."

There was a long silence.

"Renn's looking more an' more like you every day, Jes," Wirt went on. "Everyone sees it." He shook his head and sighed. "Maryland sure seems a long way off. I'm going to miss them both."

It did seem a hell of a long way off, Jesse thought. He hadn't been down to see Renn for two days now. If 'Scensia took him to Maryland, he wouldn't see him at all. He got up and walked to the pasture fence. His shirt was pressed against his body by the wind.

Wirt followed him and leaned his arm against the top rail.

"When is she planning on making this trip?"

"Two weeks."

"Two weeks? She's planning to take Renn without considering my say in it at all?"

Wirt shrugged. "If you let her go, she will."

"Let her go?" Jesse's frown deepened. "When did she ever listen to me?"

"What about the boy?" Wirt asked quietly. "He's yours. He knows he's yours, Jes. And whenever you're with him, it's plain enough to see how much that boy means to you. And Ah'm surprised that 'Scensia hasn't found out by now that you come sneakin' around to see him when she's not around. If you don't do something soon, you're going to lose them both."

Jesse watched a bluebird that had lighted on a fence post. After it flew away, he turned to Wirt. "What am I supposed to do? Order her to stay?"

"No," Wirt replied slowly. "That wouldn't do it. Especially with her feelin' the way she does right now. Not with her feelin' she hates you."

"She says she hates me?"

Suddenly dismissing any interest in the matter with an abrupt wave of his hand, Jesse growled, "Hell, I know for a fact that she doesn't- feel any other way."

"She's pretty wrought up right now," Wirt agreed. "But then no woman likes to hear that her husband is fooling around with another woman."

Jesse's eyebrows lifted as he turned to Wirt. "There's no other woman."

"That isn't the way 'Scensia has heard it. Word is going around that you are foolin' with Lieta Ainsley. 'Scensia's been quiet about it, but she's riled. Nobody dares mention your name when she's around."

"Lieta?" Jesse's face registered surprise, then annoyance. "I won't say that Lieta hasn't come around and let me know that she's willing. But I have let her know that I'm not interested."

"Well, 'Scensia's been led to believe otherwise," Wirt informed him. "And it has hurt her."

"She say so?" Jesse asked, his gaze again fixed on the meadow.

"No. But Ah reckon there's something more under all that anger," Wirt replied as he followed the direction of Jesse's gaze. "And 'Scensia doesn't deserve to live as lonely as she has been," he commented as an afterthought.

"I wouldn't think she would be lonely with all that Yankee company at the house."

"Yankee company?" Wirt queried.

"You entertain Northern friends down here, Northern *officers*, and people talk about it."

"H'm. Ah suppose they would," Wirt said. "Mind if Ah ask who's been talking about it?"

"Well, if you need to know, Lieta Ainsley. And others."

Wirt nodded slowly.

"Seems like they should have overstayed their welcome by now. Or ought to have," Jesse said and closed his lips in a hard, straight line. "Of course, my *wife* obviously doesn't think so."

" 'Scensia has been enjoying the company," confirmed Wirt. "She wanted them to stay as long as they could. Ah heard her tell them so as they were walking in the garden. Of course, they would do anything for her. And for Renn. They're devoted to the boy. They're plannin' to escort her to Maryland when she goes."

"She's agreed to that?"

"Makes sense," Wirt replied. "They're goin' back North, too. They may as well travel together."

"Sure," Jesse breathed tightly. "You kiss a man, *in public*, and I suppose it isn't a big deal traveling together."

"H'm," Wirt grunted shortly as he pulled the brim of his hat down against the sun's brightness. "You heard that, huh?" He scratched his jaw.

Jesse muttered something under his breath that Wirt couldn't catch.

"I'll admit most people down here wouldn't be welcoming Yankees with open arms," Wirt went on. And I have to admit they kind of butted into 'Scensia's business by asking where her husband was and why she and the boy were living alone. But they're generally pretty outspoken. One of them maybe went a little too far when he told 'Scensia she could do a whole lot better if she was to ask his opinion about husbands. He said the man she had married, meanin' you, of course, must be a damned fool to treat her in such a way. And then he reminded her of how disgracefully you treated her before. You know, carrying her off like you did. Twice."

"He knows all that?"

"Sure. They sit up talking for hours at night, him and 'Scensia."

Jesse's jaw thrust forward a little. "And you think she ought to be traveling North with him? A man who isn't her husband?"

"She sure isn't going to ask you to escort her," Wirt replied. "It only makes sense that she would go with her cousins."

"Her *what?*" Jesse breathed aloud, looking around at Wirt.

"Her cousins."

"The men staying at the house are her cousins?"

"They are," Wirt replied. "Why, you've met them both. Brom and Eben McCay."

"Why in hell didn't you tell me who they were before?" Jesse wanted to know.

"You never asked."

"I thought that- "

"Thought what?" Wirt asked.

"That Ascensia had met another man. They'd been seen kissing. And hugging."

"They do that," Wirt told him. "But let me guess who gave you another version of that particular piece of gossip.

"What I can't understand," Wirt went on. "Is why you would listen to *her* instead of to your own wife."

Because, Jesse thought, he had let jealousy get in the way of his common sense. Because Lieta had made it sound so believable when she described how she had overheard Ascensia telling her supposed lover that she had been caught up in the war and married for all the wrong reasons. And that she wished life could be the way it was back at Oak Haven. He didn't know how Lieta could have known about Oak Haven unless she had heard it from Ascensia herself.

"Because," he finally breathed to Wirt. "I have a habit of not thinking clearly where Ascensia is concerned."

"Well, I think she is guilty of bein' like that, too, Jes. Where you are concerned. She always was impulsive and headstrong. And stubborn like some other people I know. Ah'll tell you something else about her," Wirt went on. "She cares for you."

Jesse looked doubtful. But Wirt could see the interest back of it.

"She's confused right now. But whatever she's feeling, she's worth fighting for, isn't she?" Wirt asked.

Jesse watched a red tail hawk ride the wind currents overhead. "What am I supposed to do? Throw her across my horse and ride off with her again?"

"Well, it *is* one way to do it."

Jesse's smile faded when he realized that Wirt was serious.

"You did it before."

"Yeah," Jesse laughed under his breath. "And we almost killed each other every time."

"But underneath the killing, Jes," Wirt went on persuasively. "There was always something else."

Jesse frowned. "She wouldn't go willing."

"No," Wirt agreed. "She wouldn't go willing. She'd kick and scream. But we thought that- "

"We?" One of Jesse's dark brows lifted.

"Me and Hetty. And Quillie, too. We thought that, well, that the thing could be worked out."

"She's liable to greet me at the door with a carbine. She's shot at me before, you'll recall."

"But she missed," Wirt reminded him. "And one thing is certain, if you let her go off to Maryland, you'll lose her. And Renn. You never said anything about how things were between you those other times," Wirt went on. "But Ah reckon she came around. No matter what kind of a wolf you were to her."

Wirt continued to watch Jesse who was leaning thoughtfully against the fence.

"So?" Wirt asked with a questioning smile on his face. "You up to this last battle?"

Chapter 37

Summer yielded only gradually to autumn. Autumn lingered as if all of nature was conspiring to breathe one last spell of warmth before the winter came. It was as if the land needed time to heal its wounds. And to remember.

Ascensia remembered. So much. She closed the book she was reading and lay back on her bed. Certainly a novel called *Alone*, even though it was an interesting book, was not helping the feeling of restlessness inside her. She felt alone, too. She had the house to herself today. It was not something that happened very often.

Everyone had been busy these past two weeks. She had even felt a little left out lately. Hetty and Quillie had spent hours together finishing a dress for Ascensia last night when she had had no heart to work on it. Even Brom and Eben had been occupied elsewhere, going off with Wirt yet again this morning. Today they had taken Renn with them.

The silent house oppressed her. With everyone gone, she had had too much time to think. She had found herself haunted by ghosts of the past that she had thought she had laid aside, carefully, in the back of her mind.

She got up and walked to the window, absently smoothing the folds of the lavender calico dress she was wearing, the very one Hetty and Quillie had finished last night. By a strange coincidence, it was nearly identical to a dress she had worn long ago, when . . .

She brought her thoughts up short. She was not going to think about Jesse or the past. She was not going to do that to herself.

Crickets chirped in the grass. Golden sunshine pervaded the air with a soft warmth. And though it was September, roses were about to bloom again outside the window.

Yet a shadow was woven through it all. A shadow that seemed to deepen as the day wore to a close. She had been happy here. If only things had worked out differently. If only-

As she stood at the window, she watched the play of sunlight on the leaves outside, then frowned, bowing her head for a moment. Her only hope, the only thing she could look forward to, she reminded herself, was back at Oak Haven where she and Renn could start a new life. But even there, she thought sadly, there would be memories.

Suddenly, against her will, she was remembering a hot, sultry summer day long ago. She grew very still recalling it, recalling every detail of that day when Jesse's letter had found its way into her hands. And changed her life forever.

One corner of her mouth curved a little self-contemptuously. She had kept that letter. She had it still. She wished that she could say that she had forgotten him. Wished that Jesse didn't mean anything to her any more. She closed her eyes, remembering his eyes when he had said his vows at their wedding.

Yes, she thought bitterly. Eyes that have looked upon other women.

She stopped those thoughts. What was the use of going over all of it again? Jesse was gone. That was his decision. She couldn't spend the rest of her life waiting for him to come back. She wouldn't. It wouldn't be fair to her or to Renn. In any case, she didn't want a faithless, absent husband. She deserved better than that.

On the wooded ridge overlooking the house, a horse stamped impatiently. The man standing beside the horse suddenly swung up into the saddle. Leaning slightly forward, Jesse peered through the dense leaves to the house below.

He crossed his hands on the pommel. It had been a skillful job of scouting. And he knew what his objective was. He drew a deep breath and let it out in a sigh. He set his mouth resolutely and vowed, "Well, my sweet wife, if there's any chance in hell, I'll make you love me."

Ascensia had just walked across the room to her dresser when she became aware of someone behind her. She spun around and caught her breath sharply. Her mouth set in a straight line. "What are you doing here?"

Jesse met her gaze steadily. "I found myself wondering how my bride was doing. So I decided to come and find out."

"Oh, you showed up simply because you decided you would do so?"

"Something like that."

Jesse's dark hair was a bold contrast to the pale shirt that was clinging to his broad shoulders. He was cleanly shaven. Somehow he looked even more intensely handsome than she remembered. And that made her angrier.

She glared at him a moment longer and then paced across the room and back again, stopping before the dresser where she whirled around and stood rigidly with her back against it. "And now that you're here?"

Mist-colored eyes held hers. "I thought it would be a nice day for a ride in the country. Together." The slight lifting of one dark brow seemed to be almost a challenge, as if he expected her to fight him.

"I am not going anywhere with you," she said, meaning it.

"Sure you are."

Her mouth dropped open a little. It was followed by the slight lifting of her chin. Familiar signs.

"Just because you say so?"

"Just because."

"I won't do it," she declared.

"I intend for you to come, 'Scensia. Roped and tied, if necessary. But you will come."

He expected a protest and was not disappointed.

"You have no right to order me around," she informed him heatedly. "I am not some soldier to be- " She searched for a word. "Commanded."

"No," he agreed calmly. "You're my wife. Till death do us part. Remember?"

When he stepped towards her, she backed away, looking for a way to escape.

"Stay away from me, Jesse. Wedding vows do not give you the right to act like a- "

Her last word "savage" was gritted out. He disregarded her protests, picked her up and pitched her over his shoulder. In spite of her squirming and her threats, he carried her downstairs and out onto the back porch where he finally set her down.

She glanced quickly at the back door. Without looking at her, Jesse calmly cautioned her not to try it. His black horse was tied to the rail outside. Ignoring a string of further insults, Jesse lifted her to the back of the horse. He mounted behind her while she informed him what an outrage she considered this to be and how he hadn't changed at all. Not one bit.

While they rode, he attempted several conversations with her. He talked about the weather. And Renn. Ascensia, however, maintained a stony silence. She didn't consider this to be just a pleasant afternoon ride, even though Jesse was trying to pretend that it was. In spite of the vows they had spoken, they weren't husband and wife in the usual sense. They never had been. And he had no right acting like a husband when he had thrown those vows to the winds by taking up with another woman. So she stayed silent throughout the ride, right up until the moment that Jesse drew the horse up before a white gate that opened into the road.

Tall trees lined the long section of fence that bordered the road. Inside the fence, flowers bloomed abundantly, perfuming the air with their sweet fragrance. Through the trees, she could see a big, half stone, half frame house at the end of a long, overgrown drive.

Jesse guided the horse through the gate and straight up to the veranda of the house. He dismounted. Ascensia quickly slid off the horse before he could help her down.

The house looked deserted. The windows were bare. There were no sounds. Nor were there any other signs of habitation. Jesse stepped up onto the wide veranda and asked if she wanted to see what the house was like inside.

"But this is someone's house," she said as he opened the door.

"Sure," he replied with a mysterious air before he took her hand and drew her inside.

At the back of the house, Jesse leaned against the kitchen doorway and watched her peer cautiously around. With a little laugh at her confusion, he kissed her cheek lightly and said that he would be back after turning his horse into the pasture.

Ascensia stood where he had left her. She looked bewildered as she lifted her hand and touched her fingers to her cheek. She glanced around the kitchen and then walked into the front parlor. She also looked into the back parlor. After that she went out onto the back porch. The small room held the sun's warmth. Soft sunlight was streaming through the windows. She opened the door and looked into the back yard.

From the look of the yard and the house, Ascensia decided that whoever had lived here had left some time ago. The house was empty and the furniture was gone. Everything was overgrown and neglected. Weeds grew among the flowers. The pasture fences needed mending. The stable needed repair.

Still, the place appealed to her with its wild beauty. There was a peaceful feeling here. Everything seemed held in a spell of silence and golden sunshine and cool shadows. She lifted her face as a single bird song rang out clearly in one of the trees above her. On the faint breeze, surrounding her suddenly with a deep sense of bittersweet nostalgia, was the scent of wild roses.

She walked back to the front door and frowned as she watched Jesse latch the pasture gate. She kept watching him for a few moments, then lifted her gaze to the dark clouds rising on the horizon. They hadn't been there before.

"Be calm," she told herself. She tried and yet her heart quickened in spite of her resolve when Jesse returned to the veranda. Again he took her hand and led her to sit down beside him on the porch swing.

"All of that was a waste of time," she informed him, waving her hand in the direction of the pasture. "Since you will have to be catching your horse again and getting him ready for our ride back. And we will have to hurry judging by the look of those clouds."

He settled back in the swing and made himself comfortable as if he had no intention of hurrying anything.

"I guess we will have to wait the storm out," he said, stretching one booted foot out before him.

"It will be dark early, Jesse, and everyone will be wondering where- "

She stopped suddenly. Her mind was running over the events of the past few days. "Why, this was all planned, wasn't it? That's why Hetty insisted I stay home and finish packing. All alone."

Even the dress she was wearing was part of the plan. But how could they have possibly known this dress would evoke such a strong memory in her? She had worn one just like it at White's Ford in Leesburg, right before Jesse had sent her back north after kidnapping her the first time. Who could have planned such details? Hetty? Jesse? And why would they?

"It's true, isn't it?" She didn't give him a chance to reply. "I can't believe that they would plot like this behind my back. I can't believe anyone would *plan* to leave me at the mercy of you."

"No one meant any harm, 'Scensia," he said. "I thought I ought to have some time alone with my wife and they agreed."

"They?" she echoed in disbelief. "Did everyone agree to this? I have no doubt about Hetty's guilt." She frowned upon further reflection. "Of course Quillie would agree. Hetty could talk her into anything. Did Wirt go along with it?"

Jesse nodded. "And Eben and Brom, if you care to know."

"You have spoken to Brom?" She was surprised. Brom had had more than a few things to say about Jesse. And they had not been complementary.

"Yes," Jesse replied. "We talked for quite a while."

Well, she would have a thing or two to say to all of them when she got back. She turned her face aside, still seething over their conspiracy against her. When she looked back at Jesse, to her surprise, he had produced a wicker basket. Inside it was a bottle of champagne. He filled a glass which also magically appeared.

He smiled at her confusion and explained, "You brought me a basket of food and drink once. I thought I would return the favor. And- " he added. "We never did get the chance to properly toast our wedding."

She took the glass from him and watched in silence while he filled a glass for himself.

He was calm. He was deliberate. And that was exactly when she needed to be on guard. She knew very well that in the past, Jesse had shown the ability to disarm her, to tear down the walls she would so carefully place between them to protect herself. She didn't intend to let it happen this time.

He lifted his glass. He was about to speak when she asked abruptly, "Why are we here?"

"The last time we were together you said we needed to talk. And we never did. So- "

"I don't know what we have to say to each other," she said, frowning down at the glass in her hand. Except that it wasn't exactly true. It felt like there was a great deal left unsaid between them.

"But I suppose," she said, straightening a little. "That it is possible you feel some sort of obligation to say goodbye since I am leaving for Maryland in the morning. And then you will be free to pursue your other interests," she added because she couldn't keep from saying it.

"And what interests would that be?" he asked, watching her face.

"Lieta Ainsley, for one thing." There. She'd said it. Straight out. He should know, she thought, that she was aware of his infidelity. And then she drained her glass of champagne.

Jesse watched her over the rim of his own glass as he took a drink. "I haven't spent, nor do I intend spending, my time with Lieta."

"Really."

"I already have a wife."

She had already noticed that he was still wearing his wedding ring. That surprised her. She had taken hers off a long time ago.

"Then you are telling me that what I have heard about you and her is wrong?"

"That's just what I'm telling you," he said very soberly. "There hasn't been any other woman, 'Scensia. If you heard different, then you heard lies. We all get confused by lies now and then."

Her own gaze shifted, followed the boundary of the pasture fence. Even if he was telling her the truth, even if he hadn't been unfaithful to her, there were still other things between them. She had meant to keep the protective walls between them. In spite of her resolve, however, she felt something inside her slow down, go backward. She fought it.

She released a heavy sigh, frustrated, and closed her eyes for a moment. When she opened them again, she saw that Jesse was still watching her face closely. He poured her more champagne, lifted his own glass again and said, "Here's to truth, 'Scensia."

After the toast, he reached to take the empty glass from her hand, then got to his feet and said, "Come on. You haven't seen the upstairs rooms yet."

He led her through all the upstairs bedrooms. She looked around the last room. It was a beautiful room with a balcony. The white curtains lifted a little for the wind had risen slightly and it bore with it the faint scent of rain.

There was something sweet and poignant in the touch of the wind against her. There had been a certain sadness at the thought of leaving. It was as if she was closing a door that she would never be able to open again. And she couldn't say to herself that she wasn't feeling a kind of regret, a nameless sense of loss deep inside because of it.

She had to stop this, she told herself as she walked across the room. She had already made up her mind about going back to Maryland and she didn't intend to change it. There were good reasons for her decision.

She looked around the room, finally taking note of details that she had missed. Fresh flowers filled the vases on the dresser. There were generous bouquets of wild roses and other flowers that released their sweet fragrance into the room. She saw, too, that there were clean linens on the bed, and the pillows looked like they had been fluffed and carefully arranged.

For a moment, she was aghast that someone had attended to such details. Here. She realized that this was intended to be a seduction and that it had all been carefully planned out. To the last detail. Had Jesse seen to those things? Or had Hetty? Did everyone know except for her?

Jesse noted the changes in Ascensia's face. She had been frowning at the bed. Then she had quickly looked away. She avoided looking at him as well. He needed to give her time, he knew. After all that they had been through, she had good reason not to trust him. But he wanted to change that.

Ascensia did not want to look into Jesse's eyes. It had always seemed to be the quickest way to her downfall. She was afraid, now that they were alone, of what might happen. Of what always happened. The very thought of lying on that bed with Jesse made her feel suddenly breathless.

She fought the weakness. She was not at all certain that if he betrayed any hunger for her at all, she could resist the desires that were already, traitorously, awakening inside of her.

She had no choice, however. She was going to have to brazen the thing out. She abruptly crossed the room and sat down on the edge of the bed, the only place to sit in the room. She was determined that she would prove to herself, and to him, that she could resist this. Could resist *him*.

Jesse walked leisurely across the room and sat down beside her, though he kept a distance between them. "It rained that first night," she heard him say. "Remember, 'Scensia?"

"It seems like a very long time ago," she replied in a hushed voice. She fought the remembering.

Thunder rumbled. Softly. She turned her face to stare past the open balcony door and saw the outline of the hills in the distance.

She looked back when he said, "I can remember you standing in front of me in that prison cell," he said with a one-sided smile. "I remember your reaction when I asked you to let me see your face."

"You were too bold. You were always too bold."

"Maybe," he replied. "But it got me what I wanted. A look into the most fascinating eyes I had ever looked into."

She remembered, too, how it had been. She recalled the first time she had looked into his eyes and how he had haunted her afterwards. Even then, from that very first moment, she had felt the lure of him.

"We fought each other from the very beginning," she reminded him.

"True. We were enemies before we even looked at each other. But have you considered that if it hadn't been for the war, I probably never would have met you?"

"We could have avoided a lot of- " She searched but could not find the right word.

"Not all of it was bad, was it?"

She sighed, half in frustration. At him. At herself. "There were times when you treated me dreadfully, Jesse. You even called me a liar."

"You did lie," he reminded her.

"I never meant to hurt you, 'Scensia," he said and then breathed a low laugh that did something to her insides. "You, on the other hand, were positively bloodthirsty. You kicked me, and whipped me, not to mention you shot at me. And you slapped me. Twice."

"When did I slap you?"

"That night in Leesburg. When I kissed you. And there was that time in the tent. When I kissed you again."

"Oh," she said softly, remembering. "You see? We have always been battling."

He smiled faintly. "No. Not always. We did manage to lay down our arms now and then. Truth is," he went on. "I was glad you lied that first night. Because it meant you didn't have a Yankee husband waiting somewhere for you."

"You couldn't get rid of me fast enough," she reminded him. "You told me so often enough."

"Yeah?" There was a deeper, huskier quality to his voice. "Then I was the one lying, Ascensia."

She felt a wall crumble inside. "So much has happened," she said in a ghost of a voice.

He nodded, solemnly agreeing. "Back in that prison cell," he began again. "No one could have made either one of us believe that we would end up married. Or that you would have my baby."

He moved closer and she felt a storming of her last defenses. He reached behind her and loosened the ribbon from her heavy curls.

"The first time I saw you, I wanted to see what you looked like with your hair down," he said as he ran his hand down the length of the dark, silky strands. His hand suddenly stilled as blue-violet eyes lifted to his.

Thunder muttered. Lightning pulsed. Ascensia felt herself helplessly drawn to a place where nothing mattered beyond that room, beyond them.

Very slowly Jesse leaned towards her. His fingers lightly trailed along the side of her face. Her eyes closed as he lifted her chin. His kiss was a mere grazing of his mouth against hers. A touch that made her ache for more.

"I remember everything about that night," he whispered. "I remember how I wanted to do this." He kissed her again. "And this." He began to unfasten the buttons at the front of her dress.

"What were you thinking the first time you saw me?" His lips moved sensuously down the side of her neck.

Her breathing changed, but she managed, "That you were a most . . . insufferable Rebel." Her voice faded to a whisper as the back of his hand lightly caressed the soft swell of her breasts in the opening of her dress. "And dangerous, Jesse. I didn't know what kind of man you were."

His hands were on her shoulders now, up under her loosened dress, pushing it aside.

"I still don't know."

"Don't know what?" he asked.

"What kind of a man you are."

"A man who wants to do this," he told her as he laid her down on the bed. "And this." He began kissing her again.

He breathed her name against her hair. "There's something else we never had, honey. A wedding night. There's no war now. And I'm not going anywhere."

She could not resist the onslaught against her senses. Every one of them. She moved her body against him. She kissed him back. Jesse pulled her tightly to him, giving her one long, deeply passionate kiss before they lost themselves in each other, yielding to a last and final surrender.

A very long time later Ascensia lay quietly beside Jesse. She was listening to the sound of the rain. Thunder chased the lightning and she sighed softly as she fell asleep in her husband's arms.

She awoke to see the first of daylight seeping faintly into the bedroom. Through sleepy eyes, she watched as the light grew and the sky outside became tinged with rosy dawn. In the trees, the birds were peeping their morning songs.

Jesse was already awake. She saw him standing on the balcony. She studied him as she lay there. His profile was towards her and his chin and jaw were shadowed from a night's growth of whiskers. His shirt was open in the front, revealing his hard muscled chest and the scars she had traced last night. Her gaze wandered along his strong shoulders and arms that had warmed her and kept her close all night long.

She lay there very still, feeling very fragile in the half light. The shadows, like memories, still haunted the room. She thought about how it had been sleeping with Jesse. She recalled the relaxed drape of his arm across her. The warm comfort of his flesh and the easy rhythm of his breathing she found she remembered too well, too fondly. And how, even in his sleep, his hand would caress her very gently every now and then.

She turned from him and gazed up at the ceiling. No matter how distant and coldly indifferent she tried to be, Jesse had only to kiss her and whisper reminders to her and show her how hungry he was for her, and her anger would fade away just as if it had never existed. Just like her pride.

With a sigh, she sat up and pulled on her petticoat and chemise. She felt an inner sadness rising up inside her. Lust was the only reason Jesse had come to her. It was the only reason he ever came to her. She would be a fool to believe that it was any different this time.

Last night's tenderness was simply a clever device he used to seduce her. After a night of lovemaking, he would likely be gone before the day was over, leaving her with nothing but emptiness as he had done before. And each time the emptiness cut a little deeper Each time it was a little harder for her to bear. Each time he took a little more of her with him.

But this will be the last time, she promised herself. I will go away where he can't follow me. Where he can't . . .

Jesse looked back at her. She was sitting on the edge of the bed slowly buttoning her chemise. The light falling through the window touched her and the tumble of dark curls falling to the bed. For a moment, as she sat there not knowing that he was looking at her, her face was completely open and revealing. He could read all the vulnerability and the sadness. He turned back to look at the rising sun, his own thoughts unhidden in the early light.

Ascensia got up from the bed and went out onto the veranda. She leaned against the railing and looked below. When Jesse's arm reached out to capture her waist and pull her close to his side, she did not resist.

"Did you sleep good last night?" he asked.

She nodded but did not reply and he tried, "Nice morning."

She murmured a reply.

"It's peaceful here, isn't it?" he ventured. "Reminds me of those mornings at Oak Haven with you."

After another little pause, he said, "This place needs some work. But it has possibilities. Don't you think?"

"I suppose it does," was her answer as she pushed a stray curl back from her face and gazed vaguely down at the yard where he envisioned "possibilities."

"It would be nice to have a little bridge over the creek there. A garden would be nice to look down on in the morning. And maybe a moon garden at night."

His other hand slipped around her waist and he turned her towards him. "I like waking up with you," he said and she felt his voice run through her hands where they rested upon his bare chest.

She looked up at his face. "Jesse, why did you bring me here?" she asked suddenly.

"Because I wanted to bring you."

"Why do you keep coming back?" she asked plaintively. "I want to forget- " She bowed her head, struggling with so many conflicting emotions.

"You want to forget what?" he asked softly.

She pressed her hands against him, as if she could hold him at a distance in that way. "I am asking you to listen to me," she began unhappily. "I can't live like this. The way we have been for all these years. You don't realize how hard this is for me. I know you married my only because you felt you had to. Because of Renn. And everything happened so fast that neither one of us had time to really think it all through. But I need to- I- "

"Need what, 'Scensia?"

"More, Jesse," she whispered. "More than this. More than what happened last night."

"But you wanted last night, too."

"Yes," she admitted with an edge of bitterness in her voice. "Yes. You can make me want you. As much as you wanted me from the beginning because of revenge. I know that it was revenge motivating you."

She realized as she said it how much the words she had heard so long ago were still there, were still hurting her. And she knew, somehow, that he was realizing it, too.

"No, 'Scensia," he said, lifting her face to his. He frowned as he watched her closely. "It was only you drawing me back to Oak Haven."

"But I overheard you and Hetty talking in the garden." She closed her eyes for a moment, sorry she had blurted that out. But she felt relieved, too. The words that Jesse had spoken that night had always haunted her. They had always been between them.

He sighed and said, "When I first thought of making love to you, I wanted it to be because of him. But it wasn't. It was because of me. And you. And the way we feel about each other. The way we've always felt about each other.

"There was nothing, ever, that made me come to you but that. I'm admitting, though, that sometimes my pride kept me from letting you know that. And I didn't marry you because of Renn. I married you because I wanted you for my wife. We were pretty hard pressed for time then and I had to convince you the fastest way I knew how."

He pulled her into his embrace and she yielded a little, finding comfort in his arms. As if she could be happy there forever.

"Now, sweetheart," he said softly against her hair. "Tell me what you think of this house."

"It's nice, Jesse. It's- "

"Yours."

She looked up at him.

"It's your wedding present," he said. "I bought it for you. And for Renn. There's a fine stable. I'll show you later. And Renn sure has a liking for horses."

"How do you know that?" Ascensia asked, surprised for she knew it to be true. Renn was just like Jesse in that regard. She saw a lot of Jesse in Renn.

"I come around to see him when you're not there."

"You have been to see him? Does he know who you are?"

"Sure," Jesse grinned. "Last time he called me Pa. Though I expect he got a little coaching from Wirt. I want Renn to live in a house that can be his someday. And I want you to live in your own house. You'll be close to Hetty here. So you two can visit each other every day if you want to. 'Scensia," he went on feelingly. "You're my wife. Did you think that I wouldn't take care of you?"

He saw the old lift of her chin. "You send me money enough now. I don't want you to feel that you have to abide by some obligation to- "

"It isn't an obligation," he said. "I'm asking you to live here with me. As my wife. In our own home."

She looked past him. There was a haunted look in her eyes as she asked, "With things the same way they have been between us? With you gone until you decide you want to bed me again?"

"No," he said, shaking his head as he took her face in his hands. "We're married. Bound together. Always. It isn't just the vows we took. It's more. I think you would hardly . . . If you knew how I- Hell, 'Scensia. What I mean to say is- I love you."

She looked straight at him. She looked into eyes that matched the color of the morning mist as if she thought she hadn't heard him quite right.

"I love you," he said again and he saw the change in her face. "I guess that I started to love you when you pulled your veil back in that prison cell. I fought it a long time. But I'm not fighting anymore."

He frowned slightly, yielding finally, surrendering at last. "I can't tell you how bad it is with me. How it's been being away from you. How it's always been being away from you. I want you here with me, 'Scensia. I've been dreaming about seeing every sunset and every sunrise in your eyes, like I'm seeing it right now. And, 'Scensia, if you say you love me, I'll never walk away from you again.

"Well?" he asked softly as he gazed intently down into her eyes.

"I- " she began, overcome with emotion. "Oh, Jesse. I don't ever want you to leave me again. I want you to keep me close to you always. Always."

He held her tightly to him and she whispered her love while the morning light played on her face where it was resting against his shoulder. A gentle wind touched her dark hair and blew a strand of it across her lips which were still smiling.

The sun rose and bathed them in its warmth. The light grew full and radiant and beautiful around them while, faintly, the sweet fragrance of wild roses from the yard below perfumed the air. Rare September roses that held a promise of a lifetime ahead of them. For in the end the roses endured and could not be destroyed. Just like their love.

The end

Printed in Great Britain
by Amazon.co.uk, Ltd.,
Marston Gate.